War Goddesses
Women Warriors in Literature and Culture

Contents

Chapter 1

Introduction to the Women Warriors

1.1 Women warriors in literature and culture

For other uses, see Warrior woman (disambiguation).
Main article: Amazons
The portrayal of **women warriors** in literature and popular

Britomart Redeems Faire Amoret, *William Etty (1833)*

culture is a subject of study in history, literary studies, film studies, folklore and mythology, gender studies, and cultural studies.

1.1.1 Folklore and mythology

Medieval women helping to defend the city from attack.

See also: List of women warriors in folklore

In Hindu mythology, Chitrāngadā, wife of Arjuna, was the commander of her father's armies.

The Amazons were an entire tribe of woman warriors in Greek legend. "Amazon" has become an eponym for woman warriors and athletes.

1

In British mythology, Queen Cordelia fought off several contenders for her throne by personally leading the army in its battles.

In his *On the Bravery of Women* the Greco-Roman historian Plutarch describes how the women of Argos fought against King Cleomenes and the Spartans under the command of Telesilla in the fifth century BCE.[1][2]

1.1.2 Literature

See also: List of female action heroes

Women warriors have a long history in fiction, where they often have greater roles than their historical inspirations, such as "Gordafarid" (Persian: گردآفرید) in the ancient Persian epic poem The Shāhnāmeh.

Various other woman warriors have appeared in classic literature. Camilla in the *Aeneid* was probably the model for a group of women warriors in Renaissance epic poems: Belphoebe and Britomart in Edmund Spenser's *The Faerie Queene*, Bradamante and Marfisa in *Orlando Furioso*, Clorinda and (reluctantly) Erminia in *La Gerusalemme liberata*. There is also an ongoing debate among scholars as to whether Grendel's mother from the poem *Beowulf* was a monster or a woman warrior.

1.1.3 Media

See also: List of female action heroes

Professor Sherrie Inness in *Tough Girls: Women Warriors and Wonder Women in Popular Culture*[3] and Frances Early and Kathleen Kennedy in *Athena's Daughters: Television's New Women Warriors*,[4] for example, focus on figures such as Xena, from the television series *Xena: Warrior Princess* or Buffy Summers from *Buffy the Vampire Slayer* (who inspired the academic field Buffy Studies). In the introduction to their text, Early and Kennedy discuss what they describe as a link between the image of women warriors and girl power.[5]

1.1.4 See also

Lists

- List of women warriors in folklore
- Women in warfare and the military in the 19th century
- Women in warfare and the military in the ancient era
- Women in warfare and the military in the early modern era
- Women in warfare and the military in the medieval era

Related articles

- Amazons
- Fighter (disambiguation)
- Girls with guns
- Magical girl
- Martial arts
- Onna bugeisha
- Kunoichi
- Virago
- Counterstereotype

1.1.5 Further reading

- Alvarez, Maria. "Feminist icon in a catsuit (female lead character Emma Peel in defunct 1960s UK TV series *The Avengers*)", *New Statesman*, 14 August 1998.
- Au, Wagner James. "Supercop as Woman Warrior." *Salon.com*.
- Barr, Marleen S. *Future Females, the Next Generation: New Voices and Velocities in Feminist Science Fiction Criticism*. Lanham, Md.: Rowman & Littlefield, 2000.
- Davis-Kimball, Jeannine. *Warrior Women: An Archaeologist's Search for History's Hidden Heroines*. New York: Warner Books, 2001.
- Deuber-Mankowsky, Astrid and Dominic J. Bonfiglio (Translator). *Lara Croft: Cyber Heroine*. Minneapolis: University Of Minnesota Press, 2005.
- Early, Frances and Kathleen Kennedy, *Athena's Daughters: Television's New Women Warriors*, Syracuse University Press, 2003.
- Garner, Jack. "Strong women can be heroes, too." *Democrat and Chronicle*. 15 June 2001.
- Heinecken, Dawn. *Warrior Women of Television: A Feminist Cultural Analysis of the New Female Body in Popular Media*, New York: P. Lang, 2003.
- Hopkins, Susan, *Girl Heroes: the New Force in Popular Culture*, Pluto Press Australia, 2002.

- Inness, Sherrie A. (ed.) *Action Chicks: New Images of Tough Women in Popular Culture*, Palgrave Macmillan, 2004.

- Inness, Sherrie A. *Tough Girls: Women Warriors and Wonder Women in Popular Culture*. Philadelphia: University of Pennsylvania Press, 1999.

- Karlyn, Kathleen Rowe. "Scream, Popular Culture, and Feminism's Third Wave: 'I'm Not My Mother'. *Genders: Presenting Innovative Work in the Arts, Humanities, and Social Sciences* No. 38 (2003).

- Karras, Irene. "The Third Wave's Final Girl: Buffy the Vampire Slayer." *thirdspace* 1:2 (March 2002).

- Kennedy, Helen W. "Lara Croft: Feminist Icon or Cyberbimbo?: On the Limits of Textual Analysis". *Game Studies: The International Journal of Computer Game Research.* 2:2 (December, 2002).

- Kim, L. S. "Making women warriors: a transnational reading of Asian female action heroes in Crouching Tiger, Hidden Dragon." *Jump Cut: A Review of Contemporary Media.* No. 48, Winter, 2006.

- Kingston, Maxine Hong. *The Woman Warrior: Memoirs of a Girlhood Among Ghosts.* New York: Vintage, 1975.

- Magoulick, Mary. "Frustrating Female Heroism: Mixed Messages in Xena, Nikita, and Buffy." *The Journal of Popular Culture*, Volume 39 Issue 5 (October 2006).

- Mainon, Dominique. *The Modern Amazons: Warrior Women on Screen.* Pompton Plains, N.J. : Limelight Editions, 2006.

- McDougall, Sophia (August 15, 2013) "I hate Strong Female Characters ." *The New Statesman.* (Retrieved 8-24-13.)

- Osgerby, Bill, Anna Gough-Yates, and Marianne Wells. *Action TV: Tough-Guys, Smooth Operators and Foxy Chicks.* London: Routledge, 2001.

- Rowland, Robin. "Warrior queens and blind critics." *Canadian Broadcasting Corporation.* 31 July 2004.

- Spicuzza, Mary. "Butt-Kicking Babes." *AlterNet.* 27 March 2001.

- Tasker, Yvonne. *Action and Adventure Cinema.* New York: Routledge, 2004.

- Tasker, Yvonne.*Working Girls: Gender and Sexuality in Popular Culture.* London: Routledge 1998

- Tasker, Yvonne.*Spectacular Bodies: Gender, Genre, and the Action Cinema.* London and New York: Routledge, 1993.

- Trickey, Helyn. "Girls with Gauntlets." *Turner Network Television.*

- Ventura, Michael. "Warrior Women." *Psychology Today.* Nov/Dec 1998. 31 (6).

1.1.6   External links

- Women Warriors from 3500BC to the 20th Century - Lothene Experimental Archaeology

1.1.7   Notes

[1] "Plutarch • On the Bravery of Women — Sections I-XV". penelope.uchicago.edu. Retrieved 2014-11-18.

[2] Plant, I.M. (2004). *Women Writers of Ancient Greece and Rome: An Anthology.* University of Oklahoma Press. p. 33. ISBN 9780806136219. Retrieved 2014-11-18.

[3] *Tough Girls: Women Warriors and Wonder Women in Popular Culture*

[4] *Athena's Daughters: Television's New Women Warriors*

[5] Book review

1.2   List of women warriors in folklore

The Swedish heroine Blenda advises the women of Värend to fight off the Danish army in a painting by August Malström (1860).

The female warrior samurai Hangaku Gozen in a woodblock print by Yoshitoshi (circa 1885).

The peasant Joan of Arc (Jeanne D'Arc) led the French army to important victories in the Hundred Years' War. The only direct portrait of Joan of Arc has not survived; this artist's interpretation was painted between AD 1450 and 1500.

This is a list of women who engaged in war, found throughout mythology and folklore, studied in fields such as literature, sociology, psychology, anthropology, film studies, mass communication, cultural studies, and women's studies. A *mythological* figure does not always mean a *fictional* one, but rather, someone of whom stories have been told that have entered the cultural heritage of a people. Some women warriors are documented in the written record and as such form part of history (e.g. the Ancient Briton queen Boudica, who led the Iceni into battle against the Romans). However, to be considered a warrior, the first Asian woman in question must have belonged to some sort of military, be it recognized, like an organized army, or unrecognized, like revolutionaries.

1.2.1 Pirates and Seafarers

- Anne Bonny and Mary Read sailed alongside Calico Jack, Mary dressing as a man. Anne eventually became Jack's lover, and they had a child. In October 1720, their ship was attacked by a royal fleet. All but one of the male crew members, drunk and afraid, hid below deck as the two women fought on with the help of the unknown man. While imprisoned, Bonny is reported to have said of her doomed lover: "Sorry to see him there, but if he had fought like a man, he need not have been hanged like a dog."[1]

- Gráinne O'Malley Legendary "Pirate Queen" of Ireland. She lived during the 16th century.

- Muirisc, daughter of Úgaine Mór (Hugony the Great), the sixty-sixth high king of Ireland, c. 600 BC to AD 500.

1.2.2 Africa

Angola

- Nzinga of Ndongo and Matamba valiantly fought and held off Portuguese control of present-day Angola for over thirty years during the early 17th century.

Berber history

- Kahina or **al-Kāhina** (Classical Arabic for "female seer"; modern Maghreb Arabic **l-Kahna**, commonly romanised as **Kah(i)na**, also known as **Dihya** or **Kahya**) was a 7th-century female Berber religious and military leader, who led indigenous resistance to Arab expansion in Northwest Africa, the region then known as Numidia, known as the Maghreb today. She was born in the early 7th century and died around the end of the 7th century probably in modern day Algeria.

Burkina Faso

- Yennenga was a legendary warrior woman skilled in spear and bow, considered by the Mossi people as the mother of their empire.

Ethiopia

- Gudit (Ge'ez: Yodit, Judith) is a semi-legendary, non-Christian, Beta Israel, queen (flourished c.960) who laid waste to Aksum and its countryside, destroyed churches and monuments, and attempted to exterminate the members of the ruling Axumite dynasty. Her deeds are recorded in the oral tradition and mentioned incidentally in various historical accounts.

Ghana (then Gold Coast)

- Yaa Asantewaa was the Queen Mother of Ejisu (Asante Confederacy)—now part of modern-day Ghana. In 1900 she led the Ashanti rebellion known as the War of the Golden Stool against British colonialism.

Hausa history

- Amina Sukhera (also called Aminatu) was a Moslem princess of the royal family of the kingdom of Zazzau, in what is now northeast Nigeria, who lived c. 1533 - 1610. Her military achievements brought her great wealth and power; she was responsible for conquering many of the cities in the area surrounding her seat.

Yoruba mythology and history

- Oya is the Undergoddess of the Niger River. She is the warrior-spirit of the wind, lightning, fertility, fire, and magic. It is believed that she creates hurricanes and tornadoes, and serves as guardian of the underworld. Prior to her post-mortem deification, the historical Oya was a princess of the Oyo clan as the consort of Shango, its reigning king.

Sudanese History

- The legendary Candace of Meroe (a title, her real name never given) was a warrior queen in the Alexander Romance who caused Alexander The Great himself to retreat upon witnessing the army she'd gathered. This however may be classified a non-historical account because Alexander never reached Sudan.

- Amanirenas, however, was a historical holder of the title of Candace who fought against the Romans after their conquest of Egypt.

1.2.3 Americas

Depiction of the Aztec goddess Itzpapalotl from the Codex Borgia.

Native Americans

Fallen Leaf (often called Woman Chief by the Americans): While Fallen Leaf was a Crow warrior, she was actually born to the Gros Ventre nation and was captured by the Crow when she was 12. After she had counted coup four times in the prescribed Crow tradition, she was considered a chief and sat in the council of chiefs.

Running Eagle: she became a Blackfoot (Piegan) warrior after her husband was killed by the Crow.

Colestah: In the 1858 battle of Spokane Plains in Washington, Yakama leader Kamiakin's wife Colestah was known as a medicine woman, psychic, and warrior. Armed with a stone war club, Colestah fought at her husband's side. When Kamiakin was wounded, she rescued him, and then used her healing skills to cure him.

Buffalo Calf Road Woman: In the 1876 battle of the Rosebud in Montana, Buffalo Calf Road (aka Calf Trail Woman), the sister of Comes in Sight, rode into the middle of the warriors and saved the life of her brother. Buffalo Calf Road had ridden into battle that day next to her husband Black Coyote. This was considered to be one of the greatest acts of valor in the battle.

Moving Robe Woman: One of the best-known battles in the annals of Indian-American warfare is the 1876 Battle of the Greasy Grass in Montana where Lt. Col. George Armstrong Custer was defeated. One of those who led the counterattack against the cavalry was the woman Tashenamani (Moving Robe).

Aztec mythology

- Itzpapalotl is a fearsome skeletal warrior goddess who ruled over the paradise world of Tamoanchan.

American Civil War

- Frances Clalin, also known as Jack Williams, a mother of three from Illinois.[2]

- Sarah Pritchard, who fought with the 26th Infantry of the Confederate Army alongside her husband, until wounded. She was sent home, whereupon she switched sides and fought guerrilla style for the Union.[2]

- Albert Cashier (born Jennie Hodgers), an Irish immigrant and trans man who fought for the Union in the 95th Illinois Infantry.[2]

- Harriet Tubman escaped slave and abolitionist who in 1863 planned and lead Union troops in the Raid at Combahee Ferry

American Old West

- Calamity Jane was a frontierswoman and professional scout best known for her claim of being a close friend of Wild Bill Hickok, but also for having gained fame fighting Native Americans.

American Revolution

- Deborah Sampson, first female to ever fight in the American military (after disguising herself as a man)

- "Molly Pitchers", patriot women who manned cannons to fend off the British during the war for independence

Argentina - Bolivia

- Juana Azurduy de Padilla was a military leader during the Argentine War of Independence and Bolivian War of Independence. She was appointed commander of the patriotic Northern Army of the Revolutionary Government of the United Provinces of the Rio de la Plata after the death of her husband.

Brazil

- Maria Quitéria, dressed as a man, enlisted in the forces fighting for Brazilian Independence. Once discovered, she was promoted to cadet and afterwards alferez. Her courage was recognized by the Emperor Pedro I.

- Anita Garibaldi, fought on the Ragamuffin War

- Maria Rosa, a 15-year-old girl who fought in the Contestado War. She wore white clothes, rode a white horse and claimed that she had divine inspiration

- Maria Bonita, a member of a Cangaço band, marauders and outlaws who terrorized the Brazilian Northeast in the 1920s and 1930s. Maria Bonita means "Beautiful Maria". She has the status of a 'folk heroine' in Brazil.

1.2.4　East Asia

Historical Mongolia

- Khutulun was a 13th-century Mongol princess, the daughter of the Mongol leader Qaidu Khan and a great-great granddaughter of Genghis Khan. According to legend she was a skilled warrior and wrestler who vowed that she would only marry a man who could defeat her in wrestling. Although no man was ever able to out-wrestle her, Khutuln ended up marrying a warrior named Abtakul (possibly to squelch rumors about an incestuous relationship between her and her father). Her story was made famous by foreign chroniclers Marco Polo, and Ibn Battuta, both of whom had heard of Khutuln's legend on their travels through Asia.

Historical China

- Hua Mulan was a (possibly legendary) woman who went to war disguised as a man, and was able to return home after years of war without being found out.

- Ng Mui was a Shaolin monastery abbess who created a kung fu system especially suitable for women.

- Yim Wing-chun, often cited in Wing Chun legends as the first Wing Chun master outside the monastic tradition, was a pupil of Ng Mui.

- Fu Hao was one of the many wives of King Wu Ding of the Shang Dynasty and, unusually for that time, also served as a military general and high priestess.

- Mother Lü began a peasant rebellion.

- Li Xiu defeated rebels as a military commander.

- Lady of Yue was a famous swordswoman

- Qin Liangyu fought battles with her husband.

- Sun Shangxiang, who is often depicted as a tomboy, was the sister of the warlord Sun Quan. She received extensive martial arts training, and her maidservants were armed with weapons, which was odd for her time.

- Lady Zhurong It's unknown whether she existed, but she was the only woman portrayed in the Romance of the Three Kingdoms who took part in fighting in the war during the three kingdoms period alongside her husband.

- Mu Guiying was a woman who commanded the armies against barbarian invaders

- Princess Pingyang formed a rebel army to assist her father in overthrowing the Emperor, and was declared 'no ordinary woman' upon her death.

- Ching Shih (1775–1844) prominent pirate in middle Qing China, early 19th century. A brilliant Cantonese pirate, she commanded over 300 junks manned by 20,000 to 40,000 pirates — men, women, and even children. She challenged the empires of the time, such as the British, Portuguese, and the Qing dynasty. Undefeated, she would become one of China and Asia's strongest pirates, and one of world history's most powerful pirates. She was also one of the few pirate captains to retire from piracy.

Historical Japan

- Empress Jingu was a legendary Japanese empress and famous among the onna bugeisha (woman warrior).

- Hangaku Gozen was an onna bugeisha (woman warrior).

- Tomoe Gozen (1157?–1247?) was an onna bugeisha (woman warrior).

- Marishi-Ten the goddess of heaven, who was adopted by warriors in the 8th century as a protector and patron goddess. While devotions to Marishi-ten predate Zen, they appear to be geared towards a similar meditative mode in order to enable the warrior to achieve a more heightened spiritual level. He lost interest in the issues of victory or defeat (or life and death), thus transcending to a level where he became so empowered that he was freed from his own grasp on mortality. The end result was that he became a better warrior.

- Kaihime (presumably born 1572) was said to have fought during the Siege of Odawara and to have personally crushed a rebellion, earning her father the respect of Hideyoshi Toyotomi. However, historians aren't entirely sure if she truly did accomplish those events.

Memorial of Queen Suriyothai in the Ayutthaya Province, Thailand.

1.2.5 Southeast Asia

Historical Indonesia

- Cut Nyak Dhien, (1850-1908), leader of the Acehnese guerrilla forces during the Aceh War. Following the death of her husband Teuku Umar, she led guerrilla actions against the Dutch for 25 years. She

Monument to Thao Thep Kasattri and Thao Sri Sunthon in the Phuket Province, Thailand.

was posthumously awarded the title of National Hero of Indonesia on May 2, 1964 by the Indonesian government.[3]

- Cut Nyak Meutia, (1870-1910), commander of the Achenese guerrilla forces during the Aceh War. Together with her husband, Teuku Cik Tunong, they worked hand in hand with the Acehnese to fight against the Dutch invasion.

- Admiral Keumalahayati, (fl. 16th century), an admiral in the navy of the Aceh Sultanate, which ruled the area of modern Aceh Province, Sumatra, Indonesia.[4] She was the first woman admiral in the modern world (if Artemisia I is not included). Her troops were drawn from Aceh's widows and known as the "Inong Balee", after the Inong Balee Fortress near the city of Banda Aceh.

- Martha Christina Tiahahu, (1800-1818), a Moluccan freedom fighter and National Heroine of Indonesia. Born to a military captain, Tiahahu was active in the military from a very young age. She joined the war led by Pattimura against the Dutch colonial government when she was 17, fighting in several battles.

- Nyi Ageng Serang, (1752–1838), born under the name Raden Ajeng Kustiyah Wulaningish Retno Edhi, was a commander during the Diponegoro War. The name Nyi Ageng Serang was given to her after her father died of disease and she took over his position.[5] At the beginning of Diponegoro War in 1825, 73-year-old Nyi Ageng Serang commanded the force on a stretcher to help Pangeran Diponegoro fighting the Dutch. One of her best-known strategies was the use of *lumbu* (green taro leaves) for disguise.

- Tribhuwana Wijayatunggadewi, was a Javanese queen regnant and the third Majapahit monarch, reigning from 1328 to 1350. She appointed Gajah Mada as prime minister and pursued massive expansion of the empire. In 1331, she led the empire's army personally to the battlefield with the help of her cousin, Adityawarman, to crush the rebellion in Sadeng and Keta.

Historical Philippines

- Gabriela Silang, (1731-1761), led insurgents from Ilocos during the Philippine Revolution against Spain, after the death of her husband, Diego Silang. She was captured by Spanish colonial forces in September 1761 and executed in the town square of Vigan, reportedly after watching the executions of all her men.[6]

Historical Thailand

Somdet Phra Sri Suriyothai (Thai: สมเด็จพระศรีสุริโยทัย) was a royal consort during the 16th century Ayutthaya period of Siam (now Thailand). She is famous for having given up her life in the defense of her husband, King Maha Chakkraphat, in a battle during the Burmese-Siamese War of 1548. For the movie, see *The Legend of Suriyothai*.

Thao Thep Kasattri (ท้าวเทพกระษัตรี) and Thao Sri Sunthon (ท้าวศรีสุนทร) were styles awarded to Than Phuying Chan (ท่านผู้หญิงจัน), wife of the then recently deceased governor, and her sister, Khun Muk (คุณมุก), who defended Phuket Province in the late eighteenth century. According to popular belief, they repelled a five-week invasion by Burmaese in 1785, by dressing up as male soldiers and rallying Siamese troops. Chan and Muk were later honored by King Rama I with the Thai honorific *Thao*, as **Thao Thep Kasattri** and **Thao Sri Sunthon**, respectively.[7][8][9][10][11] The "Heroine's Monument" honouring them is situated on the main highway (402) between the Phuket International Airport and Phuket town.[12]

Historical Vietnam

- The Trung Sisters, (c. 12 - 43 AD), known in Vietnamese as *Hai Bà Trưng* ("the two Trưng ladies"'), and individually as *Trưng Trắc* (Traditional Chinese: ▯▯; pinyin: Zhēng Cè) and *Trưng Nhị* (Traditional Chinese: ▯▯; pinyin: Zhēng Èr), were two 1st century AD women leaders who repelled Chinese invasions for three years, winning several battles against considerable odds, and are regarded as national heroines of Vietnam.

- Phùng Thị Chính was a Vietnamese noble woman who fought alongside the Trưng sisters. Legend says she gave birth on the front lines and carried her newborn in one arm and a sword in the other as she fought to open the ranks of the enemy.
  - Lê Chân, general of Trưng Sisters.
- Triệu Thị Trinh described as the Vietnamese Joan of Arc.
- Tây Sơn Ngũ Phụng Thư (*Five Phoenix women generals of Tay Son dynasty*):
  - Bùi Thị Xuân, (? - 1802), wife of general Trần Quang Diệu.
  - Bùi Thị Nhạn, (? - 1802), wife of Emperor Quang Trung.
  - Trần Thị Lan, (? - 1802), wife of general Nguyễn Văn Tuyết.
  - Huỳnh Thị Cúc, (? - 1802)
  - Nguyễn Thị Dung, (? - 1802), wife of general Trương Đăng Đồ.

1.2.6 Europe

Boudica and Her Daughters *near Westminster Pier, London, commissioned by Prince Albert and executed by Thomas Thornycroft*

Britons, Roman Britain, and History of Anglo-Saxon England

Three historical women:

- Boudica was a queen of the Brythonic Celtic Iceni people of Norfolk in Eastern Britain who led a major uprising of the tribes against the occupying forces of the Roman Empire.

- Ethelfleda (alternative spelling Aethelfled, Æthelfleda, Æthelflæd) (872/879 – 918), Queen of Mercia, called "Lady of the Mercians". Daughter of Alfred the Great, she succeeded to Mercian power upon the death of her husband Aethelred, Ealdorman of Mercia (883-911), in 911. She was a skilled military leader and tactician, who defended Mercia against neighboring tribes for eight years.

- Gwenllian ferch Gruffydd was Princess consort of Deheubarth in Wales. Often accompanying her husband on "lightning raids," in 1136 she raised an army herself and led the forces in the battle near Kidwelly Castle.[13][14] Though defeated, her patriotic revolt inspired others in South Wales to rise.[13] Their battle cry became, "Revenge for Gwenllian!"[15]

Two legendary women:

- Queen Cordelia (on whom the character in Shakespeare's *King Lear* is based), battled her nephews for control of her kingdom.[16]

- Queen Gwendolen fights her husband Locrinus in battle for the throne of Britain. She defeats him and becomes queen.[17]

Celtic mythology and Irish mythology

- Andraste is a Celtic war goddess invoked[18] by Boudica while fighting against the Roman occupation of Britain in AD 61.[19]

- Medb (also: Medhbh, Meadhbh, Meab°, Meabh, Maeve, Maev) is queen of Connacht in the Ulster Cycle of Irish mythology. As recounted in *The Cattle Raid of Cooley*, she started war with Ulster.[18]

- Scathach is a legendary Scottish woman warrior who appears in the Ulster Cycle. She trains Cuchulainn.

- Aife is Scathach's rival in war; she becomes the lover of Cuchulainn and gives birth to his son Connla.

- Liath Luachra, two characters of the same name in the Fenian Cycle.

- Muirisc, legendary warrior princess, daughter of Úgaine Mór (Hugony the Great), the sixty-sixth high king of Ireland.

- Triple warrior goddess: Morrígan, Badb, and Macha (could also include Nemain and Anann)

- On St Kilda, one of the most isolated islands of Scotland, legends exist of a female warrior. A mysterious structure is known as *Taigh na Banaghaisgeich*, the 'Amazon's House'. As Martin Martin, who travelled there in 1697 recorded:

> This Amazon is famous in their traditions: her house or dairy of stone is yet extant; some of the inhabitants dwell in it all summer, though it be some hundred years old; the whole is built of stone, without any wood, lime, earth, or mortar to cement it, and is built in form of a circle pyramid-wise towards the top, having a vent in it, the fire being always in the centre of the floor; the stones are long and thin, which supplies the defect of wood; the body of this house contains not above nine persons sitting; there are three beds or low vaults that go off the side of the wall, a pillar betwixt each bed, which contains five men apiece; at the entry to one of these low vaults is a stone standing upon one end fix'd; upon this they say she ordinarily laid her helmet; there are two stones on the other side, upon which she is reported to have laid her sword: she is said to have been much addicted to hunting, and that in her time all the space betwixt this isle and that of Harries, was one continued tract of dry land.[20]

Similar stories of a female warrior who hunted the now submerged land between the Outer Hebrides and St Kilda are reported from Harris.[21]

Historical Czech Lands

- The story of Šárka and Vlasta is a legend dealing with events in the "Maidens' War" in 7th-century Bohemia.

England

- Margaret of Anjou, wife of Henry VI, emerged as the *de facto* leader of the Lancastrians during the Wars of the Roses. She introduced conscription, amassed armies, tortured and burnt to death Yorkist knights and won several battles before ultimately being defeated by the Yorkists.

- Catherine of Aragon was Queen Regent, Governor of the Realm and Captain General of the King's Forces from 30 June 1513 – 22 October 1513 when Henry VIII was fighting a war in France. When Scotland invaded, they were crushingly defeated at the Battle of

Bronze statue of Jeanne Hachette in Beauvais, by Gabriel-Vital Dubray

Flodden, with Catherine addressing the army, and riding north in full armour with a number of the troops, despite being heavily pregnant at the time. She sent a letter to Henry along with the bloodied coat of the King of Scots, James IV, who was killed in the battle.

Duchy of Brittany

- **Joanna of Flanders** (c. 1295 – September 1374), also known as **Jehanne de Montfort** and **Jeanne la Flamme**, was consort Duchess of Brittany by her marriage to John IV, Duke of Brittany. She was the daughter of Louis I, Count of Nevers and Joan, Countess of Rethel, and the sister of Louis I, Count of Flanders. Joanna organized resistance and made use of diplomatic means to protect her family and her country. In the siege of Hennebont, she took up arms, dressed in armor, and conducted the defence of the town. She eventually led a raid of soldiers outside the walls of the town and demolished one of the enemy's rear camps. She was an earlier patron for women, and a possible influence to Joan of Arc.

Illyria

- Teuta was an Illyrian queen and is frequently evoked as a fearsome "pirate queen" in art and stories dealing with Albanian past.

The Netherlands

- Kenau Simonsdochter Hasselaer (1526–1588) became a legendary folk hero for her fearless defense of the city against the Spanish invaders during the siege of Haarlem in 1573.

Albania

- Nora of Kelmendi (17th century), is also referred to as the "Helen of Albania" as her beauty also sparked a great war. She is also called the Albanian Brünhilde too, for she herself was the greatest woman warrior in the history of Albania.

- Tringe Smajl Martini, a young girl in war against the Ottoman Empire army after her father Smajl Martini, the clan leader was kidnapped. She never married, never had children, and did not have any siblings. In 1911, the New York Times described Tringe Smajli as the "Albanian Joan of Arc".

- Shote Galica (1895 - 1927), remarkable warrior of the Albanian insurgent national liberation with the goal of unification of all Albanian territories.

Historical France

- Jeanne Hachette (1456 - ?) was a French heroine known as *Jeanne Fourquet* and nicknamed *Jeanne Hachette* ('Jean the Hatchet').

- Joan of Arc (*Jeanne d'Arc* in French) asserted that she had visions from God which told her to recover her homeland from English domination late in the Hundred Years' War. The uncrowned King Charles VII sent her to the siege at Orléans as part of a relief mission. She gained prominence when she overcame the dismissive attitude of veteran commanders and lifted the siege in only nine days. She was tried and executed for heresy when she was only 19 years old. The judgment was rejected by the Pope and she was declared innocent 24 years later (and canonized in 1920).

Greek Mythology

Amazon preparing for the battle (Queen Antiope or Armed Venus) -Pierre-Eugène-Emile Hébert 1860 National Gallery of Art

- The Amazons (in Greek, Ἀμαζόνες) were a mythical and ancient nation of female warriors. Herodotus placed them in a region bordering Scythia in Sarmatia. The histories and legends in Greek mythology may be inspired by warrior women among the Sarmatians.

- Artemis (Latin Diana) is the Greek goddess of the hunt, daughter of Zeus and Leto and twin sister to Apollo. She is usually depicted bearing a bow and arrows.

- Atalanta is one of the few mortal heroines in Greek mythology. She possessed great athletic prowess: she was a skilled huntress, archer, and wrestler, and was capable of running at astounding speeds. She is said to have participated in the Argonaut expedition, and is one of the central figures in the Calydonian Boar hunt. Atalanta was renowned for her beauty and was sought by many suitors, including Melanion or Hippomenes, whom she married after he defeated her in a foot race. According to some stories, the pair were eventually turned into lions, either by Zeus or Aphrodite.

- Athena (Latin: Minerva) is the goddess of wisdom, war strategy, and arts and crafts. Often shown bearing a shield depicting the gorgon Medusa (Aegis) given to her by her father Zeus. Athena is an armed warrior goddess, and appears in Greek mythology as a helper of many heroes, including Heracles, Jason, and Odysseus.

- Enyo, a minor war goddess, delights in bloodshed and the destruction of towns, and accompanies Ares—said to be her father, in other accounts her brother—in battles.

- Hippolyta is a queen of the Amazons, and a daughter of Ares. It was her girdle that Hercules was required by Eurystheus to obtain. He captured her and brought her to Athens, where he gave her to the ruler, Theseus, to become his bride.

- Penthesilea, in a story by the Greek traveller Pausanias, is the Amazonian queen who led the Amazons against the Greeks during the Trojan War. In other stories, she is said to be the younger sister of Hippolyta, Theseus's queen, whom Penthesilea had accidentally slain while on a hunt. It was then that she joined the Trojan War to assuage her guilt. She was killed and mourned by Achilles, who greatly admired her courage, youth and beauty.

Historical Republic of Poland and Grand Duchy of Lithuania

- Emilia Plater (Emilija Pliaterytė) - Polish-Lithuanian commander in the November Uprising against Russia in the 19th century, who became a symbol of resistance and was immortalised in a poem by Adam Mickiewicz. She was a Polish-Lithuanian noble woman and a revolutionary from the lands of the partitioned Polish-Lithuanian Commonwealth. She fought in the November Uprising and is considered a national hero in Poland, Lithuania and Belarus, which were former parts of the Commonwealth. She is often referred to as the Lithuanian Joan of Arc, while actually her most widely known portrait is often mistaken for a picture of Joan of Arc herself in worldwide popular culture (as in the series *Charmed*), despite the fact that "Joan of Arc" is anachronistically portrayed in Emilia's 19th-century clothing.

- Grażyna (Gražina) - a mythical Lithuanian chieftainess Grażyna who fought against the forces of the medieval Order of the Teutonic Knights, described in an 1823 narrative poem, *Grażyna*, by Adam Mickiewicz. The woman character is believed to have been based on Mickiewicz's own sweetheart from Kaunas,

Karolina Kowalska. The name was originally conceived by Mickiewicz himself, having used the root of the Lithuanian adjective gražus, meaning "beautiful".

Portuguese Legend

- Brites de Almeida, aka *Padeira de Aljubarrota* was a Portuguese legendary figure associated with Portuguese victory at Aljubarrota Battle over Spanish forces in 1385 near Aljubarrota, Portugal. She supposedly killed seven Spanish invaders who were hidden in an oven.

- Deu-la-deu Martins, the heroine of the North. The Castilian had besieged the town of Monção for many weeks and inside the town walls, provisions were almost depleted. Knowing that the invaders also were demoralized that the town resisted for so long and without provisions themselves, Deu-la-deu ("God gave her") made loaves of bread with the little flour that remained in Monção and threw the loaves at the invaders from the walls, shouting at them defiantly "God gave these, God will give more". As a result, the Castilians gave up the siege believing that still there was a lot resistance and infinite provisions within the town walls.

Italian history, folklore and Roman Mythology

- Bellona is the Roman goddess of war: the Roman counterpart to the Greek war goddess Enyo. She prepared the chariot of her brother Mars when he was going to war, and appeared in battles armed with a whip and holding a torch.

- Bradamante is the sister of Rinaldo, and one of the heroines in Orlando Innamorato by Matteo Maria Boiardo and Orlando Furioso by Ludovico Ariosto in their handling of the Charlemagne legends. Bradamante and his lover Ruggiero were destined to become the legendary ancestors of the royal House of Este who were the patrons to both Boiardo and Ariosto. Bradamante is depicted as one of the greatest female knights in literature. She is an expert fighter, and wields a magical lance that unhorses anyone it touches. She is also one of the main characters in several novels including Italo Calvino's surrealistic, highly ironic novel *Il Cavaliere inesistente* (The Nonexistent Knight).

- Camilla was the Amazon queen of the Volsci. She was famous for her footspeed; Virgil claims that she could run across water and chase down horses. She was slain by Arruns while fighting Aeneas and the Trojans in Italy.

- Caterina Sforza (1463 – 28 May 1509), was an Italian noble woman and Countess of Forlì and Lady of Imola first with her husband, Girolamo Riario, and, after his death, as a regent of her son, Ottaviano. The descendant of a dynasty of noted condottieri, Caterina, from an early age, distinguished herself by her bold and impetuous actions taken to safeguard her possessions from possible usurpers, and to defend her dominions from attack, when they were involved in political intrigues that were a distinguishing in Italy. When Pope Sixtus IV died, rebellions and disorder immediately spread through Rome, including looting of his supporters' residences. In this time of anarchy, Caterina, who was in her seventh month of pregnancy, crossed the Tiber on horseback to occupy the rocca (fortress) of Castel Sant'Angelo on behalf of her husband. From this position, and with the obedience of the soldiers, Caterina could monitor the Vatican and dictate the conditions for the new conclave. Famous was also her fierce resistance to the Siege of Forlì by Cesare Borgia who finally was able to capture her dressed in armor and a sword in hand. Caterina's resistance was admired throughout all Italy; Niccolò Machiavelli reports that many songs and epigrams were composed in her honour. She had a large number of children, of whom only the youngest, Captain Giovanni dalle Bande Nere, inherited the forceful, militant character of his mother. In the following centuries Caterina was remembered in the folklore as *Tigre di Forlivo* (The Tiger of Forlì).

- Caterina Segurana (1506 - 15 August 1543), was an Italian woman from the County of Nice who distinguished herself during the Siege of Nice of 1543 in which France and the Ottoman Empire invaded the Duchy of Savoy. Caterina Segurana, a common washerwoman, led the townspeople into battle.

- Fantaghirò is the main character of an ancient Tuscany fairy tale named: Fanta-Ghirò persona bella, an Italian fable about a rebellious youngest daughter of a warrior king, a warrior princess. Italo Calvino talks about it in his collection of Italian fairy tales.

History of Russia|Historical Russia

- Saint Olga ruled in Kievskiy, Ukraine, from AD 945 to 960. In 945, a tribe of Drevlyane, killed her husband, King Igor. Princess Olga avenged this death four times. The first time, she buried twenty ambassadors from Drevlyane alive. The second time, she set fire to a bathhouse that was being used by another group of Drevlyane ambassadors. The third time, Princess Olga managed to get about 5,000 Drevlyane drunk, and then ordered her soldiers to assault and (presumably) kill them. Lastly, Princess Olga burned the entire city of Drevlyane, using sparrows and doves to which were attached strings of fire.

- White Tights are an urban legend about Baltic female snipers supposed to have fought against Russian forces in various recent conflicts.

- The Polinitzi are Amazon-like warrior females of the old Russian hero epics (byline).

Scandinavian folklore and Germanic paganism

- Blenda is the heroine of a legend from Småland, who leads the women of Värend in an attack on a pillaging Danish army and annihilates it.

- Freyja is a fertility goddess, the sister of the fertility god Freyr and daughter of the sea god Njörðr. Freyja is also a goddess of war, battle, death, magic, prophecy, and wealth. Freyja is cited as receiving half of the dead lost in battle in her hall Sessrúmnir, whereas Odin would receive the other half. Some scholars argue that Freyja, Frigg, and Gefion are Avatars of each other. She is also sometimes associated with the Valkyries and disir.

- Shieldmaidens in Scandinavian folklore were women who did not have the responsibility for raising a family and could take up arms to live like warriors. Many of them figure in Norse mythology. One of the most famous shieldmaidens is Hervor and she figures in the cycle of the magic sword Tyrfing.

- The Valkyries in Norse mythology are female deities, who serve Odin. The name means *choosers of the slain*.

- Þorgerðr Hölgabrúðr and Irpa are two goddesses, described as sisters, that appear at the Battle of Hjörungavágr to assist the fleet of Haakon Sigurdsson against the Jomvikings. The two goddesses produce harsh thunderstorms, ferocious squalls, and shoot arrows from their fingertips, each arrow described as killing a man, resulting in the defeat of the Jomvikings.

- Brunhild, in the *Nibelungen*, is "a royal maiden who reigned beyond the sea:

    "From sunrise to the sundown no paragon had she.
    All boundless as her beauty was her strength was peerless too,
    And evil plight hung o'er the knight who dared her love to woo.

For he must try three bouts with her; the whirling
spear to fling;
To pitch the massive stone; and then to follow
with a spring;
And should he beat in every feat his wooing well
has sped,
But he who fails must lose his love, and likewise
lose his head."

- In The saga of Hrolf Kraki, Skuld (not to be confused
  with the Norn of the same name) was a half-elven
  princess who raised an army of criminals and monsters to take over the throne of her half-brother Hrolfr
  Kraki, using necromancy to resurrect any fallen soldiers before she personally saw to Kraki's end.

Spain

*Agustina, maid of Aragon, fires a gun on the French invaders at
Saragossa.*

- Agustina de Aragón ('Agustina, maid of Aragon',
  also known as "the Spanish Joan of Arc") was a famous Spanish heroine who defended Spain during the
  Spanish War of Independence, first as a civilian and
  later as a professional officer in the Spanish Army.
  She has been the subject of much folklore, mythology, and artwork, including sketches by Goya. Her
  most famous feat was at the bloody sieges of Saragossa
  where, at the moment the Spanish troops abandoned
  their posts not to fall to nearby French bayonets, she
  ran forward, loaded a cannon, and lit the fuse, shred-
  ding a wave of attackers at point blank range. The sight
  of a lone woman bravely manning the cannons inspired
  the fleeing Spanish troops and other volunteers to return and assist her.

- La Galana ('Juana Galán') was another woman who
  fought in the Spanish War of Independence. She defended Valdepeñas, armed with a baton and aided by

the rest of the women in the village because there were
not enough men in Valdepeñas due to the war circumstances. They threw boiling water and oil through the
windows. French soldiers were delayed in arriving at
the Battle of Bailen because of this, so Spanish forces
won. Also see Valdepeñas Uprising for more information about this guerrilla action.

- La Fraila lived in Valdepeñas as Juana Galán did. During the Spanish War of Independence offered food
  and rest in Valdepeñas' hermitage to the French soldiers. When they were sleeping, La Fraila (which is
  an alias and her actual name is unknown) closed the
  doors and set the hermitage on fire using gunpowder
  as vengeance of her son's death by French army. She
  died in the fire as well.

- María Pita. She defended A Coruña against Sir Francis Drake's army.

1.2.7   Near East

Pre-Islamic Arabia|History of Arabia

- Queen Mavia, leader of the Tanukh confederation

- Queen Zenobia of Palmyra

Rashidun Caliphate|Early Islam

Khawlah bint al-Azwar was the daughter of one of the chiefs
of Bani Assad tribe, and her family embraced Islam in its
first days. The recorded history of that era mentions repeatedly the feats of Khawla in battles that took place in
Syria, Lebanon, Jordan and Palestine. In one instance, she
fought in disguise as a man to rescue her brother Derar after the Romans captured him. The Romans eventually lost
the battle and fled. When her identity was discovered, the
commander of the Moslem army was very impressed with
her courage, and he allowed her to lead the attack against
the fleeing Romans; they were defeated and the prisoners
were all released. In another battle in Ajnadin, Khawla's
spear broke, and her mare was killed, and she found herself a prisoner. But she was astonished to find that the Romans attacked the women camp and captured several of
them. Their leader gave the prisoners to his commanders,
and ordered Khawla to be moved into his tent. She was
furious, and decided that to die is more honorable than living in disgrace. She stood among the other women, and
called them to fight for their freedom and honor or die.
They took the tents' poles and pegs and attacked the Roman guards, keeping a formation of a tight circle, as she
told them. Khawla led the attack, killed the first guard with
her pole, with the other women following her. According to

Al Wakidi, they managed to kill 30 Roman soldiers, five of whom were killed by Khawla herself, including the soldier who wanted to rape her. She was a brunette, tall, slim and of great beauty, and she was also a distinguished poet.

Nusaybah bint Ka'ab, also known as Umm Ammarah (Ammarah's mother), a Hebrew woman by origin from the Banu Najjar tribe, was an early convert to Islam. Nusaybah was attending the Battle of Uhud like other women, and her intention was to bring water to the soldiers, and attend the wounded while her husband and son fought on the side of the Moslems. But after the Moslem archers disobeyed their orders and began deserting their high ground believing victory was at hand, the tide of the battle changed, and it appeared that defeat was imminent. When this occurred, Nusaybah entered the battle, carrying a sword and shield. She shielded Muhammad from the arrows of the enemy, and received several wounds while fighting. She was highly praised by Muhammad on her courage and heroism. During the battle her son was wounded and she cut off the leg of the aggressor.

Persian mythology and History of Iran|Historical Persia

- Gordafarid is one of the heroines in the *Shāhnāmeh*. She was a champion who fought against Sohrab (another Iranian hero who was the commander of the Turanian army) and delayed the Turanian troops who were marching on Persia.

- Banu Goshasp is an important heroine in Persian mythology.[22] She is the daughter of Rustam and the wife of the hero Giv.

Ancient Egypt

- Ankt may have originated in Asia Minor. Within Egypt she was later syncretized as Neith (who by that time had developed aspects of a war goddess).

- Cleopatra VII was a Hellenistic co-ruler of Egypt with her father (Ptolemy XII Auletes) and later with her brothers/husbands Ptolemy XIII and Ptolemy XIV. Her patron goddess was Isis, and thus during her reign, it was believed that she was the re-incarnation and embodiment of the goddess of wisdom.

- Sekhmet is a warrior goddess depicted as a lioness, the fiercest hunter known to the Egyptians.

- Though her reign was primarily peaceful, the pharaoh Hatshepsut fought in several battles during her younger years.

The warrior goddess Sekhmet, shown with her sun disk and cobra crown

- Nefertiti, wife of the pharaoh Akhenaten, has been at times depicted as smiting enemies in a manner similar to how a male ruler typically would.

Ahhotep, wife of Seqenenre Tao II was believed to have been in command of the army while her son Ahmose I was still young.

Mesopotamian mythology

- Ishtar is the Assyrian and Babylonian counterpart to the Sumerian Inanna and to the cognate Phoenician goddess Astarte. Anunit, Atarsamain and Esther are alternative names for Ishtar. Ishtar is a goddess of fertility, sexual love, and war.[23] In the Babylonian pantheon, she "was the divine personification of the planet Venus".[24]

- Semiramis was a legendary Assyrian empress-regnant who first came to prominence for her bravery in battle and greatly expanded her empire.

Old Testament

- Deborah, a prophetess mentioned in the *Book of Judges*, was a poet who rendered her judgments beneath a palm tree between Ramah and Bethel in the land of Benjamin. After her victory over Sisera and the Canaanite army, there was peace in the land for forty years.

Phoenician mythology

- Ashtart Phoenician "štrt" ('Ashtart); and Hebrew עשתרת (Ashtoreth, singular, or Ashtarot, plural); Greek (Astarte) is the Phoenician counterpart to the Sumerian Inanna and to the cognate Babylonian goddess Ishtar as well as the Greek Aphrodite. She is a goddess of fertility, sexual love, and war. Ashtoreth is mentioned in the Hebrew Bible as a foreign, non-Judahite goddess, the principal goddess of the homeland of the Phoenicians which is in modern day Lebanon, representing the productive power of nature. Herodotus wrote that the religious community of Aphrodite originated in Phoenicia (modern day Lebanon) and came to Greeks from there. He also wrote about the world's largest temple of Aphrodite, in one of the Phoenician cities.

Image of Durga, shown riding her tiger and attacking the demon Mahishasura

1.2.8   South Asia

Razia Sultana

- Razia Sultana, usually referred to in history as Razia Sultan or Razia Sultana, was the Sultana of Delhi in India from 1236 to 1240. She was of Turkish Seljuks ancestry and like some other Moslem princesses of the time, she was trained to lead armies and administer kingdoms if necessary. Razia Sultana, the fifth Mamluk Sultan, was the very first woman ruler in Moslem and Turkish history.

Rudrama Devi

- Rani Rudrama Devi (1259–1289) was one of the most prominent rulers of the Kakatiya dynasty on the Deccan Plateau, being one of the few ruling queens in India's history. She was born, as Rudramba, to King Ganapathideva (or Ganapatideva, or Ganapathi Devudu). As Ganapathideva had no sons, Rudramma

- Tanit is a Phoenician lunar goddess, worshiped as the patron goddess at Carthage. Her shrine excavated at Sarepta in southern Phoenicia (Carthage) revealed an inscription that identified her for the first time in her homeland (Phoenicia of the Levant) and related her securely to the Phoenician goddess Astarte/Ashtart. In Egyptian, her name means Land of Neith, Neith being a war goddess. Long after the fall of Carthage, Tanit is still venerated in North Africa under the Latin name of Juno Caelestis, for her identification with the Roman goddess Juno. Hvidberg-Hansen (Danish professor of Semitic philology), notes that Tanit is sometimes depicted with a lion's head, showing her warrior quality. In modern times the name, with the spelling "Tanith", has been used as a female given name, both for real people and, more frequently, in occult fiction. From the 5th century BC onwards, Tanit is associated with that of Ba`al Hammon. She is given the epithet pene baal ("face of Baal") and the title rabat, the female form of rab (chief).

was formally designated as a son through the ancient Putrika ceremony and given the male name of Rudradeva. When she was only fourteen years old, Rani Rudramma Devi succeeded her father. Rudramadevi was married to Veerabhadra, Eastern Chalukyan prince of Nidadavolu.[25]

Rani Velu Nachiyar

Rani Velu Nachiyar (Tamil: இராணி வேலு நாச்சியார்) was an 18th-century India Queen from Sivaganga. Rani Velu Nachiyar was the first Queen to fight against the British in India, even preceding the famous Rani Laxmibai of Jhansi.She was the princess of Ramanathapuram and the daughter of Chellamuthu Sethupathy. She married the king of Siva Gangai and they had a daughter - Vellachi Nachiar. When her husband Muthuvaduganathaperiya Udaiyathevar was killed, she was drawn into battle. Her husband and his second wife were killed by a few British soldiers and the son of the Nawab of Arcot. She escaped with her daughter, lived under the protection of Hyder Ali at Virupachi near Dindigul for eight years. During this period, she formed an army and sought an alliance with Gopala Nayaker and Hyder Ali with the aim of attacking the British. In 1780, Rani Velu Nachiyar fought the British with military assistance from Gopala Nayaker and Hyder Ali and won the battle. When Velu Nachiyar finds the place where the British stock their ammunition, she builds the first human bomb. A faithful follower, Kuyili douses herself in oil, lights herself and walks into the storehouse.[3] Rani Velu Nachiyar formed a woman's army named "udaiyaal" in honour of her adopted daughter — Udaiyaal, who died detonating a British arsenal. Nachiar was one of the few rulers who regained her kingdom and ruled it for 10 more years.

Chand Bibi

- Chand Bibi (1550–1599), also known as Chand Khatun or Chand Sultana, was an India Moslem woman warrior. She acted as the Regent of Bijapur (1580–90) and Regent of Ahmednagar (1596–99)[1]. Chand Bibi is best known for defending Ahmednagar against the Mughal forces of Emperor Akbar.

Abbakka Rani

- Abbakka Rani or Abbakka Mahadevi was the queen of Tulunadu who fought the Portuguese in the latter half of the 16th century. She belonged to the Chowta dynasty who ruled over the area from the temple town of Moodabidri.

Tarabai

- Tarabai (1675–1761) was a queen of the Maratha Empire in India.

Bibi Dalair Kaur

- Bibi Dalair Kaur was a 17th-century Sikh woman who fought against the Moghuls.

Mai Bhago

- Mai Bhago was a Sikh woman who led Sikh soldiers against the Mughals in 1704.

Malalai of Maiwand

- Malalai of Maiwand is a national folk hero of Afghanistan who rallied local Pashtun fighters against the British troops at the 1880 Battle of Maiwand.

Onake Obavva

- Onake Obavva (18th Century) was a woman who fought the forces of Hyder Ali single-handedly with a masse (Onake) in the small kingdom of Chitradurga in the Chitradurga district of Karnataka, India. She is considered to be the epitome of Kannada women pride, with the same standing as Kittur Chennamma and Keladi Chennamma.

Begum Samru

- Begum Samru (ca 1753- 1836), also known as Zebunissa, Farzana, and Joanna after baptism, started her career as a Nautch girl in 18th Century India, and eventually became the ruler of Sardhana, a principality near Meerut. Later on, she played a key role in the politics and power struggle in 18th and 19th century India. She is also regarded as the only Roman Catholic Ruler in India.

Kittur Chennamma

- Kittur Chennamma (1778–1829) was the queen of the princely state of Kittur in Karnataka. Her legacy and first victory are still commemorated in Kittur, during the Kittur Utsava of every 22–24 October. The festival is similar to the Mysore Dasara.

Rani Lakshmibai

- Rani Lakshmibai known as Jhansi Ki Rani, was the queen of the Maratha-ruled princely state of Jhansi, was one of the leading figures of the India Rebellion of 1857, and a symbol of resistance to British rule in India.

Rani Durgavati

- Rani Durgavati was born in the family of famous [Rajput] Chandel Emperor Keerat Rai.

Keladi Chennamma

- Keladi Chennamma was daughter of Siddappa Setty of Kundapur. She became the queen of Keladi Nayaka dynasty who fought the Mughal Army of Aurangzeb from her base in the kingdom of Keladi in the Shimoga district of Karnataka State, India. Her rule lasted for 25 years and Keladi kingdom was probably the last to lose autonomy to Mysore rulers and subsequently to British.

Belawadi Mallamma

- Belawadi Mallamma, to defend her husband's kingdom, she fought against the Maratha king Shivaji Maharaj.

Unniyarcha

- Unniyarcha: She was a chekava/Ezhava woman warrior from Kerala famous for her valour and beauty.

Hindu Religion

- Durga (Sanskrit: "the inaccessible"[26] or "the invincible",[27] Bengali: দুর্গা) is a form of Devi, the supreme goddess of Hinduism. According to the narrative from the Devi Mahatmya of the Markandeya Purana, the form of Durga was created as a warrior goddess to fight a demon. The nine-day holiday dedicated to Durga, *The Durga Puja,* is the biggest annual festival in Bengal and other parts of Eastern India and is celebrated by Hindus all over the world.

- Kālī (Sanskrit: काली, IPA: [kɑːliː]; Bengali: কালী; Punjabi: ਕਾਲੀ; Sinhalese: කාලි; Telugu: కాళికాదేవి; Kannada: ಕಾಳಿ ಮಾತಾ; Tamil: காளி), also known as **Kālikā** (Sanskrit: कालिका, Bengali: কালিকা), is the Hindu goddess associated with empowerment, shakti.

The name Kali comes from *kāla,* which means black, time, death, lord of death, and thus another name for Shiva. Kali means "the black one". Although sometimes presented as dark and violent, her earliest incarnation as a figure of annihilation still has some influence. In Kāli's most famous myth, Durga and her assistants, the Matrikas, wound the demon Raktabija, in various ways and with a variety of weapons in an attempt to destroy him. They soon find that they have worsened the situation, for, with every drop of blood that is spilt from Raktabija, he reproduces a clone of himself. The battlefield becomes increasingly filled with his duplicates.[28] Durga, in need of help, summons Kāli to combat the demons. It is said, in some versions, that the Goddess Durga actually assumes the form of Goddess Kāli at this time. Kali destroys Raktabija by sucking the blood from his body and putting the many Raktabija duplicates in her gaping mouth. Pleased with her victory, Kali then dances on the field of battle, stepping on the corpses of the slain. Her consort Shiva lies among the dead beneath her feet, a representation of Kali commonly seen in her iconography as *Daksinakali.*

- Other warrior goddesses include Chamunda ("the killer of demon Chanda and Munda") and the goddess group Matrikas ("Mothers").

- Vishpala (in *The Rigveda*) is a warrior queen who, after having lost a leg in battle had an iron prosthesis made. Afterwards, she returned to fight.[29]

1.2.9   See also

- List of female action heroes

- Woman warrior

- Timeline of women in early modern warfare

1.2.10   Notes

[1] ^ Druett, Joan (2000). She Captains : Heroines and Hellions of the Sea. New York: Simon & Schuster.

[2] http://www.dailymail.co.uk/news/article-2285841/ The-women-fought-men-Rare-Civil-War-pictures-female-soldiers-dres html

[3] Victory News Magazine

[4] "Admiral Keumalahayati". Retrieved May 30, 2011.

[5] Ajisaka 2008, p. 17

[6] Witeck, John. (2000.) "Women as Warriors: The Philippine Revolutionary Context." Navigating islands and continents: conversations and contestations in and around the Pacific: selected essays, pp. 4-23. Ed. Cynthia G. Franklin, Ruth Hsu, Suzanne Kosanke. Honolulu: University of Hawai'i Press.

[7] Changing Identities Among the Baba Chinese and Thai Muslims in a Tourist Paradise Khoo Su Nin (Salma) Nasution

[8] Phuket history by Richard Russell MD

[9] phuket history Gotophuket.com

[10] Thao Thep Krasatri and Thao Sri Soonthorn

[11] Thalang's defiant last stand Tipwarintron Tanaakarachod

[12] The Two Heroines Monument

[13] Lloyd, J.E. *A History of Wales; From the Norman Invasion to the Edwardian Conquest*, Barnes & Noble Publishing, Inc. 2004. pp. 80, 82-85.

[14] Kidwelly Castle by C.A. Ralegh Radford

[15] Warner, Philip. *Famous Welsh Battles*, pg 79. 1997. Barnes and Noble, Inc.

[16] Geoffrey of Monmouth, p.286

[17] Geoffrey of Monmouth, translated by Lewis Thorpe (1966). *The History of the Kings of Britain*. London, Penguin Group. p. 286.

[18] Warrior queens and blind critics

[19] Cassius Dio. Published online by Bill Thayer. Cf. also the Gaulish goddess Andarta.

[20] "A Voyage to St. Kilda" in *A Description of the Western Isles of Scotland*(1703)

[21] Maclean, Charles (1977) *Island on the Edge of the World: the Story of St. Kilda*, Canongate ISBN 0-903937-41-7 pages 27–8.

[22] Djalal Khaleghi-Motlagh), "Goshasb Banu" in Encyclopædia Iranica

[23] Wilkinson, p. 24

[24] Guirand, p. 58

[25] History of the Minor Chāḷukya Families in Medieval Āndhradēśa By Kolluru Suryanarayana

[26] "Durga." Encyclopædia Britannica. 2007. Encyclopædia Britannica Online. 25 February 2007 <http://www.britannica.com/ebc/article-9363243/Durga">.

[27] "Durga" Sanatan Society <http://www.sanatansociety.org/hindu_gods_and_goddesses/durga.htm>.

[28] D. Kinsley p. 118.

[29] "A Brief Review of the History of Amputations and Prostheses Earl E. Vanderwerker, Jr., M.D. JACPOC 1976 Vol 15, Num 5".

Chapter 2

War Goddesses (in Alphabetical Order)

2.1 Agasaya

Agasaya, "The Shrieker," was a Semitic war goddess who was merged into Ishtar in her identity as warrior of the sky.

2.2 Agrona

*Agronā is the reconstructed Proto-Celtic name for the river Aeron in Wales. The river's name literally means 'carnage'.[1] It is hypothesized that there may have been an eponymous river-goddess associated with strife or war.[2]

2.2.1 Notes

[1] Proto-Celtic—English lexicon and English—Proto-Celtic lexicon. University of Wales Centre for Advanced Welsh and Celtic Studies. (See also this page for background and disclaimers.) Cf. also the University of Leiden database.

[2] "Agrona" in Mary Jones' *Celtic Encyclopedia*.

2.2.2 Bibliography

- Ellis, Peter Berresford, *Dictionary of Celtic Mythology* (Oxford Paperback Reference), Oxford University Press, (1994): ISBN 0-19-508961-8

- MacKillop, James. *Dictionary of Celtic Mythology*. Oxford: Oxford University Press, 1998. ISBN 0-19-280120-1.

- Wood, Juliette, *The Celts: Life, Myth, and Art*, Thorsons Publishers (2002): ISBN 0-00-764059-5

2.2.3 External links

- Celtic Gods and their Associates

- Proto-Celtic — English lexicon

2.3 Alaisiagae

In Romano-British culture and Germanic polytheism, the **Alaisiagae** (possibly "Dispatching Terrors" or "All-Victorious") were a pair of Celtic and Germanic goddesses deifying victory.

2.3.1 Centres of worship

The Alaisiagae were Germanic deities who were worshipped in Roman Britain, altar-stones raised to them having been recovered in the United Kingdom at Vercovicium (Housesteads Roman Fort) at Hadrian's Wall in England.

Another centre of worship was perhaps the town of Bitburg, near the German-Belgian border, which was called "Beda Vicus," which although Latin derives from either Celtic or Germanic "Village of Beda." In Roman times, this was situated in variously Celtic and Germanic territory, west of the Rhine and subject under to various tribal groups often with mixed ethnic definitions.

2.3.2 Votive inscriptions

One of the votive inscriptions to these goddesses reads:

- DEO MARTI THINCSO ET DVABVS ALAISAGIS BEDE ET FIMMILENE ET N AVG GERM CIVES TVIHANTI VSLM

- "To the god Mars Thincsus and the two Alaisagae, Beda and Fimmilena, and the divine spirit of the emperor, the German tribesmen from Tuihantis willingly and deservedly fulfill their vow."

Mars Thicsus is thought to be the Germanic war-god Tiw who was also connected to oath-taking and the thing, a kind of judicial gathering. The name of the Germanic soldiers "Tuihantis" also attests to this connection with the one-handed sword god Tiw.

The second inscription reads: DEABVS ALAISIAGIS BAVDIHILLIE ET FRIAGABI ET N(umini) AVG(usti) N(umerus) HNAVDIFRIDI V(otum) S(olvit) L(ibens) M(erito)

The third word is often mis-reported as beginning with BO not BA in order to make it appear more Celtic and less Germanic.

- These goddesses are possibly recorded on two inscriptions in Greek recorded in *l'Année Épigraphique* for 1973.

2.3.3   Syncretism

The goddesses called the Alaisiagae are named on altar-stones from the same fort on Hadrian's Wall as being parallel with two Germanic goddesses: Celtic *Boudihillia* is equated with Germanic *Fimmilena* and Celtic *Beda* is equated with Germanic *Friagabis*. These parallel goddesses are taken to be Germanic not only because of clues in the inscriptions and the Germanic mercenaries at the wall at the time, but also because they both have an initial 'f-,' a sound not known to have developed in Celtic at this time. Equally, the two goddesses are not known to be Roman. Beda may have been an abbreviation for Ricagambeda since the two names share similar semantics. Boudihillia and Beda are more likely Celtic names however.

2.3.4   Archeological setting

The altar stones of the Alaisiagae were recovered in the Temple of Mars at Vercovicium. This roughly circular temple was found on top of Chapel Hill a little to the south of the fort, its walls of undressed stone facing with an earth and rubble infill enclosed an area measuring about 17¼ ft. across; the insubstantial foundations indicate that the superstructure was at least half-timbered. The temple was built in the early-3rd century upon the ruins of a rectangular workshop in the *vicus* which had been destroyed during the barbarian incursions of AD196. It contained altars dedicated by the commanders and men of all three units known to be stationed at Vercovicium to the god Mars Thincsus, the Romanized aspect of a Teutonic god, a common occurrence among the Roman auxiliary units. Various altars have been found at this site dedicated to Mars and/or to the Celto-Germanic goddesses Alaisiagae; named on one altar as Beda and Fimmilena, on another as Boudihillia and Friagabis.

2.3.5   Etymology

Boudihillia can be derived from the Proto-Celtic **Bōud-ī-hīlījā* meaning 'victory's fullness.' **Beda** is derived from the Proto-Celtic **Bed-ā* meaning 'burial.' **Alaisiagae** is derived from the Proto-Celtic **Ad-lājsījā-agai* meaning (in the illative) 'sending fears,' plausibly a byword for a notion of "dispatching terrors" (q.v.   ).

2.3.6   Sources

- British Museum, London, England.
- Carlisle Museum, Cumbria, England.
- Lancaster museum, Lancaster, England.
- Newcastle Museum of Antiquities, Newcastle upon Tyne, England.
- Penrith Museum, Penrith, England.
- Vercovicium Roman Museum, Housesteads, Northumberland, England.
- York Castle Museum, York, England.

2.4   Alala

For the song by Brazilian band Cansei de Ser Sexy, see Alala (song). For the sacred raven of Hawai'i, *'alalā*, see 'Alala.

Alala (Ancient Greek: Ἀλαλά; "battle-cry" or "war-cry"), was the goddess/personification/daemon of the war cry in Greek mythology. Her name means *loud cry*, esp. *war-cry*, from the onomatopoeic Greek word ἀλαλή [alalē],[1] hence the verb ἀλαλάζω (alalazō) "raise the war-cry". Greek soldiers attacked the enemy with this battle cry in order to cause panic to the enemy lines. It is reputed to be derived from the horrific sound owls make. *Alalaxios* (Ἀλαλάξιος) is an epithet of Ares. Alala is one of those deities who's name remains the same in Roman mythology as in Greek mythology, (such as Apollo's).

She is the daughter of Polemos/Bellum, the god/personification/daemon of war,[2] and according to one of Aesop's fables, her mother was Hubris/Petulantia, the female personification of arrogance.[3] Her aunt was the war goddess, Enyo/Bellona (War),[4] and her uncle was the war god, Ares/Mars. Along with her father, Polemos/Bellum, and her Aunt Enyo/Bellona, Alala is also one of her uncle, the war god, Ares', attendants out on the battlefield, along with the rest of his entourage

(Phobos & Deimos (Ares'/Mars' sons), Eris/Discordia and the Androktasiai, Makhai, Hysminai, and the Phonoi (Eris'/Discordia's children), the Spartoi, and the Keres), and their war cry was her name, *"Alale alala"*.

In World War II, during the Greco-Italian War a similar battle cry "ἀέρα" (aera) was used by the Greek soldiers. During the Fascist "Ventennio", the same war-cry (modified as "eja eja alalà", where "eja" had the same meaning of war-cry, taken from Aeschylus and Plato) was adopted by the Arditi, a special corps of the Fascist Army. It was invented by Gabriele D'Annunzio after the Capture of Fiume.

2.4.1 Quote

"Harken! O Alala, daughter of Polemos! Prelude of spears! To whom soldiers are sacrificed for their city's sake in the holy sacrifice of death." - Pindar. Dithyrambs, Frag. 78. Alala is the warrior princess, war goddess The name Alala comes from the Greek word Alalai which means warrior.

2.4.2 In popular culture

- Throughout the *Xena: Warrior Princess* franchise, the series protagonist, Xena, often utilized the signature war cry, "*Alalaes*". Her cry was an alternate writing for "Alale" (or "Alala"), who in Greek mythology was the female personification of the war cry.[5]

2.4.3 See also

- Ululation
- War-cry
- Battle cry

2.4.4 References

[1] LSJ entry ἀλαλή

[2] Theoi Project: Alala - *ALALA was the spirit (daimona) of the war cry. She was a daughter of Polemos (war personified).*

[3] Aesop, Fables 533 (from Babrius 70)

[4] Quintus Smyrnaeus, *Fall of Troy* 8. 424 ff

[5] Atsma, Aaron J. (2011). "ALALA : Goddess or Spirit of the War-Cry". *theoi.com*. Retrieved 12 July 2014.

2.5 Anahit

For other uses of "Anahit", see Anahit (disambiguation).

Anahit (Armenian: Անահիտ) was the goddess of

Armenian stamp with the image of the cast bronze head (mid-4th century BC), larger than life-size, once belonging to a statue. It was found in the 19th century near Satala, located close to the Armenian district of Erez/Yerznka. It is usually interpreted as representing either Anahit or Aphrodite. Now held in the British Museum.

fertility and healing, wisdom and water in Armenian mythology.[1] In early periods she was the goddess of war. By the 5th century BC she was the main deity in Armenia along with Aramazd.[2] The Armenian goddess Anahit is related to the similar Old Persian goddess Anahita. Anahit's worship, most likely borrowed from the Iranians during the Median invasion or the early Achaemenid period, was of paramount significance in Armenia. Unlike Iranians, Armenians fused idol-worship into the cult of Anahit. Artaxias I erected statues of Anahit, and promulgated orders to worship them. [3]

2.5.1 Armenian Anahit and Persian Anahita

According to Strabo, the "Armenians shared in the religion of the Perses and the Medes and particularly honored

Anaitis".[c16] The kings of Armenia were "steadfast supporters of the cult"[4] and Tiridates III, before his conversion to Christianity, "prayed officially to the triad Aramazd-Anahit-Vahagn but is said to have shown a special devotion to 'the great lady Anahit, ... the benefactress of the whole human race, mother of all knowledge, daughter of the great Aramazd'"[5] According to Agathangelos, tradition required the Kings of Armenia to travel once a year to the temple at Eriza (Erez) in Acilisene in order to celebrate the festival of the divinity; Tiridates made this journey in the first year of his reign where he offered sacrifice and wreaths and boughs.[c27] The temple at Eriza appears to have been particularly famous, "the wealthiest and most venerable in Armenia"[c29], staffed with priests and priestesses, the latter from eminent families who would serve at the temple before marrying.[c16] This practice may again reveal Semitic syncretic influences,[4] and is not otherwise attested in other areas. Pliny reports that Mark Antony's soldiers smashed an enormous statue of the divinity made of solid gold and then divided the pieces amongst themselves.[c19] Also according to Pliny, supported by Dio Cassius, Acilisene eventually came to be known as Anaetica.[c20] [c21] Dio Cassius also mentions that another region along the Cyrus River, on the borders of Albania and Iberia, was also called "the land of Anaitis."[c22][o]

2.5.2 Temples dedicated to Anahit

In Armenia, Anahit-worship was established in Erez, Armavir, Artashat and Ashtishat.[2] A mountain in Sophene district was known as Anahit's throne (*Athor Anahta*). The entire district of Erez, in the province of Akilisene (Ekeghiats), was called *Anahtakan Gavar*.[2]

According to Plutarch, the temple of Erez was the wealthiest and the noblest in Armenia. During the expedition of Mark Antony in Armenia, the statue was broken to pieces by the Roman soldiers. Pliny the Elder gives us the following story about it: The Emperor Augustus, being invited to dinner by one of his generals, asked him if it were true that the wreckers of Anahit's statue had been punished by the wrathful goddess. *No!* answered the general, *on the contrary, I have to-day the good fortune of treating you with one part of the hip of that gold statue.* The Armenians erected a new golden statue of Anahit in Erez, which was worshiped before the time of St. Gregory Illuminator.

The annual festivity of the month Navasard, held in honor of Anahit, was the occasion of great gatherings, attended with dance, music, recitals, competitions, etc. The sick went to the temples in pilgrimage, asking for recovery. The symbol of ancient Armenian medicine was the head of the bronze gilded statue of the goddess Anahit.[2]

2.5.3 Historians about Anahit

Commemorative coin issued by the Central Bank of Armenia devoted to Goddess Anahit

According to Agathangelos, King Trdat extolls the: *great Lady Anahit, the glory of our nation and vivifier . . .; mother of all chastity, and issue of the great and valiant Aramazd.* The historian Berossus identifies Anahit with Aphrodite, while medieval Armenian scribes identify her with Artemis. Though according to Strabo, Anahit's worship included rituals of sacred prostitution, "there is absolutely no proof, however, that this sacred prostitution was characteristic of the Armenian Anahit throughout the country, especially as native Christian writers do not mention it, although they might have used it to great advantage their attacks upon old religion".[6]

2.5.4 Relation to Avestan Aredvi Sura Anahita

The name corresponds to Avestan Anahita (Aredvi Sura Anahita), a similar divine figure.

2.5.5 See also

- Satala Aphrodite

- Anahita

- Aramazd

- Astghik

- Vahagn

- Haik

- Anat

- Sarpanit

2.5.6   References

[1] The heritage of Armenian literature, Volume 1, стр. 67, Agop Jack Hacikyan, Gabriel Basmajian, Edward S. Franchuk, Nourhan Ouzounian

[2] Hastings, James (2001). *Encyclopaedia of Religion and Ethics: Algonquins-Art*. Elibron Classics. p. 797. ISBN 978-1-4021-9433-7. Retrieved 2010-12-19.

[3] Boyce 1983, p. 1003.

[4] Boyce 1983, p. 1007.

[5] Boyce 1983, p. 1007 Cit. Agathangelos 22.

[6] Hastings, James (2001). *Encyclopaedia of Religion and Ethics: Algonquins-Art*. Elibron Classics. p. 797. ISBN 978-1-4021-9433-7. Retrieved 2010-12-19.

We have absolutely no proof, however, that this sacred prostitution was characteristic of the Armenian Anahit throughout the country, especially as native Christian writers do not mention it, although they might have used it to great advantage their attacks upon old religion.

2.5.7   External links and references

- Vahagni Tsunude Vishapakax

- Armenian Mythology from the Tour Armenia site.

- Armenian History site.

- http://www.britishmuseum.org/

- This article incorporates text from *History of Armenia* by Vahan M. Kurkjian, a publication in the public domain.

http://www.armenian-history.com/Armenian_mythology.htm

2.6   Anahita

This article is about the goddess. For other purposes, see Anahita (disambiguation). For the female given name derived from Anahita, see Anaïs.
"Nahid" redirects here. For other uses, see Nahid (disambiguation).

Anahita is the Old Persian form of the name of an Iranian goddess and appears in complete and earlier form as **Aredvi Sura Anahita** (*Arədvī Sūrā Anāhitā*); the Avestan language name of an Indo-Iranian cosmological figure venerated as the divinity of 'the Waters' (Aban) and hence associated

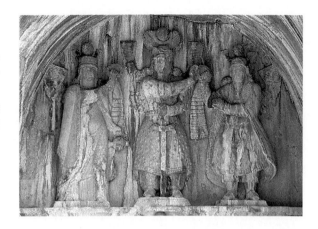

Taq-e Bostan high-relief of the investiture of Khosrow II (r. 590 to 628). The king (center) receives the ring of kingship from Mithra (right). On the left, apparently sanctifying the investiture, stands a female figure generally assumed to be Anahita (but see remark, below).

with fertility, healing and wisdom. Aredvi Sura Anahita is *Ardwisur Anahid* or **Nahid** in Middle- and Modern Persian, Anahit or Anaheed in Armenian.[1] An iconic shrine cult of Aredvi Sura Anahita, was – together with other shrine cults – "introduced apparently in the 4th century BCE and lasted until it was suppressed in the wake of an iconoclastic movement under the Sassanids."[2]

The Greek and Roman historians of classical antiquity refer to her either as **Anaïtis** or identified her with one of the divinities from their own pantheons. 270 Anahita, a silicaceous S-type asteroid is named after her.

2.6.1   Characteristics

Nomenclature

Only *Arədevī* (a word otherwise unknown, perhaps with an original meaning "moist") is specific to the divinity. It might have been derived from Arya devi[1] The words *sūra* and *anāhīta* are generic Avestan language adjectives,[3] and respectively mean "mighty" and "pure" [4][5] (or "immaculate").[1] Both adjectives also appear as epithets of other divinities or divine concepts such as Haoma[6] and the Fravashis.[7] Both adjectives are also attested in Vedic Sanskrit.[8]

As a divinity of the waters (*Abān*), the yazata is of Indo-Iranian origin, according to Lommel related to Sanskrit *Sarasvatī* that, like its Proto-Iranian equivalent **Harahvatī*, derives from Indo-Iranian **Saraswṇtī*.[1][9][10] In its old Iranian form **Harahvatī*, "her name was given to the region, rich in rivers, whose modern capital is Delhi (Avestan *Harax^v aitī*, Old Persian *Hara(h)uvati-*, Greek *Arachosia*)."[1] It might have been derived from the Goddess

Saraswati. "Like the Devi Saraswati, [Aredvi Sura Anahita] nurtures crops and herds; and is hailed both as a divinity and the mythical river that she personifies, 'as great in bigness as all these waters which flow forth upon the earth'."

In the (Middle-)Persian texts of the Sassanid and later eras, Arədvī Sūra Anāhīta appears as *Ardwisur Anāhīd*.[1] The evidence suggest a western Iranian origin of *Anāhīta*.[11] (see borrowing from Babylonia, below).

She shares characteristics with Mat Zemlya (Damp Mother Earth) in Slavic mythology.

Conflation with Ishtar

At some point prior to the 4th century BCE, this yazata was conflated with (an analogue of)[α] Semitic Ištar,[5] likewise a divinity of "maiden" fertility and from whom Aredvi Sura Anahita then inherited additional features of a divinity of war and of the planet Venus or "Zohreh" in Arabic. It was moreover the association with the planet Venus, "it seems, which led Herodotus to record that the [Persis][γ] learnt 'to sacrifice to "the heavenly goddess"' from the Assyrians and Arabians." [12][13][14]

Ishtar also "apparently"[15] gave Aredvi Sura Anahita the epithet *Banu*, 'the Lady', a typically Mesopotamian construct[15] that is not attested as an epithet for a divinity in Iran before the common era. It is completely unknown in the texts of the Avesta,[15] but evident in Sassanid-era middle Persian inscriptions (see the cult, below) and in a middle Persian *Zend* translation of *Yasna* 68.13.[16] Also in Zoroastrian texts from the post-conquest epoch (651 CE onwards), the divinity is referred to as 'Anahid the Lady', 'Ardwisur the Lady' and 'Ardwisur the Lady of the waters'.[17]

Because the divinity is unattested in any old Western Iranian language,[3] establishing characteristics prior to the introduction of Zoroastrianism in Western Iran (*c.* 5th century BCE) is very much in the realm of speculation. According to Boyce, it is "probable" that there was once a Perso–Elamite divinity by the name of *Anahiti* (as reconstructed from the Greek *Anaitis*).[18] It is then likely (so Boyce) that it was this divinity that was an analogue of Ishtar, and that it is this divinity with which Aredvi Sura Anahita was conflated.[3] Boyce concludes that "the Achaemenids' devotion to this goddess evidently survived their conversion to Zoroastrianism, and they appear to have used royal influence to have her adopted into the Zoroastrian pantheon." [19][β] According to an alternate theory, Anahita was perhaps "a *daeva* of the early and pure Zoroastrian faith, incorporated into the Zoroastrian religion and its revised canon" during the reign of "Artaxerxes I, the Constantine of that faith."[20][δ]

Cosmological entity

The cosmological qualities of the world river are alluded to in *Yasht* 5 (see in the Avesta, below), but properly developed only in the *Bundahishn*, a Zoroastrian account of creation finished in the 11th or 12th century CE. In both texts, Aredvi Sura Anahita is not only a divinity, but also the source of the world river and the (name of the) world river itself. The cosmological legend runs as follows:

All the waters of the world created by Ahura Mazda originate from the source Aredvi Sura Anahita, the life-increasing, herd-increasing, fold-increasing, who makes prosperity for all countries. This source is at the top of the world mountain Hara Berezaiti, "High Hara", around which the sky revolves and that is at the center of Airyanem Vaejah, the first of the lands created by Mazda.

The water, warm and clear, flows through a hundred thousand golden channels towards Mount Hugar, "the Lofty", one of the daughter-peaks of Hara Berezaiti. On the summit of that mountain is Lake Urvis, "the Turmoil", into which the waters flow, becoming quite purified and exiting through another golden channel. Through that channel, which is at the height of a thousand men, one portion of the great spring Aredvi Sura Anahita drizzles in moisture upon the whole earth, where it dispels the dryness of the air and all the creatures of Mazda acquire health from it. Another portion runs down to Vourukasha, the great sea upon which the earth rests, and from which it flows to the seas and oceans of the world and purifies them.

In the Bundahishn, the two halves of the name "Ardwisur Anahid" are occasionally treated independently of one another, that is, with Ardwisur as the representative of waters, and Anahid identified with the planet Venus: The water of the all lakes and seas have their origin with Ardwisur (10.2, 10.5), and in contrast, in a section dealing with the creation of the stars and planets (5.4), the *Bundahishn* speaks of 'Anahid i Abaxtari', that is, the planet Venus.[21] In yet other chapters, the text equates the two, as in "Ardwisur who is Anahid, the father and mother of the Waters" (3.17).

This legend of the river that descends from Mount Hara appears to have remained a part of living observance for many generations. A Greek inscription from Roman times found in Asia Minor reads "the great goddess Anaïtis of high Hara".[22] On Greek coins of the imperial epoch, she is spoken of as "Anaïtis of the sacred water."[21]

2.6.2 In scripture

Aredvi Sura Anahita is principally addressed in *Yasht* 5 (*Yasna* 65), also known as the Aban *Yasht*, a hymn to the waters in Avestan and one of the longer and better preserved of the devotional hymns. *Yasna* 65 is the third of

4th-6th century silver and gilt Sassanian vessel, assumed to be depicting Anahita. (Cleveland Museum of Art)

the hymns recited at the Ab-Zohr, the "offering to the waters" that accompanies the culminating rites of the Yasna service. Verses from *Yasht* 5 also form the greater part of the *Aban Nyashes*, the liturgy to the waters that are a part of the *Khordeh Avesta*.

According to Nyberg[23] and supported by Lommel[24] and Widengren,[25] the older portions of the *Aban Yasht* were originally composed at a very early date, perhaps not long after the Gathas themselves. [ζ] *Yasna* 38, which is dedicated "to the earth and the sacred waters" and is part of seven-chapter *Yasna Haptanghāiti*, is linguistically as old as the Gathas.

In the *Aban Yasht*, the river *yazata* is described as "the great spring Ardvi Sura Anahita is the life-increasing, the herd-increasing, the fold-increasing who makes prosperity for all countries" (5.1). She is "wide flowing and healing", "efficacious against the *daevas*", "devoted to Ahura's lore" (5.1). She is associated with fertility, purifying the seed of men (5.1), purifying the wombs of women (5.1), encouraging the flow of milk for newborns (5.2). As a river divinity, she is responsible for the fertility of the soil and for the growth of crops that nurture both man and beast (5.3). She is a beautiful, strong maiden, wearing beaver skins (5.3,7,20,129).

The association between water and wisdom that is common to many ancient cultures is also evident in the *Aban Yasht*, for here Aredvi Sura is the divinity to whom priests and pupils should pray for insight and knowledge (5.86). In verse 5.120 she is seen to ride a chariot drawn by four horses named "wind", "rain", "clouds" and "sleet". In newer passages she is described as standing in "statuesque stillness", "ever observed", royally attired with a golden embroidered robe, wearing a golden crown, necklace and earrings, golden breast-ornament, and gold-laced ankle-boots (5.123, 5.126-8). Aredvi Sura Anahita is bountiful to those who please her, stern to those who do not, and she resides in 'stately places' (5.101).

The concept of Aredvi Sura Anahita is to a degree blurred with that of Ashi, the Gathic figure of Good Fortune, and many of the verses of the *Aban Yasht* also appear in *Yasht* 17 (*Ard Yasht*), which is dedicated to Ashi. So also a description of the weapons bestowed upon worshippers (5.130), and the superiority in battle (5.34 et al.). These functions appears out of place in a hymn to the waters,[1] and may have originally been from *Yasht* 17.

Other verses in *Yasht* 5 have masculine instead of feminine pronouns, and thus again appear to be verses that were originally dedicated to other divinities.[26] Boyce also suggests that the new compound divinity of waters with martial characteristics gradually usurped the position of Apam Napat, the great warlike water divinity of the Ahuric triad, finally causing the latter's place to be lost and his veneration to become limited to the obligatory verses recited at the Ab-Zohr.

2.6.3   Inscriptions and classical accounts

Evidence of a cult

The earliest dateable and unambiguous reference to the iconic cult of Anahita is from the Babylonian scholar-priest Berosus, who – although writing over 70 years[η] after the reign of Artaxerxes II Mnemon[θ] – records that the emperor had been the first to make cult statues of Aphrodite Anaitis and place them in the temples of many of the empire's major cities, including Babylon, Susa, Ecbatana, Persepolis, Damascus and Sardis.[c1] Also according to Berosus, the Persians knew of no images of gods until Artaxerxes II erected those images.[c1][λ] This is substantiated by Herodotus, whose mid-5th-century-BCE general remarks on the usages of the Perses, Herodotus notes that "it is not their custom to make and set up statues and images and altars, and those that make such they deem foolish, as I suppose, because they never believed the gods, as do the Greeks, to be the likeness of men." [c23][27][28]

The extraordinary innovation of the shrine cults can thus

be dated to the late 5th century BCE (or very early 4th century BCE), even if this evidence is "not of the most satisfactory kind."[5] Nonetheless, by 330 BCE and under Achaemenid royal patronage, these cults had been disseminated throughout Asia Minor and the Levant, and from there to Armenia.[21] This was not a purely selfless act, for the temples also served as an important source of income. From the Babylonian kings, the Achaemenids had taken over the concept of a mandatory temple tax, a one-tenth tithe which all inhabitants paid to the temple nearest to their land or other source of income.[29] A share of this income called the *quppu ša šarri* or "kings chest" – an ingenious institution originally introduced by Nabonidus – was then turned over to the ruler.

Nonetheless, Artaxerxes' close connection with the Anahita temples is "almost certainly the chief cause of this king's long-lasting fame among Zoroastrians, a fame which made it useful propaganda for the succeeding Arsacids to claim him (quite spuriously) for their ancestor."[30][31]

Parsa, Elam, and Medea

Artaxerxes II's devotion to Anahita is most apparent in his inscriptions, where her name appears directly after that of Ahura Mazda and before that of Mithra. Artaxerxes' inscription at Susa reads: "By the will of Ahura Mazda, Anahita, and Mithra I built this palace. May Ahura Mazda, Anahita, and Mithra protect me from all evil" (A^{2}Hc 15–10). This is a remarkable break with tradition; no Achaemenid king before him had invoked any but Ahura Mazda alone by name although the Behistun inscription of Darius invokes Ahuramazda and "The other gods who are".[32]

The temple(s) of Anahita at Ecbatana (Hamadan) in Medea must have once been the most glorious sanctuaries in the known world.[π][c2] Although the palace had been stripped by Alexander and the following Seleucid kings,[c3] when Antiochus III raided Ecbatana in 209 BCE, the temple "had the columns round it still gilded and a number of silver tiles were piled up in it, while a few gold bricks and a considerable quantity of silver ones remained." [c4]

Polybius' reference to Alexander is supported by Arrian, who in 324 BCE wrote of a temple in Ecbatana dedicated to "Asclepius" (by inference presumed to be Anahita, likewise a divinity of healing), destroyed by Alexander because she had allowed his friend Hephaestion to die.[c5] The massive stone lion on the hill there (said to be part of a sepulcral monument to Hephaestion[ψ]) is today a symbol that visitors touch in hope of fertility.

Plutarch records that Artaxerxes II had his concubine Aspasia consecrated as priestess at the temple "to Diana of Ecbatana, whom they name Anaitis, that she might spend the remainder of her days in strict chastity."[c6] This does not however necessarily imply that chastity was a requirement of Anaitis priestesses. [v]

Isidore of Charax, in addition to a reference to the temple at Ecbatana ("a temple, sacred to Anaitis, they sacrifice there always")[c2] also notes a "temple of Artemis"[μ] at Concobar (Lower Medea, today Kangavar). Despite archaeological findings that refute a connection with Anahita,[33] remains of a 2nd-century BCE Hellenic-style edifice at Kangavar continue to be a popular tourist attraction.

Isidore also records another "royal place, a temple of Artemis, founded by Darius" at Basileia (Apadana), on the royal highway along the left bank of the Euphrates.[c7][34]

During the Hellenistic Parthian period, Susa had its "Dianae templum augustissimum"[c8] far from Elymais where another temple, known to Strabo as the "*Ta Azara*", was dedicated to Athena/Artemis[c9] and where tame lions roamed the grounds. This may be a reference to the temple above the Tang-a Sarvak ravine in present-day Khuzestan Province. Other than this, no evidence of the cult in Western Iran from the Parthian period survives, but "it is reasonable to assume that the martial features of Anāhita (Ishtar) assured her popularity in the subsequent centuries among the warrior classes of Parthian feudalism."[35]

In the 2nd century CE, the center of the cult in Parsa (Persia proper) was at Staxr (Istakhr). There, Anahita continued to be venerated in her martial role and it was at Istakhr that Sassan, after whom the Sassanid dynasty is named, served as high priest. Sassan's son, Papak, likewise a priest of that temple, overthrew the King of Istakhr (a vassal of the Arsacids), and had himself crowned in his stead. "By this time (the beginning of the 3rd century), Anāhita's headgear (*kolāh*) was worn as a mark of nobility", which in turn "suggests that she was goddess of the feudal warrior estate."[35] Ardashir (*r.* 226-241 CE) "would send the heads of the petty kings he defeated for display at her temple."[36]

During the reign of Bahram I (*r.* 272-273 CE), in the wake of an iconoclastic movement that had begun at about the same time as the shrine cult movement, the sanctuaries dedicated to a specific divinity were - by law - disassociated from that divinity by removal of the statuary and then either abandoned or converted into fire altars.[37] So also the popular shrines to Mehr/Mithra which retained the name *Darb-e Mehr* - Mithra's Gate - that is today one of the Zoroastrian technical terms for a fire temple. The temple at Istakhr was likewise converted and, according to the Kartir inscription, henceforth known as the "Fire of Anahid the Lady."[38] Sassanid iconoclasm, though administratively from the reign of Bahram I, may already have been supported by Bahram's father, Shapur I (*r.* 241-272 CE). In an inscription in Middle Persian, Parthian and Greek at Ka'ba of Zoroaster, the "Mazdean lord, ..., king of kings, ..., grandson of lord Papak" (ShKZ 1, Naqsh-e Rustam) records that he instituted fires for his daughter and three of his sons. His daughter's name: Anahid. The name of that fire: Adur-Anahid.

Notwithstanding the dissolution of the temple cults, the triad Ahura Mazda, Anahita, and Mithra (as Artaxerxes II had invoked them) would continue to be prominent throughout the Sassanid age, "and were indeed (with Tiri and Verethragna) to remain the most popular of all divine beings in Western Iran."[39] Moreover, the iconoclasm of Bahram I and later kings apparently did not extend to images where they themselves are represented. At an investiture scene at Naqsh-e Rustam, Narseh (*r.* 293-302 CE) is seen receiving his crown from a female divinity identified as Anahita. Narseh, like Artaxerxes II, was apparently also very devoted to Anahita, for in the investure inscription at Paikuli (near Khaniqin, in present-day Iraq), Narseh invokes "Ormuzd and all the yazatas, and Anahid who is called the Lady."[38]

*Naqsh-e Rustam investiture of Narseh (*r.* 293-302), in which the Sassanian king (second from right) receives the ring of kingship from Anahita (right).*

Anahita has also been identified as a figure in the investiture scene of Khusrow Parvez (*r.* 590-628 CE) at Taq-e Bostan, but in this case not quite as convincingly as for the one of Narseh.[40] But, aside from the two rock carvings at Naqsh-e Rustam and Taq-e Bostan, "few figures unquestionably representing the goddess are known."[40] The figure of a female on an Achaemenid cylinder seal has been identified as that of Anahita, as have a few reliefs from the Parthian era (250 BCE-226 CE), two of which are from ossuaries.[41]

In addition, Sassanid silverware depictions of nude or scantily dressed women seen holding a flower or fruit or bird or child are identified as images of Anahita.[42] Additionally, "it has been suggested that the colonnaded or serrated crowns [depicted] on Sasanian coins belong to Anahid."[40]

Asia Minor and the Levant

The cult flourished in Lydia even as late as end of the Hellenistic Parthian epoch.[15] The Lydians had temples to the divinity at Sardis, Philadelphia, Hieroaesarea, Hypaipa, Maeonia and elsewhere;[15] the temple at Hieroaesarea reportedly[c10] having been founded by "Cyrus" (presumably[43] Cyrus the Younger, brother of Artaxerxes II, who was satrap of Lydia between 407 and 401 BCE). In the 2nd century CE, the geographer Pausanias reports having personally witnessed (apparently Mazdean) ceremonies at Hypaipa and Hierocaesarea.[c11] According to Strabo, Anahita was revered together with Omanos at Zela in Pontus.[c12] [c13] At Castabala, she is referred to as 'Artemis Perasia'.[c14] Anahita and Omanos had common altars in Cappadocia.[c15]

Armenia and the Caucasus

Main article: Anahit

"Hellenic influence [gave] a new impetus to the cult of images [and] positive evidence for this comes from Armenia, then a Zoroastrian land."[21] According to Strabo, the "Armenians shared in the religion of the Perses and the Medes and particularly honored Anaitis".[c16] The kings of Armenia were "steadfast supporters of the cult"[34] and Tiridates III, before his conversion to Christianity, "prayed officially to the triad Aramazd-Anahit-Vahagn but is said to have shown a special devotion to 'the great lady Anahit, ... the benefactress of the whole human race, mother of all knowledge, daughter of the great Aramazd'"[44] According to Agathangelos, tradition required the Kings of Armenia to travel once a year to the temple at Eriza (Erez) in Acilisene in order to celebrate the festival of the divinity; Tiridates made this journey in the first year of his reign where he offered sacrifice and wreaths and boughs.[c27] The temple at Eriza appears to have been particularly famous, "the wealthiest and most venerable in Armenia"[c29], staffed with priests and priestesses, the latter from eminent families who would serve at the temple before marrying.[c16] This practice may again reveal Semitic syncretic influences,[34] and is not otherwise attested in other areas. Pliny reports that Mark Antony's soldiers smashed an enormous statue of the divinity made of solid gold and then divided the pieces amongst themselves.[c19] Also according to Pliny, supported by Dio Cassius, Acilisene eventually came to be known as Anaetica.[c20] [c21] Dio Cassius also mentions that another region along the Cyrus River, on the borders of Albania and Iberia, was also called "the land of Anaitis."[c22][σ]

Anahit was also venerated at Artashat (Artaxata), the capital of the Armenian Kingdom, where her temple was close to that of Tiur[φ], the divinity of oracles. At Astishat, center of the cult of Vahagn, she was revered as *voskimuyr*, the 'golden mother'.[c24] In 69 BCE, the soldiers of Lucullus saw cows consecrated to 'Persian Artemis' roaming freely at Tomisa in Sophene (on the Euphrates in South-West Armenia), where the animals bore the brand of a torch on their heads.[c25] Following Tiridates' conversion to Christianity, the cult of Anahit was condemned and iconic representations of the divinity were destroyed.[34]

Attempts have been made to identify Anahita as one of the prime three divinities in Albania, but these are questionable. However, in the territories of the Moschi in Colchis, Strabo mentions[c26] a cult of Leucothea, which Wesendonck and others have identified as an analogue of Anahita.[34] The cult of Anahita may have also influenced Ainina and Danina, a paired deities of the Caucasian Iberians mentioned by the medieval Georgian chronicles.[45]

2.6.4 Legacy

As a divinity Aredvi Sura Anahita is of enormous significance to the Zoroastrian religion, for as a representative of Aban ("the waters"), she is in effect the divinity towards whom the *Yasna* service – the primary act of worship – is directed. (see Ab-Zohr). "To this day reverence for water is deeply ingrained in Zoroastrians, and in orthodox communities offerings are regularly made to the household well or nearby stream."[46][ε]

It is "very probable"[17] that the shrine of Bibi Shahrbanu at royal Ray (Rhagae, central Medea) was once dedicated to Anahita.[17][ρ] Similarly, one of the "most beloved mountain shrines of the Zoroastrians of Yazd, set beside a living spring and a great confluence of water-courses, is devoted to Banu-Pars, "the Lady of Persia"."[47][48]

However, and notwithstanding the widespread popularity of Anahita, "it is doubtful whether the current tendency is justified whereby almost every isolated figure in Sassanid art, whether sitting, standing, dancing, clothed, or semi-naked, is hailed as her representation."[48][49]

The Armenian cult of Anahit, as well as the pre-Christian Armenian religion in general, was very closely connected to Persian Zoroastrianism,[50] but it also had significant distinct features deriving from local pagan traditions as well as from non-Zoroastrian foreign cults. In present-day Armenia, it is remembered as part of the historical mythological heritage of the nation, and the name Anahid is a popular female given name. In 1997, the Central Bank of Armenia issued a commemorative gold coin with an image of the divinity Anahit on the obverse.

As the name Nahid, the meaning is equivalent to the Pleiades (in English) and Subaru in Japanese.

2.6.5 See also

- Ab-Zohr, the Zoroastrian "purification of the waters" ceremony and the most important act of worship in Zoroastrianism.

- Aban, "the Waters", representing and represented by Aredvi Sura Anahita.

- Airyanem Vaejah, first of the mythological lands created by Ahura Mazda and the middle of the world that rests on High Hara.

- Anahita temple

- Arachosia, name of which derives from Old Iranian *Harahvatī (Avestan *Harax`aitī*, Old Persian *Hara(h)uvati-*).

- Hara Berezaiti, "High Hara", the mythical mountain that is the origin of the *Harahvatī river.

- Oxus, identified[51] as the world river that descends from the mythological High Hara.

- Sarasvati River, a manifestation of the goddess Saraswati.

2.6.6 References

Notes

Citation index

Bibliography

- Arjomand, Saïd Amir; Arjomand, Said Amir (1998), "Artaxerxes, Ardašīr, and Bahman", *Journal of the American Oriental Society* **118** (2): 245–248, doi:10.2307/605896, JSTOR 605896

- Bikerman, E. (1938), "Anonymous Gods", *The Journal of the Warburg and Courtauld Institutes* **1** (3): 187–196, doi:10.2307/750004, JSTOR 750004

- Boyce, Mary (1968), "Bībī Shahrbānū and the Lady of Pārs", *Bulletin of the School of Oriental and African Studies* (London: University of London) **30** (1): 30–44, doi:10.1017/S0041977X00099080

- Boyce, Mary (1975a), *A History of Zoroastrianism, Vol. I*, Leiden/Köln: Brill

- Boyce, Mary (1975b), "On the Zoroastrian Temple Cult of Fire", *Journal of the American Oriental Society* (Ann Arbor: AOS/UMich. Press) **95** (3): 454–465, doi:10.2307/599356, JSTOR 599356

- Boyce, Mary (1982), *A History of Zoroastrianism, Vol. II*, Leiden/Köln: Brill

- Boyce, Mary (1983), "Āban", *Encyclopædia Iranica* **1**, New York: Routledge & Kegan Paul, p. 58

- Boyce, Mary (1983), "Anāhīd", *Encyclopædia Iranica* **1**, New York: Routledge & Kegan Paul, pp. 1003–1009

- Cumont, Franz (1926), "Anahita", in Hastings, James, *Encyclopedia of Religion and Ethics* **1**, Edinburgh: T. & T. Clark

- Dandamaev, Muhammad A; Lukonin, Vladimir G (1989), *The Culture and Social Institutions of Ancient Iran*, New York: Cambridge UP, ISBN 0-521-32107-7

- Darmesteter, James (1892), "Le Zend-Avesta, I", *Annales du Musée Guimet* (Paris: Musée Guimet) **21**

- Darrow, William R (1988), "Keeping the Waters Dry: The Semiotics of Fire and Water in the Zoroastrian 'Yasna'", *Journal of the American Academy of Religion* **56** (3): 417–442, doi:10.1093/jaarel/lvi.3.417

- de Jong, Albert (1997), *Traditions of the Magi: Zoroastrianism in Greek and Latin literature*, BRILL

- Girshman, Roman (1962), *Persian art, Parthian and Sassanian dynasties*, London: Golden Press

- Gray, Louis H (1926), "A List of the Divine and Demonic Epithets in the Avesta", *Journal of the American Oriental Society* **46**: 97–153, doi:10.2307/593793, JSTOR 593793

- Jacobs, Bruno (2006), "Anahita", *Iconography of Deities and Demons in the Ancient Near East* (Electronic Pre-Publication) (PDF), Leiden: U Zürich/Brill

- Kleiss, Wolfram (2005), "Kangavar", *Encyclopædia Iranica Online* **OT 7**, Costa Mesa: Mazda Pub

- Lommel, Herman (1927), *Die Yašts des Awesta*, Göttingen-Leipzig: Vandenhoeck & Ruprecht/JC Hinrichs

- Lommel, Herman (1954), "Anahita-Sarasvati", in Schubert, Johannes; Schneider, Ulrich, *Asiatica: Festschrift Friedrich Weller Zum 65. Geburtstag*, Leipzig: Otto Harrassowitz, pp. 405–413

- MacKenzie, David Neil (1964), "Zoroastrian Astrology in the 'Bundahišn'", *Bulletin of the School of Oriental and African Studies* (London: University of London) **27** (3): 511–529, doi:10.1017/S0041977X0011835X

- Meyer, Eduard (1886), "Anaitis", *Ausführliches Lexikon der griechischen und römischen Mythologie* **I**, Leipzig: WH Roscher, pp. 330–334

- Monier-Williams, Monier (1898), *A Sanskrit-English Dictionary*, New York: OUP

- Nöldecke, Theodor (ed.) (1879), *Geschichte der Perser und Araber zur Zeit der Sasaniden*, Leiden: Brill (repr. 1973)

- Nyberg, Henrik Samuel (1938), *Die Religionen des alten Iran*, Leipzig: JC Hinrichs

- Taqizadeh, Sayyid Hasan (1938), *Old Iranian Calendars* (Prize Publication Fund, Vol. 16), London: Royal Asiatic Society

- Tsereteli, MIchael (January 1935). "The Asianic (Asia Minor) elements in national Georgian paganism". *Georgica* **1** (1): 55. Retrieved 7 August 2012.

- Widengren, Geo (1955), "Stand und Aufgaben der iranischen Religionsgeschichte: II. Geschichte der iranischen Religionen und ihre Nachwirkung", *Numen* **2** (1/2): 47–134, doi:10.2307/3269455, JSTOR 3269455

- Widengren, Geo (1965), *Die Religionen Irans* (Die Religion der Menschheit, Vol. 14), Stuttgart: Kohlhammer

2.7   Anat

For other uses, see ANAT (disambiguation).

Anat (/ˈɑːnɑːt/) or **Anath** (/ˈænəθ/; Hebrew and Phoenician ענת, *'Anōt*; Ugaritic *'nt*; Greek Αναθ, *Anath*; Egyptian *Antit*, *Anit*, *Anti*, or *Anant*) is a major northwest Semitic goddess.

2.7.1   'Anat in Ugarit

In the Ugaritic Ba'al/Hadad cycle 'Anat is a violent war-goddess, a virgin (*btlt 'nt*) who is the sister and, according to a much disputed theory, the lover of the great god Ba'al Hadad. Ba'al is usually called the son of Dagan and sometimes the son of El, who addresses 'Anat as "daughter". Either relationship is probably figurative.

'Anat's titles used again and again are "virgin 'Anat" and "sister-in-law of the peoples" (or "progenitress of the peoples" or "sister-in-law, widow of the Li'mites").

Bronze figurine of Anat wearing an atef crown with arm raised (originally holding an axe or club), dated to 1400–1200 BC, found in Syria

Cuneiform script, *(Louvre Museum) "Then Anat went to El, at the source of the rivers, in the middle of the bed of the two oceans. She bows at the feet of El, she bows and prosternates and pays him respects. She speaks and says: "the very mighty Ba'al is dead. The prince, lord of the earth, has died"" (...) "They fight like heroes. Môt wins, Ba'al wins. They bit each other like snakes. Môt wins, Ba'al wins. They jump like horses. Môt is scared. Ba'al sits on his throne".*

In a fragmentary passage from Ugarit (modern **Ras Shamra**), Syria[1] 'Anat appears as a fierce, wild and furious warrior in a battle, wading knee-deep in blood, striking off heads, cutting off hands, binding the heads to her torso and the hands in her sash, driving out the old men and townsfolk with her arrows, her heart filled with joy. "Her character in this passage anticipates her subsequent warlike role against the enemies of Baal".[2]

'Anat boasts that she has put an end to Yam the darling of El, to the seven-headed serpent, to Arsh the darling of the gods, to Atik 'Quarrelsome' the calf of El, to Ishat 'Fire' the bitch of the gods, and to Zabib 'flame?' the daughter of El. Later, when Ba'al is believed to be dead, she seeks after Ba'al "like a cow[3] for its calf" and finds his body (or supposed body) and buries it with great sacrifices and weeping. 'Anat then finds Mot, Ba'al Hadad's supposed slayer and she seizes Mot, splits him with a sword, winnows him with a

sieve, burns him with fire, grinds him with millstones and scatters the remnants to the birds.

Text *CTA* **10** tells how 'Anat seeks after Ba'al who is out hunting, finds him, and is told she will bear a steer to him. Following the birth she brings the new calf to Ba'al on Mount Zephon. Nowhere in these texts is 'Anat explicitly Ba'al Hadad's consort. To judge from later traditions 'Athtart (who also appears in these texts) is more likely to be Ba'al Hadad's consort. Complicating matters is that northwest Semitic culture permitted more than one wife and nonmonogamy is normal for deities in many pantheons.

In the North Canaanite story of *Aqhat*,[4] the protagonist Aqhat son of the judge Danel (Dn'il) is given a wonderful bow and arrows which was created for 'Anat by the craftsman god Kothar-wa-Khasis but which was given to Danel for his infant son as a gift. When Aqhat grew to be a young man, the goddess 'Anat tried to buy the bow from Aqhat, offering even immortality, but Aqhat refused all offers, calling her a liar because old age and death are the lot of all men. He then added to this insult by asking 'what would a woman do with a bow?'

Like Inanna in the Epic of Gilgamesh, 'Anat complained to El and threatened El himself if he did not allow her to take vengeance on Aqhat. El conceded. 'Anat launched her attendant Yatpan in hawk form against Aqhat to knock the breath out of him and to steal the bow back. Her plan succeeds, but Aqhat is killed instead of merely beaten and robbed. In her rage against Yatpan, (text is missing here) Yatpan runs away and the bow and arrows fall into the sea. All is lost. 'Anat mourned for Aqhat and for the curse that this act would bring upon the land and for the loss of the bow. The focus of the story then turns to Paghat, the wise younger sister of Aqhat. She sets off to avenge her brother's death and to restore the land which has been devastated by drought as a direct result of the murder. The story is incomplete. It breaks at an extremely dramatic moment when Paghat discovers that the mercenary whom she has hired to help her avenge the death is, in fact, Yatpan, her brother's murderer. The parallels between the story of 'Anat and her revenge on Mot for the killing of her brother are obvious. In the end, the seasonal myth is played out on the human level.

Gibson (1978) thinks Rahmay ('The Merciful'), co-wife of El with Athirat, is also the goddess 'Anat, but he fails to take into account the primary source documents. Use of dual names of deities in Ugaritic poetry are an essential part of the verse form, and that two names for the same deity are traditionally mentioned in parallel lines. In the same way, Athirat is called Elath (meaning "The Goddess") in paired couplets. The poetic structure can also be seen in early Hebrew verse forms.

2.7.2   Anat in Egypt

Anat first appears in Egypt in the 16th dynasty (the Hyksos period) along with other northwest Semitic deities. She was especially worshiped in her aspect of a war goddess, often paired with the goddess `Ashtart. In the *Contest Between Horus and Set*, these two goddesses appear as daughters of Re and are given in marriage to the god Set, who had been identified with the Semitic god Hadad.

During the Hyksos period Anat had temples in the Hyksos capital of Avaris and in Beth-Shan (Palestine) as well as being worshipped in Memphis. On inscriptions from Memphis of 15th to 12th centuries BCE, Anat is called "Bin-Ptah", Daughter of Ptah. She is associated with Reshpu, (*Canaanite*: Resheph) in some texts and sometimes identified with the native Egyptian goddess Neith. She is sometimes called "Queen of Heaven". Her iconography varies. She is usually shown carrying one or more weapons.

The name of Anat-her, a shadowy Egyptian ruler of this time, is derived from "Anat".

In the New Kingdom Ramesses II made 'Anat his personal guardian in battle and enlarged Anat's temple in Pi-Ramesses. Ramesses named his daughter (whom he later married) Bint-Anat 'Daughter of Anat'. His dog appears in a carving in Beit el Wali temple with the name "Anat-in-vigor" and one of his horses was named *'Ana-herte* 'Anat-is-satisfied'.

2.7.3   Anat in Mesopotamia

In Akkadian, the form one would expect *Anat* to take would be *Antu*, earlier *Antum*. This would also be the normal feminine form that would be taken by *Anu*, the Akkadian form of An 'Sky', the Sumerian god of heaven. Antu appears in Akkadian texts mostly as a rather colorless consort of Anu, the mother of Ishtar in the Gilgamesh story, but is also identified with the northwest Semitic goddess 'Anat of essentially the same name. It is unknown whether this is an equation of two originally separate goddesses whose names happened to fall together or whether Anat's cult spread to Mesopotamia, where she came to be worshipped as Anu's spouse because the Mesopotamian form of her name suggested she was a counterpart to Anu.

It has also been suggested that the parallelism between the names of the Sumerian goddess, Inanna, and her West Semitic counterpart, Ishtar, continued in Canaanite tradition as Anath and Astarte, particularly in the poetry of Ugarit. The two goddesses were invariably linked in Ugaritic scripture and are also known to have formed a triad (known from sculpture) with a third goddess who was given the name/title of Qadesh (meaning "the holy one").

2.7.4   'Anat in Israel

The goddess 'Anat is never mentioned in Hebrew scriptures as a goddess, though her name is apparently preserved in the city names Beth Anath and Anathoth. Anathoth seems to be a plural form of the name, perhaps a shortening of *bêt ªnātôt* 'House of the 'Anats', either a reference to many shrines of the goddess or a plural of intensification. The ancient hero Shamgar son of 'Anat is mentioned in Judges 3.31;5:6 which raises the idea that this hero may have been understood as a demi-god, a mortal son of the goddess. But John Day (2000) notes that a number of Canaanites known from non-Biblical sources bore that title and theorizes that it was a military designation indicating a warrior under 'Anat's protection. Asenath "holy to Anath" was the wife of the Hebrew patriarch Joseph.

In Elephantine (modern Aswan) in Egypt, the 5th century Elephantine papyri make mention of a goddess called Anat-Yahu (Anat-Yahweh) worshiped in the temple to Yahweh originally built by Jewish refugees from the Babylonian conquest of Judah. These suggest that "even in exile and beyond the worship of a female deity endured."[5] The texts were written by a group of Jews living at Elephantine near the Nubian border, whose religion has been described as "nearly identical to Iron Age II Judahite religion".[6] The papyri describe the Jews as worshiping Anat-Yahu (or AnatYahu). Anat-Yahu is described as either the wife[7] (or paredra, sacred consort)[8] of Yahweh or as a hypostatized aspect[9] of Yahweh.[10][11]

2.7.5   Anat and Athene

In a Cyprian inscription (*KAI.* 42) the Greek goddess Athêna Sôteira Nikê is equated with 'Anat (who is described in the inscription as the strength of life : *l'uzza hayim*).

Anat is also presumably the goddess whom Sanchuniathon calls Athene, a daughter of El, mother unnamed, who with Hermes (that is Thoth) counselled El on the making of a sickle and a spear of iron, presumably to use against his father Uranus. However, in the Baal cycle, that rôle is assigned to Asherah / 'Elat and 'Anat is there called the "Virgin."[12]

2.7.6   Possible late transfigurations

The goddess 'Atah worshipped at Palmyra may possibly be in origin identical with 'Anat. 'Atah was combined with 'Ashtart under the name *Atar* into the goddess 'Atar'atah known to the Hellenes as Atargatis. If this origin for 'Atah is correct, then Atargatis is effectively a combining of 'Ashtart and 'Anat.

It has also been proposed that (Indo-)Iranian Anahita meaning 'immaculate' in Avestan (*a* 'not' + *ahit* 'unclean') is a variant of *'Anat*. It is however unlikely given that the Indo-Iranian roots of the term are related to the Semitic ones and although—through conflation—Aredvi Sura Anahita (so the full name) inherited much from Ishtar-Inanna, the two are considered historically distinct.

In the Book of Zohar, 'Anat is numbered among the holiest of angelic powers under the name of Anathiel.

2.7.7   As a modern Hebrew first name

"Anat" (ענת) is a common female name in contemporary Israel, though many Israelis—including many of the women so named themselves—are not aware of it being the name of an ancient goddess. This name is often used by Russia-originated Israelis as a translation of the Russian name "Anastasia".

The name had not been used among Jews prior to the advent of Zionism.

According to Abraham Vered, researcher of Israeli popular culture, the popularity of the name might also derive from an attempt to emulate the (etymologically unconnected) European name "Annette".

2.7.8   Scc also

- Ancient Egyptian Religion

- List of Canaanite deities

- Anah, a city in Iraq possibly named in Anat's honor

2.7.9   Notes

[1] *CTA* **3 B** (= UT 'nt II)

[2] P. C. Craigie, "A Reconsideration of Shamgar Ben Anath (Judg 3:31 and 5:6)" *Journal of Biblical Literature* **91**.2 (June 1972:239-240) p 239.

[3] A *wild* cow, Albright clarifies, in *Yahweh and the Gods of Canaan.*

[4] H. L. Ginsberg, "The North-Canaanite myth of Anath and Aqhat", *Bulletin of the American Schools of Oriental Research* **97** (February 1945:3-10).

[5] Gnuse, Robert Karl (1997). *No Other Gods: Emergent Monotheism in Israel.* T&T Clark. p. 185. ISBN 978-1850756576.

[6] Noll, K.L. *Canaan and Israel in Antiquity: An Introduction.* 2001: Sheffield Academic Press. p. 248.

[7] Day, John (2002). *Yahweh and the Gods and Goddesses of Canaan.* 143: Sheffield Academic Press. ISBN 978-0826468307.

[8] Edelman, Diana Vikander (1996). *The triumph of Elohim: from Yahwisms to Judaisms.* William B. Eerdmans. p. 58. ISBN 978-0802841612.

[9] similar to the relationship of Jesus to God the Father

[10] Susan Ackerman (2004). "Goddesses". In Suzanne Richard. *Near Eastern archaeology: a reader.* Eisenbrauns. p. 394. ISBN 978-1575060835.

[11] Noll, K.L. *Canaan and Israel in Antiquity: An Introduction.* 2001: Sheffield Academic Press. p. 248.

[12] "The Myth of Baal". Archived from the original on 2009-10-25.

2.7.10   References

- Albright, W. F. (1942, 5th ed., 1968). *Archaeology and the Religion of Israel* (5th ed.). Baltimore: Johns Hopkins Press. ISBN 0-8018-0011-0.

- Day, John (2000). *Yahweh & the Gods & Goddesses of Canaan.* Sheffield, UK: Sheffield Academic Press. ISBN 1-85075-986-3.

- Gibson, J. C. L. (1978). *Canaanite Myths and Legends* (2nd ed.). T. & T. Clark: Edinburgh. Released again in 2000. ISBN 0-567-02351-6.

- Harden, Donald (1980). *The Phoenicians* (2nd ed.). London: Penguin. ISBN 0-14-021375-9.

- Kapelrud, Arvid Schou, 1969. *The violent goddess: Anat in the Ras Shamra Texts* Oslo: University Press

- *KAI = Kanaanäische und Aramäische Inscriften* (2000). H. Donner and W. Röllig (Eds.). Revised edition. Wiesbaden: Harrassowitz. ISBN 3-447-04587-6.

- Putting God on Trial - The Biblical Book of Job – A Biblical reworking of the combat motif between Yam, Anat and Baal.

- Theodor Gaster, Thespis: Ritual, Myth, and Drama in the Ancient Near East. 1950.

- The Hebrew Goddess Raphael Patai, Wayne State University Press, ISBN 0-8143-2271-9

2.8 Andarta

In Celtic polytheism, **Andarta** was a warrior goddess worshipped in southern Gaul. Inscriptions to her have been found in southern France and in Bern, Switzerland.[1] She may be related to the goddess Andate, identified with Victory in Britain according to Roman historian Cassius Dio.[2] Like the similar goddess Artio, she may have been associated with the bear.[1]

2.8.1 See also

- Andraste

2.8.2 References

Notes

[1] McKillop, James (1998), "Andarta", *A Dictionary of Celtic Mythology* ((subscription or UK public library membership required)) (online ed.), Oxford University Press, retrieved 7 August 2011 Check date values in: |access-date= (help)

[2] *Cassius Dio*, Bill Thayer, retrieved 7 August 2011

Bibliography

- MacKillop, James (1998), *Dictionary of Celtic Mythology*, Oxford University Press, ISBN 0-19-280120-1

2.9 Andraste

Andraste, also known as **Andrasta** or **Andred**, was, according to the Roman historian Dio Cassius, an Icenic war goddess invoked by Boudica in her fight against the Roman occupation of Britain in AD 60.[1] She may be the same as Andate, mentioned later by the same source, and described as "their name for Victory": i.e., the goddess Victoria.[2] Thayer asserts that she may be related to Andarta also. The goddess Victoria is related to Nike, Bellona, Magna Mater (Great Mother), Cybele, and Vacuna—goddesses who are often depicted on chariots.

Many Neopagan sources describe the hare as sacred to Andraste. This seems to derive from a misreading of the passage in Dio Cassius in which Boudica releases a hare from her gown:

> "Let us, therefore, go against [the Romans], trusting boldly to good fortune. Let us show them that they are hares and foxes trying to rule over dogs and wolves." When she [Boudica] had finished speaking, she employed a species of divination, letting a hare escape from the fold of her dress; and since it ran on what they considered the auspicious side, the whole multitude shouted with pleasure, and Boudica, raising her hand toward heaven, said: "I thank you, Andraste, and call upon you as woman speaking to woman ... I beg you for victory and preservation of liberty."[2]

The hare's release is described as a technique of divination, with an augury drawn from the direction in which it runs. This appears to be similar to the Roman methods of divination which ascribe meaning to the directions from which birds fly, with the left side being unfavorable (sinistra) and the right side favorable.[3]

2.9.1 References

Notes

[1] Kightly 1982, pp. 36–40

[2] *Cassius Dio*, Bill Thayer, retrieved 7 August 2011

[3] *Religio Romana*, "Augury".

Bibliography

- Kightly, Charles (1982), *Folk Heroes of Britain*, Thames and Hudson, ISBN 0-500-25082-0

2.9.2 External links

- Somewhat speculative page on Andraste and Boudica.

2.10 Anu (deity)

Not to be confused with Annan.

Paps of Anu; the western Pap from the eastern Pap

In Irish mythology, **Anu** (or **Ana**, sometimes given as **Anann** or **Anand**) is the name of a goddess. She may be a goddess in her own right,[1] or an alternate name for Danu. In the *Lebor Gabála Érenn*, "Anand" is given as an alternate name for Morrígu.[2] While an Irish goddess, in parts of Britain a similar figure is referred to as "Gentle Annie," in an effort to avoid offense, a tactic which is similar to referring to the fairies as "The Good People".[3] As her name is often conflated with a number of other goddesses, it is not always clear which figure is being referred to if the name is taken out of context.[1]

2.10.1 Etymology

This name may be derived the Proto-Celtic theonym **Φanon-*.[4]

2.10.2 Paps of Anu

Anu has particular associations with Munster: the twin hills known as the Paps of Anu (*Dá Chích Anann* or *the breasts of Anu*), at 52°00′55″N 9°16′09″W / 52.01528°N 9.26917°W, near Killarney,[5] County Kerry are said to have been named after this ancient goddess.[2]

2.10.3 Works cited

[1] MacKillop, James (1998) *Dictionary of Celtic Mythology* Oxford: Oxford University Press ISBN 0-19-280120-1 pp.10, 16, 128

[2] R. A. Stewart Macalister. *Lebor Gabála Érenn*. Part IV. Irish Texts Society, Dublin, 1941. § VII, First Redaction.

[3] Black Annis, Gentle Annie

[4] Proto-Celtic—English lexicon and English—Proto-Celtic lexicon. University of Wales Centre for Advanced Welsh and Celtic Studies. (See also this page for background and disclaimers.) Cf. also the University of Leiden database.

[5] The Paps of Anu - Prehistoric and Early Ireland

2.10.4 Bibliography

- MacKillop, James. *Dictionary of Celtic Mythology*. Oxford: Oxford University Press, 1998: ISBN 0-19-280120-1.

- Wood, Juliette, *The Celts: Life, Myth, and Art*, Thorsons Publishers (2002): ISBN 0-00-764059-5

2.11 Astarte

For other uses, see Astarte (disambiguation).
Astarte (Greek: Ἀστάρτη, *Astártē*) is the Hellenized form

Astarte riding in a chariot with four branches protruding from roof, on the reverse of a Julia Maesa coin from Sidon

of the Middle Eastern goddess Ishtar, worshipped from the Bronze Age through classical antiquity. The name is particularly associated with her worship in the ancient Levant among the Canaanites and Phoenicians. She was also celebrated in Egypt following the importation of Levantine cults there. The name Astarte is sometimes also applied to her cults in Mesopotamian cultures like Assyria and Babylonia.

2.11.1 Name

Astarte is one of a number of names associated with the chief goddess or female divinity of those peoples.[1] She is recorded in Akkadian as *As-dar-tu* (𒀭𒁯𒌋D), the masculine form of Ishtar.[2] The name appears in Ugaritic as *'Athtart* or *'Aṭtart* (𒀭𒁯𒌋𒌋𒌋), in Phoenician as *Ashtart* or *Aštart* (𒀭𒁯𒌋𒌋𒌋), in Hebrew as *Ashtoret* (עשתרת).[3] The Hebrews also referred to the *Ashtarot* or "Astartes" in the plural. The Etruscan Pyrgi Tablets record the name *Uni-Astre* (𒀭𒁯𒌋 𒀭𒁯𒌋𒌋𒌋).

2.11.2 Overview

Astarte was connected with fertility, sexuality, and war. Her symbols were the lion, the horse, the sphinx, the dove, and a star within a circle indicating the planet Venus. Pictorial representations often show her naked. She has been known as the deified evening star.[2]

Astarte was worshipped in Syria and Canaan beginning in the first millennium BC and was first mentioned in texts from Ugarit. She came from the same Semitic origins as the Mesopotamian goddess Ishtar, and an Ugaritic text specifically equates her with Ishtar. Her worship spread to Cyprus, where she may have been merged with an ancient Cypriot goddess. This merged Cypriot goddess may have been adopted into the Greek pantheon in Mycenaean and Dark Age times to form Aphrodite. Stephanie Budin, however, argues that Astarte's character was less erotic and more warlike than Ishtar originally was, perhaps because she was influenced by the Canaanite goddess Anat, and that therefore Ishtar, not Astarte, was the direct forerunner of the Cypriot goddess. Greeks in classical, Hellenistic, and Roman times occasionally equated Aphrodite with Astarte and many other Near Eastern goddesses, in keeping with their frequent practice of syncretizing other deities with their own.[4]

Other major centers of Astarte's worship were the Phoenician city states of Sidon, Tyre, and Byblos. Coins from Sidon portray a chariot in which a globe appears, presumably a stone representing Astarte. "She was often depicted on Sidonian coins as standing on the prow of a galley, leaning forward with right hand outstretched, being thus the original of all figureheads for sailing ships." [5] In Sidon, she shared a temple with Eshmun. Coins from Beirut show Poseidon, Astarte, and Eshmun worshipped together.

Other faith centers were Cythera, Malta, and Eryx in Sicily from which she became known to the Romans as Venus Erycina. A bilingual inscription on the Pyrgi Tablets dating to about 500 BC found near Caere in Etruria equates Astarte with Etruscan Uni-Astre, that is, Juno. At Carthage Astarte was worshipped alongside the goddess Tanit.

Lady of Galera

Donald Harden in *The Phoenicians* discusses a statuette of Astarte from Tutugi (Galera) near Granada in Spain dating to the 7th or 6th century BC in which Astarte sits on a throne flanked by sphinxes holding a bowl beneath her pierced breasts. A hollow in the statue would have been filled with milk through the head and gentle heating would have melted wax plugging the holes in her breasts, producing an apparent miracle when the milk emerged.

The Aramean goddess Atargatis (Semitic form *'Atar'atah*) may originally have been equated with Astarte, but the first element of the name Atargatis appears to be related to the Ugaritic form of Asherah's name: Athirat.

2.11.3 Astarte in Ugarit

Main article: Baal Cycle

In the Ba'al Epic of Ugarit, Athirat, the consort of the god El, plays a role. She is clearly distinguished from Ashtart in the Ugaritic documents, although in non-Ugaritic sources from later periods the distinction between the two goddesses can be blurred; either as a result of scribal error or through possible syncretism.

2.11.4 Astarte in Egypt

Astarte arrived in Ancient Egypt during the 18th dynasty along with other deities who were worshipped by northwest Semitic people. She was especially worshipped in her aspect as a warrior goddess, often paired with the goddess Anat.

In the *Contest Between Horus and Set*, these two goddesses appear as daughters of Ra and are given in marriage to the god Set, here identified with the Semitic name Hadad. Astarte also was identified with the lioness warrior goddess Sekhmet, but seemingly more often conflated, at least in part, with Isis to judge from the many images found of Astarte suckling a small child. Indeed, there is a statue of the 6th century BC in the Cairo Museum, which normally would be taken as portraying Isis with her child Horus on her knee and which in every detail of iconography follows normal Egyptian conventions, but the dedicatory inscription reads: "Gersaphon, son of Azor, son of Slrt, man of Lydda, for his Lady, for Astarte." See G. Daressy, (1905) pl. LXI (CGC 39291).

Plutarch, in his *On Isis and Osiris*, indicates that the King and Queen of Byblos, who, unknowingly, have the body of Osiris in a pillar in their hall, are *Melcarthus* (i.e. Melqart) and Astarte (though he notes some instead call the Queen *Saosis* or *Nemanūs*, which Plutarch interprets as corresponding to the Greek name *Athenais*).[6]

2.11.5 Astarte in Phoenicia

In the description of the Phoenician pantheon ascribed to Sanchuniathon, Astarte appears as a daughter of Epigeius (Greek: Uranus) and Ge (Earth), and sister of the god Elus. After Elus overthrows and banishes his father Epigeius, as some kind of trick Epigeius sends Elus his "virgin daughter" Astarte along with her sisters Asherah and the goddess who will later be called Ba`alat Gebal, "the Lady of Byblos".[7] It seems that this trick does not work, as all three become wives of their brother Elus. Astarte bears Elus children who appear under Greek names as seven daughters called the *Titanides* or *Artemides* and two sons named *Pothos* "Longing" and *Eros* "Desire". Later with Elus' consent, Astarte and Hadad reign over the land together. Astarte puts the head of a bull on her own head to symbolize Her sovereignty. Wandering through the world, Astarte takes up a star that has fallen from the sky (a meteorite) and consecrates it at Tyre.

Ashteroth Karnaim (Astarte was called Ashteroth in the Hebrew Bible) was a city in the land of Bashan east of the Jordan River, mentioned in Genesis 14:5 and Joshua 12:4 (where it is rendered solely as Ashteroth). The name translates literally to 'Ashteroth of the Horns', with 'Ashteroth'

Figurine of Astarte with a horned headdress, Louvre Museum

being a Canaanite fertility goddess and 'horns' being symbolic of mountain peaks. Figurines of Astarte have been found at various archaeological sites in Israel, showing the goddess with two horns.[8]

Astarte's most common symbol was the crescent moon (or horns), according to religious studies scholar Jeffrey Burton Russell, in his book *The Devil: Perceptions of Evil from Antiquity to Primitive Christianity*.[9]

2.11.6   Astarte in Judah

Ashtoreth is mentioned in the Hebrew Bible as a foreign, non-Judahite goddess, the principal goddess of the Sidonians or Phoenicians, representing the productive power of nature. It is generally accepted that the Masoretic "vowel pointing" adopted c. 135 AD, indicating the pronunciation *'Aštōreṯ* ("Ashtoreth," "Ashtoret") is a deliberate distortion of "Ashtart", and that this is probably because the two last syllables have been pointed with the vowels belonging to *bōšeṯ*, ("bosheth," abomination), to indicate that that word should be substituted when reading.[10] The plural form is pointed *'Aštārōṯ* ("Ashtaroth"). The biblical Ashtoreth should not be confused with the goddess Asherah, the form of the names being quite distinct, and both appearing quite distinctly in the Book of 1st Kings. (In Biblical Hebrew, as in other older Semitic languages, Asherah begins with an *aleph* or glottal stop consonant א, while 'Ashtoreth begins with an *'ayin* or voiced pharyngeal consonant ע, indicating the lack of any plausible etymological connection between the two names.) The biblical writers may, however, have conflated some attributes and titles of the two, as seems to have occurred throughout the 1st millennium Levant.[11] For instance, the title "Queen of heaven" as mentioned in *Jeremiah* has been connected with both. (In later Jewish mythology, she became a female demon of lust; for what seems to be the use of the Hebrew plural form *'Aštārōṯ* in this sense, see Astaroth).

2.11.7   Other associations

Some ancient sources assert that in the territory of Sidon the temple of Astarte was sacred to Europa. According to an old Cretan story, Europa was a Phoenician princess whom Zeus, having transformed himself into a white bull, abducted, and carried to Crete.[12]

Some scholars claim that the cult of the Minoan snake goddess who is identified with Ariadne (the "utterly pure")[13] was similar to the cult of Astarte. Her cult as Aphrodite was transmitted to Cythera and then to Greece.[14] Herodotus wrote that the religious community of Aphrodite originated in Phoenicia and came to Greeks from there. He also wrote about the world's largest temple of Aphrodite, in one of the Phoenician cities. Her name is the second name in an energy chant sometimes used in Wicca: "Isis, Astarte, Diana, Hecate, Demeter, Kali, Inanna."[15]

2.11.8   See also

- Ashteroth Karnaim, ancient city, also simply called **Ashteroth** in the Hebrew Bible.

- Attar (god)

- Ishtar

- Snake goddess

- Tanit

2.11.9   References

[1] Merlin Stone. "When God Was A Woman". (Harvest/HBJ 1976)

[2] K. van der Toorn, Bob Becking, Pieter Willem van der Horst, *Dictionary of Deities and Demons in the Bible*, p. 109-10.

[3]

[4] Budin, Stephanie L. (2004). "A Reconsideration of the Aphrodite-Ashtart Syncretism". *Numen* **51** (2): 95–145.

[5] (Snaith, *The Interpreter's Bible*, 1954, Vol. 3, p. 103)

[6] Griffiths, J. Gwyn, *Plutarch's De Iside et Osiride*, pp. 325–327

[7] *Je m'appelle Byblos*, Jean-Pierre Thiollet, H & D, 2005, p. 73. ISBN 2 914 266 04 9

[8] Raphael Patai. *The Hebrew Goddess*. (Wayne State University Press 1990). ISBN 0-8143-2271-9 p. 57.

[9] Jeffrey Burton Russell. *The Devil: Perceptions of Evil from Antiquity to Primitive Christianity*. (Cornell University Press 1977). ISBN 0-8014-9409-5 p. 94.

[10] *John Day, "Yahweh and the gods and goddesses of Canaan", p.128.* Books.google.com.au. Retrieved 2014-04-25.

[11] *Mark S. Smith, "The early history of God", p.129.* Books.google.com.au. Retrieved 2014-04-25.

[12] Lucian of Samosata. *De Dea Syria*.

[13] Barry B. Powell. *Classical Myth* with new translation of ancient texts by H. M. Howe. Upper Saddle River. New Jersey. Prentice Hall Inc. 1998. p. 368.

[14] R. Wunderlich. *The Secret of Creta*. Efstathiadis Group. Athens 1987. p. 134.

[15] BURNING TIMES/CHANT, Charles Murphy, in Internet Book of Shadows, (Various Authors), [1999], at sacred-texts.com

- Donald Harden, *The Phoenicians* (2nd ed., revised, London, Penguin 1980). ISBN 0-14-021375-9

- Georges Daressy, *Statues de Divinités*, (CGC 38001-39384), vol. II (Cairo, Imprimerie de l'Institut français d'archéologie orientale, 1905).

- Gerd Scherm, Brigitte Tast, *Astarte und Venus. Eine foto-lyrische Annäherung* (Schellerten 1996), ISBN 3-88842-603-0.

2.11.10 External links

- Britannica Online Encyclopedia - Astarte (ancient deity)

- Goddess Astarte: Goddess of Fertility, Beauty, War, and Love

- Jewish Encyclopedia - Astarte worship among the Hebrews

2.12 Athena

This article is about the Greek goddess. For other uses, see Athena (disambiguation).

"Athene", "Athina", and "Pallas Athena" redirect here. For other uses, see Athene (disambiguation), Athina (disambiguation), and Pallas Athena (disambiguation).

Athena (/əˈθiːnə/; Attic Greek: Ἀθηνᾶ, *Athēnā*, or Ἀθηναία, *Athēnaia*; Epic: Ἀθηναίη, *Athēnaiē*; Doric: Ἀθάνα, *Athānā*) or **Athene** (/əˈθiːniː/; Ionic: Ἀθήνη, *Athēnē*), often given the epithet **Pallas** (/ˈpæləs/; Παλλὰς), is the goddess of wisdom, courage, inspiration, civilization, law and justice, mathematics, strength, war strategy, the arts, crafts, and skill in ancient Greek religion and mythology. Minerva is the Roman goddess identified with Athena.[2]

Athena is portrayed as a shrewd companion of heroes and is the patron goddess of heroic endeavour. She is the virgin patroness of Athens. The Athenians founded the Parthenon on the Acropolis of her namesake city, Athens (Athena Parthenos), in her honour.[2]

Veneration of Athena was so persistent that archaic myths about her were recast to adapt to cultural changes. In her role as a protector of the city (*polis*), many people throughout the Greek world worshipped Athena as *Athena Polias* (Ἀθηνᾶ Πολιάς "Athena of the city"). While the city of Athens and the goddess Athena essentially bear the same name (*Athena* the goddess, *Athenai* the city), it is not known which of the two words is derived from the other.[3]

2.12.1 Etymology of the name and origins of her cult

Athena is associated with Athens, a plural name, because it was the place where she presided over her sisterhood, the *Athenai*, in earliest times. Mycenae was the city where the Goddess was called Mykene, and Mycenae is named in the plural for the sisterhood of females who tended her there. At Thebes she was called Thebe, and the city again a plural, Thebae (or Thebes, where the 's' is the plural formation). Similarly, at Athens she was called Athena, and the city Athenae (or Athens, again a plural).[4]

Athena had a special relationship with Athens, as is shown by the etymological connection of the names of the goddess and the city. According to mythical lore, she competed with Poseidon and she won by creating the olive tree; the Athenians would accept her gift and name the city after her. In history, the citizens of Athens built a statue of Athena as a temple to the goddess, which had piercing eyes, a helmet on her head, attired with an aegis or cuirass, and an extremely long spear. It also had a crystal shield with the head of the Gorgon on it. A large snake accompanied her and she held Nike, the goddess of victory, in her hand.

In a Mycenaean fresco, there is a composition of two women extending their hands towards a central figure who is covered by an enormous figure-eight shield and could also depict the war-goddess with her palladium, or her palladium in an aniconic representation. Therefore, Mylonas believes that Athena was a Mycenaean creation.[5] On the other hand, Nilsson claims that she was the goddess of the palace who protected the king, and that the origin of Athena was the Minoan domestic snake-goddess.[6] In the so-called Procession-fresco in Knossos which was reconstructed by the Mycenaeans, two rows of figures carrying vessels, seem to meet in front of a central figure, which is probably the Minoan palace goddess "Atano".[7]

In Mycenaean Greek, at Knossos a single inscription 𐀀𐀲𐀙𐀡𐀴𐀛𐀊 *A-ta-na po-ti-ni-ja* /Athana potniya/ appears in the Linear B tablets from the Late Minoan II-era "Room of the Chariot Tablets"; these comprise the earliest Linear B archive anywhere.[8][9] Although *Athana potniya* often is translated *Mistress Athena*, it literally means "the *Potnia* of At(h)ana", which perhaps, means *the Lady of Athens*;[10] any connection to the city of Athens in the Knossos inscription is uncertain.[11] We also find *A-ta-no-dju-wa-ja* (KO Za 1 inscription, line 1), in Linear A Minoan; the final part being regarded as the Linear A Minoan equivalent of the Linear B Mycenaean *di-u-ja* or *di-wi-ja* (*Diwia*, "divine"). *Divine* Athena also was a weaver and the deity of crafts (see *dyeus*).[12] Whether her name is attested in Eteocretan or not will have to wait for decipherment of Linear A.

Apart from these Creto-Greek attributions, Günther Neumann has suggested that Athena's name is possibly of Lydian origin;[13] it may be a compound word derived in part from Tyrrhenian *ati*, meaning *mother* and the name of the Hurrian goddess Hannahannah shortened in various places to *Ana*.

In his dialogue *Cratylus*, the Greek philosopher Plato (428–347 BC), gives the etymology of Athena's name, based on the views of the ancient Athenians and his own etymological speculations:

> That is a graver matter, and there, my friend, the modern interpreters of Homer may, I think, assist in explaining the view of the ancients. For most of these in their explanations of the poet, assert that he meant by Athena "mind" [*nous*] and "intelligence" [*dianoia*], and the maker of names appears to have had a singular notion about her; and indeed calls her by a still higher title, "divine intelligence" [θεοῦ νόησις – *theou noesis*], as though he would say: This is she who has the mind of God (*a theonoa – ἁ θεονόα*). Perhaps, however, the name Theonoe may mean "she who knows divine things" (*ta theia noousa – τὰ θεῖα νοοῦσα*) better than others. Nor shall we be far wrong in supposing that the author of it wished to identify this Goddess with moral intelligence (*en ethei noesin*), and therefore gave her the name Etheonoe; which, however, either he or his successors have altered into what they thought a nicer form, and called her Athena.
>
> — Plato, *Cratylus*, 407b

Thus for Plato her name was to be derived from Greek Ἀθε-ονόα, *Atheonóa* — which the later Greeks rationalised as from the deity's (θεός *theos*) mind (νοῦς *nous*).

Plato also noted that the citizens of Sais in Egypt worshipped a goddess whose Egyptian name was Neith,[14] and which was identified with Athena.[15] Neith was the war goddess and huntress deity of the Egyptians since the ancient Pre-Dynastic period, who was also identified with weaving. In addition, ancient Greek myths reported that Athena had visited many mythological places such as Libya's Triton River in North Africa and the Phlegraean plain.[16] Scholar Martin Bernal created the controversial[17] Black Athena theory to explain this associated origin by claiming that the conception of Neith was brought to Greece from Egypt, along with "an enormous number of features of civilization and culture in the third and second millennia".[18] The connection with Neith was later rejected by other scholars in view of formal difficulties.[19]

R. S. P. Beekes has suggested a Pre-Greek origin of the name.[20]

Some authors believe that, in early times, Athena was either an owl herself or a bird goddess in general: In the third Book of the *Odyssey*, she takes the form of a sea-eagle. These authors argue that she dropped her prophylactic owl-mask before she lost her wings. "Athena, by the time she appears in art," Jane Ellen Harrison had remarked, "has completely shed her animal form, has reduced the shapes she once wore of snake and bird to attributes, but occasionally in black-figure vase-paintings she still appears with wings."[21]

Some Greek authors have derived natural symbols from the etymological roots of Athena's names to be aether, air, earth, and moon. This was one of the primary developments of scholarly exploration in the ancient world.[22]

Miriam Robbins Dexter has suggested that, at least at some point in her history, Athena has been a solar deity.[23] Athena bears traits common with Indo-European solar goddesses, such as the possession of a mirror and the invention of weaving (for instance, the Baltic Saule possesses both these characteristics), and her association with Medusa (herself also suspected of being the remnants of a solar goddess) adds solar iconography to her cultus. Additionally, she is also equated with the Celtic Sulis, a deity whose name is derived from the common proto-Indo-European root for many solar deities. Though the sun in Greek myth is personified as the male Helios, several relictual solar goddesses are known, such as Alectrona.

2.12.2   Cult and patronages

Athenian tetradrachm representing the goddess Athena.

Athena as the goddess of philosophy became an aspect of her cult in Classical Greece during the late 5th century BC.[24] She is the patroness of various crafts, especially of weaving, as *Athena Ergane*, and was honored as such at festivals such as Chalceia. The metalwork of weapons also fell under her patronage. She led battles (*Athena Promachos* or the warrior maiden *Athena Parthenos*)[25] as the disciplined, strategic side of war, in contrast to her brother Ares, the patron of violence, bloodlust and slaughter—"the raw force of war".[26] Athena is the goddess of knowledge, purity, arts, crafts, learning, justice and wisdom. She represents intel-

A new peplos *was woven for Athena and ceremonially brought to dress her cult image (British Museum).*

ligence, humility, consciousness, cosmic knowledge, creativity, education, enlightenment, the arts, eloquence and power. She stands for Truth, Justice, and Moral values. She plays a tough, clever and independent role. Not only was this version of Athena the opposite of Ares in combat, it was also the polar opposite of the serene earth goddess version of the deity, *Athena Polias*.[25]

Athena appears in Greek mythology as the patron and helper of many heroes, including Odysseus, Jason, and Heracles. In Classical Greek myths, she never consorts with a lover, nor does she ever marry,[27] earning the title *Athena Parthenos* (Athena the Virgin). A remnant of archaic myth depicts her as the adoptive mother of Erechtheus/Erichthonius through the foiled rape by Hephaestus.[28] Other variants relate that Erichthonius, the serpent that accompanied Athena, was born to Gaia: when the rape failed, the semen landed on Gaia and impregnated her. After Erechthonius was born, Gaia gave him to Athena.

Though Athena is a goddess of war strategy, she disliked fighting without purpose and preferred to use wisdom to settle predicaments.[29] The goddess only encouraged fighting for a reasonable cause or to resolve conflict. She emphasises everyone to use intuitive wisdom rather than anger or violence. As patron of Athens she fought in the Trojan war on the side of the Achaeans.

2.12.3 Attributes and epithets

Athena's epithets include Ἀτρυτώνη, **Atrytone** (= the unwearying), Παρθένος, **Parthénos** (= virgin), and Πρόμαχος, **Promachos** (the First Fighter, i.e. *she who fights in front*).

In poetry from Homer, an oral tradition of the 8th or 7th century BC, onward, Athena's most common epithet is

Marble Greek copy signed "Antiokhos", a 1st-century BC variant of Phidias' 5th-century Athena Promachos *that stood on the Acropolis.*

Glaukopis (γλαυκῶπις), which usually is translated as, *bright-eyed* or *with gleaming eyes*.[30] The word is a combination of *glaukos* (γλαυκός, meaning *gleaming*, *silvery*, and later, *bluish-green* or *gray*)[31] and *ops* (ὤψ, *eye*, or sometimes, *face*).[32] It is interesting to note that *glaux* (γλαύξ,[33] "little owl")[34] is from the same root, presumably according to some, because of the bird's own distinctive eyes. The bird which sees well in the night is closely associated with the goddess of wisdom: in archaic images, Athena is frequently depicted with an owl (or "owl of Athena" and later under the Roman Empire, "owl of Minerva") perched on her hand. This pairing evolved in tandem so that even today the owl is a symbol of perspicacity and erudition.[2]

Unsurprisingly, the owl became a sort of Athenian mascot. The olive tree is likewise sacred to her. In earlier times, Athena may well have been a bird goddess, similar to the unknown goddess depicted with owls, wings, and bird talons

Bust of the "Velletri Pallas" type, copy after a votive statue of Kresilas in Athens (c. 425 BC)

A little Owl, sacred bird of the Goddess (Owl of Athena).

on the Burney relief, a Mesopotamian terracotta relief of the early second millennium BC.

Other epithets include: **Aethyia** under which she was worshiped in Megara.[35] The word *aethyia* (αἴθυια) signifies a *diver*, and figuratively, a *ship*, so the name must reference Athena teaching the art of shipbuilding or navigation.[36][37]

In a temple at Phrixa in Elis, which was reportedly built by Clymenus, she was known as **Cydonia**.[38]

The various Athena subgroups, or cults, all branching from the central goddess herself often proctored various initiation rites of Grecian youth, for example, the passage into citizenship by young men and for women the elevation to the status of citizen wife. Her various cults were portals of a uniform socialization, even beyond mainland Greece.[39]

In the *Iliad* (4.514), the Homeric Hymns, and in Hesiod's *Theogony*, Athena is given the curious epithet **Tritogeneia.** The meaning of this term is unclear; it could mean various things, including "Triton-born", perhaps indicating that the sea-deity was her parent according to some early myths.[40][41] In Ovid's *Metamorphoses* Athena is occasionally referred to as "Tritonia".

Another possible meaning may be *triple-born* or *third-born*, which may refer to a triad or to her status as the third daughter of Zeus or the fact she was born from Metis, Zeus, and herself; various legends list her as being the first child after Artemis and Apollo, though other legends identify her as Zeus' first child. The latter would have to be drawn from Classical myths, however, rather than earlier ones.

In her role as judge at Orestes' trial on the murder of his mother, Clytemnestra (which he won), Athena won the epithet **Areia**. Other epithets were Ageleia and Itonia.

Athena was given many other cult titles. She has the epithet **Ergane** as the patron of craftsmen and artisans. With the epithet *Parthenos* ("virgin") she was especially worshipped in the festivals of the Panathenaea and Pamboeotia where both militaristic and athletic displays took place.[42] With the epithet *Promachos* she led in battle (see Promachos). With the epithet *Polias* ("of the city"), Athena was the protector of not only Athens but also of many other cities, including Argos, Sparta, Gortyn, Lindos, and Larisa.

She was given the epithet **Hippeia** ("of the horses", "equestrian"), as the inventor of the chariot, and was worshiped under this title at Athens, Tegea and Olympia. As Athena Hippeia she was given an alternative parentage: Poseidon and Polyphe, daughter of Oceanus.[43][44] In each of these cities her temple frequently was the major temple on the acropolis.[45]

Athena often was equated with Aphaea, a local goddess of the island of Aegina, located near Athens, once Aegina was under Athenian's power. The Greek historian Plutarch (46–120 AD) also refers to an instance during the Parthenon's construction of her being called **Athena Hygieia** ("healer", *health personified*):

> A strange accident happened in the course of building, which showed that the goddess was not averse to the work, but was aiding and co-

Cult statue of Athena with the face of the Carpegna type (late 1st century BC to early 1st century CE), from the Piazza dell'Emporio, Rome.

> operating to bring it to perfection. One of the artificers, the quickest and the handiest workman among them all, with a slip of his foot fell down from a great height, and lay in a miserable condition, the physicians having no hope of his recovery. When Pericles was in distress about this, the goddess [Athena] appeared to him at night in a dream, and ordered a course of treatment, which he applied, and in a short time and with great ease cured the man. And upon this occasion it was that he set up a brass statue of Athena Hygeia, in the citadel near the altar, which they say was there before. But it was Phidias who wrought the goddess's image in gold, and he has his name inscribed on the pedestal as the workman of it.[46]

In classical times the Plynteria, or "Feast of Adorning", was observed every May, it was a festival lasting five days. During this period the Priestesses of Athena, or "Plyntrides", performed a cleansing ritual within "the Erecththeum", the personal sanctuary of the goddess. Here Athena's statue was undressed, her clothes washed, and body purified.

In Arcadia, she was assimilated with the ancient goddess Alea and worshiped as Athena Alea.

2.12.4 Mythology

Birth

After he swallowed her pregnant mother, Metis, Athena is "born" from Zeus' forehead as he grasps the clothing of Eileithyia on the right; black-figured amphora, 550–525 BC, Louvre.

Although Athena appears before Zeus at Knossos — in Linear B, as □□□□□□□, *a-ta-na po-ti-ni-ja*, "Mistress Athena"[47] — in the Classical Olympian pantheon, Athena was remade as the favorite daughter of Zeus, born fully armed from his forehead.[48] The story of her birth comes in several versions. In the one most commonly cited, Zeus lay with Metis, the goddess of crafty thought and wisdom, but he immediately feared the consequences. It had been prophesied that Metis would bear children more powerful than the sire,[49] even Zeus himself. In order to prevent this, Zeus swallowed Metis.[50] He was too late: Metis had already conceived.

Eventually Zeus experienced an enormous headache; Prometheus, Hephaestus, Hermes, Ares, or Palaemon (depending on the sources examined) cleaved Zeus' head with the double-headed Minoan axe, the *labrys*. Athena leaped from Zeus' head, fully grown and armed, with a shout — "and pealed to the broad sky her clarion cry of war. And

Ouranos trembled to hear, and Mother Gaia…" (Pindar, *Seventh Olympian Ode*). Plato, in the *Laws*, attributes the cult of Athena to the culture of Crete, introduced, he thought, from Libya during the dawn of Greek culture. Classical myths thereafter note that Hera was so annoyed at Zeus for having produced a child that she conceived and bore Hephaestus by herself, but in Philostratus the Elder, Imagines 2. 27 (trans. Fairbanks) (Greek rhetorician 3rd century AD) Hera "rejoices" at Athena's birth "as though Athena were her daughter also." In accordance with this mythological tradition, Plato, in *Cratylus* (407B), gave the etymology of her name as signifying "the mind of god", *theou noesis*. The Christian apologist of the 2nd century Justin Martyr takes issue with those pagans who erect at springs images of Kore, whom he interprets as Athena:

> "They said that Athena was the daughter of Zeus not from intercourse, but when the god had in mind the making of a world through a word (*logos*) his first thought was Athena."[51]

Other tales Some origin stories tell of Athena having been born outside of Olympus and raised by the god Triton. Fragments attributed by the Christian Eusebius of Caesarea to the semi-legendary Phoenician historian Sanchuniathon, which Eusebius thought had been written before the Trojan war, make Athena instead the daughter of Cronus, a king of Byblos who visited 'the inhabitable world' and bequeathed Attica to Athena.[52] Sanchuniathon's account would make Athena the sister of Zeus and Hera, not Zeus' daughter.

Pallas Athena

The tradition regarding Athena's parentage involves some of her more mysterious epithets: Pallas, as in the ancient-Greek Παλλάς Ἀθήνη (also Pallantias) and Tritogeneia (also Trito, Tritonis, Tritoneia, Tritogenes). A distant archaic separate entity named Pallas is invoked as Athena's father, sister, foster sister, companion, or opponent in battle. One of these is Pallas, a daughter of Triton (a sea god), and a childhood friend of Athena.[53]

In every case, Athena kills Pallas, accidentally, and thereby gains the name for herself. In one telling, they practice the arts of war together until one day they have a falling out. As Pallas is about to strike Athena, Zeus intervenes. With Pallas stunned by a blow from Zeus, Athena takes advantage and kills her. Distraught over what she has done, Athena takes the name Pallas for herself.

When Pallas is Athena's father, the events, including her birth, are located near a body of water named Triton or Tritonis. When Pallas is Athena's sister or foster-sister,

Atena farnese, Roman copy of a Greek original from Phidias' circle, c. 430 AD, Museo Archeologico, Naples

Athena's father or foster-father is Triton, the son and herald of Poseidon. But Athena may be called the daughter of Poseidon and a nymph named Tritonis, without involving Pallas. Likewise, Pallas may be Athena's father or opponent, without involving Triton.[54] On this topic, Walter Burkert says "she is the Pallas of Athens, *Pallas Athenaie*, just as Hera of Argos is *Here Argeie*.[55] For the Athenians, Burkert notes, Athena was simply "the Goddess", *hē theós* (ἡ θεός), certainly an ancient title.

Athena Parthenos: Virgin Athena

Athena never had a consort or lover and is thus known as *Athena Parthenos*, "Virgin Athena". Her most famous temple, the Parthenon, on the Acropolis in Athens takes its name from this title. It is not merely an observation of her virginity, but a recognition of her role as enforcer of rules of

The Parthenon, Temple of Athena Parthenos

sexual modesty and ritual mystery. Even beyond recognition, the Athenians allotted the goddess value based on this pureness of virginity as it upheld a rudiment of female behavior in the patriarchal society. Kerenyi's study and theory of Athena accredits her virginal epithet to be a result of the relationship to her father Zeus and a vital, cohesive piece of her character throughout the ages.[56]

This role is expressed in a number of stories about Athena. Marinus of Neapolis reports that when Christians removed the statue of the Goddess from the Parthenon, a beautiful woman appeared in a dream to Proclus, a devotee of Athena, and announced that the *"Athenian Lady"* wished to dwell with him.[57]

Erichthonius Hephaestus attempted to rape Athena, but she eluded him. His semen fell to the earth and impregnated the soil, and Erichthonius was born from the Earth, Gaia. Athena then raised the baby as a foster mother.[28]

Athena puts the infant Erichthonius into a small box (*cista*) which she entrusts to the care of three sisters, Herse, Pandrosus, and Aglaulus of Athens. The goddess does not tell them what the box contains, but warns them not to open it until she returns. One or two sisters opens the *cista* to reveal Erichthonius, in the form (or embrace) of a serpent. The serpent, or insanity induced by the sight, drives Herse and Aglaulus to throw themselves off the Acropolis.[58] Jane Harrison (*Prolegomena*) finds this to be a simple cautionary tale directed at young girls carrying the *cista* in the Thesmophoria rituals, to discourage them from opening it outside the proper context.

Another version of the myth of the Athenian maidens is told in *Metamorphoses* by the Roman poet Ovid (43 BC – 17 AD); in this late variant Hermes falls in love with Herse. Herse, Aglaulus, and Pandrosus go to the temple to offer sacrifices to Athena. Hermes demands help from Aglaulus

The Athena Giustiniani, *a Roman copy of a Greek statue of Pallas Athena with her serpent, Erichthonius*

to seduce Herse. Aglaulus demands money in exchange. Hermes gives her the money the sisters have already offered to Athena. As punishment for Aglaulus's greed, Athena asks the goddess Envy to make Aglaulus jealous of Herse. When Hermes arrives to seduce Herse, Aglaulus stands in his way instead of helping him as she had agreed. He turns her to stone.[59]

With this mythic origin, Erichthonius became the founder-king of Athens, and many beneficial changes to Athenian culture were ascribed to him. During this time, Athena frequently protected him.

Medusa and Tiresias In a late myth, Medusa, unlike her sister Gorgons, came to be viewed by the Greeks of the 5th century as a beautiful mortal that served as priestess in Athena's temple. Poseidon liked Medusa, and decided to rape her in the temple of Athena, refusing to allow her vow of chastity to stand in his way.[60] Upon discovering the desecration of her temple, Athena changed Medusa's form to match that of her sister Gorgons as punishment. Medusa's hair turned into snakes, her lower body was transformed also, and meeting her gaze would turn any living man to stone. In the earliest myths, there is only one Gorgon, but there are two snakes that form a belt around her waist.

In one version of the Tiresias myth, Tiresias stumbled upon Athena bathing, and he was struck blind by her to ensure he would never again see what man was not intended to see. But having lost his eyesight, he was given a special gift—to be able to understand the language of the birds (and thus to foretell the future).

Athena depicted on a coin of Attalus I, ruler of Pergamon; c. 200 BC.

Lady of Athens

Athena competed with Poseidon to be the patron deity of Athens, which was yet unnamed, in a version of one founding myth. They agreed that each would give the Athenians one gift and that the Athenians would choose the gift they preferred. Poseidon struck the ground with his trident and a salt water spring sprang up; this gave them a means of trade and water—Athens at its height was a significant sea power, defeating the Persian fleet at the Battle of Salamis— but the water was salty and not very good for drinking.[61]

Athena, however, offered them the first domesticated olive tree. The Athenians (or their king, Cecrops) accepted the olive tree and with it the patronage of Athena, for the olive tree brought wood, oil, and food. Robert Graves was of the opinion that "Poseidon's attempts to take possession of certain cities are political myths" which reflect the conflict between matriarchal and patriarchal religions.[61]

Other cult sites   Athena also was the patron goddess of several other Greek cities, notably Sparta, where the archaic cult of Athena Alea had its sanctuaries in the surrounding villages of Mantineia and, notably, Tegea. In Sparta itself, the temple of Athena *Khalkíoikos* (Athena "of the Brazen House", often latinized as *Chalcioecus*) was the grandest and located on the Spartan acropolis; presumably it had a roof of bronze. The forecourt of the Brazen House was the place where the most solemn religious functions in Sparta took place.

Tegea was an important religious center of ancient Greece,[62] containing the Temple of Athena Alea. The *temenos* was founded by Aleus, Pausanias was informed.[63] Votive bronzes at the site from the Geometric and Archaic periods take the forms of horses and deer; there are seal-stone and fibulae. In the Archaic period the nine villages that underlie Tegea banded together in a synoecism to form one city.[64] Tegea was listed in Homer's Catalogue of Ships as one of the cities that contributed ships and men for the Achaean assault on Troy.

Counselor

Later myths of the Classical Greeks relate that Athena guided Perseus in his quest to behead Medusa. She instructed Heracles to skin the Nemean Lion by using its own claws to cut through its thick hide. She also helped Heracles to defeat the Stymphalian Birds, and to navigate the underworld so as to capture Cerberus.

In *The Odyssey*, Odysseus' cunning and shrewd nature quickly won Athena's favour. In the realistic epic mode, however, she largely is confined to aiding him only from

Athena and Heracles on an Attic red-figure kylix, 480–470 BC.

afar, as by implanting thoughts in his head during his journey home from Troy. Her guiding actions reinforce her role as the "protectress of heroes" or as mythologian Walter Friedrich Otto dubbed her the "goddess of nearness" due to her mentoring and motherly probing.[65] It is not until he washes up on the shore of an island where Nausicaa is washing her clothes that Athena arrives personally to provide more tangible assistance. She appears in Nausicaa's dreams to ensure that the princess rescues Odysseus and plays a role in his eventual escort to Ithaca.

Athena appears in disguise to Odysseus upon his arrival, initially lying and telling him that Penelope, his wife, has remarried and that he is believed to be dead; but Odysseus lies back to her, employing skillful prevarications to protect himself.[66] Impressed by his resolve and shrewdness, she reveals herself and tells him what he needs to know in order to win back his kingdom. She disguises him as an elderly man or beggar so that he cannot be noticed by the suitors or Penelope, and helps him to defeat the suitors.

She also plays a role in ending the resultant feud against the suitors' relatives. She instructs Laertes to throw his spear and to kill the father of Antinous, Eupeithes.

Judgment of Paris

Main article: Judgement of Paris

In one myth, all the gods and goddesses as well as various mortals were invited to the marriage of Peleus and Thetis (the eventual parents of Achilles). Only Eris, goddess of discord, was not invited. She was annoyed at this, so she ar-

rived with a golden apple inscribed with the word καλλίστῃ (kallistēi, "for the fairest"), which she threw among the goddesses. Aphrodite, Hera, and Athena all claimed to be the fairest, and thus the rightful owner of the apple.

Paris is awarding the apple to Aphrodite Urteil des Paris *by Anton Raphael Mengs, c. 1857*

The goddesses chose to place the matter before Zeus, who, not wanting to favor one of the goddesses, put the choice into the hands of Paris, a Trojan prince. After bathing in the spring of Mount Ida where Troy was situated, the goddesses appeared before Paris for his decision. The goddesses undressed before him to be evaluated, either at his request or by their own choice.

Still, Paris could not decide, as all three were ideally beautiful, so they resorted to bribes. Hera tried to bribe Paris with control over all Asia and Europe, while Athena offered wisdom, fame and glory in battle, but Aphrodite came forth and whispered to Paris that if he were to choose her as the fairest he would have the most beautiful mortal woman in the world as a wife, and he accordingly chose her. This woman was Helen, who was, unfortunately for Paris, already married to King Menelaus of Sparta. The other two goddesses were enraged by this and through Helen's abduction by Paris they brought about the Trojan War.

Another interpretation is that the apple was being given to the man by the three goddesses, instead of to one of the goddesses. This is the interpretation mythologists and writers delving into more ancient Greek myths that date from before the classical period. The later interpretation is considered a variant interpretation of icons of great antiquity, to conform to the changes in the evolution of the Greek pantheon in myths.

It is suspected that the icons relate to a religious ritual in which a "king" was selected who would serve for a year (or a specified period) before being sacrificed and that the cycle would be renewed upon his death. Robert Graves was a

The apple is being given to Paris in alternative interpretations - Cornelis van Haarlem, 1628

strong proponent of this theory and it is written about in many of his publications, such as *The Greek Myths* and *The White Goddess*. This also was suggested in the early versions of an extensive analysis of Greek mythology, *The Golden Bough* by James George Frazer. In a later editions Frazer completely revised the book and left out his research and discussion of these rituals in the abbreviated edition that is known by that title today.

These interpretations relate to a concept of a *Great Goddess*, a *Mother Goddess*, and the religious worship of such a deity in very ancient Greek culture. It took a triad form, one phase being Athena along with Hera and Aphrodite and others in her matrilineal line (grandmother, mother, etc.) such as (Gaia, Rhea, Hera, Metis), and myths that arose through interpretations (or misinterpretations) of icons from earlier cultural periods. The apple would have been given to the "king" the three goddesses selected.

Roman fable of Arachne

The fable of Arachne is a late Roman addition to Classical Greek mythology[67] but does not appear in the myth repertoire of the Attic vase-painters. Arachne's name means *spider*.[68] Arachne was the daughter of a famous dyer in Tyrian purple in Hypaipa of Lydia, and a weaving student of Athena. She became so conceited of her skill as a weaver that she began claiming that her skill was greater than that of Athena herself.

Athena gave Arachne a chance to redeem herself by assuming the form of an old woman and warning Arachne not to offend the deities. Arachne scoffed and wished for a weaving contest, so she could prove her skill.

Athena wove the scene of her victory over Poseidon that had inspired her patronage of Athens. According to Ovid's

Latin narrative, Arachne's tapestry featured twenty-one episodes of the infidelity of the deities, including Zeus being unfaithful with Leda, with Europa, and with Danaë. Athena admitted that Arachne's work was flawless, but was outraged at Arachne's offensive choice of subjects that displayed the failings and transgressions of the deities. Finally, losing her temper, Athena destroyed Arachne's tapestry and loom, striking it with her shuttle.

Athena then struck Arachne with her staff, which changed her into a spider. In some versions, the destruction of her loom leads Arachne to hang herself in despair; Athena takes pity on her, and transforms her into a spider. In the aforementioned version, Arachne weaved scenes of joy while Athena weaved scenes of horror.

The fable suggests that the origin of weaving lay in imitation of spiders and that it was considered to have been perfected first in Asia Minor.

A changed status in classical mythology

In classical Greek mythology the role of Athena changed as the pantheon became organized under the leadership of Zeus. In earlier mythology she is identified as a parthenogenic daughter of a goddess, but the classical myths fashion for her a peculiar "birth from the head of Zeus" that assigns a father for Athena and eliminates a mother for her, identifying the father as a deity who at one time was portrayed as her brother. Athens may have fallen in 404 BC but the cult of Athena was so dominant in the culture that it survived the transitions seen in the mythic roles of other goddesses, albeit with a juggling of "family" relationships.

J.J. Bachofen advocated that Athena was originally a maternal figure stable in her security and poise but was caught up and perverted by a patriarchal society; this was especially the case in Athens. The goddess adapted but could very easily be seen as a god. He viewed it as "motherless paternity in the place of fatherless maternity" where once altered, Athena's character was to be crystallized as that of a patriarch.[69]

Whereas Bachofen saw the switch to paternity on Athena's behalf as an increase of power, Freud on the contrary perceived Athena as an "original mother goddess divested of her power". In this interpretation, Athena was demoted to be only Zeus's daughter, never allowed the expression of motherhood. Still more different from Bachofen's perspective is the lack of role permanency in Freud's view: Freud held that time and differing cultures would mold Athena to stand for what was necessary to them.[70]

Some modern authors classify the changes as an "androgynous compromise" that allowed her traits and what she stood for to be attributed to male and female rulers alike over the course of history (such as Marie de' Medici, Anne of Austria, Christina of Sweden, and Catherine the Great).[71]

2.12.5 Classical art

Mythological scene with Athena (left) and Herakles (right), on a stone palette of the Greco-Buddhist art of Gandhara, India

Restoration of the polychrome decoration of the Athena statue from the Aphaea temple at Aegina, c. 490 BC (from the exposition "Bunte Götter" by the Munich Glyptothek)

Classical Mosaic from a villa at Tusculum, now at Museo Pio-Clementino, Vatican

Classically, Athena is portrayed wearing a full-length chiton, and sometimes in armor, with her helmet raised high on the forehead to reveal the image of Nike. Her shield bears at its centre the aegis with the head of the gorgon (gorgoneion) in the center and snakes around the edge. It is in this standing posture that she was depicted in Phidias's famous lost gold and ivory statue of her, 36 m tall, the *Athena Parthenos* in the Parthenon. Athena also often is depicted with an owl sitting on one of her shoulders.[72]

The *Mourning Athena* is a relief sculpture that dates around 460 BC and portrays a weary Athena resting on a staff. In earlier, archaic portraits of Athena in Black-figure pottery, the goddess retains some of her Minoan-Mycenaean character, such as great bird wings although this is not true of archaic sculpture such as those of Aphaean Athena, where Athena has subsumed an earlier, invisibly numinous—*Aphaea*—goddess with Cretan connections in her *mythos*.

Other commonly received and repeated types of Athena in sculpture may be found in this list.

Apart from her attributes, there seems to be a relative consensus in late sculpture from the Classical period, the 5th century onward, as to what Athena looked like. Most noticeable in the face is perhaps the full round strong, chin with a high nose that has a high bridge as a natural extension of the forehead. The eyes typically are somewhat deeply set. The unsmiling lips are usually full, but the mouth is depicted fairly narrow, usually just slightly wider than the nose. The neck is somewhat long. The net result is a serene, serious, somewhat aloof, and very classical beauty.

An Empre style chariot clock with the goddess and Telemachus. France, c. 1810.

Euro coin commemorating 60 Years of the Second Republic of Austria, featuring Athena Promachos

2.12.6 Post-classical culture

A brief summary of Athena's evolution of myriad motifs after her dominance in Greece may be seen as follows: The rise of Christianity in Greece largely ended the worship of Greek deities and polytheism in general, but she resurfaced in the Middle Ages as a defender of sagacity and virtue so that her warrior status was still intact. (She may be found on some family crests of nobility.) During the Renaissance she donned the mantle of patron of the arts and human endeavor and finally although not ultimately, Athena personified the miracles of freedom and republic during the French Revolution. (A statue of the goddess was centered on the Place de la Revolution in Paris.)[2]

For over a century a full-scale replica of the Parthenon has stood in Nashville, Tennessee, which is known as *the Athens of the South*. In 1990, a gilded 41 feet (12.5 m) tall replica of Phidias' statue of Athena Parthenos was added. The state seal of California features an image of Athena (or Minerva) kneeling next to a brown grizzly bear.[73]

Athena is a natural patron of universities: she is the symbol of the Darmstadt University of Technology, in Germany, and the Federal University of Rio de Janeiro, in Brazil. Her image can be found in the shields of the Faculty of Philosophy and Letters and the Faculty of Sciences of the National Autonomous University of Mexico, where her owl is the symbol of the Faculty of Chemistry. Her helmet appears upon the shield of the U.S. Military Academy at West Point, New York. At Bryn Mawr College in Pennsylvania a statue of Athena (a replica of the original bronze one in the arts and archaeology library) resides in the Great Hall. It is traditional at exam time for students to leave offerings to the goddess with a note asking for good luck, or to repent for

accidentally breaking any of the college's numerous other traditions. Athena's owl also serves as the mascot of the college, and one of the college hymns is "Pallas Athena". Pallas Athena is the tutelary goddess of the international social fraternity Phi Delta Theta.[74] Her owl is also a symbol of the fraternity.[74]

Jean Boucher's statue of the seated skeptical thinker Ernest Renan caused great controversy when it was installed in Tréguier, Brittany in 1902. Renan's 1862 biography of Jesus had denied his divinity, and he had written the "Prayer on the Acropolis" addressed to the goddess Athena. The statue was placed in the square fronted by the cathedral. Renan's head was turned away from the building, while Athena, beside him, was depicted raising her arm, which was interpreted as indicating a challenge to the church during an anti-clerical phase in French official culture. The installation was accompanied by a mass protest from local Roman Catholics and a religious service against the growth of skepticism and secularism.[75]

Athena has been used numerous times as a symbol of a republic by different countries and appears on currency as she did on the ancient drachma of Athens. Athena (Minerva) is the subject of the $50 1915-S Panama-Pacific commemorative coin. At 2.5 troy oz (78 g) gold, this is the largest (by weight) coin ever produced by the U.S. Mint. This was the first $50 coin issued by the U.S. Mint and no higher was produced until the production of the $100 platinum coins in 1997. Of course, in terms of face-value in adjusted dollars, the 1915 is the highest denomination ever issued by the U.S. Mint.

French car maker Citroën named the top line of its DS models (pronounced Déesse in French, for Goddess) Pallas. It was voted the most beautiful car of all time by *Classic & Sports Car* magazine.[76]

2.12.7 Genealogy of the Olympians in classical Greek mythology

2.12.8 See also

- Athenaeum (disambiguation)

- Palladium (mythology)

2.12.9 Footnotes

[1] According to Hesiod's Theogony, Metis was Athena's mother, but, according to Homer's Iliad, after Zeus swallowed Metis because she was pregnant with Athena (to prevent the birth), Athena sprang forth from the head of Zeus nonetheless and later it was declared that she "had no mother"

[2] Deacy, Susan, and Alexandra Villing. *Athena in the Classical World*. Koninklijke Brill NV, Leiden, The Netherlands: Brill, 2001. Print.

[3] "Whether the goddess was named after the city or the city after the goddess is an ancient dispute" (Burkert 1985:139)

[4] Ruck and Staples 1994:24.

[5] G. Mylonas, *Mycenae and the Mycenaean world*, Princeton University Press, Princeton 1965, p. 159.

[6] Also the later Greek Athena was closely related with the snakes and the birds: M. Nilsson,*Die Geschichte der griechischen Religion*, C.F.Beck Verlag, München 1967, pp. 347, 433.

[7] A. Fururmark, "The Thera catastrophe-Consequences for the European civilization", p. 672. In: *Thera and the Aegean world I*, London 1978.

[8] KN V 52 (text 208 in Ventris and Chadwick).

[9] "Palaeolexicon, Word study tool of ancient languages". Palaeolexicon.com. Retrieved 2010-08-25.

[10] Palaima, p. 444.

[11] Burkert, p. 44.

[12] Ventris and Chadwick [page missing]

[13] Günther Neumann, "Der lydische Name der Athena. Neulesung der lydischen Inschrift Nr. 40". In: *Kadmos* **6** (1967).

[14] "The citizens have a deity for their foundress; she is called in the Egyptian tongue Neith, and is asserted by them to be the same whom the Hellenes call Athena; they are great lovers of the Athenians, and say that they are in some way related to them." (*Timaeus* 21e)

[15] Besides *Timaeus* 21e, cf. also Herodotus, *Histories* 2:170–175.

[16] Aeschylus. *Eumenides* v.292–293. Cf. the tradition that she was the daughter of Neilos: see, e.g. Clement of Alexandria *Protr.* 2.28.2; Cicero, *De Natura Deorum*. 3.59.

[17] Jacques Berlinerblau, *Heresy in the University: The Black Athena Controversy and the Responsibilities of American Intellectuals*, Rutgers University Press, 1999, p. 93ff.

[18] M. Bernal, *Black Athena: The Afroasiatic Roots of Classical Civilization* (New Brunswick: Rutgers University Press, 1987), pp. 21, 51–53.

[19] Jasanoff, Jay H. and Nussbaum, Alan, Word games: the Linguistic Evidence in Black Athena, in: Mary R. Lefkowitz, Guy MacLean Rogers (eds.), *Black Athena Revisited*, The University of North Carolina Press, 1996, p. 194.

[20] R. S. P. Beekes, *Etymological Dictionary of Greek*, Brill, 2009, p. 29.

[21] Harrison 1922:306. (Harrison 1922:307, fig. 84: Detail of a cup in the Faina collection). Archived 5 November 2004 at the Wayback Machine

[22] Gerhard Johrens (1981), *Athenahymnus*, pp. 438–452.

[23] Dexter, Miriam Robbins. Proto-Indo-European Sun Maidens and Gods of the Moon. Mankind Quarterly 25:1 & 2 (Fall/Winter, 1984), pp. 137–144.

[24] Walter Burkert, *Greek Religion* 1985:VII "Philosophical Religion" treats these transformations.

[25] C.J. Herrington, *Athena Parthenos and Athena Polias*. Manchester: Manchester University Press, 1955

[26] Darmon."Athena and Ares". Chicago and London: University of Chicago Press, 1978.

[27] S. Goldhill. *Reading Greek Tragedy* (Aesch.Eum.737). Cambridge: Cambridge University Press, 1986.

[28] Pseudo-Apollodorus, *Bibliotheke* 3.14.6.

[29] Loewen, Nancy. *Athena*. ISBN 0-7368-0048-4.

[30] γλαυκῶπις in Liddell and Scott.

[31] γλαυκός in Liddell and Scott.

[32] ὤψ in Liddell and Scott.

[33] Thompson, D'Arcy Wentworth. *A glossary of Greek birds*. Oxford, Clarendon Press 1895, pp 45-46.

[34] γλαύξ in Liddell and Scott.

[35] Pausanias, i. 5. § 3; 41. § 6

[36] John Tzetzes, *ad Lycophr., l.c.*

[37] Schmitz, Leonhard (1867). Smith, William, ed. "Dictionary of Greek and Roman Biography and Mythology" **1**. Boston, MA. p. 51. |contribution= ignored (help)

[38] Smith, *Dictionary of Greek and Roman Biography and Mythology.*

[39] P.Schmitt,"Athena Apatouria et la ceinture: Les aspects féminins des apatouries à Athènes" in *Annales:Economies, Societies, Civilisations* (1059-1073). London: Thames and Hudson, 2000.

[40] Karl Kerenyi suggests that "Tritogeneia did not mean that she came into the world on any particular river or lake, but that she was born of the water itself; for the name Triton seems to be associated with water generally." (Kerenyi, p. 128).

[41] Τριτογένεια in Liddell and Scott.

[42] Robertson, Noel.*Festivals and Legends:The Formation of Greek Cities in the Light of Public Ritual.*Toronto:University of Toronto Press,1992.

[43] "POLYPHE: Oceanid nymph of Rhodes in the Aegean; Greek mythology". Theoi.com. Retrieved 2010-08-25.

[44] "TITLES OF ATHENA: Ancient Greek religion". Theoi.com. Retrieved 2010-08-25.

[45] Burkert, p. 140.

[46] Plutarch, *Life of Pericles*, 13.8

[47] Knossos tablet V 52 (John Chadwick, *The Mycenaean World*, [Cambridge] 1976:88, fig 37.) *Athana Potnia* does not appear at Mycenaean Pylos, where the mistress goddess is *ma-te-re te-i-ja, Mater Theia,* literally "Mother Goddess".

[48] Jane Ellen Harrison's famous characterization of this myth-element as, "a desperate theological expedient to rid an earth-born Kore of her matriarchal conditions" (Harrison 1922:302) has never been refuted nor confirmed.

[49] Compare the prophecy concerning Thetis.

[50] Hesiod, *Theogony* 890ff and 924ff.

[51] Justin, *Apology* 64.5, quoted in Robert McQueen Grant, *Gods and the One God*, vol. 1:155, who observes that it is Porphyry "who similarly identifies Athena with 'fore-thought'".

[52] ""Sacred Texts: Ancient Fragments", ed. and trans. I. P. Cory, 1832: "The Theology of the Phœnicians from San-choniatho"". Sacred-texts.com. Archived from the original on 5 September 2010. Retrieved 2010-08-25.

[53] "Pallas". Theoi.com. Retrieved 2011-07-24.

[54] Graves, Robert, *The Greek Myths I*, "The Birth of Athena", 8.a., p. 51. The story comes from Libyan (modern Berbers) where the Greek Athena and the Egyptian Neith blend into one deity. The story is not often referenced because some of the details are contradicted by other, better-documented theories. Frazer, vol. 2 p.41

[55] Burkert, p. 139.

[56] K.Kerenyi,*Die Jungfrau und Mutter der griechischen Religion. Eine Studie uber Pallas Athene.*Zurich:Rhein Verlag, 1952.

[57] Marinus of Samaria, *"The Life of Proclus or Concerning Happiness"*, Translated by Kenneth S. Guthrie (1925), pp.15–55:30, retrieved 21 May 2007.Marinus, *Life of Proclus*

[58] Graves, Robert, *The Greek Myths I*, "The Nature and Deeds of Athena" 25.d.

[59] Ovid, *Metamorphoses*, X. Aglaura, Book II, 708–751; XI. The Envy, Book II, 752–832.

[60] "Medusa in Myth and Literary History". Archived from the original on 23 January 2010. Retrieved 2010-01-06.

[61] Graves 1960:16.3p 62.

[62] "This sanctuary had been respected from early days by all the Peloponnesians, and afforded peculiar safety to its suppliants" (Pausanias, *Description of Greece* iii.5.6)

[63] Pausanias, *Description of Greece* viii.4.8.

[64] Compare the origin of Sparta.

[65] W.F.Otto,*Die Gotter Griechenlands(55-77).*Bonn:F.Cohen, 1929

[66] Trahman in *Phoenix*, p. 35.

[67] The Arachne narrative is in Ovid's *Metamorphoses* (vi.5-54 and 129-145) and mentioned in Virgil's *Georgics*, iv, 246.

[68] ἀράχνη, ἀράχνης. Liddell, Henry George; Scott, Robert; *A Greek–English Lexicon* at the Perseus Project.

[69] J.J. Bachofen."Mother Right:An investigation of religious and juridical character of matriarchy in the ancient world",*Myth, Religion and Mother Right.*London:Routledge and Kegan Paul,1967.

[70] Shearer,*Athene*,224-235.

[71] F.Zeitlin,"The Dynamics of Misogyny:Myth and Mythmaking in the Oresteia",*Arethusa*15(1978), 182.

[72] The owl's role as a symbol of wisdom originates in this association with Athena.

[73] "Symbols of the Seal of California". LearnCalifornia.org. Retrieved 2010-08-25.

[74] "Phi Delta Theta International - Symbols". phidelta-theta.org. Archived from the original on 7 June 2008. Retrieved 2008-06-07.

[75] "Musee Virtuel Jean Boucher". Jeanboucher.net. Retrieved 2010-08-25.

[76] "1955 Citroen DS – The Most Beautiful Car of All Time". Motorcities.com. Retrieved 9 July 2009.

2.12.10 References

Ancient sources

- Apollodorus, *Library, 3,180*

- Augustine, *De civitate dei xviii.8–9*

- Cicero, *De natura deorum iii.21.53, 23.59*

- Eusebius, *Chronicon 30.21–26, 42.11–14*

- Lactantius, *Divinae institutions i.17.12–13, 18.22–23*

- Livy, *Ab urbe condita libri vii.3.7*

- Lucan, *Bellum civile ix.350*

Modern sources

- Burkert, Walter, 1985. *Greek Religion* (Harvard).

- Graves, Robert, (1955) 1960. *The Greek Myths* revised edition.

- Kerenyi, Karl, 1951. *The Gods of the Greeks* (Thames and Hudson).

- Harrison, Jane Ellen, 1903. *Prolegomena to the Study of Greek Religion.*

- Palaima, Thomas, 2004. "Appendix One: Linear B Sources." In Trzaskoma, Stephen, et al., eds., *Anthology of Classical Myth: Primary Sources in Translation* (Hackett).

- Ruck, Carl A.P. and Danny Staples, 1994. *The World of Classical Myth: Gods and Goddesses, Heroines and Heroes* (Durham, NC).

- Telenius, Seppo Sakari, (2005) 2006. *Athena-Artemis* (Helsinki: Kirja kerrallaan).

- Trahman, C.R., 1952. "Odysseus' Lies ('Odyssey', Books 13-19)" in *Phoenix*, Vol. 6, No. 2 (Classical Association of Canada), pp. 31–43.

- Ventris, Michael and John Chadwick, 1973. *Documents in Mycenaean Greek* (Cambridge).

- Friel, Brian, 1980. *Translations*

- Smith, William; *Dictionary of Greek and Roman Biography and Mythology*, London (1873). "Athe'na"

2.12.11 External links

- Theoi.com Cult of Athena —Extracts of classical texts

- Roy George, "Athena: The sculptures of the goddess" —A repertory of Greek and Roman types

- Temples of Athena

2.13 Ayao

Ayao is an orisha in the Santería pantheon. She is the orisha of the air. Ayao is considered to reside in both the forest and in the eye of the tornado. She works closely with Osain and is a fierce warrior. Ayao has among her implements a crossbow with a serpent, a quill and nine stones. She is commonly placed next to her sister, Oya. Her colors are brown and green. Ayao's cult was thought to be lost among various adherents; however, a growing number of olorichas have her in their possession.

2.14 Badb

Badb would commonly take the form of the hooded crow.

In Irish mythology, the **Badb** (Old Irish, pronounced ['baðβ]) or **Badhbh** (Modern Irish, pronounced ['bəiv])—meaning "crow"—is a war goddess who takes the form of a crow, and is thus sometimes known as **Badb Catha** ("battle crow"). She is known to cause fear and confusion among soldiers to move the tide of battle to her favoured side. Badb may also appear prior to a battle to foreshadow the extent of the carnage to come, or to predict the death of a notable person. She would sometimes do this through wailing cries, leading to comparisons with the bean-sídhe (banshee).

With her sisters, Macha and the Morrígan, Badb is part of a trio of war goddesses known as the *Morrígna*.[1][2][3]

2.14.1   Representations in legends

In Irish legends, Badb is associated with war and death, appearing either to foreshadow imminent bloodshed or to participate in battles, where she creates confusion among the soldiers. As a harbinger of doom, she appears in a number of different guises. In *Togail Bruidne Dá Derga*, she takes the form of an ugly hag who prophesies Conaire Mór's downfall.[4] She appears in a similar guise in *Togail Bruidne Dá Choca* to foretell the slaying of Cormac Condloinges, as well as taking the form of a "washer at the ford"—a woman washing Cormac's chariot and harness in a ford in what was considered an omen of death.[4][5] The cries of Badb may also be an ill omen: Cormac's impending death is foreshadowed with the words "The red-mouthed badbs will cry around the house, / For bodies they will be solicitous" and "Pale badbs shall shriek".[6] In this role she has much in common with the bean-sídhe.[7]

She was also regularly depicted as an active participant in warfare; indeed, the battlefield was sometimes referred to as "the garden of the Badb".[8] During the First Battle of Mag Tuired, Badb—along with her sisters, Macha and Morrígan—fights on the side of the Tuatha Dé Danann. Using their magic, the three sisters incite fear and confusion among the Fir Bolg army, conjuring "compact clouds of mist and a furious rain of fire" and allowing their enemies "neither rest nor stay for three days and nights".[9] Badb plays a similar role in the Táin Bó Cúailnge, terrorising and disorienting the forces of Queen Medb and causing many to fall on their own weapons.[6] She would often take the form of a screaming raven or crow, striking fear into those who heard her,[10] and could also be heard as a voice among the corpses on a battlefield.[4]

Following the defeat of the Formorians by the Tuatha Dé Danann in the Second Battle of Mag Tuired, Badb (or the Morrígan daughter of Ernmas)[3] instead of predicting doom, now sings a prophecy celebrating the victory and a time of peace,

Sith co nem. Nem co doman. Doman fo ním,
nert hi cach, án

forlann, lan do mil, mid co saith. Sam hi
ngam, gai for sciath, sciath
for durnd. Dunad lonngarg; longait-tromfoíd fod
di uí ross forbiur
benna abu airbe imetha.   Mess for crannaib,
craob do scis scis do áss
saith do mac mac for muin, muinel tairb tarb di
arccoin odhb do
crann, crann do ten. Tene a nn-ail. Ail a n-uír
uích a mbuaib boinn a
mbru. Brú lafefaid ossglas iaer errach, foghamar
forasit etha. Iall do
tir, tir co trachd lafeabrae. Bidruad rossaib síraib
rithmár, 'Nach scel
laut?' Sith co nemh, bidsirnae .s.[2]
Peace to sky. Sky to earth. Earth under sky, strength in each, a
cup full, full of honey, mead in plenty. Summer in winter, spear over shield, shield
over fist. Fort of spears; a battle-cry, land for sheep, bountiful forests
mountains forever, magic enclosure. Mast on branches, branches heavy, heavy with fruit,
wealth for a son, a gifted son, strong neck of bull, a bull for a poem, a knot on
a tree, wood for fire. Fire from stone. Stone from earth, wealth from cows, belly of
the Brú. Doe cries from mist, stream of deer after spring, corn in autumn, upheld by peace.
Warrior band
for the land, prosperous land to the shore. From wooded headlands, waters rushing, "What news

have you?" Peace to the sky, life and land everlasting. Peace.

Then she delivers a prophecy of the eventual end of the world, "foretelling every evil that would be therein, and every disease and every vengeance. Wherefore then she sang this lay below.":[3]

I shall not see a world that will be dear to me.

Summer without flowers,
Kine will be without milk,
Women without modesty,
Men without valour,
Captures without a king.

... ...

Woods without mast,
Sea without produce,

... ...

Wrong judgments of old men,
False precedents of brehons,
Every man a betrayer,
Every boy a reaver.
Son will enter his father's bed,
Father will enter his son's bed,
Everyone will be his brother's brother-in-law.

... ...

An evil time!
Son will deceive his father,

Daughter will deceive her mother.[11]

2.14.2 Kinship

Badb is often identified as one of the Morrígna, a trio of Irish war goddesses, although there exist a number of conflicting accounts on this subject. In *Lebor Gabála Érenn*, Badb, Macha and Morrígan make up the Morrígna trinity and are named as daughters of the farming goddess Ernmas.[1] According to this version, she is also the sister of Ériu, Banba and Fódla, the three matron goddesses of Ireland, who give their names to the land.[1] Other accounts identify the trio as daughters of the druid Cailitin and his wife.[12]

Lebor Gabála Érenn also states that Badb is one of the two wives of the war god Neit.[1] Less commonly, she has been described as the wife of the Fomorian king Tethra.[7]

Similar deities

In her role as a terrifying battlefield goddess and harbinger of doom, Badb closely resembles Nemain. Like Badb, Nemain is identified as a wife of Neit and is sometimes listed as one of the three Morrígna. Writers have sometimes used their names interchangeably, suggesting that they may in fact be a single goddess.[7] On the other hand, W. M. Hennessy notes that Badb and Nemain were said to have different sets of parents, suggesting that they may not be entirely identical figures.[6]

Badb also appears to be closely related to the Gaulish goddess Catubodua, or Bodua.[7]

2.14.3 Etymology

Pointing to variants such as Irish *badhbh* 'hoodie crow, a fairy, a scold,' Early Irish *badb*, 'crow, demon,' *Badba*, Welsh *bod*, 'kite,' the Gaulish name *Bodv-*, in *Bodvognatus* and the Welsh name *Bodnod*, Macbain (1982) suggests **bodwā-* as the Proto-Celtic ancestral form. However, Julius Pokorny (1959:203) suggests **badwā-* on the basis of similar data. Both MacBain (1982) and Julius Pokorny (1959:203) correlate the element with Norse *böð*, genitive *boðvar*, 'war,' and Anglo-Saxon *beadu*, genitive *beadwe*, 'battle,' suggesting that the word originally denoted 'battle' or 'strife.' Julius Pokorny (1959:203) presents the element as an extended form of the Proto-Indo-European root **bhedh-* 'pierce, dig.' To this root Pokorny also links the Sanskrit *bádhate*, 'oppress,' and the Lithuanian *bádas*, 'famine'.

W. M. Hennessy argues that the word *bodb* or *badb* originally meant *rage*, *fury*, or *violence*, and came to mean a witch, fairy, or goddess, represented in folklore by the scald-crow, or royston-crow. Peter O'Connell's 1819 *Irish Dictionary* defines the Badb as a "*bean-sidhe*, a female fairy, phantom, or spectre, supposed to be attached to certain families, and to appear sometimes in the form of squall-crows, or royston-crows" and *badb-catha* as "*Fionog*, a royston-crow, a squall crow". Other entries relate to her triple nature: "*Macha*, i. e. a royston-crow; *Morrighain*, i. e. the great fairy; *Neamhan*, i. e. *Badb catha nó feannóg*; a *badb catha*, or royston-crow."[13]

2.14.4 See also

- Irish mythology in popular culture
- Boa Island
- Clídna
- Mongfind

2.14.5 Footnotes

[1] Macalister, R.A.S. (trans.) (1941). *Lebor Gabála Érenn: Book of the Taking of Ireland Part 1-5*. Dublin: Irish Texts Society.

[2] *Cath Maige Tuired*: The Second Battle of Mag Tuired, Text 166, Author: Unknown

[3] Elizabeth A. Gray (ed. & trans.), *Cath Maige Tuired: The Second Battle of Mag Tuired*, section 167, 1982

[4] Koch, John T. (December 2005). *Celtic Culture: a historical encyclopedia*. Santa Barbara, Calif.: ABC-CLIO. p. 220. ISBN 978-1-85109-440-0.

[5] Davidson, Hilda Ellis (1988). *Myths and Symbols in Pagan Europe: early Scandinavian and Celtic Religions*. Syracuse, NY: Syracuse University Press. p. 99. ISBN 978-0-8156-2441-7.

[6] Hennessy, W. M., "The Ancient Irish Goddess of War", *Revue Celtique* 1, 1870–72, pp. 32–37

[7] Mackillop, James (2004). *A Dictionary of Celtic Mythology*. New York: Oxford University Press. p. 30. ISBN 978-0-19-860967-4.

[8] Sjoestedt, Mary-Louise (2000). *Celtic Gods and Heroes*. Mineola, NY: Dover Publications. p. 32. ISBN 978-0-486-41441-6. (reissue of *Gods and Heroes of the Celts*. London: Methuen, 1949)

[9] Fraser, J. (ed. & trans.), "The First Battle of Moytura", *Ériu* 8, pp. 1–63, 1915

[10] Leeming, David (November 2007). *The Oxford Companion to World Mythology*. New York: Oxford University Press. ISBN 978-0-19-515669-0.

[11] Stokes, Whitley (ed. & trans.), "The Second Battle of Moytura", *Revue Celtique* 12, 1891, pp. 52–130, 306–308; Elizabeth A. Gray (ed. & trans.), *Cath Maige Tuired: The Second Battle of Mag Tuired*, section 167, 1982

[12] Monaghan, Patricia (2004). *The Encyclopedia of Celtic Mythology and Folklore*. New York City: Facts on File, Inc. p. 31. ISBN 978-0-8160-4524-2.

[13] Walter Yeeling Evans-Wentz, *The Fairy-faith in Celtic Countries*, 1911, pp. 304–305

2.14.6 References

- Ó Cuív, Brian (1968). *Irish Sagas*; ed. Myles Dillon. Cork: Mercier.

- MacBain, Alexander. (1982) *An Etymological Dictionary of the Gaelic Language*. Gairm Publications.

- Pokorny, Julius (1959). *Indogermanisches etymologisches Wörterbuch*

2.15 Banba

For the Clannad album, see Banba (album).

In Irish mythology, **Banba** (modern spelling: **Banbha**, pronounced [ˈbʲanʲəvʲə]), daughter of Ernmas of the Tuatha Dé Danann, is a patron goddess of Ireland.

She was part of an important triumvirate of patron goddesses, with her sisters, Ériu and Fódla. According to Seathrún Céitinn she worshipped Macha, who is also sometimes named as a daughter of Ernmas. The two goddesses may therefore be seen as equivalent. Céitinn also refers to a tradition that Banbha was the first person to set foot in Ireland before the flood, in a variation of the legend of Cessair.

In the 'Tochomlad mac Miledh a hEspain i nErind: no Cath Tailten',[1] it is related that as the Milesians were journeying through Ireland, 'they met victorious Banba among her troop of faery magic hosts' on Senna Mountain, the stony mountain of Mes. A footnote identifies this site as Slieve Mish in Chorca Dhuibne, County Kerry. The soil of this region is a non-leptic podzol . If the character of Banbha originated in an earth-goddess, non-leptic podzol may have been the particular earth-type of which she was the deification.

The LÉ Banba (CM11), a ship in the Irish Naval Service (now decommissioned), was named after her.

Initially, she could have been a goddess of war as well as a fertility goddess.

2.15.1 References

[1] The Progress of the Sons of Mil from Spain to Ireland TCD H.4.22, Celtic Literature Collective

2.16 Bastet

For other uses, see Bastet (disambiguation).

Bastet was a goddess in ancient Egyptian religion, worshiped as early as the Second Dynasty (2890 BC). As **Bast**, she was the goddess of warfare in Lower Egypt, the Nile River delta region, before the unification of the cultures of ancient Egypt. Her name is also spelled **Baast**, **Ubaste**, and **Baset**.[1]

The two uniting cultures had deities that shared similar roles and usually the same imagery. In Upper Egypt, Sekhmet was the parallel warrior lioness deity to Bast. Often similar deities merged into one with the unification, but that did not occur with these deities with such strong roots in their cultures. Instead, these goddesses began to diverge. During the Twenty-Second Dynasty (c. 945–715 BC), Bast had changed from a lioness warrior deity into a major protector deity represented as a cat.[2] **Bastet**, the name associated with this later identity, is the name commonly used by scholars today to refer to this deity.

2.16.1 Name

Bastet, the form of the name which is most commonly adopted by Egyptologists today because of its use in later

Photograph of an alabaster cosmetic jar topped with a lioness, representing Bast, an 18th dynasty burial artifact from the tomb of Tutankhamun circa 1323 BC - Cairo Museum

dynasties, is a modern convention offering one possible reconstruction. In early Egyptian, her name appears to have been *b?stt*. In Egyptian writing, the second *t* marks a feminine ending, but was not usually pronounced, and the aleph ? (*?*) may have moved to a position before the accented syllable, *?bst*.[3] By the first millennium, then, *b?stt* would have been something like ***Ubaste** (< ***Ubastat**) in Egyptian speech, later becoming Coptic *Oubaste*.[3]

During later dynasties, Bast was assigned a lesser role in the pantheon bearing the name Bastet, but retained. Thebes became the capital of Ancient Egypt during the 18th Dynasty. As they rose to great power the priests of the temple of Amun, dedicated to the primary local deity, advanced the stature of their titular deity to national prominence and shifted the relative stature of others in the Egyptian pantheon. Diminishing her status, they began referring to Bast with the added suffix, as "Bastet" and their use of the new name was well-documented, becoming very familiar to researchers. By the 22nd dynasty the transition had occurred in all regions.

The town of Bast's cult (see below) was known in Greek as *Boubastis* (Βούβαστις). The Hebrew rendering of the name for this town is *Pî-beset* ("House of Bastet"), spelled without *Vortonsilbe*.[3]

What the name of the goddess means remains uncertain.[3] One recent suggestion by Stephen Quirke (*Ancient Egyptian Religion*) explains it as meaning "She of the ointment jar". This ties in with the observation that her name was written with the hieroglyph "ointment jar" (*b?s*) and that she was associated with protective ointments, among other things.[3] Also compare the name alabaster which might, through Greek, come from the name of the goddess.

She was the goddess of protection against contagious diseases and evil spirits.[4]

She is also known as The Eye of Ra.

2.16.2   From lioness-goddess to cat-goddess

Bastet first appears in the 3rd millennium BC, where she is depicted as either a fierce lioness or a woman with the head of a lioness.[5] Images of Bast were often created from a local stone, named alabaster today. The lioness was the fiercest hunter among the animals in Africa, hunting in cooperative groups of related females.

Originally she was viewed as the protector goddess of Lower Egypt. As protector, she was seen as defender of the pharaoh, and consequently of the later chief male deity, Ra, who was also a solar deity, gaining her the titles *Lady of Flame* and *Eye of Ra*.

Her role in the Egyptian pantheon became diminished as Sekhmet, a similar lioness war deity, became more dominant in the unified culture of Lower and Upper Egypt known as the *Two Lands*.

In the first millennium BC, when domesticated cats were popularly kept as pets, Bastet began to be represented as a woman with the head of a cat. In the 2nd millennium, domestic cats appeared as Bastet's sacred animal. After the 11th century BCE, Bast was commonly depicted as a woman with the head of a cat or lioness, often carrying a sistrum (sacred rattle) and an aegis. When the Greeks started to settle in Egypt, around the 5th century BCE, Bastet started to gain some of the characteristics of Artemis, such as transitioning from a sun goddess to a moon goddess. (Citation needed; information needs to be reordered in correct chronological sequence)

2.16.3   Bubastis

Bast was a local deity whose cult was centered in the city of Bubastis, now Tell Basta, which lay in the Delta near what is known as Zagazig today.[5][6] The town, known in Egyptian as *pr-b☐stt* (also transliterated as Per-Bast), carries her name, literally meaning "House of Bast". It was known in Greek as *Boubastis* (Βούβαστις) and translated into Hebrew as *Pî-beset*. In the biblical Book of Ezekiel 30:17, the town appears in the Hebrew form Pibeseth.[5]

Temple

Herodotus, a Greek historian who traveled in Egypt in the 5th century BC, describes Bast's temple at some length:[7]

> Save for the entrance, it stands on an island; two separate channels approach it from the Nile, and after coming up to the entry of the temple, they run round it on opposite sides; each of them a hundred feet wide, and overshadowed by trees. The temple is in the midst of the city, the whole circuit of which commands a view down into it; for the city's level has been raised, but that of the temple has been left as it was from the first, so that it can be seen into from without. A stone wall, carven with figures, runs round it; within is a grove of very tall trees growing round a great shrine, wherein is the image of the goddess; the temple is a square, each side measuring a furlong. A road, paved with stone, of about three furlongs' length leads to the entrance, running eastward through the market place, towards the temple of Hermes; this road is about 400 feet wide, and bordered by trees reaching to heaven.

The description offered by Herodotus and several Egyptian texts suggest that water surrounded the temple on three (out of four) sides, forming a type of lake known as *isheru*, not too dissimilar from that surrounding the temple of the mother goddess Mut in Karnak at Thebes.[5] Lakes known as *isheru* were typical of temples devoted to a number of leonine goddesses who are said to represent one original goddess, daughter of the Sun-God Re / Eye of Re: Bast, Mut, Tefnut, Hathor, and Sakhmet.[5] Each of them had to be appeased by a specific set of rituals.[5] One myth relates that a lioness, fiery and wrathful, was once cooled down by the water of the lake, transformed into a gentle cat, and settled in the temple.[5]

Festival

Herodotus also relates that of the many solemn festivals held in Egypt, the most important and most popular one was that celebrated in Bubastis in honour of the goddess, whom he calls Bubastis and equates with the Greek goddess Artemis.[8][9] Each year on the day of her festival, the town is said to have attracted some 700,000 visitors ("as the people of the place say"), both men and women (but not children), who arrived in numerous crowded ships. The women engaged in music, song, and dance on their way to the place, great sacrifices were made and prodigious amounts of wine were drunk, more than was the case throughout the year.[10] This accords well with Egyptian sources which prescribe that leonine goddesses are to be appeased with the "feasts of drunkenness".[3] However, a festival of Bastet was celebrated already in the New Kingdom at Bubastis. The block statue of the wab-priest of Sekhmet named Nefer-ka (sculpted under Amenhotep III, Eighteenth Dynasty, around 1380 BC) provides written evidence for this. The inscription suggests that the king (i.e., Amenhotep III) was personally present at the event and had great offerings made to the deity.

The goddess Bast was sometimes depicted holding a ceremonial sistrum in one hand and an aegis in the other—the aegis usually resembling a collar or gorget embellished with a lioness head.

Bast was a lioness goddess of the sun throughout most of Ancient Egyptian history, but later she was changed into the cat goddess (Bastet). She also was changed to a goddess of the moon by Greeks occupying Ancient Egypt toward the end of its civilization. In Greek mythology, Bast also is known as *Ailuros*.

2.16.4 History and connection to other deities

The lioness represented the war goddess and protector of both lands that would unite as Ancient Egypt. As divine mother, and more especially as protector, for Lower Egypt, Bast became strongly associated with Wadjet, the patron goddess of Lower Egypt. She eventually became **Wadjet-Bast**, paralleling the similar pair of patron (Nekhbet) and lioness protector (Sekhmet) for Upper Egypt. Bast fought an evil snake named Apep.

As the fierce lion god Maahes of nearby Nubia later became part of Egyptian mythology and assigned the role of the son of Bast, during the time of the New Kingdom, Bast was held to be the daughter of Amun Ra, a newly ascending deity in the Egyptian pantheon during that late dynasty. Bast became identified as his mother in the Lower Egypt, near the delta. Similarly the fierce lioness war goddess Sekhmet, became identified as the mother of Maahes in the Upper Egypt.

Cats in ancient Egypt were revered highly, partly due to their ability to combat vermin such as mice, rats -

Wadjet-Bast, with a lioness head of Bast, the solar disk, and the cobra that represents Wadjet

which threatened key food supplies -, and snakes, especially cobras. Cats of royalty were, in some instances, known to be dressed in golden jewelry and were allowed to eat from their owners' plates. Turner and Bateson estimate that during the 22nd dynasty c.945-715 BC, Bast worship changed from being a lioness deity into being a major cat deity.[2] With the unification of the two Egypts, many similar deities were merged into one or the other, the significance of Bast and Sekhmet, to the regional cultures that merged, resulted in a retention of both, necessitating a change to one or the other.

The Ancient Egyptian pantheon was evolving constantly. During the 18th dynasty Thebes became the capital of Ancient Egypt and because of that, their patron deity became paramount. The priests of the temple of Amun shifted the relative stature of other deities in the Egyptian pantheon. Diminishing the status of Bast, they began referring to her with the added suffix, as "Bastet" and their use of the new name became very familiar to Egyptologists.

In the temple at Per-Bast some cats were found to have been mummified and buried, many next to their owners. More

than 300,000 mummified cats were discovered when Bast's temple at Per-Bast was excavated. The main source of information about the Bast cult comes from Herodotus who visited Bubastis around 450 BC during after the changes in the cult. He equated Bastet with the Greek Goddess Artemis. He wrote extensively about the cult. Turner and Bateson suggest that the status of the cat was roughly equivalent to that of the cow in modern India. The death of a cat might leave a family in great mourning and those who could would have them embalmed or buried in cat cemeteries - pointing to the great prevalence of the cult of Bastet. Extensive burials of cat remains were found not only at Bubastis, but also at Beni Hasan and Saqqara. In 1888, a farmer uncovered a plot of many hundreds of thousands of cats in Beni Hasan.[2]

2.16.5 Later perception

Later scribes sometimes renamed her *Bastet*, a variation on *Bast* consisting of an additional feminine suffix to the one already present (the "t" of Bast), thought to have been added to emphasize pronunciation; perhaps it is a diminutive name applied as she receded in the ascendancy of Sekhmet in the Egyptian pantheon. Since *Bast* literally meant, *(female) of the ointment jar*, Her name was related with the lavish jars in which Egyptians stored their perfume.

Bast thus gradually became regarded as the goddess of perfumes, earning the title, *perfumed protector*. In connection with this, when Anubis became the god of embalming, Bast, as goddess of ointment, came to be regarded as his wife. The association of Bast as mother of Anubis, was broken years later when Anubis became identified as the son of Nephthys.

Lower Egypt's loss in the wars between Upper and Lower Egypt led to a decrease in the ferocity of Bast. Thus, by the Middle Kingdom she came to be regarded as a domestic cat rather than a lioness. Occasionally, however, she was depicted holding a lioness mask, hinting at her potential ferocity and perhaps, a reminder of her origin.

Because domestic cats tend to be tender and protective of their offspring, Bast also was regarded as a good mother, and she was sometimes depicted with numerous kittens. Consequently, a woman who wanted children sometimes wore an amulet showing the goddess with kittens, the number of which indicated her own desired number of children.

Eventually, her position as patron and protector of Lower Egypt led to her being identified with the more substantial goddess Mut, whose cult had risen to power with that of Amun, and eventually being syncretized with her as *Mut-Wadjet-Bast*. Shortly after, in the constantly evolving pantheon, Mut also absorbed the identities of the Sekhmet-

Ancient Egyptian statue of Bastet after becoming represented as a domestic cat

The Gayer-Anderson cat, believed to be a representation of Bastet

Nekhbet pairing as well.

This merging of identities of similar goddesses has led to considerable confusion, leading to some attributing to Bast the title *Mistress of the Sistrum* (more properly belonging to Hathor, who had become thought of as an aspect of the later emerging Isis, as had Mut), and the Greek idea of her as a lunar goddess (more properly an attribute of Mut) rather than the solar deity she was. The native Egyptian rulers were replaced by Greeks during an occupation of Egypt in the Ptolemaic dynasty that lasted almost 300 years.

The Ptolemys adopted many Egyptian beliefs and customs, but always "interpreted" them in relation to their own Greek culture. These associations sought to link the antiquity of Egyptian culture to the newer Greek culture, thereby lending parallel roots and a sense of continuity. Indeed, much confusion occurred with subsequent generations; the identity of Bast slowly merged among the Greeks during their occupation of Egypt, who sometimes named her **Ailuros** (Greek for *cat*), thinking of Bast as a version of Artemis, their own moon goddess.

Thus, to fit their own cosmology, to the Greeks Bast is thought of as the sister of Horus, whom they identified as Apollo (Artemis' brother), and consequently, the daughter of the later emerging deities, Isis and Ra. Roman occu-

pation of Egypt followed in 30 BC, and their pantheon of deities also was identified with the Greek interpretations of the Ancient Egyptians. The introduction of Christianity and Muslim beliefs followed as well, and by the 6th century AD only a few vestiges of Ancient Egyptian religious beliefs remained, although the cult of Isis had spread to the ends of the Roman Empire.

2.16.6   See also

- Other (non-Iranian) variants of Lion and Sun

2.16.7   Notes

[1] Badawi, Cherine. *Footprint Egypt*. Footprint Travel Guides, 2004.

[2] Serpell, "Domestication and History of the Cat", p. 184.

[3] Te Velde, "Bastet", p. 165.

[4] http://www.shira.net/egypt-goddess.htm#Bastet

[5] Te Velde, "Bastet", p. 164.

[6] Bastet Egyptian Museum

[7] Herodotus, Book 2, chapter 138.

[8] Herodotus, Book 2, chapter 59.

[9] Herodotus, Book 2, chapter 137.

[10] Herodotus, Book 2, chapter 60.

2.16.8 References

Primary sources

- Herodotus, ed. H. Stein (et al.) and tr. AD Godley (1920), *Herodotus 1. Books 1 and 2*. Loeb Classical Library. Cambridge, Mass.

- Egyptian temples

- E. Bernhauer, "Block Statue of Nefer-ka", in: M. I. Bakr, H. Brandl, Faye Kalloniatis (eds.): Egyptian Antiquities from Kufur Nigm and Bubastis. Berlin 2010, pp. 176–179 ISBN 978-3-00-033509-9.

Secondary sources

- Velde, Herman te (1999). "Bastet". In Karel van der Toorn, Bob Becking and Pieter W. van der Horst. *Dictionary of Demons and Deities in the Bible* (2nd ed.). Leiden: Brill Academic. pp. 164–5. ISBN 90-04-11119-0.

- Serpell, James A. "Domestication and History of the Cat". In Dennis C. Turner and Paul Patrick Gordon Bateson. *The Domestic Cat: the Biology of its Behaviour*. pp. 177–192.

2.16.9 Further reading

- Malek, Jaromir (1993). *The Cat in Ancient Egypt*. London: British Museum Press.

- Otto, Eberhard (1972–1992). "Bastet". In W. Helck; et al. *Lexicon der Ägyptologie* **1**. Wiesbaden. pp. 628–30.

- Quaegebeur, J. (1991). "Le culte de Boubastis - Bastet en Egypte gréco-romaine". In L. Delvaux and E. Warmenbol. *Les divins chat d'Egypte*. Leuven. pp. 117–27.

- Quirke, Stephen (1992). *Ancient Egyptian Religion*. London: British Museum Press.

- Bakr, Mohamed I. and Brandl, Helmut (2010). "Bubastis and the Temple of Bastet". In M. I. Bakr, H. Brandl, F. Kalloniatis (eds.). *Egyptian Antiquities from Kufur Nigm and Bubastis*. Cairo/Berlin. pp. 27–36. ISBN 978-3-00-033509-9

- Bernhauer, Edith (2014). "Stela Fragment (of Bastet)". In M. I. Bakr, H. Brandl, F. Kalloniatis (eds.). *Egyptian Antiquities from the Eastern Nile Delta*. Cairo/Berlin. pp. 156–157. External link in |chapter= (help) ISBN 978-3-00-045318-2

2.16.10 External links

- Exhaustive scholarly essay on the goddess

- "Temple to cat god found in Egypt", BBC News.

2.17 Bellona (goddess)

See Bellona for other meanings of this word.

"Bellona", by Rodin.

Bellona was an Ancient Roman goddess of war. She was called the sister of Mars, and in some sources, his wife or an associate of his female cult partner Nerio.[1] Bellona's main attribute is the military helmet worn on her head, and she often holds a sword, a shield, or other weapons of battle.

Politically, all Roman Senate meetings relating to foreign war were conducted in the Templum Bellonæ (Temple of Bellona) on the Collis Capitolinus outside the *pomerium*, near the Temple of Apollo Sosianus. The fetiales, a group of priest advisors, conducted ceremonies to proclaim war and peace, and announced foreign treaties at the columna bellica, in front of her temple.[1]

2.17.1   Etymology

The name Bellona is transparently derived from the Latin word *bellum* "war"—the older form *Duellona* demonstrates its antiquity, showing the same sound change as *duellum*.

2.17.2   Attributes

In art, she is portrayed with a helmet on her head, usually wearing a breastplate or plate armour, bearing a sword, spear, shield, or other weaponry, sometimes holding a flaming torch or sounding the Horn of Victory and Defeat. In heraldic crests, she may be shown as a goddess with spread feathered wings bearing a helmet or coronet.

Ammianus Marcellinus, in describing the Roman defeat at the Battle of Adrianople refers to "Bellona, blowing her mournful trumpet, was raging more fiercely than usual, to inflict disaster on the Romans".

Bellona, & count's coronet, c. 1863 floor tile, southern England.[2]

2.17.3   In later culture

Near the beginning of Shakespeare's *Macbeth* (I.ii.54), Macbeth is introduced as a violent and brave warrior when the Thane of Ross calls him "Bellona's bridegroom" (i.e. Mars). In *Henry IV, Part I*, Hotspur describes her as "the fire-eyed maid of smoky war" (IV.i.119). And in The Two Noble Kinsmen (1613), set in pre-Roman Athens, the sister of Hippolyta will solicit her divine aid for Theseus against Thebes (I.iii.13).

The goddess has also proved popular in post-Renaissance art as a female embodiment of military virtue, and an excellent opportunity to portray the feminine form in armour and helmet.

Bellona appears in the prologue of Rameau's opera, *Les Indes Galantes*.

The composer Francesco Bianchi and the librettist Lorenzo da Ponte together created a Cantata first performed in London on 11 March 1797 & called Le nozze del Tamigi e Bellona, (The Wedding of the Thames and Bellona), to mark the British naval victory over the Spanish at the Battle of Cape St Vincent.

Also, the "Temple of Bellona" was a popular choice of name for the small mock-temples that were a popular feature of 18th- and 19th-century English landscaped gardens (e.g. William Chambers's 1760 Temple of Bellona for Kew Gardens, a small Doric temple with a four-column facade to contain plaques honouring those who served in the Seven Years' War of 1756–64).

First World War poet Edgell Rickwood wrote a poem "The Traveller" where he marches toward the front line in company of Art, the God Pan and the works of essayist Walter Pater. As they approach the active war, they meet Bellona. One by one the pleasurable companions are forced to flee by the violence of war, until Bellona rejoices in having him to herself.

Samuel R. Delany's 1975 novel *Dhalgren* is set in the city of Bellona.

The detective novel *The Unpleasantness at the Bellona Club* by Dorothy L Sayers is set at a fictional London club whose membership is composed of active or retired military officers, and is named after the goddess.

Bellona also appears as a playable character in Hi-Rez Studios' mythology based video game called Smite.

- Salis family (origin Grisons) crest, late 19th-century version on an album cover.

- Bronze sculpture of Bellona, 17th century, Royal Castle in Warsaw.

- Salis crest, an English version on silver entree dish cover, 1865.

- Early 19th-century Salis crest on cloth

- Bellona on the badge of the Volunteer Training Corps in World War I

- Bellona, part of a circa 1845 window by Thomas Willement for Captain the Hon. C. L. M. Fane De Salis.

2.17.4 References

[1] Encyclopædia Britannica. "Bellona". Retrieved 25 March 2014.

[2] Elizabeth Darby, "A French Sculptor in Wiltshire: Henri de Triqueti's Panel in the Church of St Michael & All Angels, Teffont Evias." The Wiltshire Archaeological and Natural History Magazine. Vol.95 (2002).

2.17.5 External links

- Images of Bellona in the Warburg Institute Iconographic Database

2.18 Bia (mythology)

In Greek mythology, **Bia**, (in Greek: Βία, "Violence"), was the personification of force and raw energy, daughter of Pallas and Styx,[1] and sister of Nike, Kratos, and Zelus.[2]

She and her siblings were constant companions of Zeus.[3] They achieved this honour after supporting Zeus in the war of the Titans along with their mother.[4] Bia is one of the characters named in the Greek tragedy *Prometheus Bound*, written by Aeschylus, where Hephaestus is compelled by the gods to bind Prometheus after he was caught stealing fire and offering the gift to mortals.

2.18.1 References

[1] Hesiod. *Theogony*, 375-383.

[2] Hesiod, *Theogony* 383–5.

[3] Hesiod, *Theogony* 386–7.

[4] Hesiod, *Theogony* 389–94.

2.18.2 External links

- Theoi Mythology, Bia

2.19 Brigantia (goddess)

A statuette in the Museum of Brittany, Rennes, probably depicting Brigantia: c. 2nd century BCE

Brigantia was a goddess in Celtic (Gallo-Roman and Romano-British) religion of Late Antiquity.

Through *interpretatio Romana*, she was equated with *Victoria*. The tales connected to the characters of Brigid and Saint Brigid in Irish mythology and legend have been argued to be connected to Brigantia although the figures themselves remain distinct.

2.19.1   Etymology

Further information: Brigantes

The name *Brigantia* continues the feminine PIE *bhṛg'hntī*, from a root *berg'h* "high, lofty, elevated". The name is in origin an adjectival epithet simply meaning "the high one", "the elevated one".

An exact cognate is found in the Germanic *Burgundi* (Proto-Germanic *burgundī*, compare *Bornholm*), in Sanskrit *bṛhatī*, and in Avestan *bərəzaitī*, both feminine adjectives meaning "high" (Sanskrit Brhati also being a female given name, as is Old High German *Purgunt*). The ethnonym *Brigantes* may either translate to "the high, noble ones" or to "highlanders" (IEW, s.v. "bhereg'h-").

2.19.2   Evidence for Brigantia

Inscriptions

Seven inscriptions to Brigantia are known, all from Britain (Epigraphik-Datenbank Clauss/Slaby). At Birrens (the Roman Blatobulgium), Dumfries and Galloway, in Scotland, is an inscription:

> Brigantiae s(acrum) Amandus / arc(h)itectus ex imperio imp(eratum) (fecit) (*RIB* 02091).

Brigantia is assimilated to *Victoria* in two inscriptions, one from Castleford in Yorkshire (AE 1892, 00098; RIB 00628) and one from Greetland near Halifax, also in Yorkshire (RIB 00627). The later may be dated to 208 AD by mention of the consuls:

> D(eae) Vict(oriae) Brig(antiae) / et num(inibus) Aauugg(ustorum) / T(itus) Aur(elius) Aurelian/us d(onum) d(edit) pro se / et suis s(e) mag(istro) s(acrorum) // Antonin[o] / III et Geta [II] / co(n)ss(ulibus)

At Corbridge on Hadrians Wall - in antiquity, Coria - Brigantia has the divine epithet *Caelestis* ("Heavenly, Celestial") and is paired with Jupiter Dolichenus (AE 1947, 00122; RIB 01131):

Altar to Jupiter Dolichenus and Caelestis Brigantia from Corbridge, on a 1910 postcard

> Iovi aeterno / Dolicheno / et caelesti / Brigantiae / et Saluti / C(aius) Iulius Ap/ol(l)inaris / l(centurio) leg(ionis) VI iuss(u) dei

There is an inscription at Irthington, Yorkshire DEAE NYMPHAE BRIGANTIAE—"divine nymph Brigantia" (Nicholson).

Garret Olmstead (1994) noted numismatic legends in Iberian script, BRIGANT_N (or PRIKANT_N, as Iberic script does not distinguish voiced and unvoiced consonants) inscribed on a Celtiberian coin, suggesting a cognate Celtiberian goddess.

Iconography

At Birrens (the Roman Blatobulgium), archaeologists have found a Roman-era stone bas-relief of a female figure; she is crowned like a tutelary deity, has a Gorgon's head on her breast, and holds a spear and a globe of victory like the Roman goddesses Victoria and Minerva (Green 1996, p. 197).

The inscription mentioned above assures the identification of the statue as Brigantia rather than Minerva. A statue found in Brittany also seems to depict Brigantia with the attributes of Minerva.

Toponomy

There are several placenames deriving from '**Brigantium**', the neuter form of the same adjective of which the feminine became the name of the goddess. Association of these with the goddess is however dubious, since the placenames are easily explained as referring to a "high fort" or "high place" in the literal sense.

Lisa Bitel (2001) noted a wide spread through toponymy:

> The town of Bregenz, at the eastern end of Lake Constance in Austria, retains the older name of Brigantion, a tribal capital of a people called the Brigantii, possibly after a goddess Brigant. The rivers Brent in England, Braint in Wales, and Brigid in Ireland are all related linguistically and maybe religiously to the root Brig/Brigant ... Ptolemy, a second-century geographer, did mention a tribe calling itself the Brigantes in Leinster. But nothing remains of the Irish Brigantes except this single tribal name on a Greek's map, the river Brigid, and much later literary references to saints and supernatural figures named Brigit.

Other towns which may also preserve this theonym include Brigetio in Hungary (Green 1986 p. 161), also Brianconnet and Briançon, both in Provence-Alpes-Côte d'Azur, France. In antiquity, Briançon was called Brigantio and was the first town on the Via Domitia. It is attested by an inscriptions mentioning munic(ipii) Brigantien(sium) (the town of Brigantio)(CIL 12, 00095) and Bri/gantione geniti (the Briganti people)(CIL 12, 00118). At Brianconnet, an inscription mentions ord(o) Brig(antorum) (AE 1913, 00014). There, oak trees were particularly venerated.

The ancient name of Bragança in Trás-os-Montes, Portugal, was Brigantia. The inhabitants today are still called *brigantinos*. Braga is another town in Portugal. It is the capital of the district of the same name in the province of Minho. A short distance up the coast, the cities of A Coruña and Betanzos in present day Galicia (which together with the area of present day Portugal north of the Douro river formed the Roman and later medieval kingdom of Gallaecia or Callaecia) were respectively named Brigantia and Brigantium. According to the Lebor Gabála Érenn (The Book of the Taking of Ireland) Breogán found the city called Brigantia, and built a tower there from the top of which his son

Íth glimpses Ireland and then sets sail across the Celtic Sea to invade and settle it.

2.19.3 References

- Année Epigraphique (AE), yearly volumes.

- Bitel, Lisa M. (2001) "St. Brigit of Ireland: From Virgin Saint to Fertility Goddess" on-line)

- Claus, Manfredd; *Epigraphik-Datenbank Clauss / Slaby*, Johann Wolfgang Goethe-Universität Frankfurt. Online epigraphic search tool

- Ellis, Peter Berresford (1994) *Dictionary of Celtic Mythology* Oxford Paperback Reference, Oxford University Press, ISBN 0-19-508961-8

- Gree, Miranda (1986) *The Gods of the Celts.* Stroud, Sutton Publishing. ISBN 0-7509-1581-1

- Green, Miranda (1996) *Celtic Goddesses: Warriors, Virgins, and Mothers* New York, pp 195–202.

- MacKillop, James (1998) *Dictionary of Celtic Mythology*. Oxford, Oxford University Press. ISBN 0-19-280120-1.

- Olmstead, Garret (1994) *The Gods of the Celts and Indo-Europeans* Budapest, pp 354–361

- *Roman Inscriptions of Britain* (RIB).

- Wood, Juliette (2002) *The Celts: Life, Myth, and Art.* Thorsons. ISBN 0-00-764059-5

2.19.4 External links

- Brighid: What Do We Really Know? by Francine Nicholson includes a section on Brigantia and a picture of the Birrens bas-relief.

2.20 Cathubodua

Cathubodua (Proto-Celtic: *Katu-bodwā*, "battle crow") is the name of a Gaulish goddess inferred from a single inscription at Mieussy in Haute Savoie, eastern France,[1] which actually reads ATHVBODVAE AVG SERVILIA TERENTIA S L M.[2] The text's restitution as *Cathubodua* depends on the assumptions that an initial C has been lost and that the personal names ATEBODVAE, ATEBODVVS and ATEBODVI in 3 other inscriptions in modern Austria and Slovenia[3] are unrelated.

She appears to be identical to the Irish goddess Badb Catha. Nicole Jufer and Thierry Luginbühl provisionally link Cathubodua with other apparently martial goddesses attested elsewhere, such as **Boudina, Bodua,** and **Boudiga,** whose names share roots meaning either 'fighting' or 'victory'.[4] She would therefore be comparable to the Roman Victoria and the Greek goddess Nike and possibly the Nordic goddess Sigyn.

2.20.1 A related Roman legend?

A story of the Roman wars against the Gauls of the 4th century BC, recorded by Livy, Aulus Gellius and Dionysius of Halicarnassus, may preserve a reference to her. A Roman soldier, Marcus Valerius, accepted a challenge to single combat with a Gaulish champion. When the fight began, a crow landed on Valerius's helmet and began to attack the Gaul, who, terrified by this divine intervention, was easily beaten. Valerius adopted the cognomen "Corvus" (crow), and as Marcus Valerius Corvus went on to be a famous general and politician of the Roman Republic.[5]

2.20.2 Name and etymology

In the Gaulish language, the name Cathubodua is believed to mean *battle-crow*.[6][1]

Etymological lexical forms reconstructed in the University of Wales' Proto-Celtic lexicon, suggest that the name is likely to be ultimately derived from the Proto-Celtic *Katu-bodwā*, a word that could be interpreted as 'battle-fighting'.[7] Nonetheless it is this second element *bodwā* which appears to be the Proto-Celtic root of the later form of the name Badhbh. The masculine form *bodwos* ('fighting') developed in Gaelic into Bodb.

2.20.3 References

[1] "Cathubodua". *L'Arbre Celtique*. 2015. Retrieved 2015-05-13.

[2] W. M. Hennessey (1870). *The Ancient Irish Goddess of War*.

[3] *CIL* III, 5247; *CIL* III, 4732; *CIL* III, 5386;

[4] Jufer, N. and T. Luginbühl (2001). *Répertoire des dieux gaulois*. Paris, Editions Errance.

[5] Titus Livius. *Periochae*. Book 7:10.

[6] Georges Dottin (1918) *La Langue Gauloise, Grammaire, Textes et Glossaire*. Paris Librairie C. Klincksieck. p. 235 and 244

[7] Proto-Celtic—English lexicon. University of Wales Centre for Advanced Welsh and Celtic Studies. (See also this page for background and disclaimers.)

2.21 Chamunda

For the village in Nepal, see Chamunda, Nepal. For the skipper butterfly genus, see Chamunda (butterfly).

Chamunda (Sanskrit: चामुण्डा, *Cāmuṇḍā*), also known as **Chamundi**, **Chamundeshwari** and **Charchika**, is a fearsome aspect of Devi, the Hindu Divine Mother and one of the seven Matrikas (mother goddesses). She is also one of the chief Yoginis, a group of sixty-four or eighty-one Tantric goddesses, who are attendants of the warrior goddess Durga.[2] The name is a combination of Chanda and Munda, two monsters whom Chamunda killed. She is closely associated with Kali, another fierce aspect of Devi.[3] She is sometimes identified with goddesses Parvati, Chandi or Durga as well. The goddess is often portrayed as haunting cremation grounds or fig trees. The goddess is worshipped by ritual animal sacrifices along with offerings of wine and in the ancient times, human sacrifices were offered too. Originally a tribal goddess, Chamunda was assimilated in Hinduism and later entered the Jain pantheon too. Though in Jainism, the rites of her worship include vegetarian offerings, and not the meat and liquor offerings.

2.21.1 Origins

Ramakrishna Gopal Bhandarkar says that Chamunda was originally an indigenous goddess worshipped by the Munda peoples of the Vindhya range of central India. These tribes were known to offer goddesses animal as well as human sacrifices along with ritual offerings of liquor. These methods of worship were retained in Tantric worship of Chamunda, after assimilation in Hinduism. He proposes the fierce nature of this goddess is due of her association with Vedic Rudra (identified as Shiva in modern Hinduism), identified with fire god Agni at times.[4] Wangu also backs the theory of the tribal origins of the goddess.[5]

2.21.2 Iconography

The black or red coloured Chamunda is described as wearing a garland of severed heads or skulls (*Mundamala*). She is described as having four, eight, ten or twelve arms, holding a Damaru (drum), trishula (trident), sword, a snake, skull-mace (*khatvanga*), thunderbolt, a severed head and *panapatra* (drinking vessel, wine cup) or skull-cup (kapala), filled with blood. Standing on a corpse of a man (*shava* or *preta*) or seated on a defeated demon or corpse (*pretasana*), she is described as having a skeletal body with three eyes, a terrifying face, drooping breasts, protruding teeth, long nails and a sunken belly. She has a scorpion sitting on her navel like a decoration. Chamunda is depicted adorned by

Chamunda, 11th-12th century, National Museum, Delhi. The ten-armed Chamunda is seated on a corpse, wearing a necklace of severed heads.

ornaments of bones, skulls, serpents and scorpions, symbols of disease and death. She also wears a *Yajnopavita* (a sacred thread worn by mostly Hindu male priests) of skulls. She wears a *jata mukuta*, that is, headdress formed of piled, matted hair tied with snakes or skull ornaments. Sometimes, a crescent moon is seen on her head.[6][7] Her socket eyes are described as burning the world with flames. She is accompanied by fiends and goblins.[7][8] She is also shown surrounded by skeletons or ghosts and beasts like jackals, who are shown eating the flesh of the corpse which the goddess sits or stands on. The jackals and her fearsome companions are sometimes depicted as drinking blood from the skull-cup or blood dripping from the severed head, implying that Chamunda drinks the blood of the defeated enemies.[9] This quality of drinking blood is a usual characteristic of all Matrikas, and Chamunda in particular. At times, she is depicted seated on an owl, her vahana (mount or vehicle). Her

banner figures an eagle.[7]

These characteristics, a contrast to usual Hindu goddess depiction with full breasts and a beautiful face, are symbols of old age, death, decay and destruction.[10]

2.21.3 Hindu legends

The Goddess Ambika (here identified with: Durga or Chandi) Leading the Eight Matrikas in Battle Against the Demon Raktabija, Folio from a Devi Mahatmya - (top row, from the left) Narashmi, Vaishnavi, Kumari, Maheshvari, Brahmi. (bottom row, from left) Varahi, Aindri and Chamunda, drinking the blood of demons (on right) arising from Raktabija's blood and Ambika.

In Hindu scripture Devi Mahatmya, Chamunda emerged as *Chandika Jayasundara* from an eyebrow of goddess *Kaushiki*, a goddess created from "sheath" of Durga and was assigned the task of eliminating the demons Chanda and Munda, generals of demon kings Shumbha-Nishumbha. She fought a fierce battle with the demons, ultimately killing them.[11] Goddess Chandika Jayasundara took the slain heads of the two demons to goddess Kaushiki, who became immensely pleased. Kaushiki blessed Chandika Jayasundara and bestowed upon her the title of "Chamunda", to commemorate the latter's victory over the demons.

According to a later episode of Devi Mahatmya, Durga created Matrikas from herself and with their help slaughtered the demon army of Shumbha-Nisumha. In this version, Kali is described as a Matrika who sucked all the blood of the demon Raktabija. Kali is given the epithet Chamunda in the text.[12] Thus, the Devi Mahatmya identifies Chamunda with Kali.

In Varaha Purana, the story of Raktabija is retold, but here each of Matrikas appears from the body of another Matrika. Chamunda appears from the foot of the lion-headed goddess Narshmi. Here, Chamunda is considered a representation of the vice of tale-telling (*pasunya*). The Varaha Purana text clearly mentions two separate goddesses Chamunda and Kali, unlike Devi Mahatmya.[7]

According to another legend, Chamunda appeared from

the frown of the benign goddess Parvati to kill demons Chanda and Munda. Here, Chamunda is viewed as a form of Parvati.[13]

Matsya Purana tells a different story of Chamunda's origins. She with other matrikas was created by Shiva to help him kill the demon Andhakasura, who has an ability - like Raktabija - to generate from his dripping blood. Chamunda with the other matrikas drinks the blood of the demon ultimately helping Shiva kill him.[7] Ratnakara, in his text Haravijaya, also describes this feat of Chamunda, but solely credits Chamunda, not the other matrikas of sipping the blood of Andhaka. Having drunk the blood, Chamunda's complexion changed to blood-red.[14] The text further says that Chamunda does a dance of destruction, playing a musical instrument whose shaft is Mount Meru, the spring is the cosmic snake Shesha and gourd is the crescent moon. She plays the instrument during the deluge that drowns the world.[8]

2.21.4   Association with Matrikas

Chamunda is included in the *Saptamatrika* (seven Matrikas or mothers) lists in the Hindu texts like Mahabharata (Chapter 'Vana-parva'), Devi Purana and Vishnudharmottara Purana. She is often depicted in the Saptamatrika group in sculptures, examples of which are Ellora and Elephanta caves. Though she is always portrayed last (rightmost) in the group, she is sometimes referred to as the leader of the group.[15] While other Matrikas are considered as Shaktis (powers) of male divinities and resemble them in their appearance, Chamunda is the only Matrika who is a Shakti of the great Goddess Devi rather than a male god. She is also the only Matrika who enjoys independent worship of her own; all other Matrikas are always worshipped together.[16]

Devi Purana describe a pentad of Matrikas who help Ganesha to kill demons.[17] Further, sage Mandavya is described as worshipping the *Mātrpañcaka* (the five mothers), Chamunda being one of them. The mothers are described as established by creator god Brahma for saving king Harishchandra from calamities.[18] Apart from usual meaning of Chamunda as slayer of demons Chanda and Munda, Devi Purana gives a different explanation: *Chanda* means terrible while *Munda* stands for Brahma's head or lord or husband.[19]

In Vishnudharmottara Purana - where the Matrikas are compared to vices - Chamunda is considered as a manifestation of depravity.[20] Every matrika is considered guardian of a compas direction. Chamunda is assigned the direction of south-west.[13]

Chamunda, being a Matrika, is considered one of the chief Yoginis, who are considered to be daughters or manifesta-

Chamunda, British Museum. Odisha, 8th - 9th century AD India.

tions of the Matrikas. In the context of a group of sixty-four yoginis, Chamunda is believed to have created seven other yoginis, together forming a group of eight. In the context of eighty-one yoginis, Chamunda heads a group of nine yoginis.[2]

2.21.5   Hindu worship

A South Indian inscription describes ritual sacrifices of sheep to Chamunda.[21] In Bhavabhuti's eighth century Sanskrit play, Malatimadhva describes a devotee of the goddess trying to sacrifice the heroine to Chamunda's temple, near a cremation ground, where the goddess temple is situated.[22] A stone inscription at Gangadhar, Rajasthan, deals with a construction to a shrine to Chamunda and the other Matrikas, "who are attended by Dakinis (female demons)" and rituals of daily Tantric worship (*Tantrobhuta*) like the ritual of *Bali* (offering of grain).[23]

Many Kshatriyas and even the Jain community worship her

Found in Jajpur dated 8th Century AD

Chamundeshwari Temple

also as her Kuladevi "family deity". The Chapa dynasty worshiped her as their kuladevi.The Kutch Gurjar Kshatriyas also worship her as kuladevi and temples are located in Sinugra and Chandiya. Alungal family, a lineage of Mukkuva caste - (Hindu caste of Shudra origin) in Kerala - also worship chamundi in Chandika form, as Kuladevta and temple is situated in Thalikulam village of Thrissur, Kerala . This is an example of Chamunda worship across different caste sects.

Temples

In the Kangra district of Himachal Pradesh, around 10 kilometres (6.2 mi) west of Palampur, is the renowned Chamunda Devi Temple which depicts scenes from the

Devi Mahatmya, the Ramayana and the Mahabharata. The goddess's image is flanked by the images of Hanuman and Bhairava. Another temple, Chamunda Nandikeshwar Dham, also found in Kangra, is dedicated to Shiva and Chamunda. According to a legend, Chamunda was enshrined as chief deity "Rudra Chamunda", in the battle between the demon Jalandhara and Shiva. In Gujarat, two Chamunda shrines are located on the hills of Chotila and Panera. Kichakeshwari Temple, located near the Baripada, Charchika Temple, near Banki and Vaital Deula in Bhubaneswar, Odisha. Another temple is Chamundeshwari Temple on Chamundi Hill, Mysore. Here, the goddess is identified with Durga, who killed the buffalo demon. Chamundeshwari or Durga, the fierce form of Shakti, a tutelary deity held in reverence for centuries by the Maharaja of Mysore. The *Chamunda Mataji temple* in Mehrangarh Fort, Jodhpur, was established in 1460 after the idol of the goddess Chamunda - the Kuladevi and iṣṭa-devatā (tutelary deity) of the Parihar rulers - was moved from the old capital of Mandore by the then-ruler Jodha of Mandore. The goddess is still worshipped by the royal family of Jodhpur and other citizens of the city. The temple witnesses festivities in Dussehra - the festival of the goddess. Another temple, Sri Chamundeshwari Kshetram is located near Jogipet, in Medak District in Telangana State.

Jodhpur temple

2.21.6   In Jainism

Early Jainism was dismissive of Chamunda, a goddess who demands blood sacrifice, which is against the principle of Jain vegetarianism. Some Jain legends portray Chamunda as a goddess defeated by monks like Jinadatta and Jinaprabhasuri.[24]

Another legend tells the story of conversion of Chamunda into a Jain goddess. According to this story, Chamunda sculpted the Mahavira image for the temple in Osian, Jodhpur and was happy with the conversions of the Oswals to Jainism. At the time of Navratri, a festival that celebrates the Divine Mother, Chamunda expected animal sacrifices from the converted Jains. The vegetarian Jains, however, were unable to meet her demand. Ratnaprabhasuri intervened, and as a result, Chamunda accepted vegetarian offerings, forgoing her demand for meat and liquor. Ratnaprabhsuri further named her *Sacciya*, one who had told the truth, as Chamunda had told him the truth that a rainy season stay in Osian would be beneficial for him. She also became the protective goddess of the temple and remained the clan goddess, Kuladevi, of the Oswals. The Sachiya Mata Temple in Osian was built in her honour.[25] Some Jain scriptures warn of dire consequences of worship of Chamunda by the Hindu rites and rituals.[26]

2.21.7   References

[1] Nalin, David R. (2004-06-15). "The Cover Art of the 15 June 2004 Issue". Clinical Infectious Diseases.

[2] Wangu p.114

[3] Wangu p.72

[4] *Vaisnavism Saivism and Minor Religious Systems* By Ramkrishna G. Bhandarkar, p.205, Published 1995, Asian Educational Services, ISBN 81-206-0122-X

[5] Wangu p.174

[6] See:

- Kinsley p. 147, 156. Descriptions as per Devi Mahatmya , verses 8.11-20
- "Sapta Matrikas (12th C AD)". Department of Archaeology and Museums, Government of Andhra Pradesh. Archived from the original on July 1, 2007. Retrieved 2008-01-08.
- Donaldson, T. "Chamunda, The fierce, protective eight-armed mother.". British Museum.
- "Chamunda, the Horrific Destroyer of Evil [India, Madhya Pradesh] (1989.121)". In Timeline of Art History. New York: The Metropolitan Museum of Art, 2000–. http://www.metmuseum.org/toah/ho/07/ssn/ho_1989.121.htm (October 2006)
- Kalia, pp.106–109.

[7] Goswami, Meghali; Gupta, Ila; Jha, P. (March 2005). "Sapta Matrikas In Indian Art and their significance in Indian Sculpture and Ethos: A Critical Study" (PDF). *Anistoriton Journal*. Anistoriton. Retrieved 2008-01-08. "Anistoriton is an electronic Journal of History, Archaeology and ArtHistory. It publishes scholarly papers since 1997 and it is freely available on the Internet. All papers and images since vol. 1 (1997) are available on line as well as on the free Anistorion CD-ROM edition."

[8] Kinsley p.147

[9] "Durga: Avenging Goddess, Nurturing Mother ch.3, Chamunda". Norton Simon Museum.

[10] Wangu p.94

[11] Gopal, Madan (1990). K.S. Gautam, ed. *India through the ages*. Publication Division, Ministry of Information and Broadcasting, Government of India. p. 81.

[12] Kinsley p. 158, Devi Mahatmya verses 10.2-5

[13] Moor p.118

[14] Handelman pp.132–33

[15] Handelman p.118

[16] Kinsley p.241 Footnotes

[17] Pal in Singh p.1840, Chapters 111-116

[18] Pal in Singh p.1840, Chapter 116(82-86)

[19] Pal p.1844

[20] Kinsley p. 159

[21] Kinsley p.146

[22] Kinsley p.117

[23] Joshi, M.C. in Harper and Brown, p.48

[24] *Encyclopaedia of Jainism* By Narendra Singh, Published 2001, Anmol Publications PVT. LTD., ISBN 81-261-0691-3, p.705

[25] Babb, Lawrence A. *Alchemies of Violence: Myths of Identity and the Life of Trade in Western India*, Published 2004, 254 pages, ISBN 0-7619-3223-2 pp.168–9, 177-178.

[26] *Encyclopaedia of Jainism* By Narendra Singh p.698

2.21.8 Further reading

- Wangu, Madhu Bazaz (2003). *Images of Indian Goddesses*. Abhinav Publications. 280 pages. ISBN 81-7017-416-3.

- Pal, P. The Mother Goddesses According to the Devipurana in Singh, Nagendra Kumar, *Encyclopaedia of Hinduism*, Published 1997, Anmol Publications PVT. LTD.,ISBN 81-7488-168-9

- Kinsley, David (1988). *Hindu Goddesses: Vision of the Divine Feminine in the Hindu Religious Traditions.* University of California Press. ISBN 0-520-06339-2

- Kalia, Asha (1982). *Art of Osian Temples: Socio-Economic and Religious Life in India, 8th-12th Centuries A.D.* Abhinav Publications. ISBN 0-391-02558-9.

- Handelman, Don. with Berkson Carmel (1997). *God Inside Out: Siva's Game of Dice*, Oxford University Press US. ISBN 0-19-510844-2

- Moor, Edward (1999). *The Hindu Pantheon*, Asian Educational Services, ISBN 81-206-0237-4. First published: 1810.

2.21.9 External links

- Shri Sachchiyay Mataji (Shri Osiya Mataji) A form (avatar) of Chamunda Devi

- Chamunda Devi Temple (Chamunda Nandikeshwar Dham), Himachal Pradesh

2.22 Chandraghanta

In Hinduism, **Chandraghanta** is the third form of Goddess Durga. Her name Chandra-Ghanta, means "one who has a half-moon shaped like a bell". She is also known as Chandrakhanda, Chandika or Ramchandi. Her worship takes place on the third day of Navaratri (the nine divine nights of Navadurga). She is believed to reward people with her grace, bravery and courage. By her grace all the sins, distresses, physical sufferings, mental tribulations and ghostly hurdles of the devotees are eradicated.

2.22.1 Legend

After Lord Shiva gave Parvati his word that he would not marry any woman, her sufferings overwhelmed him so much that he gave up, followed by a tearful reunion, and then agrees to marry her. Soon, the joyous moment of Parvati's life comes. Shiva brings a procession of gods, mortals, ghosts, ghouls, goblins, sages, ascetics, Aghoris and Shivaganas to the gates of King Himavan's palace to take away his bride Parvati, on the occasion of his remarriage. Shiva arrives at King Himavan's palace in a terrorizing form and Parvati's mother Mainavati faints in terror. Parvati appears to Shiva and sees his fearsome form, so to save her parents and other family members she transforms herself into Goddess Chandraghanta.

Chandraghanta persuaded Shiva to re-appear in a charming form, on listening to the Goddess, Shiva appears as a prince decorated with countless jewels. Parvati revived her mother, father and friends then Shiva and Parvati get married and made promises to one another.

Chandraghanta with her weapons

She has eight hands holding a Trishula (trident), Gada (mace), bow-arrow, khadak (sword), Kamal (lotus), Ghanta (bell) and kamandal (waterpot), while one of her hands remains in blessing posture or abhayamudra. She rides a tiger or lion as her vehicle, which represents bravery and courage, she wears a half moon on her forehead and has a third eye in the middle of her forehead. Her complexion is golden. Shiva sees Chandraghanta's form as a great example of beauty, charm and grace. She rides a tiger or lion as her vehicle, representing bravery. This is a terrible aspect and is roaring in anger. This form of Durga is not completely different from earlier forms. It shows that when provoked she can be malevolent. Her malevolent form is said to be Chandi or Chamunda Devi. She is otherwise the very embodiment of serenity.

The devotees who adore and worship her develop an aura of divine splendor. Their persons emit invisible power-waves which exercise a great impact on those who come in contact with them. They easily achieve success in life. Chandraghanta is ready to destroy the wicked, but to her devotees she is a kind and compassionate Mother showering peace and prosperity. During the battle between her and the demons, the horrible sound produced by her bell sent thousands of wicked demons to the abode of the Death God. She is ever in a warring posture which shows her eagerness to destroy the foes of her devotees so that they may live in peace and prosperity. Divine vision is acquired by her grace. If a devotee happens to enjoy divine fragrance and hears diverse sounds, he is said to be blessed by the Mother.

Durga incarnated as Kaushiki, the daughter of Lord Shiva and Parvati, in order to vanquish demons Shumbh and Nishumbh and their hordes. The beauty of Kaushiki was to lure demons to their doom. Shumbh wanted to marry Kaushiki to his brother Nishumbh and thus sent demon Dhumralochan to bring her. When she resisted, Dhumralochan attacked her. Enraged, Parvati assumed a warrior form, seated on a tiger and defeated Dhumralochan and his entire army.[1]

2.22.2 References

[1] "Goddess Chandraghanta". *DrikPanchang*. Retrieved 26 February 2015.

2.23 Cihuateteo

In Aztec mythology, the **Cihuateteo** (Classical Nahuatl: *Cihuātēteoh* "Divine Women", singular Classical Nahuatl: *Cihuātēotl*) were the spirits of human women who died in childbirth (*mociuaquetzque*). Childbirth was considered a form of battle, and its victims were honored as fallen warriors. Their physical remains were thought to strengthen soldiers in battle while their spirits became the much-feared Cihuateteo who accompanied the setting sun in the west. They also haunted crossroads at night, stealing children and

A terracotta statue of Cihuateotl, the Aztec goddess of women who died during childbirth.

causing sicknesses, especially seizures and madness, and seducing men to sexual misbehavior.

Their images appear with the beginning day signs of the five western trecena, (*1 Deer, 1 Rain, 1 Monkey, 1 House,* and *1 Eagle*) during which they were thought to descend to the earth and cause particularly dangerous mischief. They are depicted with skeletal faces and with eagle claws for hands.

They are associated with the goddess Cihuacoatl and are sometimes considered envoys of Mictlan, the world of the dead. Cihuateteo are servants of the Aztec moon deities Tezcatlipoca and Tlazolteotl.

2.23.1 See also

- Black Sun (mythology)
- Erinyes
- La Llorona

2.23.2 References

2.24 Durga

For other uses of "Durga", see Durga (disambiguation).
"Mahishasuramardini" redirects here. For the radio

programme of All India Radio, see Mahisasuramardini (radio programme).

"Jagadamba" redirects here. For the upcoming Indian film, see Jagadamba (film).

Durga (Hindustani pronunciation: [ˈd̪ʊrɡaː], Sanskrit: दुर्गा *Durgā* "Invincible"[1]) is the principle form of the Goddess, also known as Devi and Shakti in Hinduism.[2] Durga the mahashakti, the form and formless, is the root cause of creation, preservation and annihilation. According to legend, Durga Manifested herself for the slaying of the buffalo demon Mahisasura from Brahma, Vishnu, Shiva, and the lesser gods, who were otherwise powerless to overcome him. She is pure Shakti, having manifested herself within the gods so that she may fulfil the tasks of the universe via them. At times of distress, such as the mahishasura episode, to protect the universe she manifests herself via the gods.

2.24.1 Origins and development

Ramprasad Chanda writes the following about the development of Durga from primitive goddess to her current form: [3]

> ...it is possible to distinguish two different strata – one primitive and the other advanced. The primitive form of Durga is the result of syncretism of a mountain-goddess worshiped by the dwellers of the Himalaya and the Vindhyas, a goddess worshiped by the nomadic Abhira shepherd, the vegetation spirit conceived as a female, and a war-goddess. As her votaries advanced in civilization the primitive war-goddess was transformed into the personification of the all-destroying time (Kali), the vegetation spirit into the primordial energy (Adya Sakti) and the saviouress from "samsara" (cycle of rebirths) , and gradually brought into line with the Brahmanic mythology and philosophy.

The delusion of the supreme soul is otherwise called Shakti (power). From this power, generates all forms of knowledge of the world and it is accepted as vital cause of creation, existence and destruction. According to 'Shree Durga Shaptshati- Rahasyam', the original power is Mahalaxmi that created three pairs of Supreme Powers. They are Brahma, Vishnu and Shiva as male and Saraswati, Laxmi and Parvati as female, and they married respectively. Maha Saraswati is well known as Brahmani, Mahalaxmi as Vaishnavi and Mahakali as Maheswari. Durga Shakti is the original cause of all the present or past worldly occurrences. Durga Shakti is called as Adhyashakti, Paramatma Shakti or Ati Prakrutika Shakti. She is creating and controlling

other two powers: Natural and General. Natural Power is called as Atma Shakti, Prakrutika Shakti, Pancha Mahabhuta Shakti etc. This Shakti creates and controls the General Energy. General Energies are called Jada Shakti or Tamashakti. By the blessings of Durga Shakti, the mother of the Universe, man is able to get his emancipation or salvation and indulge in enjoyments in performance of his daily activities. So Vyasadev, the eminent poet of "Devi Bhagwat", has aptly described "Rudrahinam Vishnuhinam na vadanti janastatha Shaktihinam Yathasarbe probodhanti Naradhamam". The powerless persons are despised as mean persons. So, by being devoted to the Supreme, we should be strong and powerful by her grace.

2.24.2 Stories

Shiva Purana gives an account of the origin of Durga. At the beginning of time, Lord Shiva invoked Durga, the primordial energy from his left half to create. Together they created their eternal abode, Shivaloka, also known as Kashi. Thereafter, they created Vishnu and Brahma.

Durga on a lion

As per Shiva Purana and Devi Mahatmyah, Mahishasura,

the son of demon Rambha, unleashed reign of terror on earth. When gods intervened, Mahishasura defeated gods and banished them from heaven. Vanquished gods went to Trideva- Brahma, Vishnu and Shiva. As they narrated their woeful tale, immense mass of light manifested from Lord Vishnu's mouth, which was joined by similar rays that emerged from the enraged faces of gods. This mass of light transformed into a woman. Then all the Gods gave their divine weapon to that supreme power. Adishakti remanifested as Durga to slay Mahishasura. Armed with celestial weapons of all deities and decked with divine ornaments, Durga rode into the battle field and challenged demons for battle. Mahishasura's entire army, led by demons like Chikshur, Chamar, Asiloma, Vidalaksha, Durdhara, Durmukha, Mahahanu and many more attacked Durga at once. But Durga slew all of them with unparalleled cruelty. An enraged Mahishasura attacked Durga in guise of a buffalo. But Durga bound it with ropes. The buffalo morphed into a lion and leapt on Durga, but she beheaded it with her sword. At this, Mahishasura began to fight in form of a swordsman. Durga pinned him down with a torrent of arrows. Mahishasura now assumed form of a giant elephant and tugged at Durga's lion. Durga lopped off its trunk with her sword and freed her lion. The elephant turned into a buffalo and charged at Durga. Sipping from her wine cup, Durga flung her trident and beheaded Mahishasura, finally killing him.

2.24.3 Worship

Main article: Durga Puja

The four-day-long (Saptami to Dashami) Durga Puja

Maa Durga

is the biggest annual festival in Bengal, Assam, Odisha, Jharkhand and Nepal, where it is known as Dashain. It is celebrated likewise with much fervour in various parts of India, especially the Himalayan region, but is celebrated in

A traditional Durga idol at a pandal in Kolkata.

various forms throughout the Hindu universe.

An idol of Durga Pooja, comprising Goddess Durga, her daughters Laxmi, Saraswati and her sons Ganesha, Karitik

The day of Durga's victory is celebrated as Vijayadashami (Bijoya in Bengali), Dashain (Nepali) or Dussehra (in Hindi) – these words literally mean "the Victory on the Tenth (day)".[4]

In Andhra Pradesh she is also worshipped as Kanaka Durgammathalli,where there is also famous temple for Goddess Kanaka Durga in Indrakeeladri,Vijayawada.She is also known by the name of Chandi Bhavani.

In Kashmir she is worshipped as *shaarika* (the main temple is in Hari Parbat in Srinagar).

The actual period of the worship however may be on the preceding nine days (Navaratri) followed by the last day called *Vijayadashami* in North India or five days in Bengal (from the sixth to tenth day of the waxing-moon fortnight).[5] Nine aspects of Durga known as Navadurga are meditated upon, one by one during the nine-day festival by devout Shakti worshippers. Durga Puja also includes the worship of Shiva, who is Durga's consort (Durga is an aspect of Goddess Parvati), in addition to Lakshmi, Saraswati with Ganesha and Kartikeya, who are considered to be Durga's children.[6] Worship of mother nature is done, through nine types of plant (called "Kala Bou"), including a plantain (banana) tree, which represent nine divine forms of Goddess Durga.[7] In South India especially, Andhra Pradesh Dussera Navaratri is also celebrated and the goddess is dressed each day as a different devi – Shailputri Bramhacharini chandi chandraghantaetc. – for the nine days.

In North India, the tenth day, is celebrated as *Dussehra*, the day Rama emerged victorious in his battle against the demon, Ravana – gigantic straw effigies of Ravana are burnt in designated open spaces (e.g. Delhi's Ram Lila grounds), watched by thousands of families and little children.

In Mysore (which originated from Mahishasooru) in Karnataka, she is worshipped as Chamundeshwari, the patron goddess of the city during Dussehra (Dasara).

In Gujarat it is celebrated as the last day of Navaratri, during which the Garba dance is performed to celebrate the victory of Mahishasura-mardini, Durga.

The Goddess Durga is worshipped in her peaceful form as Maha Gauri, The Fair Lady, Shree Shantadurga also known as Santeri, is the patron Goddess of Goa. She is worshipped by all Goan Hindus.

In Maharashtra, Tulja Bhavani, Hedavde Mahalaxmi and Ambabai are worshipped as Mahishasur Mardini, who is the patron goddess of the land. Bhavani is known as Tulaja, Amba,[8] Renuka, Yamai Saptshrungi and Jogai in different places of Maharashtra. She is the inspirational goddess of Raja Shivaji. As per legends, Bhavani appeared after Shivaji prayed to her and blessed him to be able to make Hindustan or the then India (ruled by the Mughals) independent – the kingdom he established eventually became the Hindu Pad Padshahi (sometimes also called the Maratha Empire), which comprised all the land ruled by the Mughals and brought India back under Hindu sovereignty.

In Bangladesh also, the four-day long Sharadiya Durga Puja (Bengali: শারদীয়া দুর্গা পূজা, 'autumnal Durga worship') is the biggest religious festivals for the Hindus and celebrated across the country with *Vijayadashami* being a national holiday.

The prominence of Durga Puja increased gradually during the British Raj in Bengal.[9] After the Hindu reformists identified Durga with India, she became an icon for the Indian independence movement.

2.24.4 Western references

Some early Western accounts refer to a deity known as Deumus, Demus or Deumo. Western (Portuguese) sailors first came face to face with the murti of Deumus at Calicut on the Malabar Coast and they concluded it to be the deity of Calicut. Deumus is sometimes interpreted as an aspect of Durga in Hindu mythology and sometimes as deva.

It is described that the ruler of Calicut (Zamorin) had a murti of Deumus in his temple inside his royal palace.[10][11] The temple was two paces wide in each of the four sides and three paces high, with a wooden door covered with gods carved in relief. At the centre of the temple, there was a metal idol of Deumus placed in a seat, which was also made of metal.

Western accounts also describe the ruler of Calicut worshiping an ultimate god called Tamerani ("Tamburan"). The accounts also describes a misunderstood form of the "hook-swinging" ritual once commonly performed as part of some popular Hindu religious festivals.

2.24.5 Notable temples of Durga

In India

Image of Durga in a small temple next to Rewalsar Lake, Himachal Pradesh, India

Assam

- Deopani Temple, in Golaghat district, Assam

Andhra Pradesh

- Kanaka Durga Temple in Vijayawada

Delhi:

- Shri Adya Katyani Shakti Peeth Mandir in Chattarpur

Goa

- Shanta Durga temple in Goa

Gujarat

- [12] Arasuri Ambaji Temple in Gujarat
- Umiya Mataji Temple at Unjha & Sidsar
- Kali Mataji Temple in Pavagadh
- Chamunda Mataji in Chotila

Himachal Pradesh

- Shoolini Devi temple at Solan Himachal Pradesh

Jammu

- Bahu Fort Temple in Jammu
- Bala Sundri Temple in Billawar Jammu
- ChiChi Mata Temple in Jammu
- Kol Kandoli Temple in Jammu
- Mahamaya Temple in Jammu
- Sukrala Mata Temple in Jammu
- Vaishno Devi Temple in Katra Jammu

Karnataka

- Chamundeshwari Temple, Mysore Karnataka
- Kateel Durgaparameshwari Temple, near Mangalore, Karnataka
- Kollur Sri Mookambika Temple, near Udupi, Karnataka

Kerala

- Adichikkavu Sree Durga Devi Kshetram, Pandanad, Kerala
- Ammathiruvadi Temple, Thrissur, Kerala

- Vengoor Sree Durga Devi Temple, near Perumbavoor-Kerala
- Kumaranalloor Devi Temple, Kottayam, Kerala
- Padappad Sree Devi Temple, Thiruvalla, Kerala
- Bhagavathinada Sree Durga Temple, Venganoor, Trivandrum, Kerala
- Sankhumugham Durga Temple, Trivandrum, Kerala
- Aruvikkara Durga Temple, Trivandrum, Kerala
- Kalarivathikkal Devi Temple, Kannur, Kerala
- Pattathil Durga & Bhadra Temple, Vallikunnam, Kerala

Maharashtra

- Tulja Bhavani Temple, in Tuljapur, Maharashtra
- Hedavde Mahalaxmi Temple, in Hedavde near Mumbai close to Virar on Nh8 Highway, Maharashtra
- Saptashrungi Devi Temple, Vani/Nanduri, Nashik

Odisha

- Biraja Temple, Jajpur, Odisha
- Durga Temple, Baideshwar, Odisha
- Katak Chandi Temple, Cuttack, Odisha
- Kichakeshwari Temple, Odisha
- Manikeshwari Temple, Bhawanipatna, Odisha.

Punjab

- Durgiana Temple, Amritsar

Rajasthan

- Ambika Mata Temple in the village of Jagat near Mount Abu in Rajasthan
- Shila Devi temple at Amber, Jaipur, Rajasthan
- Aai Mata Temple at Bilara Dist Jodhpur
- Mata Tripura Sundari at Banswara

Madhya Pradesh

- Bhadwa Mata Temple at Bhadwa Mata near Neemuch

Tamil Nadu

- Durgai Amman Temple, Patteeswaram, Kumabakonam, Tamil Nadu

- Raja Durga Temple, Thiruvarur, Tamil Nadu

- Vana Durga Parameshwari Temple, Kathiramangalam, Mayiladuthurai, Tamil Nadu

- Vana Durga Temple, Valarpuram, Sriperumpudur, Tamil Nadu

- Bhagavathi Amman Temple, Kanyakumari, Tamil Nadu

- Durgai Amman Temple, Eduthanur,villupuram Dist., Tamil Nadu

Tripura

- Udaipur, Tripura

Uttar Pradesh

- Vindhyachal temple at Mirzapur

West Bengal

- Kanak Durga Temple, Chikligarh, Medinipur, West Bengal

- Nava Durga Temple, Kolkata, West Bengal

- 23 Palli Durga Temple, Kolkata, West Bengal

- Sarbamongala Mandir, Burdwan, West Bengal

- Durga Mandir, Malbazar, West Bengal

Outside India

- Dhakeshwari Temple in Dhaka, Bangladesh

- Prambanan Temple, Indonesia

- Sri Santha Durga Devi Army Camp in Sungai Petani, Malaysia

- Sri Thurgha Parameswary Amman Alayam, Kampung Tumbuk Pantai, Tanjong Sepat,in Selangor, Malaysia

2.24.6 See also

- Ayindri

- Devi-Bhagavata Purana

- Devi Mahatmya

- Durga Puja

- Shaktism

- Jwaladevi Temple

2.24.7 References

[1] "Durga,". Encyclopædia Britannica Online. Retrieved 7 October 2009.

[2] "Hindu Goddesses : Durga - Hindu goddess that kills your demons". Sanatansociety.org. Retrieved 2015-10-22.

[3] McDaniel, June (2004). *Offering Flowers, Feeding Skulls: Popular Goddess Worship in West Bengal*. Oxford University Press. ISBN 0-19-516791-0. p. 214.

[4] Esposito, John L.; Darrell J. Fasching; Todd Vernon Lewis (2007). *Religion & globalization: world religions in historical perspective*. Oxford University Press. p. 341. ISBN 0-19-517695-2.

[5] Parmita Borah (2 October 2011). "Durga Puja – a Celebration of Female Supremacy". EF News International. Retrieved 26 October 2011.

[6] Kinsley, David (1988). *Hindu Goddesses: Vision of the Divine Feminine in the Hindu Religious Traditions*. University of California Press. ISBN 0-520-06339-2. p. 95.

[7] "Kolabou". Bangalinet.com. Retrieved 2013-06-25.

[8] Gopal, Madan (1990). K.S. Gautam, ed. *India through the ages*. Publication Division, Ministry of Information and Broadcasting, Government of India. p. 64.

[9] "Article on Durga Puja".

[10] Jörg Breu d. Ä. zugeschrieben, Idol von Calicut, in: Ludovico de Varthema, 'Die Ritterlich und lobwürdig Reisz', Strassburg 1516. (Bild: Völkerkundemuseum der Universität Zürich

[11] *A briefe collection and compendious extract of straunge and memorable thinges, gathered out of the* Cosmographye *of Sebastian Munster, wherein is made a plaine description of diuers and straunge lawes, rites, maners and properties of sondrye nations, and a short report of straunge histories of diuers men, and of the nature and properties of certaine fovvles, fishes, beastes, monsters, and sondry countryes and places,* published in London in 1574 by Tomas Marshe

[12] Ambaji

2.24.8 Further reading

- Amazzone, Laura (2010). *Goddess Durga and Sacred Female Power*. University Press of America, Lanham. ISBN 0761853146.

- Bandyopadhyay, Pranab (1993). *Mother Goddess Durga*. United Writers, Calcutta. ISBN 81-85328-13-7.

- Kinsley, David (1986). *Hindu Goddesses: Vision of the Divine Feminine in the Hindu Religious Traditions*. Motilal Banarsidass Publ., Delhi. ISBN 81-208-0379-5.

- Sen Ramprasad (1720–1781). *Grace and Mercy in Her Wild Hair: Selected Poems to the Mother Goddess*. Hohm Press. ISBN 0-934252-94-7.

2.24.9 External links

- Durga at DMOZ

- 108 names of Durga from the Durgāsaptaśatī

2.25 Enyo

For other uses, see Enyo (disambiguation).

Enyo (/ɨˈnaɪoʊ/; Greek: Ἐνυώ) was a goddess of war and destruction in Greek mythology, the companion and lover of the war god Ares. She is also identified as his sister Eris, and daughter of Zeus and Hera,[1] in a role closely resembling that of Eris; with Homer in particular representing the two as the same goddess. She is also accredited as the mother of the war god Enyalius, by Ares.[2] However, the name Enyalius or Enyalios can also be used as a title for Ares himself.[3]

As goddess of war, Enyo is responsible for orchestrating the destruction of cities, often accompanying Ares into battle,[4] and depicted "as supreme in war".[5] During the fall of Troy, Enyo inflicted terror and bloodshed in the war, along with Eris ("Strife"), and Phobos ("Fear") and Deimos ("Dread"), the two sons of Ares.[6] She, Eris, and the two sons of Ares are depicted on Achilles's shield.[6]

Enyo was involved in the war of the Seven Against Thebes and Dionysus's war with the Indians as well.[7][8] Enyo so delighted in warfare that she even refused to take sides in the battle between Zeus and the monster Typhon:

> Eris (Strife) was Typhon's escort in the mellay, Nike (Victory) led Zeus into battle... impartial Enyo held equal balance between the two

sides, between Zeus and Typhon, while the thunderbolts with booming shots revel like dancers in the sky.[9]

The Romans identified Enyo with Bellona, and she also has similarities with the Anatolian goddess Ma.

At Thebes and Orchomenos, a festival called Homolôïa, which was celebrated in honour of Zeus, Demeter, Athena and Enyo, was said to have received the surname of Homoloïus from Homoloïs, a priestess of Enyo.[10] A statue of Enyo, made by the sons of Praxiteles, stood in the temple of Ares at Athens.[11] Among the Graeae in Hesiod[12] there is one called Enyo.

Enyo was also the name of one of the Graeae, three sisters who shared one eye and one tooth among them, along with **Deino** ("Dread") and **Pemphredo** ("Alarm").[13]

2.25.1 Genealogy of the Olympians in Greek mythology

2.25.2 References

- This article incorporates text from a publication now in the public domain: Leonhard Schmitz (1870). "Enyo". In Smith, William. *Dictionary of Greek and Roman Biography and Mythology*.

2.25.3 Footnotes

[1] Quintus Smyrnaeus, *Fall of Troy*, 8.424

[2] Eustathius on Homer 944

[3] Willcock, Malcolm M. (1976). *A companion to the Iliad : based on the translation by Richard Lattimore* ([9th print.] ed.). Chicago: University of Chicago Press. p. 58. ISBN 0-226-89855-5.

[4] Homer, Iliad 5. 333, 592

[5] Pausanias, *Description of Greece* 4. 30. 5

[6] Quintus Smyrnaeus, *Fall of Troy*

[7] Statius, *Thebaid*

[8] Nonnus, *Dionysiaca*

[9] Nonnus, *Dionysiaca* 2. 358 and 2. 475 ff

[10] Suidas s. v.; comp. Müller, Orchomen. p. 229, 2nd edit. (cited by Schmitz)

[11] Pausanias, *Description of Greece*, I. 8. § 5. (cited by Schmitz)

[12] Theogony 273 (cited by Schmitz)

[13] Harris, Stephen L., and Gloria Platzner. *Classical Mythology: Images and Insights* (Third Edition). California State University, Sacramento. Mayfield Publishing Company. 2000, 1998, 1995, pp. 273–274, 1039.

2.26 Eris (mythology)

This article is about the Greek goddess of chaos. For the god of love, see Eros.
"Discordia" redirects here. For other uses, see Discordia (disambiguation).

Eris (/ˈɪərɪs, ˈɛrɪs/; Greek: Ἔρις, "Strife")[1] is the Greek goddess of chaos, strife, and discord. Her name is the equivalent of Latin **Discordia**, which means "discord". Eris' Greek opposite is Harmonia, whose Latin counterpart is Concordia. Homer equated her with the war-goddess Enyo, whose Roman counterpart is Bellona. The dwarf planet Eris is named after the goddess, as is the religion Discordianism.

2.26.1 Characteristics in Greek mythology

El Juicio de Paris *by Enrique Simonet, 1904*

In Hesiod's *Works and Days* 11–24, two different goddesses named Eris are distinguished:

> So, after all, there was not one kind of Strife alone, but all over the earth there are two. As for the one, a man would praise her when he came to understand her; but the other is blameworthy: and they are wholly different in nature. For one fosters evil war and battle, being cruel: her no man loves; but perforce, through the will of the deathless gods, men pay harsh Strife her honour due.
>
> But the other is the elder daughter of dark Night

Golden apple of discord *by Jakob Jordaens, 1633*

Das Urteil des Paris *by Anton Raphael Mengs, c. 1757*

> (Nyx), and the son of Cronus who sits above and dwells in the aether, set her in the roots of the earth: and she is far kinder to men. She stirs up even the shiftless to toil; for a man grows eager to work when he considers his neighbour, a rich man who hastens to plough and plant and put his house in good order; and neighbour vies with his neighbour as he hurries after wealth. This Strife is wholesome for men. And potter is angry with potter, and craftsman with craftsman, and beggar is jealous of beggar, and minstrel of minstrel.

In Hesiod's *Theogony* (226–232), Strife, the daughter of Night, is less kindly spoken of as she brings forth other personifications as her children:

> But abhorred *Eris* ("Strife") bare painful *Ponos* ("Toil/Labor"), *Lethe* ("Forgetfulness") and *Limos* ("Famine") and tearful *Algos* ("Pains/Sorrows"), *Hysminai* ("Fightings/Combats") also, *Makhai* ("Battles"), *Phonoi* ("Murders/Slaughterings"), *Androctasiai*

("Manslaughters"), *Neikea* ("Quarrels"), *Pseudologoi* ("Lies/Falsehoods"), *Amphilogiai* ("Disputes"), *Dysnomia* ("Lawlessness") and *Ate* ("Ruin/Folly"), all of one nature, and *Horkos* ("Oath") who most troubles men upon earth when anyone wilfully swears a false oath.

The other Strife is presumably she who appears in Homer's *Iliad* Book IV; equated with Enyo as sister of Ares and so presumably daughter of Zeus and Hera:

> Strife whose wrath is relentless, she is the sister and companion of murderous Ares, she who is only a little thing at the first, but thereafter grows until she strides on the earth with her head striking heaven. She then hurled down bitterness equally between both sides as she walked through the onslaught making men's pain heavier. She also has a son whom she named Strife.

Enyo is mentioned in Book 5, and Zeus sends Strife to rouse the Achaeans in Book 11, of the same work.

The most famous tale of Eris recounts her initiating the Trojan War by causing the Judgement of Paris. The goddesses Hera, Athena and Aphrodite had been invited along with the rest of Olympus to the forced wedding of Peleus and Thetis, who would become the parents of Achilles, but Eris had been snubbed because of her troublemaking inclinations.

She therefore (as mentioned at the *Kypria* according to Proclus as part of a plan hatched by Zeus and Themis) tossed into the party the Apple of Discord, a golden apple inscribed τῇ καλλίστῃ (Ancient Greek: *tē(i) kallistē(i)*) – "For the most beautiful one", or "To the Fairest One" – provoking the goddesses to begin quarreling about the appropriate recipient. The hapless Paris, Prince of Troy, was appointed to select the fairest by Zeus. The goddesses stripped naked to try to win Paris' decision, and also attempted to bribe him. Hera offered political power; Athena promised infinite wisdom; and Aphrodite tempted him with the most beautiful woman in the world: Helen, wife of Menelaus of Sparta. While Greek culture placed a greater emphasis on prowess and power, Paris chose to award the apple to Aphrodite, thereby dooming his city, which was destroyed in the war that ensued.

In Nonnus' *Dionysiaca*, 2.356, when Typhon prepares to battle with Zeus:

> Eris ("Strife") was Typhon's escort in the melée, Nike ("Victory") led Zeus to battle.

Another story of Eris includes Hera, and the love of Polytekhnos and Aedon. They claimed to love each other more than Hera and Zeus were in love. This angered Hera, so she sent Eris to rack discord upon them. Polytekhnos was finishing off a chariot board, and Aedon a web she had been weaving. Eris said to them, "Whosoever finishes thine task last shall have to present the other with a female servant!" Aedon won. But Polytekhnos was not happy by his defeat, so he came to Khelidon, Aedon's sister, and raped her. He then disguised her as a slave, presenting her to Aedon. When Aedon discovered this was indeed her sister, she chopped up Polytekhnos' son and fed him to Polytekhnos. The gods were not pleased, so they turned them all into birds.

2.26.2 Cultural influences

Discordianism

Main article: Discordianism

Eris has been adopted as the patron deity of the modern Discordian religion, which was begun in the late 1950s by Gregory Hill and Kerry Wendell Thornley under the pen names of "Malaclypse the Younger" and "Omar Khayyam Ravenhurst". The Discordian version of Eris is considerably lighter in comparison to the rather malevolent Graeco-Roman original. A quote from the *Principia Discordia*, the first holy book of Discordianism, attempts to clear this up:

> One day Mal-2 consulted his Pineal Gland and asked Eris if She really created all of those terrible things. She told him that She had always liked the Old Greeks, but that they cannot be trusted with historic matters. "They were," She added, "victims of indigestion, you know."[2]

The story of Eris being snubbed and indirectly starting the Trojan War is recorded in the *Principia*, and is referred to as the Original Snub. The *Principia Discordia* states that her parents may be as described in Greek legend, or that she may be the daughter of Void. She is the Goddess of Disorder and Being, whereas her sister Aneris (called the equivalent of Harmonia by the Mythics of Harmonia) is the goddess of Order and Non-Being. Their brother is Spirituality.[3]

The concept of Eris as developed by the *Principia Discordia* is used and expanded upon in the science fiction work *The Illuminatus! Trilogy* by Robert Shea and Robert Anton Wilson (in which characters from *Principia Discordia* appear). In this work, Eris is a major character.[4]

The classic fairy tale *Sleeping Beauty* is partly inspired by Eris's role in the wedding of Peleus and Thetis. Like Eris, a malevolent fairy curses a princess after not being invited to the princess' christening.[5][6]

2.26.3 In popular culture

Eris serves as the main antagonist of the 2003 DreamWorks animated film *Sinbad: Legend of the Seven Seas* where she is voiced by Michelle Pfeiffer. She controls a vast army of creatures resembling constellations, three of which being Cetus, a giant kraken, the sirens, water spirits, and the Roc, a giant white bird. She appears a black-haired woman, with blue skin, with a short-sleeved dress, and tendrils of pink smoke for legs.

In the television show, *Hercules: the Legendary Journeys* and its spin-off *Xena: Warrior Princess*, Discord is a recurring antagonist, Ares's henchwoman and pseudo gun moll. Strife was reimagined as a male character, also a flunky of Ares.

In the Cartoon Network original series, *The Grim Adventures of Billy and Mandy*, Eris (voiced by Rachael MacFarlane) is a recurring character, often seen with her Golden Apple of Discord. She is an antagonist, though she is represented in a comedic fashion.

In the video game, "Glory of Heracles", Eris is a playable character, although her story is changed a bit, with her being a child, then later being romantically involved with Prometheus.

Eris makes a cameo appearance in the fantasy novel *The House of Hades* as one of the several children of Nyx seen in the book.

In Kelly McCullough's *Ravirn* series Eris is the pole power of chaos opposing Fate as the pole of order.

In The New 52 relaunched Wonder Woman title, Eris was renamed "Strife". She is sarcastic, venomous, and a drinker, though both Diana and Hermes consider her mentality to be like that of a spiteful child.[7]

In EVE Online, Eris is the name of the Gallente Interdictor.

In the Light Novel *Mushoku Tensei* Eris is one of the main protagonists with a very short temper.

In the Freedom City setting, Eris is a high power level antagonist, particularly for player characters with supernatural ties.

2.26.4 Genealogy of the Olympians in Greek mythology

It should be noted that this genealogy of the Olympians is based primarily on the ancient work *The Theogony*; other sources include *The Iliad* and *The Odyssey*, which contain different genealogies.

2.26.5 See also

- Aneris
- Discordian Works
- Eris (dwarf planet)

2.26.6 References

[1] Of uncertain etymology; connections with the verb ὀρίνειν *orinein*, "to raise, stir, excite," and the proper name Ἐρινύες *Erinyes* have been suggested; R. S. P. Beekes has rejected those derivations and suggested a Pre-Greek origin (*Etymological Dictionary of Greek*, Brill, 2009, p. 459).

[2] "The Principia Discordia". Ology.org. 1997-04-21. Retrieved 2012-06-14.

[3] "Page 57". Principia Discordia. Retrieved 2012-06-14.

[4] "Robert Anton Wilson: Searching For Cosmic Intelligence" by Jeffrey Elliot Interview discussing novel (URL accessed 21 February 2006)

[5] H. J. Rose (2006). *A Handbook of Greek Mythology, Including Its Extension to Rome*. Kessinger Publishing. ISBN 978-1-4286-4307-9. Retrieved 2007-11-06.

[6] Maria Tatar (Ed.) (2002). *The Annotated Classic Fairy Tales*. W. W. Norton & Company. ISBN 978-0-393-05163-6. Retrieved 2007-11-06.

[7] http://www.comicvine.com/eris/4005-15769/

2.26.7 External links

- Goddess Eris at Theoi.com, ancient texts and art
- Hesiod's *Works And Days*
- Hesiod's *Theogony*
- Homer's *Iliad*
- Homer's Iliad at Gutenberg (there are many different translations at Gutenberg)

2.27 Erzulie

In Vodou, **Erzulie** (sometimes spelled **Erzili** or **Ezili**) is a family of lwa, or spirits.

The Black Madonna of Częstochowa, the inspiration typically used in the depiction of Erzulie Dantor

2.27.1 Maîtresse Mambo Erzulie Fréda Dahomey

Erzulie Fréda Dahomey, the Rada aspect of Erzulie, is the Haitian African spirit of love, beauty, jewelry, dancing, luxury, and flowers. She wears three wedding rings, one for each husband - Damballa, Agwe and Ogoun. Her symbol is a heart, her colours are pink, blue, white and gold, and her favourite sacrifices include jewellery, perfume, sweet cakes and liqueurs. Coquettish and very fond of beauty and finery, Erzulie Freda is femininity and compassion embodied, yet she also has a darker side; she is seen as jealous and spoiled and within some Vodoun circles is considered to be lazy. During ritual possession, she may enter the body of either a man or a woman. She enjoys the game of flirtation and seduces people without distinguishing between sexes. In Christian iconography she is often identified with the Mater Dolorosa, as well as another Lwa Metres Ezili. She is conceived of as never able to attain her heart's most fervent desire. For this reason she always leaves a service in tears. Her syncretic iconographical depiction is usually based on

that of the Virgin and Child, because she is the mother of Ti. Common syncretizations include Iyalorde Oxum as she relate to that Yoruba Vodu goddess of Erotic Love, Gold and Femininity.

2.27.2 Erzulie Dantor

In her Petro nation aspect as *Erzulie Dantor* she is often depicted as a scarred and buxom black woman, holding a child protectively in her arms. She is a particularly fierce protector of women and children. She is often identified with lesbian women.

A common syncretic depiction of Erzulie Dantor is St Jeanne d'Arc, who is displayed carrying or supporting a sword. Another is as the Black Madonna of Częstochowa, as she is represented as being dark-skinned. Her colours are red, gold and navy blue. Her symbols are a pierced heart and knives or swords. Her favourite sacrifices include black pigs, *griot* (seasoned fried pork), and rum.

Ti Jean Petro is her son and sometimes considered her lover or husband.

2.27.3 Erzulie Family

Rada

- **Erzulie Freda** (Lady Erzulie) - The vain and flirty goddess of love. Her "horses" tend to cry tears of longing and regret. She is syncretized with Our Lady of Sorrows (the Virgin Mary as suffering mother).

- **Erzulie Balianne** (Erzulie the Gagged) - "Silences" (heals or calms) hearts. Keeps secrets or ensures that secrets will not be revealed. Helps people to forget past loves and overcome passionate emotions. Her "horses" tend to speak as if they have a gag in their mouth. She is syncretized with The Immaculate Heart.

- **Erzulie Mansur** (Erzulie the Blessed) - Represents maternal love and protects children from harm.

- **Granne Erzulie** (Grandma Erzulie) - Represents the wisdom granted by experience and maturity and grandmotherly kindness and love. She is syncretized with St. Anne, the mother of the Virgin Mary.

Petro

- **Erzulie D'en Tort** or *Erzulie Dantor* (Erzulie of the Wrongs) Protects women and children and deals revenge against those who wrong them.

- **Erzulie Mapiangue** (Erzulie the Suckler) Deals with the pain of childbirth and the protection of unborn and newborn babies. Her "horses" tend to get in a fetal position or birthing position and cry tears of pain. Common syncretization is as the Virgin and Infant of Prague, which wear matching red velvet robes and gold crowns.

- **Erzulie Yeux Rouge** or *Erzulie Ge-Rouge* (Red-Eyed Erzulie) Takes revenge on unfaithful lovers. Her "horses" cry tears of bitter sadness.

- **Erzulie Toho** Aids the jealous or slighted in love. Her "horses" cry tears of anger.

Others

- **Erzulie La Flambeau** (Erzulie of the Torch)

- **Erzulie Wangol** (Erzulie of the Sacred Banner)

2.27.4 Similar spirits in the pantheon

- **La Sirène** or **Mami Wata** is associated with **Erzulie** and sometimes is displayed in Erzulie's roles as mother, lover, and protector. Her husband is Agwe, the King of the Sea and patron of sailors and fishermen.

- **Marinette Bras-Chèche** or *Marinette Bwa Chech* ("Marinette of the Dry Arms"), a Kongo Loa, is similar to *Erzulie Dantor*. She represents revolt and misfortune and is prayed to either placate her wrath or direct her fury at another. She is in the form of a skeleton or rotting corpse and is syncretically represented by the *Anima Sola* ("Forsaken Soul").

- **Mai-Louise** is an Ibo goddess.

- **Ti-Quitta / Ti Kitha**, a Loa of sexuality and fertility, is one of the Quitta Loas. One of her aspects is *Ti Quitta Demembre* (Dismembered Quitta).

- **Maman Brigitte** ("Mother Brigitte"), is a Guede goddess who is the wife of **Baron Samedi** and protector of gravestones or funerary markers. She is syncretically represented by St Brigit.

- **Tsillah Wedo** is associated with **Erzulie**. She is depicted as a beautiful virgin of great wealth.

2.27.5 Other aspects

2.27.6 Erzulie in popular culture

Music

- A 1988 solo album by free-jazz pianist Cecil Taylor is called *Erzulie Maketh Scent*.

- "Mistress of Erzulie" was the first track on Alannah Myles' 1995 album "A-lan-nah."

- Erzulie (Freda) is also a character in the Broadway musical *Once On This Island* as the beautiful goddess of love.

- In the Steely Dan song "Two Against Nature" (the third track from the album of the same name), the narrator describes Madame Erzulie as a succubus who "bangs you silly but leaves a nasty bite."

Literature

- A powerful swamp witch/voodoo woman in Terry Pratchett's Discworld novel *Witches Abroad* is named Erzulie Gogol. She is the lover of Genua's former ruler, Baron Saturday (Baron Samedi).

- In the *Buffy the Vampire Slayer* comic *Past Lives, part 4*, Erzulie is invoked to clear a room of all magic.

Erzulie, Papa Legba and Baron Samedi all appear in the WildCats original comic series, assisting Voodoo.

- There is discussion of a portrait of Maitresse Erzulie in Zadie Smith's novel 'On Beauty' (2005).

Television

- In *The Spectacular Spider-Man* animated series, "Ezili" is the surname of the villain Calypso, a voodoo practitioner who had no last name in the original comics.

2.27.7 Notes

2.28 Freyja

For other uses, see Freyja (disambiguation).

In Norse mythology, **Freyja** (/ˈfreɪə/; Old Norse for "(the) Lady") is a goddess associated with love, sexuality, beauty, fertility, gold, seiðr, war, and death. Freyja is the owner of the necklace Brísingamen, rides a chariot pulled by two cats, keeps the boar Hildisvíni by her side, possesses a cloak of falcon feathers, and, by her husband Óðr, is the mother of two daughters, Hnoss and Gersemi. Along with her brother Freyr (Old Norse the "Lord"), her father Njörðr, and her mother (Njörðr's sister, unnamed in sources), she is a member of the Vanir. Stemming from Old Norse *Freyja*, modern

Nuzzled by her boar Hildisvíni, Freyja gestures to a jötunn in an illustration (1895) by Lorenz Frølich

forms of the name include **Freya, Freija, Frejya, Freyia, Fröja, Frøya, Frøjya, Freia, Freja, Frua** and **Freiya**.

Freyja rules over her heavenly afterlife field Fólkvangr and there receives half of those that die in battle, whereas the other half go to the god Odin's hall, Valhalla. Within Fólkvangr is her hall, Sessrúmnir. Freyja assists other deities by allowing them to use her feathered cloak, is invoked in matters of fertility and love, and is frequently sought after by powerful jötnar who wish to make her their wife. Freyja's husband, the god Óðr, is frequently absent. She cries tears of red gold for him, and searches for him under assumed names. Freyja has numerous names, including *Gefn, Hörn, Mardöll, Sýr, Valfreyja,* and *Vanadís*.

Freyja is attested in the *Poetic Edda*, compiled in the 13th century from earlier traditional sources; in the *Prose Edda* and *Heimskringla*, the two latter written by Snorri Sturluson in the 13th century; in several Sagas of Icelanders; in the short story *Sörla þáttr*; in the poetry of skalds; and into the modern age in Scandinavian folklore, as well as the name for Friday in many Germanic languages.

Scholars have theorized about whether Freyja and the goddess Frigg ultimately stem from a single goddess common among the Germanic peoples; about her connection to the valkyries, female battlefield choosers of the slain; and her relation to other goddesses and figures in Germanic mythology, including the thrice-burnt and thrice-reborn Gullveig/Heiðr, the goddesses Gefjon, Skaði, Þorgerðr Hölgabrúðr and Irpa, Menglöð, and the 1st century CE "Isis" of the Suebi. Freyja's name appears in numerous place names in Scandinavia, with a high concentration in southern

Sweden. Various plants in Scandinavia once bore her name, but it was replaced with the name of the Virgin Mary during the process of Christianization. Rural Scandinavians continued to acknowledge Freyja as a supernatural figure into the 19th century, and Freyja has inspired various works of art.

2.28.1   Etymology

Freya *(1882) by Carl Emil Doepler*

The name *Freyja* is transparently "lady" and ultimately derives from Proto-Germanic **fraw(j)ōn*. *Freyja* is cognate with, for example, Old Saxon *frūa* "lady, mistress" and Old High German *frouwa* (compare modern German *Frau* "lady").[1] The theonym *Freyja* is thus considered to have been an epithet in origin, replacing a personal name that is now unattested.[2] As a result, either the original name became entirely taboo or another process occurred in which the goddess is a duplicate or hypostasis of another known goddess; see "Relation to Frigg and other goddesses and figures" below.

See also: List of names of Freyja

2.28.2   Attestations

Poetic Edda

In the *Poetic Edda*, Freyja is mentioned or appears in the poems *Völuspá Grímnismál, Lokasenna, Þrymskviða, Oddrúnargrátr,* and *Hyndluljóð*.

Völuspá contains a stanza that mentions Freyja, referring to her as "Óð's girl"; Freyja being the wife of her husband, Óðr. The stanza recounts that Freyja was once promised to an unnamed builder, later revealed to be a jötunn and subsequently killed by Thor (recounted in detail in *Gylfaginning* chapter 42; see *Prose Edda* section below).[3] In the poem *Grímnismál*, Odin (disguised as *Grímnir*) tells the young Agnar that every day Freyja allots seats to half of those that are slain in her hall Fólkvangr, while Odin owns the other half.[4]

The poem *Þrymskviða* features Loki borrowing Freyja's cloak of feathers and Thor dressing up as Freyja to fool the lusty jötunn Þrymr. In the poem, Thor wakes up to find that his powerful hammer, Mjöllnir, is missing. Thor tells Loki of his missing hammer, and the two go to the beautiful court of Freyja. Thor asks Freyja if she will lend him her cloak of feathers, so that he may try to find his hammer. Freyja agrees:

Freyja and Loki flyte in an illustration (1895) by Lorenz Frølich

While Freyja's cats look on, the god Thor is unhappily dressed as Freyja in Ah, what a lovely maid it is! *(1902) by Elmer Boyd Smith*

In the poem *Lokasenna*, where Loki accuses nearly every female in attendance of promiscuity and/or unfaithfulness, an aggressive exchange occurs between Loki and Freyja. The introduction to the poem notes that among other gods and goddesses, Freyja attends a celebration held by Ægir. In verse, after Loki has flyted with the goddess Frigg, Freyja interjects, telling Loki that he is insane for dredging up his terrible deeds, and that Frigg knows the fate of everyone, though she does not tell it. Loki tells her to be silent, and says that he knows all about her—that Freyja is not lacking in blame, for each of the gods and elves in the hall have been her lover. Freyja objects. She says that Loki is lying, that he is just looking to blather about misdeeds, and since the gods and goddesses are furious at him, he can expect to go home defeated. Loki tells Freyja to be silent, calls her a malicious witch, and conjures a scenario where Freyja was once astride her brother when all of the gods, laughing, surprised the two. Njörðr interjects—he says that a woman having a lover other than her husband is harmless, and he points out that Loki has borne children, and calls Loki a pervert. The poem continues in turn.[5]

Loki flies away in the whirring feather cloak, arriving in the land of Jötunheimr. He spies Þrymr sitting on top of a mound. Þrymr reveals that he has hidden Thor's hammer deep within the earth and that no one will ever know where the hammer is unless Freyja is brought to him as his wife. Loki flies back, the cloak whistling, and returns to the courts of the gods. Loki tells Thor of Þrymr's conditions.[8]

The two go to see the beautiful Freyja. The first thing that Thor says to Freyja is that she should dress herself and

put on a bride's head-dress, for they shall drive to Jötunheimr. At that, Freyja is furious—the halls of the gods
shake, she snorts in anger, and from the goddess the necklace Brísingamen falls. Indignant, Freyja responds:

The gods and goddesses assemble at a thing and debate how
to solve the problem. The god Heimdallr proposes to dress
Thor up as a bride, complete with bridal dress, head-dress,
jingling keys, jewelry, and the famous Brísingamen. Thor
objects but is hushed by Loki, reminding him that the new
owners of the hammer will soon be settling in the land of
the gods if the hammer isn't returned. Thor is dressed as
planned and Loki is dressed as his maid. Thor and Loki go
to Jötunheimr.[11]

In the meantime, Thrym tells his servants to prepare for the
arrival of the daughter of Njörðr. When "Freyja" arrives
in the morning, Thrym is taken aback by her behavior; her
immense appetite for food and mead is far more than what
he expected, and when Thrym goes in for a kiss beneath
"Freyja's" veil, he finds "her" eyes to be terrifying, and he
jumps down the hall. The disguised Loki makes excuses for
the bride's odd behavior, claiming that she simply has not
eaten or slept for eight days. In the end, the disguises successfully fool the jötnar and, upon sight of it, Thor regains
his hammer by force.[12]

In the poem *Oddrúnargrátr*, Oddrún helps Borgny give birth
to twins. In thanks, Borgny invokes vættir, Frigg, Freyja,
and other unspecified deities.[13]

*Reclining atop her boar Hildisvíni, Freyja visits Hyndla in an illus-
tration (1895) by Lorenz Frølich*

Freyja is a main character in the poem *Hyndluljóð*, where
she assists her faithful servant Óttar in finding information
about his ancestry so that he may claim his inheritance. In
doing so, Freyja turns Óttar into her boar, Hildisvíni, and,
by means of flattery and threats of death by fire, Freyja successfully pries the information that Óttar needs from the jötunn Hyndla. Freyja speaks throughout the poem, and at
one point praises Óttar for constructing a hörgr (an altar of
stones) and frequently making blót (sacrifices) to her:

Prose Edda

Freja *by John Bauer (1882–1918)*

Freyja appears in the *Prose Edda* books *Gylfaginning* and
Skáldskaparmál. In chapter 24 of *Gylfaginning*, the en-
throned figure of High says that after the god Njörðr split
with the goddess Skaði, he had two beautiful and mighty
children (no partner is mentioned); a son, Freyr, and a
daughter, Freyja. Freyr is "the most glorious" of the gods,
and Freyja "the most glorious" of the goddesses. Freyja
has a dwelling in the heavens, Fólkvangr, and that whenever
Freyja "rides into battle she gets half the slain, and the other
half to Odin [...]." In support, High quotes the *Grímnismál*
stanza mentioned in the *Poetic Edda* section above.[16]

High adds that Freyja has a large, beautiful hall called
Sessrúmnir, and that when Freyja travels she sits in a chariot
and drives two cats, and that Freyja is "the most approach-
able one for people to pray to, and from her name is derived the honorific title whereby noble ladies are called *fru-
vor* [noble ladies]." High adds that Freyja has a particular
fondness for love songs, and that "it is good to pray to her
concerning love affairs."[16]

In chapter 29, High recounts the names and features of various goddesses, including Freyja. Regarding Freyja, High
says that, next to Frigg, Freyja is highest in rank among
them and that she owns the necklace Brísingamen. Freyja is
married to Óðr, who goes on long travels, and the two have
a very fair daughter by the name of Hnoss. While Óðr is absent, Freyja stays behind and in her sorrow she weeps tears
of red gold. High notes that Freyja has many names, and explains that this is because Freyja adopted them when looking for Óðr and traveling "among strange peoples." These
names include Gefn, Hörn, Mardöll, Sýr, and Vanadís.[17]

Freyja plays a part in the events leading to the birth of
Sleipnir, the eight-legged horse. In chapter 42, High recounts that, soon after the gods built the hall Valhalla, a
builder (unnamed) came to them and offered to build for
them in three seasons a fortification so solid that no jötunn

would be able to come in over from Midgard. In exchange, the builder wants Freyja for his bride, and the sun and the moon. After some debate the gods agree, but with added conditions. In time, just as he is about to complete his work, it is revealed that the builder is, in fact, himself a jötunn, and he is killed by Thor. In the mean time, Loki, in the form of a mare, has been impregnated by the jötunn's horse, Svaðilfari, and so gives birth to Sleipnir. In support, High quotes the *Völuspá* stanza that mentions Freyja.[18] In chapter 49, High recalls the funeral of Baldr and says that Freyja attended the funeral and there drover her cat-chariot, the final reference to the goddess in *Gylfaginning*.[19]

At the beginning of the book *Skáldskaparmál*, Freyja is mentioned among eight goddesses attending a banquet held for Ægir.[20] Chapter 56 details the abduction of the goddess Iðunn by the jötunn Þjazi in the form of an eagle. Terrified at the prospect of death and torture due to his involvement in the abduction of Iðunn, Loki asks if he may use Freyja's "falcon shape" to fly north to Jötunheimr and retrieve the missing goddess. Freyja allows it, and using her "falcon shape" and a furious chase by eagle-Þjazi, Loki successfully returns her.[21]

Heimdallr returns the necklace Brísingamen to Freyja *(1846) by Nils Blommér*

In chapter 6, a means of referring to Njörðr is provided that refers to Frejya ("father of Freyr and Freyja"). In chapter 7, a means of referring to Freyr is provided that refers

to the goddess ("brother of Freyja"). In chapter 8, ways of referring to the god Heimdallr are provided, including "Loki's enemy, recoverer of Freyja's necklace", inferring a myth involving Heimdallr recovering Freyja's necklace from Loki.[22]

In chapter 17, the jötunn Hrungnir finds himself in Asgard, the realm of the gods, and becomes very drunk. Hrungnir boasts that he will move Valhalla to Jötunheimr, bury Asgard, and kill all of the gods—with the exception of the goddesses Freyja and Sif, who he says he will take home with him. Freyja is the only one of them that dares to bring him more to drink. Hrungnir says that he will drink all of their ale. After a while, the gods grow bored of Hrungnir's antics and invoke the name of Thor. Thor immediately enters the hall, hammer raised. Thor is furious and demands to know who is responsible for letting a jötunn in to Asgard, who guaranteed Hrungnir safety, and why Freyja "should be serving him drink as if at the Æsir's banquet."[23]

In chapter 18, verses from the 10th century skald's composition *Þórsdrápa* are quoted. A kenning used in the poem refers to Freyja.[24] In chapter 20, poetic ways to refer to Freyja are provided; "daughter of Njörðr", "sister of Freyr", "wife of Óðr", "mother of Hnoss", "possessor of the fallen slain and of Sessrumnir and tom-cats", possessor of Brísingamen, "Van-deity", Vanadís, and "fair-tear deity".[25] In chapter 32, poetic ways to refer to gold are provided, including "Freyja's weeping" and "rain or shower [...] from Freyja's eyes".[26]

Chapter 33 tells that once the gods journeyed to visit Ægir, one of whom was Freyja.[26] In chapter 49, a quote from a work by the skald Einarr Skúlason employs the kenning "Óðr's bedfellow's eye-rain", which refers to Freyja and means "gold".[27]

Chapter 36 explains again that gold can be referring to as Freyja's weeping due to her red gold tears. In support, works by the skalds Skúli Þórsteinsson and Einarr Skúlason are cited that use "Freyja's tears" or "Freyja's weepings" to represent "gold". The chapter features additional quotes from poetry by Einarr Skúlason that references the goddess and her child Hnoss.[28] Freyja receives a final mention in the *Prose Edda* in chapter 75, where a list of goddesses is provided that includes Freyja.[29]

Heimskringla

The *Heimskringla* book *Ynglinga saga* provides an euhemerized account of the origin of the gods, including Freyja. In chapter 4, Freyja is introduced as a member of the Vanir, the sister of Freyr, and the daughter of Njörðr and his sister (whose name is not provided). After the Æsir–Vanir War ends in a stalemate, Odin appoints Freyr and Njörðr as priests over sacrifices. Freyja becomes

Freja (1901) by Anders Zorn

the priestess of sacrificial offerings and it was she who introduced the practice of seiðr to the Æsir, previously only practiced by the Vanir.[30]

In chapter 10, Freyja's brother Freyr dies, and Freyja is the last survivor among the Æsir and Vanir. Freyja keeps up the sacrifices and becomes famous. The saga explains that, due to Freyja's fame, all women of rank become known by her name—*frúvor* ("ladies"), a woman who is the mistress of her property is referred to as *freyja*, and *húsfreyja* ("lady of the house") for a woman who owns an estate.[31]

The chapter adds that not only was Freyja very clever, but that she and her husband Óðr had two immensely beautiful daughters, Gersemi and Hnoss, "who gave their names to our most precious possessions."[31]

Other

Freyja is mentioned in the sagas *Egils saga*, *Njáls saga*, *Hálfs saga ok Hálfsrekka*, and in *Sörla þáttr*.

Egils saga

In *Egils saga*, when Egill Skallagrímsson refuses to eat, his daughter Þorgerðr (here anglicized as "Thorgerd") says she

will go without food and thus starve to death, and in doing so will meet the goddess Freyja:

> Thorgerd replied in a loud voice, "I have had no evening meal, nor will I do so until I join Freyja. I know no better course of action than my father's. I do not want to live after my father and brother are dead."[32]

Hálfs saga ok Hálfsrekka

In the first chapter of the 14th century legendary saga *Hálfs saga ok Hálfsrekka*, King Alrek has two wives, Geirhild and Signy, and cannot keep them both. He tells the two women that he would keep whichever of them that brews the better ale for him by the time he has returned home in the summer. The two compete and during the brewing process Signy prays to Freyja and Geirhild to Hött ("hood"), a man she had met earlier (earlier in the saga revealed to be Odin in disguise). Hött answers her prayer and spits on her yeast. Signy's brew wins the contest.[33]

Freyja in the Dwarf's Cave (1891) by Louis Huard

Sörla þáttr

In *Sörla þáttr*, a short, late 14th century narrative from a later and extended version of the *Óláfs saga Tryggvasonar* found in the *Flateyjarbók* manuscript, an euhmerized account of the gods is provided. In the account, Freyja is described as having been a concubine of Odin, who bartered sex to four dwarfs for a golden necklace. In the work, the Æsir once lived in a city called Asgard, located in a region called "Asialand or Asiahome". Odin was the king of the realm, and made Njörðr and Freyr temple priests. Freyja was the daughter of Njörðr, and was Odin's concubine. Odin deeply loved Freyja, and she was "the fairest of woman of that day." Freyja had a beautiful bower, and when the door was shut no one could enter without Freyja's permission.[34]

Chapter 1 records that one day Freyja passed by an open stone where dwarfs lived. Four dwarfs were smithying a golden necklace, and it was nearly done. Looking at the necklace, the dwarfs thought Freyja to be most fair, and she the necklace. Freyja offered to buy the collar from them with silver and gold and other items of value. The dwarfs said that they had no lack of money, and that for the necklace the only thing she could offer them would be a night with each of them. "Whether she liked it better or worse", Freyja agreed to the conditions, and so spent a night with each of the four dwarfs. The conditions were fulfilled and the necklace was hers. Freyja went home to her bower as if nothing happened.[35]

As related in chapter 2, Loki, under the service of Odin, found out about Freyja's actions and told Odin. Odin told Loki to get the necklace and bring it to him. Loki said that since no one could enter Freyja's bower against her will, this wouldn't be an easy task, yet Odin told him not to come back until he had found a way to get the necklace. Howling, Loki turned away and went to Freyja's bower but found it locked, and that he couldn't enter. So Loki transformed himself into a fly, and after having trouble finding even the tiniest of entrances, he managed to find a tiny hole at the gable-top, yet even here he had to squeeze through to enter.[35]

Having made his way into Freyja's chambers, Loki looked around to be sure that no one was awake, and found that Freyja was asleep. He landed on her bed and noticed that she was wearing the necklace, the clasp turned downward. Loki turned into a flea and jumped onto Freyja's cheek and there bit her. Freyja stirred, turning about, and then fell asleep again. Loki removed his flea's shape and undid her collar, opened the bower, and returned to Odin.[36]

The next morning Freyja woke and saw that the doors to her bower were open, yet unbroken, and that her precious necklace was gone. Freyja had an idea of who was responsible. She got dressed and went to Odin. She told Odin of the malice he had allowed against her and of the theft of her necklace, and that he should give her back her jewelry.[37]

Odin said that, given how she obtained it, she would never get it back. That is, with one exception: she could have it back if she could make two kings, themselves ruling twenty kings each, battle one another, and cast a spell so that each time one of their numbers falls in battle, they will again spring up and fight again. And that this must go on eternally, unless a Christian man of a particular stature goes into the battle and smites them, only then will they stay dead. Freyja agreed.[37]

2.28.3 Post-Christianization and Scandinavian folklore

Ripe rye in Northern Europe

Although the Christianization of Scandinavia beheld a new institution in Scandinavia, the church, that sought to demonize the native gods, belief and reverence in the gods, including Freyja, remained into the modern period and melded into Scandinavian folklore. Britt-Mari Näsström comments that Freyja became a particular target under Christianization:

> Freyja's erotic qualities became
> an easy target for the new religion,

in which an asexual virgin was the ideal woman [...] Freyja is called "a whore" and "a harlot" by the holy men and missionaries, whereas many of her functions in the everyday lives of men and women, such as protecting the vegetation and supplying assistance in childbirth were transferred to the Virgin Mary.[38]

However, Freyja did not disappear. In Iceland, Freyja was called upon for assistance by way of Icelandic magical staves as late as the 18th century, and as late as the 19th century, Freyja is recorded as retaining elements of her role as a fertility goddess among rural Swedes.[39]

The Old Norse poem *Þrymskviða* (or its source) continued into Scandinavian folk song tradition, where it was euhemerized and otherwise transformed over time. In Iceland, the poem became known as *Þrylur*, whereas in Denmark the poem became *Thor af Havsgaard* and in Sweden it became *Torvisan* or *Hammarhämtningen*.[38] A section of the Swedish *Torvisan*, in which *Freyja* has been transformed into "the fair" (*den väna*) *Frojenborg*, reads as follows:

In the province of Småland, Sweden, an account is recorded connecting Freyja with sheet lightning in this respect. Writer Johan Alfred Göth recalled a Sunday in 1880 where men were walking in fields and looking at nearly ripened rye, where Måns in Karryd said: "Now Freyja is out watching if the rye is ripe". Along with this, Göth recalls another mention of Freyja in the countryside:

> When as a boy I was visiting the old Proud-Katrina, I was afraid of lightning like all boys in those days. When the sheet lightning flared at the night, Katrina said: "Don't be afraid little child, it is only Freyja who is out making fire with steel and flintstone to see if the rye is ripe. She is kind to people and she is only doing it to be of service, she is not like Thor, he slays both people and livestock, when he is in the mood" [...] I later heard several old folks talk of the same thing in the same way.[40]

In Värend, Sweden, Freyja could also arrive at Christmas night and she used to shake the apple trees for the sake of a good harvest and consequently people left some apples in the trees for her sake. However, it was dangerous to leave

the plough outdoors, because if Freyja sat on it, it would no longer be of any use.[40]

2.28.4 Eponyms

*Freyja's hair—*Polygala vulgaris*—a species of the genus* Polygala*.*

Several plants were named after Freyja, such as *Freyja's tears* and *Freyja's hair* (*Polygala vulgaris*), but during the process of Christianization, the name of the goddess was replaced with that of the Virgin Mary.[41] In the pre-Christian period, the Orion constellation was called either Frigg's distaff or Freyja's distaff (Swedish *Frejerock*).[41]

Place names in Norway and Sweden reflect devotion to the goddess, including the Norwegian place name Frøihov (originally **Freyjuhof*, literally "Freyja's hof") and Swedish place names such as Frövi (from **Freyjuvé*, literally "Freyja's vé").[42] In a survey of toponyms in Norway, M. Olsen tallies at least 20 to 30 location names compounded with *Freyja*. Three of these place names appear to derive from **Freyjuhof* ('Freyja's hof'), whereas the goddess's name is frequently otherwise compounded with words for 'meadow' (such as *-þveit*, *-land*) and similar land formations. These toponyms are attested most commonly on the west coast though a high frequency is found in the southeast.[43]

Place names containing *Freyja* are yet more numerous and varied in Sweden, where they are widely distributed. A particular concentration is recorded in Uppland, among which a number derive from the above-mentioned **Freyjuvé* and also *Freyjulundr* ('Freyja's sacred grove'), place names that indicate public worship of Freyja. In addition, a variety of place names (such as *Frøal* and *Fröale*) have been seen as containing an element cognate to Gothic *alhs* and Old English *ealh* ("temple"), although these place names may be otherwise interpreted. In addition, *Freyja* appears as a compound element with a variety of words for geographic features such as fields, meadows, lakes, and natural objects such as rocks.[44]

The Freyja name *Hörn* appears in the Swedish place names Härnevi and Järnevi, stemming from the reconstructed Old Norse place name **Hörnar-vé* (meaning "Hörn's vé").[45]

2.28.5 Archaeological record and historic depictions

A 7th-century phalara found in a "warrior grave" in what is now Eschwege in northwestern Germany features a female figure with two large braids flanked by two "cat-like" beings and holding a staff-like object. This figure has been interpreted as Freyja.[46] This image may be connected to various B-type bracteates, referred to as the Fürstenberg-type, that may also depict the goddess; they "show a female figure, in a short skirt and double-looped hair, holding a stave or sceptre in her right hand and a double-cross feature in the left".[46]

A 12th century depiction of a cloaked but otherwise nude woman riding a large cat appears on a wall in the Schleswig Cathedral in Schleswig-Holstein, Northern Germany. Beside her is similarly a cloaked yet otherwise nude woman riding a distaff. Due to iconographic similarities to the literary record, these figures have been theorized as depictions of Freyja and Frigg respectively.[47]

2.28.6 Theories

Relation to Frigg and other goddesses and figures

Due to numerous similarities, scholars have frequently connected Freyja with the goddess Frigg. The connection with Frigg and question of possible earlier identification of Freyja with Frigg in the Proto-Germanic period (Frigg and Freyja origin hypothesis) remains a matter of scholarly discourse.[48] Regarding a Freyja-Frigg common origin hypothesis, scholar Stephan Grundy comments that "the problem of whether Frigg or Freyja may have been a single goddess originally is a difficult one, made more so by the scantiness of pre-Viking Age references to Germanic goddesses, and the diverse quality of the sources. The best that can be done is to survey the arguments for and against their identity, and to see how well each can be supported."[49]

Like the name of the group of gods to which Freyja belongs, the Vanir, the name *Freyja* is not attested outside of Scandinavia, as opposed to the name of the goddess *Frigg*, who is attested as a goddess common among the Germanic peoples, and whose name is reconstructed as Proto-Germanic **Frijjō*. Similar proof for the existence of a common Germanic goddess from which *Freyja* descends does not exist, but scholars have commented that this may simply be due to lack of evidence.[48]

In the *Poetic Edda* poem *Völuspá*, a figure by the name of Gullveig is burnt three times yet is three times reborn. After her third rebirth, she is known as Heiðr. This event is generally accepted as precipitating the Æsir–Vanir War. Starting with scholar Gabriel Turville-Petre, scholars such as Rudolf Simek, Andy Orchard, and John Lindow have theorized that Gullveig/Heiðr is the same figure as Freyja, and that her involvement with the Æsir somehow led to the events of the Æsir–Vanir War.[50]

Outside of theories connecting Freyja with the goddess Frigg, some scholars, such Hilda Ellis Davidson and Britt-Mari Näsström, have theorized that other goddesses in Norse mythology, such as Gefjon, Gerðr, and Skaði, may be forms of Freyja in different roles and/or ages.[51]

Receiver of the slain

Freyja and her afterlife field Fólkvangr, where she receives half of the slain, has been theorized as connected to the valkyries. Scholar Britt-Mari Näsström points out the description in *Gylfaginning* where it is said of Freyja that "whenever she rides into battle she takes half of the slain," and interprets *Fólkvangr* as "the field of the Warriors". Näsström notes that, just like Odin, Freyja receives slain heroes who have died on the battlefield, and that her house is Sessrumnir (which she translates as "filled with many seats"), a dwelling that Näsström posits likely fills the same function as Valhalla. Näsström comments that "still, we must ask why there are two heroic paradises in the Old Norse view of afterlife. It might possibly be a consequence of different forms of initiation of warriors, where one part seemed to have belonged to Óðinn and the other to Freyja. These examples indicate that Freyja was a war-goddess, and she even appears as a valkyrie, literally 'the one who chooses the slain'."[52]

Siegfried Andres Dobat comments that "in her mythological role as the chooser of half the fallen warriors for her death realm Fólkvangr, the goddess Freyja, however, emerges as the mythological role model for the Valkyrjar [*sic*] and the dísir."[53]

The "Oriental" hypothesis

Gustav Neckel, writing in 1920, connects Freyja to the Phrygian goddess Cybele. According to Neckel, both goddesses can be interpreted as "fertility goddesses" and other potential resemblances have been noted. Some scholars have suggested that the image of Cybele subsequently influenced the iconography of Freyja, the lions drawing the former's chariot becoming large cats. These observation became an extremely common observation in works regarding Old Norse religion until at least the early 1990s. In her book-length study of scholarship on the topic of Freyja, Britt-Mari Näsström (1995) is highly critical of this deduction; Näsström says that "these 'parallels' are due to sheer ignorance about the characteristics of Cybele; scholars have not troubled to look into the resemblances and differences between the two goddesses, if any, in support for their arguments for a common origin."[54]

2.28.7   Modern influence

Freia—a combination of Freyja and the goddess Iðunn—from Richard Wagner's opera Der Ring des Nibelungen *as illustrated (1910) by Arthur Rackham*

Into the modern period, Freyja was treated as a Scandinavian counterpart to the Roman Venus in, for example, Swedish literature, where the goddess may be associated with romantic love or, conversely, simply as a synonym for "lust and potency".[55] In the 18th century, Swedish poet Carl Michael Bellman referred to Stockholm prostitutes as "the children of Fröja".[38] In the 19th century, Britt-Mari Näsström observes, Swedish Romanticism focused less on Freyja's erotic qualities and more on the image of "the pining goddess, weeping for her husband".[38]

Freyja is mentioned in the first stanza ("it is called old Denmark and it is Freja's hall") of the civil national anthem of Denmark, *Der er et yndigt land*, written by 19th century Danish poet Adam Gottlob Oehlenschläger in 1819.[56] In addition, Oehlenschläger wrote a comedy entitled *Freyjas alter* (1818) and a poem *Freais sal* featuring the goddess.[57]

The 19th century German composer Richard Wagner's *Der Ring des Nibelungen* opera cycle features *Freia*, the goddess Freyja combined with the apple-bearing goddess Iðunn.[58]

In late 19th century and early 20th century Northern Europe, Freyja was the subject of numerous works of art, including *Freyja* by H. E. Freund (statue, 1821–1822), *Freja sökande sin make* (painting, 1852) by Nils Blommér, *Freyjas Aufnahme uner den Göttern* (charcoal drawing, 1881), and *Frigg; Freyja* (drawing, 1883) by Carl Ehrenberg, *Freyja* (1901) by Carl Emil Doepler d. J., and *Freyja and the Brisingamen* by J. Doyle Penrose (painting, 1862–1932).[57] Like other Norse goddesses, her name was applied widely in Scandinavia to, for example, "sweetmeats or to stout carthorses".[59] *Vanadís*, one of Freyja's names, is the source of the name of the chemical element vanadium, so named because of its many colored compounds.[60]

Starting in the early 1990s, derivatives of *Freyja* began to appear as a given name for girls.[59] According to the Norwegian name database from the Central Statistics Bureau, around 500 women have Frøya (the modern, Norwegian spelling of the goddess's name) as a first name in the country. There are several similar names that likely have the same origin, such as the more widespread Frøydis.[61]

Freyja is one of the incarnated goddesses in the New Zealand comedy/drama "The Almighty Johnsons". The part of "Agnetha/Freyja" is played by Alison Bruce[62]

2.28.8   See also

- List of Germanic deities

- Frigg

2.28.9   Notes

[1] Orel (2003), p. 112.

[2] Grundy (1998), pp. 55–56.

[3] Larrington (1999), p. 7.

[4] Larrington (1999), p. 53.

[5] Larrington (1999), pp. 84,90.

[6] Thorpe (1866), p. 62.

[7] Bellows (1923), p. 175.

[8] Larrington (1999), p. 98.

[9] Thorpe (1866), p. 64.

[10] Bellows (1923), p. 177.

[11] Larrington (1999), pp. 99–100.

[12] Larrington (1999), pp. 100–101.

[13] Larrington (1999), p. 206.

[14] Thorpe (1866), p. 108.

[15] Bellows (1923), p. 221.

[16] Faulkes (1995), p. 24.

[17] Faulkes (1995), pp. 29–30.

[18] Faulkes (1995), pp. 35–36.

[19] Faulkes (1995), p. 50.

[20] Faulkes (1995), p. 59.

[21] Faulkes (1995), p. 60.

[22] Faulkes (1995), pp. 75–76.

[23] Faulkes (1995), p. 68.

[24] Faulkes (1995), p. 85.

[25] Faulkes (1995), p. 86.

[26] Faulkes (1995), p. 95.

[27] Faulkes (1995), p. 119.

[28] Faulkes (1995), p. 98.

[29] Faulkes (1995), p. 157.

[30] Hollander (2007), p. 8.

[31] Hollander (2007), p. 14.

[32] Scudder (2001), p. 151.

[33] Tunstall (2005).

[34] Morris & Morris (1911), p. 127.

[35] Morris & Morris (1911), p. 128.

[36] Morris & Morris (1911), pp. 128–129.

[37] Morris & Morris (1911), p. 129.

[38] Näsström (1995), p. 21.

[39] For Freyja in Iceland, see Flowers (1989), pp. 73,80. For Freyja in Sweden, see Schön (2004), pp. 227–228.

[40] Schön (2004), pp. 227–228.

[41] Schön (2004), p. 228.

[42] Simek (2007), p. 91 and Turville-Petre (1964), pp. 178–179.

[43] Turville-Petre (1964), p. 178.

[44] Turville-Petre (1964), pp. 178–179.

[45] Simek (2007), pp. 156–157 and Turville-Petre (1964), p. 178.

[46] Gaimster (1998), pp. 54–55.

[47] Jones & Pennick (1995), pp. 144–145.

[48] Grundy (1998), pp. 56–66.

[49] Grundy (1998), p. 57.

[50] Simek (2007), pp. 123–124, Lindow (2002), p. 155, and Orchard (1997), p. 67.

[51] Davidson (1998), pp. 85–86.

[52] Näsström (1999), p. 61.

[53] Dobat (2006), p. 186.

[54] Näsström (1995), pp. 23–24.

[55] Näsström (1995), pp. 21–22.

[56] Andersen (1899), p. 157.

[57] Simek (2007), p. 91.

[58] Simek (2007), p. 90.

[59] Näsström (1995), p. 22.

[60] Wiberg, Wiberg & Holleman (2001), p. 1345. A suburb of Minneapolis, MN, an area settled heavily by Scandinavians, is called "Vanadis Heights."

[61] "Names". Statistics Norway.

[62] "The Almighty Johnsons". *http://www.tv3.co.nz/ 0108---I-Can-Give-You-Frigg/tabid/1737/articleID/ 69747/Default.aspx#http://cdn.tv3.co.nz/tv/AM/ 2011/3/28/69747/TAJ-ep8a-(Alison-Bruce-as-A.jpg?crop=auto&maxwidth=620&maxheight=415.*

2.28.10   References

- Andersen, Vilhelm (1899). *Adam Oehlenschläger: et livs poesi* (in Danish). Nordiske forlag, E. Bojesen.

- Bellows, Henry Adams (Trans.) (1923). *The Poetic Edda*. American-Scandinavian Foundation.

- Davidson, Hilda Ellis (1998). *Roles of the Northern Goddess*. Routledge. ISBN 0-415-13611-3.

- Dobat, Siegfried Andres (2006). "Bridging mythology and belief: Viking Age functional culture as a reflection of the belief in divine intervention". In Andren, A.; Jennbert, K.; Raudvere, C. *Old Norse Religion in Long Term Perspectives: Origins, Changes and Interactions, an International Conference in Lund, Sweden, June 3–7, 2004*. Nordic Academic Press. ISBN 91-89116-81-X.

- Faulkes, Anthony (Trans.) (1995). *Edda*. Everyman. ISBN 0-460-87616-3.

- Gaimster, Märit (1998). *Vendel Period Bracteates on Gotland*. Almqvist & Wiksell International. ISBN 91-22-01790-9.

- Grundy, Stephan (1998). "Freyja and Frigg". In Billington, Sandra; Green, Miranda. *The Concept of the Goddess*. Routledge. ISBN 0-415-19789-9.

- Hollander, Lee Milton (Trans.) (2007). *Heimskringla: History of the Kings of Norway*. University of Texas Press. ISBN 978-0-292-73061-8.

- Flowers, Stephen (1989). *The Galdrabók: An Icelandic Grimoire*. Samuel Weiser, Inc. ISBN 0-87728-685-X.

- Larrington, Carolyne (Trans.) (1999). *The Poetic Edda*. Oxford University Press. ISBN 0-19-283946-2.

- Lindow, John (2002). *Norse Mythology: A Guide to the Gods, Heroes, Rituals, and Beliefs*. Oxford University Press. ISBN 0-19-515382-0.

- Jones, Prudence; Pennick, Nigel (1995). *A History of Pagan Europe*. Routledge. ISBN 9780415091367.

- Morris, William (Trans.); Morris, May (1911). *The Collected Works of William Morris: Volume X, Three Northern Love Stories and the Tale of Beowulf*. Longmans Green and Company.

- Näsström, Britt-Mari (1995). *Freyja - the Great Goddess of the North*. Almqvist & Wiksell International. ISBN 91-22-01694-5.

- Näsström, Britt-Mari (1999). "Freyja – The Trivalent Goddess". In Sand, Reenberg Erik; Sørensen, Jørgen Podemann. *Comparative Studies in History of Religions: Their Aim, Scope and Validity*. Museum Tusculanum Press. ISBN 87-7289-533-0.

- Orchard, Andy (1997). *Dictionary of Norse Myth and Legend*. Cassell. ISBN 0-304-34520-2.

- Orel, Vladimir (2003). *A Handbook of Germanic Etymology*. Brill Publishers. ISBN 90 04 12875 1.

- Schön, Ebbe (2004). *Asa-Tors hammare, Gudar och jättar i tro och tradition* (in Swedish). Fält & Hässler, Värnamo.

- Scudder, Bernard (Trans.) (2001). "Egils saga". *The Sagas of Icelanders*. Penguin Group. ISBN 0-14-100003-1.

- Simek, Rudolf (2007). *Dictionary of Northern Mythology*. translated by Angela Hall. D.S. Brewer. ISBN 0-85991-513-1.

- Thorpe, Benjamin (Trans.) (1866). *The Elder Edda of Saemund Sigfusson*. Norrœna Society.

- Tunstall, Peter (Trans.) (2005). *The Saga of Half & His Heroes*.

- Turville-Petre, E. O. G. (1964). *Myth and Religion of the North: The Religion of Ancient Scandinavia*. Holt, Rinehart and Winston.

- Wiberg, Egon; Wiberg, Nils; Holleman, Arnold Frederick (2001). *Holleman-Wiberg's Inorganic Chemistry*. Academic Press. ISBN 0-12-352651-5.

2.28.11   External links

- Media related to Freyja at Wikimedia Commons

2.29   Hysminai

The **Hysminai** (Ancient Greek: ὑσμῖναι; singular: ὑσμίνη **hysmine** "battle, conflict, combat"[1]) are figures in Greek mythology. Descendants of Eris, they are personifications of battle.[2][3] Quintus Smyrnaeus[4] wrote of them in Book V of the *Fall of Troy* in a passage translated by Arthur Way:

> Around them hovered the relentless Fates;
> Beside them Battle incarnate onward pressed
> Yelling, and from their limbs streamed blood and
> sweat.[5]

2.29.1 See also

- Androktasiai

- Makhai

2.29.2 References

[1] "ὑσμίνη": Lexicon entry in LSJ

[2] Hesiod, *Theogony* 226 ff

[3] Scull, Sarah Amelia (1880). *Greek mythology systematized*. Porter & Coates. p. 42. Retrieved 2 April 2010.

[4] Quintus Smyrnaeus, *Fall of Troy* 5. 25 ff

[5] Quintus (Smyrnaeus) (1913). *The fall of Troy*. Translated, Arthur S. Way. W. Heinemann. p. 213. Retrieved 2 April 2010.

2.30 Inanna

Inanna (/ɪˈnænə/ or /ɪˈnɑːnə/; Cuneiform: 𒀭𒈹 (Old Babylonian) or ⤚⟶⟍⟊ (Neo-Assyrian) ^{D}MUŠ₃; Sumerian: Inanna; Akkadian: Ištar; Unicode: U+12239) was the Sumerian goddess of love, fertility, and warfare, and goddess of the E-Anna temple at the city of Uruk, her main centre.

Part of the front of Inanna's temple from Uruk

2.30.1 Origins

Inanna was the most prominent female deity in ancient Mesopotamia.[1] As early as the Uruk period (ca. 4000–3100 BC), Inanna was associated with the city of Uruk. The famous Uruk Vase (found in a deposit of cult objects of the Uruk III period) depicts a row of naked men carrying various objects, bowls, vessels, and baskets of farm products, and bringing sheep and goats, to a female figure facing the ruler. This figure was ornately dressed for a divine marriage, and attended by a servant. The female figure holds the symbol of the two twisted reeds of the doorpost, signifying Inanna behind her, while the male figure holds a box and stack of bowls, the later cuneiform sign signifying *En*, or high priest of the temple. Especially in the Uruk period, the symbol of a ring-headed doorpost is associated with Inanna.[1]

Seal impressions from the Jemdet Nasr period (ca. 3100–2900 BC) show a fixed sequence of city symbols including those of Ur, Larsa, Zabalam, Urum, Arina, and probably Kesh. It is likely that this list reflects the report of contributions to Inanna at Uruk from cities supporting her cult. A large number of similar sealings were found from the slightly later Early Dynastic I phase at Ur, in a slightly different order, combined with the rosette symbol of Inanna, that were definitely used for this purpose. They had been used to lock storerooms to preserve materials set aside for her cult.[2] Inanna's primary temple of worship was the Eanna, located in Uruk (c.f. Worship).

Etymology

Inanna's name derives from *Lady of Heaven* (Sumerian: nin-an-ak). The cuneiform sign of Inanna (𒈹); however, is not a ligature of the signs *lady* (Sumerian: nin; Cuneiform: 𒊩𒌆 SAL.TUG₂) and *sky* (Sumerian: an; Cuneiform: 𒀭 AN).[3] These difficulties have led some early Assyriologists to suggest that originally Inanna may have been a Proto-Euphratean goddess, possibly related to the Hurrian mother goddess Hannahannah, accepted only latterly into the Sumerian pantheon, an idea supported by her youthfulness, and that, unlike the other Sumerian divinities, at first she had no sphere of responsibilities.[4] The view that there was a Proto-Euphratean substrate language in Southern Iraq before Sumerian is not widely accepted by modern Assyriologists.[5]

2.30.2 Worship

Along the Tigris and Euphrates rivers were many shrines and temples dedicated to Inanna. The *House of Heaven* (Sumerian: e₂-anna; Cuneiform: 𒂍𒀭 E₂.AN) temple[6] in Uruk[7] was the greatest of these, where sacred prostitution was a common practice.[8] In addition, according to Leick 1994 persons of asexual or hermaphroditic bodies and feminine men were particularly involved in the worship and ritual practices of Inanna's temples (see *gala*). The deity of this fourth-millennium city was probably originally An. After its dedication to Inanna the temple seems to have housed priestesses of the goddess. The high priestess would choose for her bed a young man who represented the shepherd Dumuzid, consort of Inanna, in a hieros gamos or sacred marriage, celebrated during the annual Akitu (New Year) ceremony, at the spring Equinox. According to Samuel Noah Kramer in *The Sacred Marriage Rite,* in late Sumerian history (end of the third millennium) kings established their legitimacy by taking the place of Dumuzi in the temple for one night on the tenth day of the New Year festival.[9] A Sacred Marriage to Inanna may have conferred legitimacy on a number of rulers of Uruk. Gilgamesh is reputed to have refused marriage to Inanna, on the grounds of her misalliance with such kings as Lugalbanda and Damuzi.

One version of the star symbol of Inanna/Ishtar

2.30.3   Iconography

Inanna's symbol is an eight-pointed star or a rosette.[10] She was associated with lions – even then a symbol of power – and was frequently depicted standing on the backs of two lionesses. Her cuneiform ideogram was a hook-shaped twisted knot of reeds, representing the doorpost of the storehouse (and thus fertility and plenty).[11]

Inanna as the planet Venus

Inanna was associated with the planet Venus, which at that time was regarded as two stars, the "morning star" and the "evening star." There are hymns to Inanna as her astral manifestation. It also is believed that in many myths about Inanna, including *Inanna's Descent to the Underworld* and *Inanna and Shukaletuda,* her movements correspond with the movements of Venus in the sky. Also, because of its

positioning so close to Earth, Venus is not visible across the dome of the sky as most celestial bodies are; because its proximity to the sun renders it invisible during the day. Instead, Venus is visible only when it rises in the East before sunrise, or when it sets in the West after sunset.[12]

Because the movements of Venus appear to be discontinuous (it disappears due to its proximity to the sun, for many days at a time, and then reappears on the other horizon), some cultures did not recognize Venus as single entity, but rather regarded the planet as two separate stars on each horizon as the morning and evening star. The Mesopotamians, however, most likely understood that the planet was one entity. A cylinder seal from the Jemdet Nasr period expresses the knowledge that both morning and evening stars were the same celestial entity.[13] The discontinuous movements of Venus relate to both mythology as well as Inanna's dual nature.[13] Inanna is related like Venus to the principle of connectedness, but this has a dual nature and could seem unpredictable. Yet as both the goddess of love and war, with both masculine and feminine qualities, Inanna is poised to respond, and occasionally to respond with outbursts of temper. Mesopotamian literature takes this one step further, explaining Inanna's physical movements in mythology as corresponding to the astronomical movements of Venus in the sky.

Inanna's Descent to the Underworld explains how Inanna is able to, unlike any other deity, descend into the netherworld and return to the heavens. The planet Venus appears to make a similar descent, setting in the West and then rising again in the East.

In *Inanna and Shukaletuda,* in search of her attacker, Inanna makes several movements throughout the myth that correspond with the movements of Venus in the sky. An introductory hymn explains Inanna leaving the heavens and heading for *Kur,* what could be presumed to be, the mountains, replicating the rising and setting of Inanna to the West. Shukaletuda also is described as scanning the heavens in search of Inanna, possibly to the eastern and western horizons.[13]

Inanna was associated with the eastern fish of the last of the zodiacal constellations, Pisces. Her consort Dumuzi was associated with the contiguous first constellation, Aries.[14]

2.30.4   Character

Inanna is the goddess of love. In the Babylonian epic of Gilgamesh, Gilgamesh points out Inanna's infamous ill-treatment of her lovers. Inanna also has a very complicated relationship with her lover, Dumuzi, in "Inanna's Descent to the Underworld".[15]

She also is one of the Sumerian war deities: "She stirs confusion and chaos against those who are disobedient to her, speeding carnage and inciting the devastating flood, clothed in terrifying radiance. It is her game to speed conflict and battle, untiring, strapping on her sandals."[16] Battle itself is sometimes referred to as "the dance of Inanna."

Consider her description in one hymn: "When the servants let the flocks loose, and when cattle and sheep are returned to cow-pen and sheepfold, then, my lady, like the nameless poor, you wear only a single garment. The pearls of a prostitute are placed around your neck, and you are likely to snatch a man from the tavern."[17] Inanna also was associated with rain and storms and with the planet Venus, the morning and evening star,[11] as was the Greco-Roman goddess Aphrodite or Venus.

2.30.5 Myths

Enmerkar and the Lord of Aratta

Inanna has a central role in the myth of Enmerkar and the Lord of Aratta.[18] A major theme in the narrative is the rivalry between the rulers of Aratta and Uruk for the heart of Inanna. Ultimately, this rivalry results in natural resources coming to Uruk and the invention of writing. The text describes a tension between the cities:

> The lord of Aratta placed on his head the golden crown for Inana. But he did not please her like the lord of Kulaba (A district in Uruk). Aratta did not build for holy Inana (*sic.*; Alternate spelling of 'Inanna') — unlike the Shrine E-ana (Temple in Uruk for Inanna).[19]

Text Summary: The city Aratta is structured as a mirror image of Uruk, only Aratta has natural resources (i.e. gold, silver, lapis lazuli) that Uruk needs. Enmerkar, king in Uruk, comes to Inanna requesting that a temple be built in Uruk with stones from Aratta, and she orders him to find a messenger to cross the Zubi mountains and go to the Lord of Aratta demanding precious metals for the temple.[20] The messenger makes the journey and all the peoples he passes along the way praise Inanna. He makes his demands, and the Lord of Aratta refuses, saying that Aratta will not submit to Uruk. He is upset, however, to learn that Inanna is pleased with the Shrine E-ana.[21] The Lord of Aratta issues a challenge to Enmerkar to bring barley to Aratta because Aratta is currently experiencing a severe famine. Enmerkar mobilizes men and donkeys to deliver the food. Still, the Lord of Aratta will not submit.[22] A series of riddles, or challenges, follows. Enermerkar, with the wisdom of Enki succeeds at every task. Eventually, the Lord of Aratta challenges Enmerkar to have a champion from each city fight in single combat.[23] By this point, however, the messenger is tired. Enmerkar gives him a message, but he is unable to repeat it verbally. So, the messenger writes it down, thus inventing writing:

> (Enmerkar's) speech was substantial, and its contents extensive. The messenger, whose mouth was heavy, was not able to repeat it. Because the messenger, whose mouth was tired, was not able to repeat it, the lord of Kulaba patted some clay and wrote the message as if on a tablet. Formerly, the writing of messages on clay was not established. Now, under that sun and on that day, it was indeed so. The lord of Kulaba inscribed the message like a tablet.[24]

The Lord of Aratta cannot read the text, but the god Ishkur causes rains to end the drought in Aratta. The Lord of Aratta decides that his city has not been forsaken after all.[25] The champion of Aratta dresses in a "garment of lion skins," possibly a reference to Inanna.[26] The end of the text is unclear, but it seems that the city of Uruk is able to access Aratta's resources.

Inanna and the Mes

According to one story, Inanna tricked the god of culture, Enki, who was worshipped in the city of Eridu, into giving her the Mes. The Mes were documents or tablets which were blueprints to civilization. They represented everything from abstract notions like Victory and Counsel and Truth to technologies like weaving to writing to social constructs like law, priestly offices, kingship, and even prostitution. They granted power over, or possibly existence to, all the aspects of civilization (both positive and negative). Inanna traveled to Enki's city Eridu, and by getting him drunk, she got him to give her hundreds of Mes, which she took to her city of Uruk. Later, when sober, Enki sent mighty Abgallu (the seven sages, half-fish, half-human demigods that counselled the antediluvian god-kings) to stop her boat as it sailed the Euphrates and retrieve his gifts, but she escaped with the Mes and brought them to her city. This story may represent the historic transfer of power from Eridu to Uruk.

Inanna and Ebih

This myth depicts Inanna's confrontation with and ultimate destruction of Mount Ebih (Jebel Hamrin, in modern-day Iraq),[27] which has refused to recognize her superiority.

The story begins with an introductory hymn to praise Inanna.[28] The goddess then journeys about the world, until she comes across Mount Ebih, and is subsequently angered by its seeming lack of respect and natural beauty, and rails at the mountain:

Mountain, because of your elevation, because of your height,
Because of your goodness, because of your beauty,
Because you wore a holy garment,
Because An organized(?) you,
Because you did not bring (your) nose close to the ground,
Because you did not press (your) lips in the dust.[1]

1. ^ Karahashi, Fumi (April 2004). "Fighting the Mountain: Some Observations on the Sumerian Myths of Inanna and Ninurta". *Journal of Near Eastern Studies* **63** (2): 111–8. JSTOR 422302.

She petitions to the god An to allow her to destroy the mountain. An refuses, but Inanna proceeds to attack and destroy the mountain regardless, utterly annihilating it and leaving sad destruction in her wake. In the conclusion of the myth, she tells Ebih why she attacked it.

Inanna and Shukaletuda

Inanna and Shukaletuda begins with a hymn to Inanna which praises her as the planet Venus (as it appears in the sky).

The story then goes on to introduce the reader to Shukaletuda, a gardener who is terrible at his job and partially blind. All of his plants die, with the exception of one poplar tree. Shukaletuda prays to the deities for guidance in his work. To his surprise, the goddess Inanna, sees his one poplar tree and decides to rest under the shade of its branches. While Inanna is asleep, Shukaletuda decides it would be a good idea to undress and rape her. The goddess awakes and realizes she was violated in her sleep. She is furious and determined to bring her attacker to justice. In a fit of rage, Inanna unleashes plagues upon the Earth to punish and identify her attacker. She turns water to blood in an attempt to punish her rapist. Shukaletuda, terrified for his life, asks his father for advice on how to escape Inanna's wrath. His father tells him to hide in the city, amongst the hordes of people and blend in. Inanna searches the mountains of the East for her attacker, and is not able to find him. She then releases a series of storms and closes the roads to the city, and is still unable to find Shukaletuda in the mountains. After her plagues, Inanna is still not able to find her rapist and asks Enki for help in revealing him. Inanna threatens to leave her temple at Uruk unless Enki helps her find her attacker. He consents, and allows her to "fly across the sky like a rainbow". Inanna finally finds Shukaletuda. He attempts to make his excuses for his crime against her, but she will have nothing to do with it and kills him.[13]

This myth and Shukaletuda is cited as a Sumerian Astral myth, as the movements of Inanna to only the mountains correspond with the movements of the planet Venus. When Shukaletuda was praying to the goddess, he may have been looking toward Venus in the horizon.[13]

Inanna and Gudam

This fragmentary myth focuses on the actions of Gudam, who is described as a fierce warrior, who dined on flesh and drank blood instead of beer.[29] Gudam walks through Uruk, killing many and damaging the Eanna temple, until a "fisherman of Inanna" turns his axe against him and defeats him. Gudam, humbled, pleads to Inanna for forgiveness, promising to praise her through words and offerings.

Inanna and An

This myth, also fragmentary, begins with a conversation between Inanna and her brother Utu. She laments the fact that the Eanna temple is not of their domain, and resolves to reach or secure it. The text becomes increasingly fragmentary at this point in the narrative, but appears to describe her difficult passage through a marshland to reach it, while being advised by a fisherman as to the best route.

Ultimately she reaches her father, Anu. While he is shocked by her arrogance in attempting to capture the Eanna temple for herself, he nevertheless concedes that she has succeeded and it is now her domain. The text ends with an exaltation of her qualities and powers.[30] This myth may represent an eclipse in the authority of the priests of Anu in Uruk, and a transfer of power to the priests of Inanna.

Inanna's descent to the underworld

The story of Inanna's descent to the underworld is a relatively well-attested and reconstructed composition.

In Sumerian religion, the *Underworld* was conceived of as a dreary, dark place; a home to deceased heroes and ordinary people alike. While everyone suffered an eternity of poor conditions, certain behavior while alive, notably creating a family to provide offerings to the deceased, could alleviate conditions somewhat.

Inanna's reason for visiting the underworld is unclear. The reason she gives to the gatekeeper of the underworld is that she wants to attend the funeral rites of Ereshkigal's husband, here said to be Gud-gal-ana. Gugalana was the Bull of Heaven in The Epic of Gilgamesh, which was killed by Gilgamesh and Enkidu. To further add to the confusion, Ereshkigal's husband typically is the plague god, Nergal.

In this story, before leaving Inanna instructed her minister and servant, Ninshubur, to plead with the deities Enlil, Sin, and Enki to save her if anything went amiss. The attested laws of the underworld dictate that, with the exception of appointed messengers, those who enter it could never leave.

Inanna dresses elaborately for the visit, with a turban, a wig, a lapis lazuli necklace, beads upon her breast, the 'pala dress' (the ladyship garment), mascara, pectoral, a golden ring on her hand, and she held a lapis lazuli measuring rod. These garments are each representations of powerful *mes* she possesses. Perhaps Inanna's garments, unsuitable for a funeral, along with Inanna's haughty behavior, make Ereshkigal suspicious.[31]

Following Ereshkigal's instructions, the gatekeeper tells Inanna she may enter the first gate of the underworld, but she must hand over her lapis lazuli measuring rod. She asks why, and is told 'It is just the ways of the Underworld'. She obliges and passes through. Inanna passes through a total of seven gates, at each one removing a piece of clothing or jewelry she had been wearing at the start of her journey, thus stripping her of her power.

When she arrives in front of her sister, she is naked. "After she had crouched down and had her clothes removed, they were carried away. Then she made her sister Erec-ki-gala rise from her throne, and instead she sat on her throne. The Anna, the seven judges, rendered their decision against her. They looked at her – it was the look of death. They spoke to her – it was the speech of anger. They shouted at her – it was the shout of heavy guilt. The afflicted woman was turned into a corpse. And the corpse was hung on a hook."

Ereshkigal's hatred for Inanna could be referenced in a few other myths. Ereshkigal, too, is bound by the laws of the underworld; she can not leave her kingdom of the underworld to join the other 'living' deities, and they can not visit her in the underworld, or else they can never return. Inanna symbolized erotic love and fertility, and contrasts with Ereshkigal.

Three days and three nights passed, and Ninshubur, following instructions, went to Enlil, Nanna, and Enki's temples, and demanded they save Inanna. The first two deities refused, saying it was her own doing, but Enki was deeply troubled and agreed to help. He created two asexual figures named *gala-tura* and the *kur-jara* from the dirt under the fingernails of the deities. He instructed them to appease Ereshkigal; and when asked what they wanted, they were to ask for Inanna's corpse and sprinkle it with the food and water of life. However, when they come before Ereshkigal, she is in agony like a woman giving birth, and she offers them what they want, including life-giving rivers of water and fields of grain, if they can relieve her; nonetheless they take only the corpse.

Things went as Enki said, and the *gala-tura* and the *kur-jara* were able to revive Inanna. Demons of Ereshkigal's followed (or accompanied) Inanna out of the underworld, and insisted that she wasn't free to go until someone took her place. They first came upon Ninshubur and attempted to take her. Inanna refused, as Ninshubur was her loyal servant, who had rightly mourned her while she was in the underworld. They next came upon Cara, Inanna's beautician, still in mourning. The demons said they would take him, but Inanna refused, as he too had mourned her. They next came upon Lulal, also in mourning. The demons offered to take him, but Inanna refused.

They next came upon Dumuzi, Inanna's husband. Despite Inanna's fate, and in contrast to the other individuals who were properly mourning Inanna, Dumuzi was lavishly clothed and resting beneath a tree. Inanna, displeased, decrees that the demons shall take him, using language which echoes the speech Ereshkigal gave while condemning her. Dumuzi is then taken to the underworld.

In other recensions of the story, Dumuzi tries to escape his fate, and is capable of fleeing the demons for a time, as the deities intervene and disguise him in a variety of forms. He is eventually found. However, Dumuzi's sister, out of love for him, begged to be allowed to take his place. It was then decreed that Dumuzi spent half the year in the underworld, and his sister take the other half. Inanna, displaying her typically capricious behavior, mourns his time in the underworld. This she reveals in a haunting lament of his deathlike absence from her, for "[he] cannot answer . . . [he] cannot come/ to her calling . . . the young man has gone."[32] Her own powers, notably those connected with fertility, subsequently wane, to return in full when he returns from the netherworld each six months. This cycle then approximates the shift of seasons.

Additional discussion of Inanna's descent to the underworld, with new interpretation since discoveries of additional material in 1963, is included at Tammuz_(deity)#Dumuzid_and_Inanna.

Interpretations of the Inanna descent myth Additionally, the myth may be described as a union of Inanna with her own "dark side", her twin sister-self, Ereshkigal, as when she ascends it is with Ereshkigal's powers, while Inanna is in the underworld it is Ereshkigal who apparently takes on fertility powers, and the poem ends with a line in praise, not of Inanna, but of Ereshkigal. It is in many ways a praise-poem dedicated to the more negative aspects of Inanna's domain, symbolic of an acceptance of the necessity of death to the continuance of life. It can also be interpreted as being about the psychological power of a descent into the unconscious, realizing one's own strength through an episode of seeming powerlessness, and/or an acceptance of one's own negative qualities, as is discussed by Joseph Campbell.[33]

Another recent interpretation, by Clyde Hostetter, indicates that the myth is an allegorical report of related movements of the planets Venus, Mercury, and Jupiter; and those of the waxing crescent Moon in the Second Millennium, beginning with the Spring Equinox and concluding with a meteor shower near the end of one synodic period of Venus.[34]

Joshua Mark argues that it is most likely that the moral of the *Descent of Inanna* was that there are always consequences for one's actions. "The Descent of Inanna, then, about one of the gods behaving badly and other gods and mortals having to suffer for that behavior, would have given to an ancient listener the same basic understanding anyone today would take from an account of a tragic accident caused by someone's negligence or poor judgment: that, sometimes, life is just not fair."[35]

2.30.6   Related deities

Inanna's Akkadian counterpart is Ishtar. In different traditions Inanna is the daughter of Anu or she is the daughter of the moon god Sin. In various traditions, her siblings include the sun god Utu, the rain god Ishkur, and Ereshkigal, Queen of the Underworld. Her personal assistant is Ninshubur. She is never considered to have a permanent spouse, although Dumuzi is her lover. Yet, she is responsible for sending Dumuzi to the Underworld in "Inanna's Descent to the Underworld." Inanna also is regarded in astral traditions as the morning and evening star.[15] The cult of Inanna may also have influenced the deities Ainina and Danina of the Caucasian Iberians mentioned by the medieval Georgian Chronicles.[36]

2.30.7   Modern relevance

Since Inanna embodies the traits of independence, self-determination, and strength in an otherwise patriarchal Sumerian pantheon, she has become the subject of feminist theory.[37] Indeed, in one analysis of "Inanna and the huluppu tree", the author points out how she was implicitly "tamed and controlled", even "demoted", implying her prior importance as a female role model.[38] Another modern work explores the idea that Inanna was once regarded in parts of Sumer as the mother of all humanity.[39]

On January 2012 the Israeli feminist artist, Liliana Kleiner, presented in Jerusalem an exhibition of paintings of Inana, inspired by the above.[40]

Ancient cuneiform texts consisting of "Hymns to Inanna" have been cited as early examples of the archetype of a powerful, sexual female displaying dominating behaviors

and forcing Gods and men into submission to her.[41] Archaeologist and historian Anne O Nomis notes that Inanna's rituals included cross-dressing of cult personnel, and rituals "imbued with pain and ecstasy, bringing about initiation and journeys of altered consciousness; punishment, moaning, ecstasy, lament and song, participants exhausting themselves with weeping and grief."[42]

2.30.8   In popular culture

- A major leitmotif in Rufi Thorpe's 2014 novel *The Girls of Corona del Mar* concerns the narrator's translation of epic poetry concerning Inanna and the narrator's identification with the goddess.

- The goddess Inanna was a major character in John Myers Myers 1981 fantasy novel, *The Moon's Fire-Eating Daughter*

- The black metal band Beherit wrote a song called, "The Gate of Inanna", featured in their 1994 album *H418ov21.C*

- Tori Amos' song Caught a Lite Sneeze features backing vocals during the chorus of her singing Inanna's name.

- Rock band The Tea Party feature a song called "Inanna" on their 1995 album *The Edges of Twilight*

- Alice Notley's feminist poetry epic, *The Descent of Alette* (1996), takes inspiration from the myth of Inanna's descent into the underworld

- *Inanna: An Opera of Ancient Sumer* (2003) is a three-act classical opera by American composer John Craton

- *The Self Laudatory Hymn of Inanna and Her Omnipotence* by Michael Nyman, performed by James Bowman and Fretwork on Time Will Pronounce (1993), the text of which comes from *Ancient Near Eastern Texts Relating to the Old Testament* [43]

- Inanna is glancingly mentioned in *The Queen of the Damned* by Anne Rice (1988). "And this was Akasha...a worshipper of the great goddess Inanna...." p. 286

- In researching Inanna and Enki, the characters of Juanita and Hiro discover the underlying plot of *Snow Crash* by Neal Stephenson (1992).

- Inanna is worshipped by the women in *The Red Tent* by Anita Diamant (1997).

- Inanna is reincarnated as a so far male-presenting person in "The Wicked + The Divine" (2014).

2.30.9 Dates (approximate)

2.30.10 See also

- Anat

- Hannahannah

- Ishtar

- Nanaya

- Astarte

- Aphrodite

- Venus

- Isis

- Madonna

- Anann

- Lillith

- Enheduanna

2.30.11 Notes

[1] Black, Jeremy; Green, Anthony (1992). *Gods, Demons and Symbols of Ancient Mesopotamia: An Illustrated Dictionary*. University of Texas Press. ISBN 0-292-70794-0.

[2] Van der Mierop, Marc (2007). *A History of the Ancient Near East: 3,000–323 BCE*. Blackwell. ISBN 978-1-4051-4911-2.

[3] Wolkstein & Noah Kramer 1993 – a modern, poetic reinterpretation of Inanna myths

[4] Harris, Rivkah (February 1991). "Inanna-Ishtar as Paradox and a Coincidence of Opposites". *History of Religions* **30** (3): 261–278. doi:10.1086/463228. JSTOR 1062957.

[5] Rubio, Gonzalo (1999). "On the Alleged "Pre-Sumerian Substratum"". *Journal of Cuneiform Studies* **51**: 1–16. JSTOR 1359726.

[6] é-an-na = sanctuary ('house' + 'Heaven'[='An'] + genitive) (Halloran 2009)

[7] modern-day Warka, Biblical Erech

[8] Morris Silver. "Temple/Sacred Prostitution in Ancient Mesopotamia Revisited". Academia.edu. Retrieved 2013-08-13.

[9] Encounters in the Gigunu

[10] Black & Green 1992, pp. 156, 169–170

[11] Thorkild 1976

[12] http://www.universetoday.com/22570/venus-the-morning-star/

[13] Cooley, Jeffrey L. (2008). "Inana and Šukaletuda: a Sumerian Astral Myth". *KASKAL* **5**: 161–172. ISSN 1971-8608.

[14] Foxvog, D. (1993). "Astral Dumuzi". In Hallo, William W.; Cohen, Mark E.; Snell, Daniel C.; et al. *The Tablet and the scroll: Near Eastern studies in honor of William W. Hallo* (2nd ed.). CDL Press. p. 106. ISBN 0962001392.

[15] Black & Green 1992, pp. 108–9

[16] Enheduanna pre 2250 BCE "A hymn to Inana (Inana C)". *The Electronic Text Corpus of Sumerian Literature*. 2003. lines 18–28. 4.07.3.

[17] *Voices From the Clay: the development of Assyro-Babylonian Literature*. University of Oklahoma Press, Norman, 1965.

[18] "Enmerkar and the lord of Aratta". *The Electronic Text Corpus of Sumerian Literature*. 2006. 1.8.2.3.

[19] Enmerkar and the lord of Aratta, lines 25–32

[20] Enmerkar and the lord of Aratta, lines 33–104; 108–133

[21] Enmerkar and the lord of Aratta, lines 160–241

[22] Enmerkar and the lord of Aratta, lines 242–372

[23] Enmerkar and the lord of Aratta, lines 373–461

[24] Enmerkar and the lord of Aratta, lines 500–514

[25] Enmerkar and the lord of Aratta, lines 536–577

[26] Especially her Akkadian counterpart Ishtar was represented with the lion as her beast. C.f. Black & Green 1992, p. 109

[27] Postgate, Nicholas (2004). *Early Mesopotamia: Society and Economy at the Dawn of History*. Taylor & Francis. p. 9. ISBN 978-0-415-24587-6.

[28] Attinger, Pascal. Inana et Ebih. *Zeitschrift fur Assyriologie*. 3 1988, pp 164–195

[29] "Inana and Gudam". *The Electronic Text Corpus of Sumerian Literature*. 2003. 1.3.4.

[30] "Inana and An". *The Electronic Text Corpus of Sumerian Literature*. 2003. 1.3.5.

[31] Kilmer, Anne Draffkorn (1971). "How was Queen Ereshkigal tricked? A new interpretation of the Descent of Ishtar". *Ugarit-Forschungen* **3**: 299–309.

[32] Sandars, Nancy K. (1989). *Poems of Heaven and Hell from Ancient Mesopotamia*. Penguin. pp. 162, 164–5. ISBN 0140442499.

[33] Joseph Campbell, *The Hero with a Thousand Faces* (Novato, California: New World Library, 2008), pp. 88–90.

[34] Clyde Hostetter, *Star Trek to Hawa-i'i* (San Luis Obispo, California: Diamond Press, 1991), p. 53)

[35] Mark, Joshua J. (2011). "Inanna's Descent: A Sumerian Tale of Injustice". Ancient History Encyclopedia

[36] Tseretheli, Michael (1935). "The Asianic (Asia Minor) elements in national Georgian paganism". *Georgica* **1** (1): 55–56.

[37] e.g. Frymer-Kensky 1992

[38] Stuckey 2001

[39] White 2013

[40] Hebrew review by Michal Sadan and photos of Inana paintings

[41] "Inana and Ebih". *The Electronic Text Corpus of Sumerian Literature*. 2001. cited in Anne O Nomis (2013). "The Warrior Goddess and her Dance of Domination". *The History & Arts of the Dominatrix*. Mary Egan Publishing. p. 53. ISBN 9780992701000.

[42] See "A Hymn to Inana (Inana C)". *The Electronic Text Corpus of Sumerian Literature*. 2006. lines 70–80. cited in Anne O Nomis 2013, pp. 59–60 Dominatrix Rituals of Gender, Transformation, Ecstasy and Pain

[43] trans. S.N. Kramar, Pritchard, James B., ed. (1969). *Ancient Near Eastern Texts Relating to the Old Testament* (3rd ed.). Princeton University Press. ISBN 0691035032.

2.30.12   References

- Enheduanna. "The Exaltation of Inanna (Inanna B): Translation". *The Electronic Text Corpus of Sumerian Literature*. 2001.

- Frymer-Kensky, Tikva Simone (1992). *In the Wake of the Goddesses: Women, Culture, and the Biblical Transformation of Pagan Myth*. Free Press. ISBN 0029108004.

- Fulco, William J., S.J. "Inanna." In Eliade, Mircea, ed., *The Encyclopedia of Religion*. New York: Macmillan Group, 1987. Vol. 7, 145–146.

- George, Andrew, ed. (1999). *The Epic of Gilgamesh: the Babylonian epic poem and other texts in Akkadian and Sumerian*. Penguin. ISBN 0-14-044919-1.

- "Inana's descent to the nether world: translation". *The Electronic Text Corpus of Sumerian Literature*. Faculty of Oriental Studies, University of Oxford. 2001.

- Jacobsen, Thorkild (1976). *The Treasures of Darkness: A History of Mesopotamian Religion*. Yale University Press. ISBN 978-0-300-02291-9.

- Noah Kramer, Samuel (1988). *History Begins at Sumer: Thirty-Nine Firsts in Recorded History* (3rd ed.). University of Pennsylvania Press. ISBN 978-0-8122-1276-1.

- Leick, Gwendolyn (2013) [1994]. *Sex and Eroticism in Mesopotamian Literature*. Routledge. ISBN 978-1-134-92074-7.

- Mitchell, Stephen. *Gilgamesh:A New English Translation*. New York: Free Press (Div. Simon & Schuster), 2004.

- Stuckey, Johanna (2001). "Inanna and the Huluppu Tree, An Ancient Mesopotamian Narrative of Goddess Demotion". In Devlin-Glass, Frances; McCredden, Lyn. *Feminist Poetics of the Sacred*. American Academy of Religion. ISBN 978-0-19-514468-0.

- White, Gavin (2013). *The Queen of Heaven. A New Interpretatation of the Goddess in Ancient Near Eastern Art*. Solaria. ISBN 978-0955903717.

- Wolkstein, Diana; Noah Kramer, Samuel (1983). *Inanna: Queen of Heaven and Earth*. Harper. ISBN 0-06-090854-8.

- Santo, Suzanne Banay (January 15, 2014). *From the Deep: Queen Inanna Dies and Comes Back to Life Again*. Toronto, Ontario, Canada: Red Butterfly Publications. p. 32. ISBN 9780988091412.

2.30.13   Further reading

- Black, Jeremy (2004). *The Literature of Ancient Sumer*. Oxford University Press. ISBN 978-0-19-926311-0.

- "The Electronic Text Corpus of Sumerian Literature". Faculty of Oriental Studies, University of Oxford. 2003.

- Halloran, John A. (2009). "Sumerian Lexicon Version 3.0".

- Voorbij de Zerken: a Dutch book which "contains" both Ereshkigal and Inanna.

- Pereira, Sylvia Brunton (1981). *Descent to the Goddess*. Inner City Books. ISBN 978-0-919123-05-2. A Jungian interpretation of the process of psychological 'descent and return', using the story of Inanna as translated by Wolkstein & Kramer 1983.

- Ancient Mesopotamian Gods and Goddesses: Inana/Ištar (goddess)

- Clickable map of Mesopotamia

2.31 Ioke (mythology)

In Greek mythology, **Ioke** (Ἰωκή) was the spirit and personification of pursuit. In the *Iliad*, she is one of several warlike personifications portrayed on Athena's aegis, other ones being Phobos, Eris and Alke, alongside the head of Medusa.[1]

The Ancient Greek word ἰωκή is a rare doublet for διωκή "rout, pursuit", from the common verb διώκω "drive, pursue, chase away".[2]

2.31.1 References

[1] Homer, *Iliad*, 5. 738 ff

[2] H. G. Liddel, R. Scott. A Greek-English Lexicon. 10th edition with a revised supplement. Oxford, Clarendon press, 1996, p. 847

2.31.2 External links

- Theoi Project - Ioke

2.32 Ishtar

For other uses, see Ishtar (disambiguation).

Ishtar (English pronunciation /ˈɪʃtɑːr/; Transliteration: ^D*IŠTAR*; Akkadian: 𒀭𒈹 ; Sumerian) is the East Semitic Akkadian, Assyrian and Babylonian goddess of fertility, love, war, and sex.[1] She is the counterpart to the Sumerian Inanna, and the cognate for the Northwest Semitic Aramean goddess Astarte.

2.32.1 Characteristics

Ishtar was the goddess of love, war, fertility, and sexuality.

Ishtar was the daughter of Anu.[2] She was particularly worshipped in northern Mesopotamia, at the Assyrian cities of Nineveh, Ashur and Arbela (Erbil).[2]

Besides the lions on her gate, her symbol is an eight-pointed star.[3]

Old Babylonian period Queen of Night relief, often considered to represent an aspect of Ishtar.

In the Babylonian pantheon, she "was the divine personification of the planet Venus".[2]

Ishtar had many lovers; however, as Guirand notes,

> "Woe to him whom Ishtar had honoured! The fickle goddess treated her passing lovers cruelly, and the unhappy wretches usually paid dearly for the favours heaped on them. Animals, enslaved by love, lost their native vigour: they fell into traps laid by men or were domesticated by them. 'Thou has loved the lion, mighty in strength', says the hero Gilgamesh to Ishtar, 'and thou hast dug for him seven and seven pits! Thou hast loved the steed, proud in battle, and destined him for the halter, the goad and the whip.'
>
> Even for the gods Ishtar's love was fatal. In her youth the goddess had loved Tammuz, god of the harvest, and—if one is to believe Gilgamesh —this love caused the death of Tammuz.[2]

Her cult may have involved sacred prostitution,[4] though this is debatable. Guirand referred to her holy city Uruk as the "town of the sacred courtesans" and to her as the "courtesan of the gods".[2]

Ishtar holding her symbol, Louvre Museum

2.32.2 Descent into the underworld

One of the most famous myths[5] about Ishtar describes her descent to the underworld. In this myth, Ishtar approaches the gates of the underworld and demands that the gatekeeper open them:

> If thou openest not the gate to let me enter,
> I will break the door, I will wrench the lock,
> I will smash the door-posts, I will force the doors.
> I will bring up the dead to eat the living.
> And the dead will outnumber the living.

The gatekeeper hurried to tell Ereshkigal, the Queen of the Underworld. Ereshkigal told the gatekeeper to let Ishtar enter, but "according to the ancient decree".

The gatekeeper let Ishtar into the underworld, opening one gate at a time. At each gate, Ishtar had to shed one article of clothing. When she finally passed the seventh gate, she was naked. In rage, Ishtar threw herself at Ereshkigal, but Ereshkigal ordered her servant Namtar to imprison Ishtar and unleash sixty diseases against her.

One type of depiction of Ishtar/Inanna

After Ishtar descended to the underworld, all sexual activity ceased on earth. The god Papsukal reported the situation to Ea, the king of the gods. Ea created an intersex being called Asu-shu-namir and sent it to Ereshkigal, telling it to invoke "the name of the great gods" against her and to ask for the bag containing the waters of life. Ereshkigal was enraged when she heard Asu-shu-namir's demand, but she had to give it the water of life. Asu-shu-namir sprinkled Ishtar with this water, reviving her. Then, Ishtar passed back through the seven gates, getting one article of cloth-

The lion was her symbol (detail of the Ishtar Gate)

ing back at each gate, and was fully clothed as she exited the last gate.

Here there is a break in the text of the myth, which resumes with the following lines:

> If she (Ishtar) will not grant thee her release,
> To Tammuz, the lover of her youth,
> Pour out pure waters, pour out fine oil;
> With a festival garment deck him that he may play on the flute of lapis lazuli,
> That the votaries may cheer his liver. [his spirit]
> Belili [sister of Tammuz] had gathered the treasure,
> With precious stones filled her bosom.
> When Belili heard the lament of her brother, she dropped her treasure,
> She scattered the precious stones before her,
> "Oh, my only brother, do not let me perish!
> On the day when Tammuz plays for me on the flute of lapis lazuli, playing it for me with the porphyry ring.
> Together with him, play ye for me, ye weepers and lamenting women!
> That the dead may rise up and inhale the incense."

Formerly, scholars[2][6] believed that the myth of Ishtar's descent took place after the death of Ishtar's lover, Tammuz: they thought Ishtar had gone to the underworld to rescue Tammuz. However, the discovery of a corresponding myth[7] about Inanna, the Sumerian counterpart of Ishtar, has thrown some light on the myth of Ishtar's descent, including its somewhat enigmatic ending lines. According to the Inanna myth, Inanna can only return from the underworld if she sends someone back in her place. Demons go with her to make sure she sends someone back. However, each time Inanna runs into someone, she finds him to

be a friend and lets him go free. When she finally reaches her home, she finds her husband Dumuzi (Babylonian Tammuz) seated on his throne, not mourning her at all. In anger, Inanna has the demons take Dumuzi back to the underworld as her replacement. Dumuzi's sister Geshtinanna is grief-stricken and volunteers to spend half the year in the underworld, during which time Dumuzi can go free. The Ishtar myth presumably had a comparable ending, Belili being the Babylonian equivalent of Geshtinanna.[8]

There are intriguing parallels in the Graeco-Roman myths of Orpheus and Persephone.

2.32.3 Ishtar in the Epic of Gilgamesh

The *Epic of Gilgamesh* contains an episode[9] involving Ishtar which portrays her as bad-tempered, petulant and spoiled by her father.

She asks the hero Gilgamesh to marry her, but he refuses, citing the fate that has befallen all her many lovers:

> Listen to me while I tell the tale of your lovers. There was Tammuz, the lover of your youth, for him you decreed wailing, year after year. You loved the many-coloured Lilac-breasted Roller, but still you struck and broke his wing [...] You have loved the lion tremendous in strength: seven pits you dug for him, and seven. You have loved the stallion magnificent in battle, and for him you decreed the whip and spur and a thong [...] You have loved the shepherd of the flock; he made meal-cake for you day after day, he killed kids for your sake. You struck and turned him into a wolf; now his own herd-boys chase him away, his own hounds worry his flanks."[10]

Angered by Gilgamesh's refusal, Ishtar goes up to heaven and complains to her father the high god Anu that Gilgamesh has insulted her. She demands that Anu give her the Bull of Heaven. Anu points out that it was her fault for provoking Gilgamesh, but she warns that if he refuses, she will do exactly what she told the gatekeeper of the underworld she would do if he didn't let her in:

> If you refuse to give me the Bull of Heaven [then] I will break in the doors of hell and smash the bolts; there will be confusion [i.e., mixing] of people, those above with those from the lower depths. I shall bring up the dead to eat food like the living; and the hosts of the dead will outnumber the living."[11]

Anu gives Ishtar the Bull of Heaven, and Ishtar sends it to attack Gilgamesh and his friend Enkidu. Gilgamesh and Enkidu kill the Bull and offer its heart to the Assyro-Babylonian sun-god Shamash.

While Gilgamesh and Enkidu are resting, Ishtar stands upon the walls of the city (which is Uruk) and curses Gilgamesh. Enkidu tears off the Bull's right thigh and throws it in Ishtar's face, saying, "If I could lay my hands on you, it is this I should do to you, and lash your entrails to your side."[12] (Enkidu later dies for this impiety.) Then Ishtar called together "her people, the dancing and singing girls, the prostitutes of the temple, the courtesans,"[12] and had them mourn for the Bull of Heaven.

2.32.4 Comparisons with other deities

Like Ishtar, the Greek Aphrodite and the Aramean Northwestern Semitic Astarte were love goddesses. Donald A. Mackenzie, an early popularizer of mythology, draws a parallel between the love goddess Aphrodite and her "dying god" lover Adonis[13] on one hand, and the love goddess Ishtar and her "dying god" lover Tammuz on the other.[14] Some scholars have suggested that

> the myth of Adonis was derived in post-Homeric times by the Greeks indirectly from the Eastern Semites of Mesopotamia (Assyria and Babylonia), via the Aramean and Canaanite Western Semites, the Semitic title 'Adon', meaning 'lord', having been mistaken for a proper name. This theory, however, cannot be accepted without qualifications.[15]

Joseph Campbell, a more recent scholar of comparative mythology, equates Ishtar, Inanna, and Aphrodite, and he draws a parallel between the Egyptian goddess Isis who nurses Horus, and the Assyrian-Babylonian goddess Ishtar who nurses the god Tammuz.[16]

2.32.5 In other media

Art

The artwork *The Dinner Party* features a place setting for Ishtar.[17]

Books, comics and other literature

In the book and movie *Generation P* by Viktor Pelevin, Ishtar and her legends are one of the main storylines. Ishtar is also a love interest for Destruction of The Endless in

Neil Gaiman's *Sandman* comic book series. In the Japanese manga *Red River*, a young Japanese girl is transported to ancient Hattusa and is mistaken as Ishtar. Ishtar is also seen as a goddess side character helping out the main heroine of the Japanese manga *Loose Relation Between Wizard & Apprentice* to awaken the protagonist's sexual desires.

Movies

Ishtar appears in the movies *Blood Feast* (1963) and *Blood Diner* (1987), although she is referred to as an Egyptian god. The sequel to *Blood Feast*, *Blood Feast 2: All U Can Eat* (2002) also features Ishtar, but it is explained that she is Babylonian, even though "everyone seems to think she's Egyptian." In the movie *The Mole People* (1956), some explorers find an ancient Sumerian people living beneath a mountain, and the people think that Ishtar has sent the explorers. In the movie *Venus Wars*, the antagonist's army is called the Ishtar Army, named from the real Venusian continent "Ishtar Terra". There is also a movie called Ishtar, but the title refers to a fictional country.

Religion

The name Ishtar (including Istar) is still sometimes used as a given name by the Assyrian Christian ethnic minority in Iraq and its surrounds.

Video games

- Ishtar (☒☒☒☒☒, Ishutaru) is a recurring demon/persona in the Japanese *Shin Megami Tensei* video game series, based on Babylonian lore. She appears in 6 games in the series in different iterations.

- In the video game *Catherine*, Ishtar appears as the hostess of a program called "Golden Playhouse" and tells the player the tale of Vincent Brooks, starting the game.

- Ishtar is a character in Namco's video game *The Tower of Druaga* and its sequels. She assists the heroes, Gilgamesh and Ki, on their quest.

- Ishtar is a side character that journeys along with Enoch within El Shaddai: Ascension of the Metatron.

- In the MMORPG *Eve Online*, the *Ishtar* is a Heavy Assault Cruiser of the *Gallente* faction that often draws on mythology for ship names, an advanced combat ship that relies on drones as its primary weapon.

- In the Japanese-exclusive Super Nintendo game *Live A Live*, Ishtar is a strong monster and a minion of the demon lord in the final chapter, appearing as a blonde-haired, masculine young man, holding a heart and attached at the torso to a snake-like creature that is ingesting (or consummating with) its own tail.[18]

- In the video game *Destiny*, Ishtar is a name of a map on planet Venus, a statue of Ishtar appears on this map.[19]

- In the Super Nintendo game Fire Emblem: Genealogy of the Holy War, Ishtar is the daughter of Lord Bloom, King of the Manster District, and Duke of Freege. She is renowned as a powerful thunder mage, due to her being a descendant of the Crusader Tordo. Her status led to her betrothal to the nefarious crown prince of Grannvale, Prince Julius.

2.32.6 See also

- Astaroth

- Gingira

- Inanna

- Lillith

2.32.7 Notes

[1] Wilkinson, p. 24

[2] Guirand, p. 58

[3] Black, Jeremy and Green, Anthony (1992). *Gods, Demons, and Symbols of Ancient Mesopotamia: An Illustrated Dictionary*. ISBN 0-292-70794-0 pp. 156, 169–170.

[4] Day, John (2004). "Does the Old Testament Refer to Sacred Prostitution and Did It Actual Exist in Ancient Israel?". In McCarthy, Carmel; Healey, John F. *Biblical and Near Eastern Essays: Studies in Honour of Kevin J. Cathcart*. Cromwell Press. pp. 2–21. ISBN 0-8264-6690-7. pp. 15-17.

[5] Jastrow

[6] Mackenzie, p. 95–98

[7] Wolkstein and Kramer, p. 52–89

[8] Kirk, p. 109

[9] *Gilgamesh*, p. 85–88

[10] *Gilgamesh*, p. 86

[11] *Gilgamesh*, p. 87

[12] *Gilgamesh*, p. 88

[13] Mackenzie, p. 83

[14] Mackenzie, p. 103

[15] Mackenzie, p. 84

[16] Campbell, p. 70

[17] Place Settings. Brooklyn Museum. Retrieved on 2015-08-06.

[18] http://shrines.rpgclassics.com/snes/lal/finalenem.shtml

[19] https://www.artstation.com/artwork/destiny-ishtar-statue-game-mesh

2.32.8 References

- Campbell, Joseph. *The Masks of God: Occidental Mythology*. New York: Penguin Books, 1976.

- *The Epic of Gilgamesh*. Trans. N. K. Sandars. Harmondsworth: Penguin, 1985.

- Guirand, Felix. "Assyro-Babylonian Mythology". *New Larousse Encyclopedia of Mythology* (trans. Aldington and Ames, London: Hamlyn, 1968), pp. 49–72.

- Jastrow, Morris. "Descent of the Goddess Ishtar into the Lower World" (*The Civilization of Babylonia and Assyria*, 1915). Sacred-Texts. 2 June 2002.

- Kirk, G. S. *Myth: Its Meaning and Functions in Ancient and Other Cultures*. Berkeley: Cambridge UP, 1973.

- Mackenzie, Donald A. *Myths of Babylonia and Assyria*. London: Gresham, 1915.

- Wilkinson, Philip. *Illustrated Dictionary of Mythology*. NY: Dorling Kindersley, 1998.

- Wolkstein and Kramer. *Inanna: Queen of Heaven and Earth*. New York: Harper & Row, 1983.

- Holy Bible: King James Version. Thomas Nelson Camden, 1972.

2.32.9 Further reading

- Powell, Barry. *Classical Myth: Sixth Edition*. Upper Saddle River, NJ: Prentice Hall, 2008.

- The myth of Ishtar's descent into the underworld being read aloud in Babylonian.

2.32.10   External links

- Ancient Mesopotamian Gods and Goddesses: Inana/Ištar (goddess)

- Assyrian origins: discoveries at Ashur on the Tigris: antiquities in the Vorderasiatisches Museum, Berlin, an exhibition catalog from The Metropolitan Museum of Art Libraries (fully available online as PDF), which contains material on Ishtar

2.33   Kaalratri

The combined 9 forms of Durga create Navdurga--who killed the demon Mahishasura

Maa Kala Ratri is the seventh form amongst the Navadurga or the nine forms of the Hindu goddess Parvati or (Shakti). She is worshipped during the nine nights of Navratri celebrations.[1] The seventh day of Navratri pooja (ritual) is dedicated to Durga Kalaratri and she is considered the most violent form[2] of Goddess Durga. Kalaratri is the one of the fiercest forms of Durga and her appearance itself evokes fear.

This form of Goddess is believed to be the destroyer of all demon entities, ghosts, spirits and negative energies, who flee upon knowing of her arrival.[3]

2.33.1   Mythology

Kaal Ratri means the One who is "the Death of Kaal". Here Kaal is dedicated as time & death and *ratri* means night. Kaal Ratri is the one who destroys ignorance and removes darkness. This form primarily depicts that life also has a dark side – the violence of Mother Nature, creating havoc and removing all dirt. She is also known as *Shubhamkari* or "good-doing".

2.33.2   Story

Once there were two demons named Shumbha and Nishumbha, who invaded devaloka and defeated the demigods; Indra the ruler of the demigods, along with the demigods went to The Himalayas for getting help, to get back their abode. They prayed to goddess Parvati. Parvati heard their prayer, while she was bathing, so she created another goddess Chandi or Ambika to help them out. Goddess Chandi then went to kill the cruel demons. In the battlefield when Chanda-Munda sent by Shumbha and Nishumbha, came to battle her, she created a dark goddess Kali or Kaalratri. Kali killed them acquiring the name Chamunda. A demon named Rakhtbeej arrived, who had the boon that if any drop of blood of him fell on the ground another Rakhtbeej would be created. When Kaalratri attacked on him, his blood would create several clones of him. This way it was impossible to defeat him. So while battling, furious Kaalratri whenever attacked him drank his blood to prevent it from falling down and thus she killed Raktabeej and helping goddess Chandi to kill Shumbha and Nishumbha and give back the demigods a safe place to live.

Another legend says that, once there was a demon named Durgasur who tried to attack Kailash, the abode of Parvati in the absence of Shiva. Parvati got to know about this and created Kaalratri and said her to go and warn Durgasur, when Kaalratri reached there Durgasur's guards tried to capture her but she grew big in her original form and said Durgasur that his death was nearby. After that when Durgasur came to invade Kailash, Parvati battled him and killed him gaining the name Durga. Here Kaalratri serves as an agent who gives the message and warning from Parvati to Durgasur.

The complexion of Maa Kalaratri is like dark night with bountiful hair and heavenly shaped form, and, she has four hands. The left two hands holds a scimitar and a thunderbolt, and the right two are in the mudras of "giving" (varadamudra) and "protecting" (abhayamudra). She wears a necklace that shines like the moon. Kalaratri has three eyes which emanate rays like lightning. Flames appear through her nostrils when she inhales or exhales.[4] Her mount is the donkey, often considered as a donkey's corpse.

Blue, red and white colors should be used to wear on this day.

The appearance of Maa Kalaratri can be seen as being very dangerous for evil-doers. But she always bears good fruits for her devotees who are not afraid of her and all should avoid fear when faced with her, for she removes the darkness of worry from life of her *bhaktas* or worshipers. Her worship on 7th day of Navratri has very much a high importance to Yogis and Sādhakas. Yogis & Sādhaka penance on Shahtra Chakra on this day. For the worshipers on this day door opens of every siddhi, power and practice in the universe.

2.33.3 Temples

- Kalratri -Varanasi Temple, D.8/17, Kalika Galli, which is a lane parallel to Annapurna – Vishwanath

2.33.4 See also

- Kaal Bhairav

2.33.5 References

[1] The Seventh form of Durga

[2] "Maa Kaal Ratri". jai-maa-durge.blogspot.com. Retrieved 19 December 2012.

[3] Saraswati, Yogi Ananda. "Kalaratri". vedicgoddess.weebly.com. Retrieved 19 December 2012.

[4] Rampuri, Baba. "Navdurga – the nine forms of Durga". rampuri.com. Retrieved 19 December 2012.

2.34 Katyayini

Katyayini is the sixth form amongst the Navadurga or the nine forms of Hindu goddess Parvati or (Shakti), worshipped during the Navratri celebrations.[1] this is the second name given for Parvati in amarakosha, the Sanskrit lexicon. (uma katyayani gaouri kali haimavathi iiswari) In Shaktism she is associated with the fierce forms of Shakti or Durga, a Warrior goddess, which also includes Bhadrakali and Chandika,[2] and traditionally she is associated with the colour red, as with Goddess Durga, the primordial form of Shakti, a fact also mentioned in Patanjali's *Mahabhashya* on Pāṇini, written in 2nd BCE.[3]

She is first mentioned in the Taittiriya Aranyaka part of the Krishna Yajurveda. Skanda Purana mentions her being created out of the spontaneous anger of Gods, which eventually led to slaying the demon, Mahishasura, mounted of the lion given to her by Goddess Gauri. This occasion is celebrated during the annual Durga Puja festival in most parts of India.[4]

Her exploits are described in the *Devi-Bhagavata Purana* and *Devi Mahatmyam*, part of the Markandeya Purana attributed to sage Markandeya Rishi, who wrote it in Sanskrit ca. 400-500 CE. Over a period of time, her presence was also felt in Buddhist and Jain texts and several Tantric text, especially the Kalika Purana (10th century), which mentions *Uddiyana* or *Odradesa* (Odisha), as the seat of Goddess Katyayani and Lord Jagannath .[5]

In Hindu traditions like Yoga and the Tantra, she is ascribed to the sixth Ajna Chakra or the 'Third eye chakra', and her blessings are invoked by concentrating on this point.[1]

2.34.1 Mythology

According to ancient legends, she was born a daughter of Katyayana Rishi, born in the Katya lineage, thus called Katyayani, "daughter of Katyayana" . Elsewhere in texts like the Kalika Purana, it is mentioned that it was Rishi Kaytyayana who first worshipped her, hence she came to known as '*Katyayani*. In either case, she is a demonstration or apparition of the Durga, and is worshipped on the sixth day of Navratri festival.[1][6]

Devi Mahatmya *in Sanskrit, the central text of Shaktism, dated 11 CE*

The *Vamana Purana* mentions the legend of her creation in great detail: "When the gods had sought Vishnu in their distress, he, and at his command Shiva, Brahma, and the other gods, emitted such flames from their eyes and countenances that a mountain of effulgence was formed, from which became manifest Katyayini, refulgent as a thousand suns, having three eyes, black hair, and eighteen arms. Siva gave her his trident, Vishnu a Sudarshan Chakra or discus, Varuna a shankha, a conch-shell, Agni a dart, Vayu a bow, Surya a quiver full of arrows, Indra a thunderbolt, Kuvera a mace, Brahma a rosary and water-pot, Kala a shield and sword, Visvakarma a battle-axe and other weapons. Thus armed, and adored by the gods, Katyayini proceeded to the Vindhya hills. There, the asuras Chanda and Munda saw her, and captivated by her beauty they so described her to Mahishasura, their king, that he was anxious to obtain her. On asking for her hand, she told him she must be won in fight. He came, and fought; at length Durga dismounted from her lion, and sprang upon the back of Mahisha, who was in the form of a buffalo, and with her tender feet so smote him on the head that he fell to the ground senseless, when she cut off his head with her sword, and hence was called *Mahishasuramardini*, the Slayer of Mahishasura.,[4] the legend also finds mention in *Varaha Purana*, and the classical text of Shaktism the *Devi-Bhagavata Purana*[7]

According to 'Tantras, she revealed through the North face, which is one six Faces of Shiva. This face is s blue in color and with three eyes, and also revealed the Devis, Dakshinakalika, Mahakali, Guhyakah, Smashanakalika, Bhadrakali, Ekajata, Ugratara (fierce Tara), Taritni, Chhinnamasta, Nilasarasvati (Blue Saraswati), Durga, Jayadurga, Navadurga, Vashuli, Dhumavati, Vishalakshi, Gauri, Bagalamukhi, Pratyangira, Matangi, Mahishasuramardini, their rites and Mantras.[8]

Elsewhere in history, Katyayani and Maitreyi are mentioned as a wives of Sage Yajnavalkya (याज्ञवल्क्य) of Vedic India, credited with the authorship of the Shatapatha Brahmana[9]

2.34.2 Worship

The *Bhagavata Purana* in 10th Canto, 22nd Chapter, describes the legend of *Katyayani Vrata*, where young marriageable daughters (gopis) of the cowherd men of Gokula in Braja, worshipped Goddess Katyayani and took a *vrata* or vow, during the entire month of *Margashirsha*, the first month of the winter season, to get Lord Krishna as their husband. During the month, they ate only unspiced khichri, and after bathing in the Yamuna at sunrise, made an earthen deity of the goddess on the riverbank, and worshipped the idol with aromatic substances like sandalwood pulp, and lamps, fruits, betel nuts, newly grown leaves, and fragrant garlands and incense. This follows the episode where Krishna takes away their clothes while they were bathing in the Yamuna River.[10][11]

She is worshiped as the Adi shakti swaroop who if you make vow of fasting, would give you the husband you have wished and prayed for. The fasting, called Kātyāyanī-vrata is made for a whole month, offering such things as sandal, flowers, incense, etc.

"During the month of Mārgaśīrṣa, every day early in the morning the young daughters of the cowherds (gopis) would take one another's hands and, singing of Krishna's transcendental qualities, go to the Yamunā (Jamuna) to bathe. Desiring to obtain Krishna as their husband, they would then worship the goddess Kātyāyanī with incense, flowers and other items".

Each day they rose at dawn. Calling out to one another by name, they all held hands and loudly sang the glories of krishna while going to the Kālindī (Kalindi—personified Jamuna) to take their bath.

The Adolescent Virgin Goddess in the southern tip of India, Devi Kanya Kumari is said to be the avatar of Devi Katyayani. She is the goddess of penance and Sanyas. During the Pongal (Thai Pongal), a harvest festival, which coincides with the Makara Sankranthi, and is celebrated in Tamil Nadu, young girls prayed for rain and prosperity and throughout the month, they avoided milk and milk products. Women used to bath early in the morning, and worshiped the idol of Goddess Katyayani, carved out of wet sand. The penance ended on the first day of the month of Thai (January–February) in Tamil calendar.[12]

2.34.3 Temples

- Sri Katyayani Peeth Temple, Vrindavan , (U.P) [13]

- Sri Katyayani Baneshwar Temple, Aversa, Karnataka, built in AD 1510, original idols brought from Goa during Portuguese rule [14]

- Chhatarpur Temple, Delhi, built 1974.

- Sri Kartyayani Temple, Cherthala, Alappuzha, Kerala, India

- Sri Katyayani Temple, Kolhapur, Maharashtra, India

- Sri Kathyayini Amman Temple, Marathurai, Thanjavure, Tanjore District, , Tamil Nadu ,[15][16]

- Sri Katyayani Shakthipeeth Adhar Devi (Arbuda Devi) Temple, Mount Abu, Aravali Range, Rajasthan, India.,[17][18]

2.34.4 References

[1] The Sixth form of Durga

[2] *Religious beliefs and practices of North India during the early medieval period*, by Vibhuti Bhushan Mishra. Published by BRILL, 1973. ISBN 90-04-03610-5. *Page 22.*

[3] *Devī-māhātmya: the crystallization of the goddess tradition*, by Thomas B. Coburn. Published by Motilal Banarsidass Publ., 1988. ISBN 81-208-0557-7. *Page 240.*

[4] CHAPTER VII. UMĀ. *Hindu Mythology, Vedic and Puranic*, by W.J. Wilkins. 1900. *page 306*

[5] Uddiyana Pitha *Iconography of the Buddhist Sculpture of Orissa: Text*, by Thomas E. Donaldson, Indira Gandhi National Centre for the Arts. Abhinav Publications, 2001. ISBN 81-7017-406-6. *Page 9.*

[6] Forms of Durga

[7] *The triumph of the goddess: the canonical models and theological visions of the Devī-Bhāgavata Purāṇa*, by Cheever Mackenzie Brown. SUNY Press, 1990. ISBN 0-7914-0363-7. *Page 97.*

[8] Chapter Six: Shakti and Shakta *Shakti and Shâkta*, by Arthur Avalon (Sir John Woodroffe), 1918.

[9] LECTURE II - THE MYSTICISM OF THE UPANISHADS *Hindu Mysticism*, by S.N. Dasgupta, 1927.

[10] Sri Katyayani Vrata Story Bhagavata Purana 10th Canto 22nd Chapter.

[11] *Ancient Indian tradition & mythology: Puranas in translation*, by Jagdish Lal Shastri, Arnold Kunst, G. P. Bhatt, Ganesh Vasudeo Tagare. Published by Motilal Banarsidass, 1970. *Page 1395.*

[12] History of Pongal Festival

[13] http://www.katyayanipeeth.org.in

[14] http://www.shreekatyayani.org/

[15] Temple details and description from Dinamalar composition on temples

[16] http://temple.dinamalar.com/en/new_en.php?id=1531

[17] http://hill-temples.blogspot.in/2010/07/adhar-arbuda-devi-temple.html

[18] http://astrobix.com/hindumarg/69-अरबुदा_देवी_मन्दिर_ _Arbuda_Devi_Temple__Arbuda_Devi_Mandir_ _Arbuda_Devi.html

2.34.5 External links

- Katyayani Peeth, Vrindavan

- Eulogy to Katyayani, ascribed to Pandava Brothers from Devi Purana

2.35 Kaumari

Kaumari is also known as Kumari, Kartikeyani, Karthikeyani, Jagadambika Jagdamba and/or Ambika is the power of Kumar (Kartikeya), the God of war. Kaumari rides a peacock and has four or twelve arms. She holds a spear, axe, scimitar, trident, bow, arrow, sword, shield, mace, lotus, longsword, discus and conch shell.she killed the deamons with her axe trident javelin etc. she is famous in the jagdamba form

2.36 Korravai

Kotrawi (Kotṛawi) was the ancient goddess of war and victory and mother of Murugan, the Hindu god of war, now patron god of Tamil Nadu.[1] The earliest references to Korrawi are found in the ancient Tamil grammar Tolkappiyam, considered to be the earliest work of the ancient Sangam literature. Korrawi is identified with goddess Durga. In early iconography, Korrawi is presented as fierce and bloodthirsty .

To illustrate Korrawi's place in the metaphysical world of the earliest sources, Kersenboom-Story provides a "tentative" fivefold classification of the disposition of the major spiritual powers.

> According to the early Tamil literature, the divine manifests itself in various shapes, shades and degrees of intensity. In most cases it is thought of as a power that is highly ambivalent: possibly benevolent, but usually dangerous and even malevolant. The most striking aspect of man's relation to these different manifestations is his attempt to control them by means of some type of 'dramatic performance'. True evil is too powerful to be dealt with by humans and has to be subdued by the god Murugaṇ. ... Tentatively, we classify the manifestations of the divine as follows:
>
> 1. benevolent: the god Murugaṇ; the king
> 2. mildly ambivalent: hero-stone; *kantu* (stump of a tree)
> 3. ambivalent: *aṇaṇku* 'sacred power'
> 4. dangerous: *pēy*, *pūtam* (demon); Korṛavai
> 5. evil: *cūr*, Cūraṇ[2]

2.36.1 See also

- Hindu deities

2.36.2 Notes and references

[1] "Korrawi was perhaps the earliest and the most widely worshipped goddess of the ancient Tamil people." Tiwari (1985).

[2] Kersenboom-Story (1987): 10–11.

2.36.3 Bibliography

- Mahalakshmi, R. (2009). "Caṅkam literature as a social prism: an interrogation". Chapter 3 (29–41) in

Brajadulal Chattopadhyaya (editor). *A Social History of Early India*. Pearson Education, India.

- Harle, James C. (1963). "Durgā, Goddess of Victory". *Artibus Asiae* **26** (3/4): 237–246. doi:10.2307/3248984. JSTOR 3248984.

- Kersenboom-Story, Saskia C. (1987). *Nityasumaṅgalī: devadasi tradition in South India*. Motilal Banarsidass.

- Kinsley, David R. (1988). *Hindu goddesses: visions of the divine feminine in the Hindu religious tradition*. Hermeneutics: Studies in the History of Religions **12**. University of California Press.

- Tiwari, Jagdish Narain (1985). *Goddess Cults in Ancient India (with special reference to the first seven centuries A.D.)*. Sundeep Prakashan. [Adapted from his PhD thesis accepted by the Australian National University in 1971.]

2.37   Lua (goddess)

In Roman mythology, **Lua** was a goddess to whom soldiers sacrificed captured weapons.[1] She is sometimes referred to as "Lua Saturni", which makes her a consort of Saturn.[1] It may be that Lua was merely an alternative name for Ops.[2]

2.37.1   References

[1] Daly, Kathleen N.; Rengel, Marian (2009). *Greek and Roman Mythology, A to Z*. Infobase Publishing. p. 88. ISBN 1438128002. Retrieved 2014-07-05.

[2] Myth Index - Lua

2.38   Macha

For other uses, see Macha (disambiguation).

Macha (Irish pronunciation: [ˈmaxə]) is a goddess of ancient Ireland, associated with war, horses, sovereignty, and the sites of Armagh and Eamhain Mhacha in County Armagh, which are named after her. A number of figures called Macha appear in Irish mythology, legend and historical tradition, all believed to derive from the same deity. The name is presumably derived from Proto-Celtic *makajā denoting "a plain" (genitive *makajās "of the plain").[1]

"Macha Curses the Men of Ulster", Stephen Reid's illustration from Eleanor Hull's The Boys' Cuchulainn *(1904)*

2.38.1   Macha, daughter of Partholón

A poem in the *Lebor Gabála Érenn* mentions Macha as one of the daughters of Partholón, leader of the first settlement of Ireland after the flood, although it records nothing about her.[2]

2.38.2   Macha, wife of Nemed

Various sources record a second Macha as the wife of Nemed, leader of the second settlement of Ireland after the flood. She was the first of Nemed's people to die in Ireland – twelve years after their arrival according to Geoffrey Keating,[3] twelve days after their arrival according to the *Annals of the Four Masters*.[4] She is said to have given her name to the city of Armagh (*Ard Mhacha*—"Macha's high place") – where she was buried.

2.38.3 Macha, daughter of Ernmas

Macha, daughter of Ernmas, of the Tuatha Dé Danann, appears in many early sources. She is often mentioned together with her sisters, "Badb and Morrigu, whose name was Anand."[5] The three (with varying names) are often considered a triple goddess associated with war.[6] *O'Mulconry's Glossary*, a thirteenth-century compilation of glosses from medieval manuscripts preserved in the *Yellow Book of Lecan*, describes Macha as "one of the three *morrígna*" (the plural of *Morrígan*), and says the term *Mesrad Machae*, "the mast [acorn crop] of Macha", refers to "the heads of men that have been slaughtered." A version of the same gloss in MS H.3.18 identifies Macha with Badb, calling the trio "raven women" who instigate battle.[7] Keating explicitly calls them "goddesses",[8] but medieval Irish tradition was keen to remove all trace of pre-Christian religion. Macha is said to have been killed by Balor of the Evil Eye during the battle with the Fomorians.[9][10]

2.38.4 Macha Mong Ruad

Macha Mong Ruad ("red mane"), daughter of Áed Rúad, was, according to medieval legend and historical tradition, the only queen in the List of High Kings of Ireland. Her father rotated the kingship with his cousins Díthorba and Cimbáeth, seven years at a time. Áed died after his third stint as king, and when his turn came round again, Macha claimed the kingship. Díthorba and Cimbáeth refused to allow a woman to take the throne, and a battle ensued. Macha won, and Díthorba was killed. She won a second battle against Díthorba's sons, who fled into the wilderness of Connacht. She married Cimbáeth, with whom she shared the kingship. She pursued Díthorba's sons alone, disguised as a leper, and overcame each of them in turn when they tried to have sex with her, tied them up, and carried the three of them bodily to Ulster. The Ulstermen wanted to have them killed, but Macha instead enslaved them and forced them to build the stronghold of Emain Macha (Navan Fort near Armagh), to be the capital of the Ulaid, marking out its boundaries with her brooch (explaining the name *Emain Macha* as *eó-muin Macha* or "Macha's neck-brooch").[11] Macha ruled together with Cimbáeth for seven years, until he died of plague at Emain Macha, and then a further fourteen years on her own, until she was killed by Rechtaid Rígderg.[12][13] The *Lebor Gabála* synchronises her reign to that of Ptolemy I Soter (323–283 BC).[14] The chronology of Keating's *Foras Feasa ar Éirinn* dates her reign to 468–461 BC, the *Annals of the Four Masters* to 661–654 BC.

Marie-Louise Sjoestedt writes of this figure: "In the person of this second Macha we discover a new aspect of the local goddess, that of the warrior and dominator; and this is combined with the sexual aspect in a specific manner which reappears in other myths, the male partner or partners being dominated by the female."[15]

2.38.5 Macha, wife of Cruinniuc

Macha, daughter of Sainrith mac Imbaith, was the wife of Cruinniuc, an Ulster farmer. After Cruinniuc's first wife died, she appeared at his house and, without speaking, began acting as his wife. As long as they were together Cruinniuc's wealth increased. When he went to a festival organised by the king of Ulster, she warned him that she would only stay with him so long as he did not mention her to anyone, and he promised to say nothing. However, during a chariot race, he boasted that his wife could run faster than the king's horses. The king heard, and demanded she be brought to put her husband's boast to the test. Despite being heavily pregnant, she raced the horses and beat them, giving birth to twins on the finish line. Thereafter the capital of Ulster was called *Emain Macha*, or "Macha's twins" (in spite of the conflicting story according to which Emain Macha was named after "Macha's neck brooch"). She cursed the men of Ulster to suffer her labour pains in the hour of their greatest need, which is why none of the Ulstermen but the semi-divine hero Cúchulainn were able to fight in the *Táin Bó Cuailnge* (Cattle Raid of Cooley).[16] This Macha is particularly associated with horses—it is perhaps significant that twin colts were born on the same day as Cúchulainn, and that one of his chariot-horses was called Liath Macha or "Macha's Grey"—and she is often compared with the Welsh mythological figure Rhiannon.

2.38.6 See also

- Cliodna
- Grian
- Mongfind

2.38.7 References

[1] Proto-Celtic lexicon Archived 27 September 2007 at the Wayback Machine

[2] *Lebor Gabála Érenn* §38

[3] Geoffrey Keating, *Foras Feasa ar Éirinn* 1.7

[4] *Annals of the Four Masters* M2850

[5] *Lebor Gabála Érenn* §62, 64

[6] James MacKillop, *Dictionary of Celtic Mythology*, Oxford University Press, 1998, pp. 281–282

[7] Angelique Gulermovich Epstein, *War Goddess: The Morrí-gan and her Germano-Celtic Counterparts*, September 1998, pp. 49–52.

[8] Geoffrey Keating, *Foras Feasa ar Éirinn* 1.11

[9] *Lebor Gabála Érenn §60, 62, 64*

[10] Whitley Stokes (ed & trans), *The Second Battle of Moytura*, p. 101

[11] Eugene O'Curry, *Lectures on the Manuscript Materials of Ancient Irish History*, 1861, Appendix No. XXXVIII

[12] Geoffrey Keating, *Foras Feasa ar Éirinn* 1.27-1.28

[13] *Annals of the Four Masters* M4532-4546

[14] R. A. Stewart Macalister (ed. & trans.), *Lebor Gabála Érenn: The Book of the Taking of Ireland Part V*, Irish Texts Society, 1956, p. 263-267

[15] Sjoestedt, Marie-Louise; (Translated by Myles Dillon) (1982). *Gods and Heroes of the Celts* (second ed.). Berkeley, CA: Turtle Island Foundation. pp. 28–9. ISBN 0-913666-52-1.

[16] "The Debility of the Ulstermen"

2.39 Maheshvari

Maheshwari is the power of Lord Mahesh (Shiva), also known as Maheshwar. Maheshwari is also known by the names Raudri, Rudrani, Shankari, Shivaa and Maheshi, derived from Shiva's few names of Rudra, Shiv, Shankar and Mahesh. Maheshwari is depicted seated on Nandi (the bull) and has two, four or six hands. The white complexioned, the three eyed Goddess holds a trident, drum, a garland of beads, drinking vessel, axe and a skull-bowl. She is adorned with serpent bracelets, the crescent moon and a headdress formed of piled, matted hair, with a serpent on it. And just like Lord Shiva, she also wears a serpent around her neck.

2.40 Matrikas

This article is about Hindu goddesses called *mātṛkā*s. For other use, see matrka.

Matrikas (**Matrika** singular, Sanskrit: mātṛkā, मातृका "mother"), also called **Matara** (Sanskrit: mātaraḥ plural, मातर:) and **Matri** (mātṛ, मातृ singular), is a group of Hindu goddesses who are always depicted together.[2] Since they are usually depicted as a heptad, they are called **Saptamatrika(s)** (Sanskrit: saptamātṛkāḥ, सप्तमातृका:, "seven mothers"): Brahmani, Vaishnavi, Maheshvari, Indrani, Kaumari, Varahi, Chamunda and Narasimhi. However, they

may sometimes be eight (**Ashtamatrika(s)**: ashtamātṛkāh, अष्टमातृका:, "eight mothers").[3] Whereas in South India, Saptamatrika worship is prevalent, the Ashtamatrika are venerated in Nepal.[4]

The Matrikas assume paramount significance in the goddess-oriented sect of Hinduism, Tantrism.[5] In Shaktism, they are "described as assisting the great Shakta Devi (goddess) in her fight with demons."[6] Some scholars consider them Shaiva goddesses.[7] They are also connected with the worship of warrior god Skanda.[8] In most early references, the Matrikas are described as having inauspicious qualities and often described as dangerous. They come to play a protective role in later mythology, although some of their inauspicious and wild characteristics still persist in these accounts.[9] Thus, they represent the prodigiously fecund aspect of nature as well as its destructive force aspect.[10]

In the 6th century encyclopedia Brihat-Samhita, Varahamihira says that "Mothers are to be made with cognizance of (different major Hindu) gods corresponding to their names."[11] They are associated with these gods as their spouses or their energies (*Shaktis*).[10] Originally believed to be a personification of the seven stars of the star cluster the Pleiades, they became quite popular by the seventh century and a standard feature of goddess temples from the ninth century onwards.[12]

2.40.1 Origins and development

According to Jagdish Narain Tiwari and Dilip Chakravati, the Matrikas were existent as early as the Vedic period and the Indus Valley civilization. Coins with rows of seven feminine deities or priestesses are cited as evidence for the theory.[13][14] A Hindu text known as the Rigveda (IX 102.4) speaks of a group of seven Mothers who control the preparation of Soma, but the earliest clear description appears in some layers of the epic Mahabharata (dated to 1st century AD).[15][16] Wangu believes that Matrika description in Mahabharata, is rooted in the group of seven females depicted on Indus valley seals.[5] It was assumed that the people locally worshipped these goddesses, such an example is also described in Zimmer Heinrich book *The Art Of Indian Asia*, about the seven shrines of seven Mother Goddesses worshipped locally. By the fifth century, all these goddesses were incorporated in mainstream orthodox Hinduism as Tantric deities.[17][18] David Kinsley proposes that the Matrikas may be non-Aryan or at least non-Brahmanical (orthodox Hinduism), local village goddesses, who were being assimilated in the mainstream. He cites two reasons for his assertion: their description in Mahabharata as dark in colour, speaking foreign languages and living in "peripheral areas" and their association with non-Brahmanical god

Varahi, one of the Matrikas

Skanda and his father, Shiva, who though Vedic has non-Brahmanical attributes.[19] Sara L. Schastok suggests that Matrikas maybe inspired by the concept of Yakshas, who are associated with Skanda and Kubera – both are often portrayed with the Matrikas.[20] In contrast to Indus valley origins theory, Bhattacharyya notes:

> [The] cult of the Female Principle was a major aspect of Dravidian religion, The concept of Shakti was an integral part of their religion [...] The cult of the *Sapta Matrika*, or Seven Divine Mothers, which is an integral part of the Shakta religion, may be of Dravidian inspiration.[21]

The Sapta-Matrikas were earlier connected with Skanda (Kumara) and in later times, associated with the sect of Shiva himself.[8] During the Kushana period (1st to 3rd century), the sculptural images of the matrikas first appear in stone. The Kushana images merged from the belief in *Balagraha* (lit "destroyers of children") worship related to conception, birth, diseases and protection of children. The Balagraha tradition included the worship of the infant Skanda with the Matrikas. The goddesses were considered as personifications of perils, related to children and thus, were pacified by worship. The Kushana images emphasize the maternal as well as destructive characteristics of the Matrikas through their emblems and weapons. They appear to be an undifferentiated sculptural group but develop in standard and complex iconographic representation during the following Gupta period.[22]

In the Gupta period (3rd to 6th century A.D.), folk images of Matrikas became important in villages.[23] The diverse folk goddesses of the soldiers like Matrikas were acknowledged by the Gupta rulers and their images were carved on royal monuments in order to strengthen the loyalty and adherence of the armed forces.[24] The Gupta kings Skandagupta and Kumaragupta I (c. second half of fifth century) made Skanda (Kumara)[b] their model and elevated the position of Skanda's foster mothers, the Matrikas from a cluster of folk goddesses to court goddesses.[25] Since the fourth century, Parhari, Madhya Pradesh had a rock-cut shrine been solely devoted to the Sapta Matrika.[26]

The Western Ganga Dynasty (350–1000 CE) kings of Karnataka built many Hindu temples along with *saptamatrika* carvings[27] and memorials, containing sculptural details of *saptamatrikas*.[28] The evidence of Matrika sculptures is further pronounced in the Gurjara–Patiharas (8th to 10th century A.D.) and Chandella period (8th to 12th century A.D.).[29] The Chalukyas claimed to have been nursed by the Sapta Matrikas. It was a popular practice to link South Indian royal family lineage to a Northern kingdom in ancient times.[30] During the Chalukya period (11th to 13th century), all Matrikas continued to figure among the deity sculptures of this period. The Kadambas and Early Chalukyas from the fifth century praise the Matrikas in their preambles, as giver of powers to defeat enemies.[31][32] In most of the relevant texts, their exact number has not been specified, but gradually their number and names became increasingly crystallized and seven goddesses were identified as matrikas, albeit some references indicate eight or even sixteen Matrikas.[33] Laura Kristine Chamberlain (now Laura K. Amazzone) cites:

> The inconsistency in the number of Matrikas found in the valley [Indus] today (seven, eight, or nine) possibly reflects the localization of goddesses [.] Although the Matrikas are mostly grouped as seven goddesses over the rest of the Indian Subcontinent, an eighth Matrikas has

sometimes been added in Nepal to represent the eight cardinal directions. In Bhaktapur, a city in the Kathmandu Valley, a ninth Matrika is added to the set to represent the center.[34]

2.40.2 Iconography

The Goddess Ambika (here identified with: Durga or Chandi) Leading the Eight Matrikas in Battle Against the Demon Raktabija, Folio from a Devi Mahatmya – (top row, from the left) Narasinhmi, Vaishnavi, Kaumari, Maheshvari, Brahmani. (bottom row, from left) Varahi, Aindri and Chamunda or Kali, Ambika. on the right, demons arising from Raktabija's blood

The iconographical features of the Matrikas have been described in Hindu scriptures such as Puranas and Agamas and the epic Mahabharata. Puranas like Varaha Purana, Agni Purana,[35] Matsya Purana, Vishnudharmottara Purana and Devi Mahatmya, a part of Markandeya Purana as well as Agamas such as Amsumadbhedagama, Surabhedagama, Purvakarnagama and Rupamandana describe the Matrikas.

The **Ashta-Matrika** or **Ashta-Matara** as described in Devi Mahatmya is given below.[36]

1. **Brahmani** (Sanskrit: ब्रह्माणी, Brahmânī) or **Brahmi** (Sanskrit: ब्राह्मि, Brāhmī) is the Shakti (power) of the creator god Brahma. She is depicted yellow in colour and with four heads. She may be depicted with four or six arms. Like Brahma, she holds a rosary or noose and kamandalu (water pot) or lotus stalk or a book or bell and is seated on a hamsa (identified with a swan or goose) as her vahana (mount or vehicle). She is also shown seated on a lotus with the hamsa on her banner. She wears various ornaments and is distinguished by her basket-shaped crown called *karaṇḍa mukuṭa*.

2. **Vaishnavi** (Sanskrit: वैष्णवी, Vaiṣṇavī), the power of the preserver-god Vishnu, is described as seated on the Garuda (eagle-man) and having four or six arms. She holds Shankha (conch), chakra (Discus), mace and lotus and bow and sword or her two arms are in *varada* mudra (Blessing hand gesture) and *abhaya* mudra ("No-fear" hand gesture). Like Vishnu, she is heavily adorned with ornaments like necklaces, anklets, earrings, bangles etc. and a cylindrical crown called *kirita mukuṭa*.

3. **'Maheshvari'** (Sanskrit: माहेश्वरी, Māheśvarī) is the power of god Shiva, also known as Maheshvara. Maheshvari is also known by the names **Raudri**, **Rudrani** and **Maheshi**, derived from Shiva's names Rudra and Mahesh. Maheshvari is depicted seated on Nandi (the bull) and has four or six hands. The white complexioned, *Trinetra* (three eyed) goddess holds a Trishula (trident), Damaru (drum), Akshamala (A garland of beads), Panapatra (drinking vessel) or axe or an antelope or a kapala (skull-bowl) or a serpent and is adorned with serpent bracelets, the crescent moon and the *jaṭā mukuṭa* (A headdress formed of piled, matted hair).

4. **Indrani** (Sanskrit: इन्द्राणी, Indrāṇī), also known as **Aindri**, (Sanskrit: ऐन्द्री, Aindrī), **Mahendri**, **Shakri**, **Shachi'** and **Vajri**, is the power of the Indra, the Lord of the heaven. Seated on a charging elephant, Aindri, is depicted dark-skinned, with two or four or six arms. She is depicted as having two or three or like Indra, a thousand eyes. She is armed with the Vajra (thunderbolt), goad, noose and lotus stalk. Adorned with variety of ornaments, she wears the *kirita mukuṭa*.

5. **'Kaumari'** (Sanskrit: कौमारी, Kaumārī), also known as **Kumari**, **Karttikeyani** and **Ambika**[37] is the power of Kumara (Kartikeya or Skanda), the god of war. Kaumari rides a peacock and has four or twelve arms. She holds a spear, axe, a Shakti (power) or Tanka (silver coins) and bow. She is sometimes depicted six-headed like Kumara and wears the cylindrical crown.

6. **Varahi** (Sanskrit: वाराही, Vārāhī) or **Vairali** is described as the power of Varaha – the boar-headed form of Vishnu or Yama – the god of death, has a boar head on a human body and rides a ram or a buffalo. She holds a Danda (rod of punishment) or plough, goad, a Vajra or a sword, and a Panapatra. Sometimes, she carries a bell, chakra, chamara (a yak's tail) and a bow. She wears a crown called *karaṇḍa mukuṭa* with other ornaments.

7. **Chamunda** (Sanskrit: चामुण्डा, Cāmuṇḍā), also known as **Chamundi** and **Charchika** is the power of Devi (Chandi). She is very often identified with Kali and is similar in her appearance and habit.[38] The identification with Kali is explicit in Devi

Mahatmya.[39] The black coloured Chamunda is described as wearing a garland of severed heads or skulls (Mundamala) and holding a Damaru (drum), trishula (trident), sword and pānapātra (drinking-vessel). Riding a jackal or standing on a corpse of a man (*shava* or *preta*), she is described as having three eyes, a terrifying face and a sunken belly.

8. '**Narasimhi**' (Sanskrit: नारसिंही, Nārasiṃhī), power of Narasimha (lion-man form of Vishnu), is a woman-lion and throws the stars into disarray by shaking her lion mane.

Though the first six are unanimously accepted by texts, the name and features of the seventh and eighth Matrika are disputed. In Devi-Mahatmya, Chamunda is omitted after the Saptamatrika list,[40] while in sculpture in shrines or caves and the Mahabharata, Narasimhi is omitted. The Varaha Purana names **Yami** – the Shakti of Yama, as the seventh and **Yogishwari** as the eighth Matrika, created by flames emerging from Shiva's mouth.[41] In Nepal, the eighth Matrika is called **Maha-Lakshmi** or **Lakshmi** is added omitting Narasimhi. In lists of nine Matrikas, Devi-Purana mentions **Gananayika** or Vinayaki – the Shakti of Ganesha, characterized by her elephant head and ability to remove obstacles like Ganesha and **Mahabharavi** omitting Narasimhi.[42]

2.40.3 Legends

There are several Puranic texts related to the origin of Matrikas. Matsya Purana, Vamana Purana, Varaha Purana, Kurma Purana and the Suprabhedagama contain references to Matrikas, and this asserts their antiquity.[43]

According to the Shumbha-Nishumbha story of Devi Mahatmya, Matrikas appear as Shaktis from the bodies of the gods – Brahma, Shiva, Skanda, Vishnu, Indra;[44] having form of each, approached Chandika (identified with Devi) with whatever form, ornaments and vehicle the god possessed. In that form, they slaughter the demon army.[7][45] Thus, the Matrikas are goddesses of the battlefield. They are described as assistants of Durga having sinister as well as propitious characteristics.[39] After the battle, the Matrikas dance drunk with their victim's blood.[46] This description is repeated with little variation in Devi Bhagavata Purana.[47] and Vamana Purana.[48] The Devi-Bhagavata Purana mentions three other goddesses, Shaktis of other gods in addition to Saptamatrikas making a group of 10 Matrikas.[49]

According to latter episode of Devi Mahatmya, Durga created Matrikas from herself and with their help slaughtered the demon army. In this version, Kali is described as a Matrika, who sucked all the blood of demon Raktabija.

9th–10th century granite Chola statue of Matrika Maheshvari, seen with a trident in a hand, adorned by serpent ornaments and her vahana (mount), the bull Nandi is seen on her seat — Musée Guimet, Paris.

Kali is given the epithet Chamunda in the text. When demon Shumbha challenges Durga to a single combat, she absorbs the Matrikas in herself and says that they are her different forms.[50] In the Vamana Purana too, the Matrikas arise from different parts of Devi and not from male gods although they are described and named after the male deities.[51]

In Matsya Purana, Shiva had created seven Matrikas to combat the demon Andhaka, who had the ability to duplicate from each drop of his blood that falls from him when he is wounded.[c] The Matrikas drink up his blood and help Shiva defeat the demon. After the battle, the Matrikas begin a rampage of destruction by starting to devour other gods, demons and peoples of the world. Narasimha, Vishnu's man-lion incarnation, creates a host of thirty-two benign goddesses who calm down the terrible, fire-breathing Matrikas. Narasimha commanded the Matrikas to protect the world, instead of destroying it and thus be worshipped by mankind. At the end of the episode, Shiva's terrible form Bhairava is enshrined with the images of the Matrikas at the place where the battle took place.[52][53] This story is retold in Vishnudharmottara Purana.[54] Vishnudharmottara Purana further relates them with vices or inauspicious emotions like envy, pride, anger etc.[55]

In Varaha Purana, they are created from the distracted mind of goddess Vaishnavi, who loses her concentration while doing asceticism. They are described as lovely and act as the goddesses' attendants on the battlefield.[56] In Bhagavata Purana, when beings created by Vishnu are enlisted; the Matrikas are listed with rakshasas (demons), bhutas (ghosts), pretas, dakinis and other dangerous beings. In the same text, milkmaids offer a prayer for protection of the infant-god Krishna from the Matrikas.[57]

The Devi Purana(6th – 10th century) mentions a group of sixteen matrikas and six other types of Matrikas mentioned, apart from the Saptamatrikas.[58] It introduces the *Loka-matara* (mothers of the world), a term used in the Mahab-harata, in the very first chapter. Kind to all creatures, the Matrikas are said to reside in various places for the bene-fit of children.[59] The text paradoxically describes the Ma-trikas as being created by various gods like Brahma, Vishnu, Shiva, Indra as well as being their mothers.[60] Devi Purana describe a pentad of Matrikas, who help Ganesha to kill demons.[61] Further, sage Mandavya is described as wor-shipping the *Mātṛpañcaka* (the five mothers) named Am-bika (Kaumari), Rudrani, Chamunda, Brahmi and Vaish-navi and who have been established by Brahma; for saving king Harishchandra from calamities. The Matrikas direct the sage to perform worship of *Mātṛchakra*(interpreted as a Yantra or Mandala or a circular shrine to the Matrikas), established by Vishnu on the Vindhya mountains, by meat and ritual sacrifice.[62]

A Hoysala sculpture of Chamunda, Halebidu. Surrounded by skele-tons, the goddess has large nails and protruding teeth and wears a garland of skulls.

Mahabharata

The Mahabharata narrates in different chapters the birth of warrior-god Skanda (the son of Shiva and Parvati) and his association with the Matrikas – his adopted mothers.

In one version, Indra (king of gods) sends the goddesses called "mothers of the world" to kill him.[15] However, upon seeing Skanda, instead they follow their maternal instincts and raise him.[5] In the chapter *Vana-parva* version, the Saptamatrikas are mentioned.[15][63] Later in the Mahab-harata; when absorption of these indigenous goddesses in the Brahmanic pantheon was initiated, a standardized group of seven goddesses – the Saptamatrikas, Shaktis or powers of Brahmanic gods are mentioned as Brahmi, Maheshvari, Kumari, Vaishnavi, Varahi, Indrani and Chamunda.[5]

In other accounts of Skanda's birth in Mahabharata, eight ferocious goddesses emerge from Skanda, when struck by Indra's Vajra (thunderbolt). These are Kāki, Halimā, Mālinī, Bṛhalī, Āryā, Palālā and Vaimitrā, which Skanda accepted as his mothers, who stole other children – a char-acteristic of the Matrikas.[64]

Another account mentions the *Maha-matrikas* (the great mothers), a group of the wives of six of the Saptarishis (7 great sages), who were accused of being Skanda's real mothers and thus abandoned by their husbands. They request Skanda to adopt them as his mothers. Skanda agrees and grants them two boons: to be worshipped as great goddesses and permission to torment children as long as they are younger than 16 years and then act as their protectors.[64] These six goddesses as well as the Saptama-trikas are identified or associated with Vedic Krittikas, the constellation Pleiades.[65]

The Shalya Parva of the Mahabharata mentions character-istics of a host of Matrikas, who serve Skanda. Ninety-two of them are named but the text says there exist more. The Shalya Parva describes them as young, cheerful, most of them fair but having dangerous features like long nails and large teeth. They are said to fight like Indra in battles, invoking terror in minds of enemies; speak different for-eign tongues and lives in inaccessible places away from hu-man settlements like crossroads, caves, mountains, springs, forests, riverbanks and cremation grounds.[66][67][68] Notable among these lists of Matrikas is *Putana*, a goddess who tried to kill the infant Krishna (an incarnation of Vishnu) by suckling him with poisoned breast milk and consequently killed by Krishna.[69]

2.40.4 Depictions

Bronze group with (from left) Ganesha; Brahmi, Kumari, Vaishnavi – the 3 Matrikas, and Kubera taken at the British Museum; Originally from Eastern India, Dedicated in 43rd year of reign of Pala king Mahipala I (about AD 1043)

The textual description of Matrikas is generally awesome, frightening and ferocious. In the Mahabharata, all the seven mothers are described as fatal or serve as threats to foetuses or infants. They are described as living in trees, crossroads, caves and funeral grounds and they are terrible as well as beautiful.[5] But, in the sculptural portrayal, they are depicted quite differently as protectors and benevolent mothers. They are armed with the same weapons, wear the same ornaments, and ride the same vahanas and carry the same banners as their corresponding male deities.

The Saptamatrkas are generally carved in relief on a rectangular stone slab in the sequential order of Brahmani, Maheshvari, Kumari, Vaishnavi, Varahi, Indrani and Chamunda, being flanked by two male figures – a terrible form of Shiva (Virabhadra) and his son Ganesha in both sides (first – on their right and last – on their left). Thus, the Matrikas are considered Saivite goddesses.[7] They are often depicted on the lintel slabs of the main door of a Shiva temple – mainly in Jaunsar-Bawar region, with their respective mounts forming the pedestal.[10] Sometimes, they are occupied by the couple Uma-Maheshvara (Parvati and Shiva). The earliest instance of their portrayal with Uma-Maheshvara is at Desha Bhattarika, Nepal although now the Matrika images have withered away.[70] The 12th century Sanskrit author Kalhana mentions worship of Matrikas with Shiva in Kashmir, his work Rajatarangini.[71]

Three panels of Saptamatrikas appear near the Shiva cave at Udayagiri, Bhopal.[72] They are also depicted in the Shaiva

Nataraja–Shiva (left) with Virabhadra and the first three Matrikas. Matrikas are depicted with children – Ellora

caves of Elephanta and Ellora (Caves 21, 14, 16 and 22).[73] In sixth century Rameshvara cave (Cave 21) at Ellora, "With the terrific aspect repressed entirely, the matrikas are depicted as benign and are worshipped in adulation. Sensuous, elegant, tender, beautiful adolescents, they are yet haughty and grand, quintessentially the creatrix."[74] Karrtikkeyi (Kumari) is depicted with a child on her lap and even Varahi is depicted with a human head, rather than the usual boar one.[75] In Ravana-ka-kai cave (Cave 14), each of the matrikas is with a child.[76] In eighth century Kailash Temple (cave 16) – dedicated to Shiva – of Rashtrakuta period, the Matrikas appear on the southern boundary of the temple.[26] As the influence of Tantra rose, the fertility area and upper parts of body in the Matrika sculptures were stressed.[77]

In each of the four depictions at Ellora, the matrikas are accompanied by Virabhadra, Ganesha and also on their left (besides Ganesha) by Kala (Time personified or Death).[78] The presence of Kala in form of a skeleton, seems to indicate the darker aspect of the matrikas' nature.[76] At Osian, the Matrikas is flanked by Ganesha and Kubera (the treasurer of the gods and a devotee of Shiva) while Virabhadra sits in the middle of the group.[79] In Gupta and post-Gupta art, like in 6th Century caves of Shamalaji, the Matrikas are accompanied by Shiva's son Skanda.

2.40.5 Associations

Yoginis

Often the Matrikas are confused with the Yoginis, a group of sixty-four or eighty-one Tantric goddesses.[80] In Sanskrit literature the Yoginis have been represented as the attendants or various manifestations of goddess Durga engaged in fighting with the demons Shumbha and Nishumbha, and the principal Yoginis are identified with the Matrikas.[81]

Kaumari, folio from Devi Mahatmya.

Other Yoginis are described as born from one or more Matrikas. The derivation of sixty-four Yoginis from eight Matrikas became a common tradition, by mid- 11th century. The Mandala (circle) and chakra of Yoginis were used alternatively. The eighty-one Yoginis evolve from a group of nine Matrikas, instead of seven or eight. The Saptamatrika (Brahmi, Maheshvari, Kumari, Vaishnavi, Varahi, Indrani and Chamunda) joined by Chandika and Mahalakshmi form the nine Matrika cluster. Each Matrika is considered to be a Yogini and is associated with eight other Yoginis resulting in the troupe of eighty-one (nine times nine).[82] Thus, Yoginis are considered as manifestations or daughters of the Matrikas.[83]

The yoginis also occupy an important place in Tantra, one of their chief temples in India are in 'Ranipur-Jharial' and the 'Chaushathi Jogini' (the 64 yoginis) temple near Bhubaneswar, Odisha. The rise of Yogini cult is also analogous to the rise of the Matrikas' cult. Bhattacharyya sums it this way: "The growing importance of Shaktism [of the matrikas and yoginis in the first millennium CE] brought them into greater prominence and distributed their cult far and wide. [...] The primitive Yogini cult was also revived on account of the increasing influenced of the cult of the Seven Mothers."[81]

Script Characters

Matrika (Sanskrit *mātṛkā*) is also a term used to denote features of Indic scripts (also in combination with aksara, matrikaksara), though there is considerable variation in the precise interpretation of the term from one author to another. Sometimes it denotes a single character, the entire collection of characters (an "alphabet"), the alphabetic "matrix" used as a collation tool,[84] vowels in particular (considered erroneous by Georg Bühler), or the sound of the syllable represented by the character.[85] Various traditions identify the script matrikas with the personified divine Matrikas.

According to K.C. Aryan, the number of Matrikas is determined in the structure of the Devanagari alphabet. First is the (A) group which contains the vowels, then the (Ka), (Cha), (Ta), (ta), (Pa), (Ya) and (Ksha) groups. The seven mother goddesses (*Saptamatrikas*) correspond to the seven consonant groups; when the vocalic (A) group is added to it, the eight mother goddesses (*Ashtamatrikas*) are obtained.[86] The Shaktas hold that the Mothers preside over impurities (*mala*) and over sounds of the language. The Mothers were identified with fourteen vowels plus the *anusarva* and *visarga* – making their number sixteen.[87]

In Tantra, the fifty or fifty-one letters including vowels as well as consonants from A to Ksha, of the Devanagari alphabet itself, the *Varnamala* of bija, have been described as being the Matrikas themselves. It is believed that they are infused with the power of the Divine Mother herself. The Matrikas are considered to be the subtle form of the letters *(varna)*. These letters combined make up syllables *(pada)* which are combined to make sentences *(vakya)* and it is of these elements that mantra is composed. It is believed that the power of mantra derives from the fact that the letters of the alphabet are in fact forms of the goddess.[88] The 50 Matrika Kalas are given in the same account as follows: Nivritti, Pratishtha, Vidya, Shanti, Indhika, Dipika, Mochika, Para, Sukshma, Sukshmamrita, Jnanamrita, Apyppayani, Vyapini, Vyomarupa, Ananta, Srishti, Riddhi, Smriti, Medha, Kanti, Lakshmi, Dyuti, Sthira, Sthiti, Siddhi, Jada, Palini, Shanti, Aishvarya, Rati, Kamika, Varada, Ahladini, Pritih, Dirgha, Tikshna, Raudri, Bhaya, Nidra, Tadra, Kshudha, Krodhini, Kriya, Utkari, Mrityurupa, Pita, Shveta, Asita, Ananta.[89] Sometimes, the Matrikas represent a diagram written in the letter, believed to possess magical powers.[90]

2.40.6 Worship

In India

According to Leslie C. Orr, the Saptamatrika, who first appeared in South India in the eighth century, had once temples dedicated exclusively to them, but the ninth century onwards, they were demoted to status of "deities of the entourage" (*parivara devata*) of Shiva. Their images moved from the sanctums to corners of temple complexes and now they are as guardian deities in small village shrines.[91] The Saptamatrikas are worshipped as *Saptakanyakas* (the celestial nymphs) in most South Indian Shiva temples. But the Selliyamman temple at Alambakkam in Tiruchirapalli district (In 1909 called Trichonopoly district) is important in worship of the Matrikas. Here once stood a temple dedicated to the Saptamatrika, which was replaced by the

Shrine of the "Seven Mothers" in Ramanathapuram District, Tamil Nadu.

Vaishnavi or Bishnuvi (top) and Brahmayani in the Bhairab Naach

present temple.[92]

In India, shrines of the Saptamatrikas are located in "the wilderness", usually near lakes or rivers, and are made of seven vermilion smeared stones. It is believed that the Matrikas kill fetuses and newborns unless pacified with bridal finery and prayers by women.[93] Devdutt Pattanaik says: "The cult of the Seven Mothers is found all over India. ... Pregnant women and nursing mothers worship them. When these goddesses are angry, they make women barren and strike newborns with fatal fevers. When they are appeased, they ensure the health and happiness of children."[94] A prominent Saptamatrika temple is located near Baitarani River,in Jajpur.

The Saptamatrika images are worshipped by women on *Pithori* – new moon day, with the 64 yoginis represented by rice flour images or supari nuts. The goddesses are worshipped by ceremonial offerings of fruit and flower and mantras.[95]

In Nepal

The Matrikas function both as city protectors and individual protectors in both Hinduism and Buddhism. The Astha matrika are considered as Ajimas (grandmother goddesses, who are feared as bringer of disease and misfortune as well act as protectresses) in the Newar pantheon. Temples (*pithas* i.e. seats) of the ashta matrika built in and around Kathmandu are considered powerful places of worship.[96]

The *pithas* are usually open-air shrines, but may be closed structures too. In these *pithas*, the Matrikas are worshipped with their followers (*ganas*) in form of stone statues or natural stones, while in *dyochems* (god-houses) in towns and villages, they are represented in brass images. The brass images (*utsav-murtis*) are paraded around town and placed at their respective *pithas* once every year. Like Vishnudharmottara Purana (discussed in Legends), the Matrikas are considered as representing a vice and are worshipped by *pithapuja* (a pilgrimage around the *pithas*) to free oneself from them.[97] Though each *pitha* is primarily dedicated to a Matrika, the other Matrikas are also worshipped as subordinate deities.[98] The *pithas*, which are "theoretically located at the outer boundaries of the city" are said to form a protective mandala around the city and assisted to a certain compass point.[99] In other temples like the ones dedicated to Pacali Bhairava, the Asthamatrikas are worshipped as a circle of stones.[98] In Bhaktapur, the Ashtamatrikas are believed to the preserver goddesses of the city guarding the eight geometrical directions. Mary Sluser says "Not only do the Mātṛkās guard the compass points but they are also regarded as regents of the sky." [100] Sometimes, they are paired with the Ashta Bhairava (Eight aspects of Bhairava) and sculpted on temple roofs or terraces. Nepali Buddhists worship the Matrikas as described in Dharanisamgrahas.[101]

The Malla king of Nepal Srinivasa Malla built the Patan durbar (court) in 1667 AD and is believed to have seen the Matrikas dance in the durbar one night. The king ordered that the Ashta-matrika be worshipped during the Ashwin Navaratri and cost is defrayed by the durbar. The custom continues til this day.[102] Another festival *Ghorajatra* is celebrated in Patan with animal sacrifices to the

Matrikas.[103]

In the Kathmandu valley of Nepal, the Ashta-matrikas with a central village goddess are worshipped as protectors of the city or town. They are identified with the guardians of directions (*digpala*), places (*lokapala*) or lands (*kshatrapala*), satiated by blood sacrifice. Newar Buddhists associate the Matrikas with 24 human qualities, which can mastered by visiting three sets of eight Matrika *pithas*.[104]

Tantric worship

Saptamatrika with Ganesha, at Panchalingeshvara temple in Karnataka.

The 7th century Sanskrit author Banabhatta mentions the propitiation of Matrikas by a Tantric ascetic in his Harshacharita.[105] The text mentions use of *mātrmandala* (mandala of the Matrikas) or *Yantra* along with a special *anusthana* (ritual) to cure the ailing king.[106] The text describes "young nobles [..](of the king) burning themselves with lamps to propitiate the Matrikas in a temple dedicated to the Matrikas (*matr-grha*). Banabhatta's Kadambari, Bhasa's Cārudatta, Shudraka's Mrichakatika mention the ritual offerings of food and shrines of Matrikas at crossroads.[31] Other offerings include flowers and clothes and meat and wine for some Matrikas. Tantric works like Tantraraja-Tantra (unknown date, author) and Kulacūḍāmaṇi discuss the worship of Matrikas as Shaktis or letters of the alphabet.[107] A process of this worship, *Matrika-nyasa* (lit. "installation of the Mothers"), is described in Devi Gita, part of Devi Bhagavata Purana.[108] It involves installation of powers of Matrikas – as letters of the alphabet – in one's body, by "feeling the deity worshipped in different parts of the body" like head, face, anus and legs and reciting mantras.[109] The *Hrillekha-matrika-nyasa*, a more specialized form of *Matrika-nyasa*, combines the installation of "most powerful set of all letters (Matrikas)" with the seed syllable *Hrīṃ* of Goddess Bhuvaneshvari.[110]

Stone inscriptions of Tantric worship of The Matrikas are found in Gangadhar, Rajasthan(by king Vishvavarman- 423 C.E., identified as the first epigraphic evidence of Tantra worship); in Bihar (by Guptas – fifth century) and in Deogarh, Uttar Pradesh (by Svāmibhaṭa – sixth century).[31] The Gangadhar inscripture deals with a construction to a

shrine to Chamunda and the other Matrikas, "who are attended by Dakinis (female demons)" and rituals of daily Tantric worship (*Tantrobhuta*) like the ritual of *Bali* (offering of grain).[106]

The eight Matrikas are said to reside the second line of *bhupura* in Sri Chakra. They are frequently aligned with the Eight Bhairavas, as in *Jñānārṇava Tantra*. The Svacchaṇḍa Tantra(1.33) explains that the primary function of Matrikas is to preside eight groups (*vargas*) of letters of Devanagari alphabet, while Brahmayāmala states they issue originate from the vowels.[111]

Rituals and goals of worship

The Natya Shastra (13.66) recommends worship to Matrikas before setting up the stage and before dance performances.[19] Indra declares in chapter 90 of Devi Purana that the Matrikas are the best among all deities and should be worshipped in cities, villages, towns and shields.[112] Matrikas are generally to be worshipped on all occasions with Navagraha (the nine planets) and the Dikpala (Guardians of the directions) and at night with the Goddess.[113]

The Matsya Purana and Devi Purana prescribe that Matrika shrines should be north-facing and be placed in northern part of a temple-complex.[114] The temples of the Matrikas are found earliest dating to the fourth century and from textual evidence, it is predicated that "there must be impressive shrines all over the [Indian] subcontinent".[115] Although circular Mandalas and Chakras are mentioned in religious texts, most existing shrines are rectangular in nature. Pal speculates that earlier circular shrines, which open to the sky or under trees of less durable material were replaced by the Guptas in stone as rectangular shrines.[71]

The Devi Purana mentions the Matrikas or *Deva Shaktis* (powers of the gods) as group of seven or more, who should be worshipped for Mukti (liberation) by all, but particularly kings for powers of domination.[72] The Saptamatrika are worshipped for "personal and spiritual renewal" with Mukti as the ultimate goal as well as for powers to control and rule and earthly desires (Bhukti).[116] Also important are the banners of the Saptamatrikas, which are carved outside the Udayagiri caves. These banners are called "Indra's sisters" in the Devi Purana. The Purana lists them as: swan, bull, peacock, conch, discus, elephant and skeleton – attributes of the Matrikas. A king installing these banners is believed to get mukti and bhukti. As per the Nitisara, Matrikas acted as the king's tangible Shaktis and conferred the power to conquer and rule.[117]

2.40.7 Notes

[1] Wangu p.99

[2] Kinsley .151

[3] "Mantras to the Aṣṭamātṛkās". *http://cudl.lib.cam.ac.uk*. Cambridge Digital Library. Retrieved 2 February 2015.

[4] van den Hoek in Nas, p.362

[5] Wangu p.41

[6] Bhattacharyya, N. N., *History of the Sakta Religion*, Munshiram Manoharlal Publishers Pvt. Ltd. (New Delhi, 1974, 2d ed. 1996), p. 126.

[7] Wangu p.75

[8] The Iconography and Ritual of Śiva at Elephanta By Charles Dillard Collins p.143

[9] Kinsley (1988) p.151

[10] Jain p.162

[11] Brhatsamhita, Ch.57, v.56. Panda, S.S. (September 2004). "Sakti Cult in Upper Mahanadi Valley" (PDF). *Orissa Review*. Government of Orissa. Retrieved 2008-01-08.

[12] Wangu Glossary p.187

[13] Jagdish Narain Tiwari, "Studies in Goddess Cults in Northern India, with Reference to the First Seven Centuries AD" p.215-244; as referred in Kinsley p.151

[14] Dilip Chakravati in *Archaeology and World Religion* By Timothy Insoll, Published 2001, Routledge, ISBN 0-415-22154-4, pp.42–44

[15] Kinsley p.151

[16] Pal in Singh p.1836

[17] Zimmer Heinrich, 1960,2001 The Art Of Indian Asia, Its Mythology and Transformations.Motilal Banarsidas Publication. New Delhi (Page B4C,257,135)

[18] Harper in Harper and Brown, p.48

[19] Kinsley p.155

[20] Schastok pp.58–60

[21] Bhattacharyya, N. N., *History of the Sakta Religion*, Munshiram Manoharlal Publishers Pvt. Ltd. (New Delhi, 1974, 2d ed. 1996).

[22] Wangu pp.58–59

[23] Wangu p.67

[24] Wangu p. 68

[25] Wangu p.76

[26] Berkson p.212

[27] Kamath, Suryanath U. (2001) [1980]. *A concise history of Karnataka : from pre-historic times to the present*. Bangalore: Jupiter books. LCCN 80905179. OCLC 7796041. p51

[28] Kamath (2001), p52

[29] Goswami, Meghali; Gupta, Dr.Ila; Jha, Dr. P. of IIT, Roorkee (March 2005). "Sapta Matrikas In Indian Art and their significance in Indian Sculpture and Ethos: A Critical Study" (PDF). *Anistoriton Journal*. Anistoriton. Retrieved 2008-01-08. "Anistoriton is an electronic Journal of History, Archaeology and ArtHistory. It publishes scholarly papers since 1997 and it is freely available on the Internet. All papers and images since vol. 1 (1997) are available on line as well as on the free Anistorion CD-ROM edition."

[30] Dr. Suryanath U. Kamath (2001), A Concise History of Karnataka from pre-historic times to the present, Jupiter books, MCC (Reprinted 2002), p60

[31] Lorenzen, David in Harper and Brown, p.29

[32] Harper in Harper and Brown, p.121

[33] Kinsley p.156

[34] Cited in Laura Kristine Chamberlain. "Durga and the Dashain Harvest Festival: From the Indus to Kathmandu Valleys" in ReVision, Summer 2002, vol. 25, no. 1, p.26

[35] Agni Purana, Tr. by M.N. Dutta, Calcutta, 1903–04,Ch.50.18.22.

[36] See:

- Kinsley p.156, IAST Names and Descriptions as per Devi Mahatmya , verses 8.11–20
- "Sapta Matrikas (12th C AD)". Department of Archaeology and Museums, Government of Andhra Pradesh. Archived from the original on July 1, 2007. Retrieved 2008-01-08.
- Other names from Devi Purana: Pal in Singh p.1844 and Descriptions: p.1846
- Kalia, pp.106–109.

[37] Singh p.1840, Ambika is used as another name for Kaumari in Devi Purana.

[38] Kinsley p.241 Footnotes

[39] Wangu p.72

[40] Singh p.1858

[41] Kalia, p.108

[42] Pal in Singh p.1846

[43] The stories are quoted in (Rao, T.A. Gopinatha, Elements of Hindu Iconography, Vol.I, Part-II, 2nd Edition, Indological Book House, Varanasi, 1971, pp.379–383).

[44] Kinsley p. 156, Devi Mahatmya verses 8.11–20

[45] Kinsley p. 156, Devi Mahatmya verses 8.38, 44, 49, 62

[46] Kinsley p. 156, Devi Mahatmya verses 8.62

[47] Kinsley p. 156, verses 5.28–29 and It names 10 goddesses and then says that some shaktis of other gods also came to battle.

[48] Kinsley p. 156, verses 30

[49] Kinsley p.242

[50] Kinsley p. 158, Devi Mahatmya verses 10.2–5

[51] Kinsley p. 158,verses 30.3–9

[52] Kinsley p. 158-159, verses 179.8–90

[53] Pal in Singh p.1835-6

[54] Kinsley p. 159, verses 1.225

[55] Kinsley p. 159, verses 17.33–37

[56] Kinsley p. 159, Verses 44.1–96

[57] Kinsley p. 159, verses 2.10.37–39 and 10.63.6 ff., 10.6,27–29

[58] Pal in Singh p.1839

[59] Pal in Singh p.1835

[60] Pal in Singh p.1844

[61] Pal in Singh p.1840, Chapters 111–116

[62] Pal in Singh p.1840, Chapter 116(82–86)

[63] Mahabharata verses 215.16 – 215.18, two of the goddesses are described in 215.21–22

[64] Kinsley p.152

[65] Harper in Harper and Brown, p.116

[66] Kinsley p.153

[67] Pattanaik pp.132–3

[68] Vaishampayana said... The Mahabharata translated by Kisari Mohan Ganguli (1883 −1896), Book 9: Shalya Parva: Section 46.

[69] Kinsley p.154

[70] Singh p.1855

[71] Pal in Singh p.1858

[72] Harper in Harper and Brown, p.117

[73] Berkson p.87

[74] Berkson p.134

[75] For images see Berkson pp.136 – 144

[76] Berkson p.186

[77] Berkson pp.186–7

[78] Berkson p.135

[79] Kalia p.109

[80] Dehejia, Vidya, *Yogini Cult and Temples*

[81] Bhattacharyya, N. N., *History of the Sakta Religion*, Munshiram Manoharlal Publishers Pvt. Ltd. (New Delhi, 1974, 2d ed. 1996), p. 128.

[82] Wangu p.114

[83] Banerji p.296

[84] Cox, Colette (1992). "The unbroken treatise: Scripture and argument in early Buddhist scholasticism". In Williams, M.A.; Cox, C.; Jaffee, M. *Innovation in Religions Traditions: Essays in the Interpretation of Religions Change.* de Gruyter. p. 152.

[85] Bühler, G. (1881). "Palaeographical remarks on the Horiuzi palm leaf MSS.". In Müller, F.M. *Anecdota Oxoniensia: Texts, Documents, and Extracts Chiefly from Manuscripts in the Bodleian and the Oxford Libraries.* Clarendon Press. p. 67, note 2.

[86] Aryan (1980), p. 9

[87] Jain p.163

[88] Aryan (1980), pp. 24–28

[89] Woodroffe, p. 103

[90] Banerji p.61

[91] Leslie C. Orr, *Gods and Worshippers on South Indian sacred ground* in *The World in the Year 1000* By James Heitzman and Wolfgang Schenkluhn, pp.244–5, Published 2004, University Press of America, 338 pages, ISBN 0-7618-2561-4.

[92] *The Madras Epigraphical Department*, Annual Report 1909-10 p. 285 as quoted in pp.285–6 *South Indian shrines illustrated* By P. V. Jagadisa Ayyar. Published 1993, Asian Educational Services,ISBN 81-206-0151-3

[93] Pattanaik p.131

[94] "SaptaMatrikas and Matrikas". Shakti Sadhana Group. 27 March 2006. Retrieved 2008-01-08.

[95] The Hindu Religious Year By Muriel Marion Underhill; Published 1991; Asian Educational Services, 194 pages, ISBN 81-206-0523-3, p.110

[96] The Rough Guide to Nepal By David Reed, James McConnachie p.521 Published 2002 Rough Guides ISBN 1-85828-899-1

[97] van den Hoek, Bert in Nas, p.362

[98] van den Hoek, Bert in Nas, p.367-8

[99] van den Hoek, Bert in Nas, p.364

[100] White p.61

[101] Pal in Singh p.1851

[102] p.245 History of Nepal: With an Introductory Sketch of the Country and People of Nepal. By Daniel Wright Published 1996,Asian Educational Services,340 pages,ISBN 81-206-0552-7

[103] Nepal Handbook By Tom Woodhatch Published 1999 Footprint Travel Guides 572 pages ISBN 0-658-00016-0

[104] Hiltebeitel p. 260

[105] Banerji p.34

[106] Joshi, M.C. in Harper and Brown, p.48

[107] Banerji p.148 and 205

[108] Brown, p.292 Verses 10.6–8

[109] Banerji p.27

[110] Brown, p.293-4

[111] Brooks p.143-4

[112] Singh p.1850

[113] Singh p.1850-51

[114] Pal in Singh p.1850-1

[115] Pal in Singh p.1854

[116] Harper in Harper and Brown, p.122

[117] Harper in Harper and Brown, p.125-7

b. ^ Note that the Gupta rulers took the names of the deity Skanda as their own names

c. ^ This very ability is possessed by Raktabija of the Devimahatmya and Vamana Purana.

2.40.8 References

- Aryan, K.C. (1980). *The Little Goddesses (Matrikas)*. New Delhi: Rekha Prakashan. ISBN 81-900002-7-6.

- Berkson, Carmel (1992). *Ellora, Concept and Style*. Abhinav Publications. ISBN 81-7017-277-2.

- Jain, Madhu; O. C. Handa (1995). *The Abode of Mahashiva: Cults and Symbology in Jaunsar-Bawar in the Mid – Himalayas*. Indus Publishing. ISBN 81-7387-030-6.

- Kinsley, David (1998) [1988]. *Hindu Goddesses: Vision of the Divine Feminine in the Hindu Religious Traditions*. Motilal Banarsidass Publ. ISBN 81-208-0394-9.

- Panikkar, Shivaji K (1997). "Saptamatrka Worship and Sculptures: An Iconological Interpretation of Conflicts and Resolutions in the Storied Brahmanical Icons". *Perspectives in Indian Art and Archaeology* **3** (1 ed.). ISBN 81-246-0074-0.

- Van den Hoek, Bert (1993). "Kathmandu as a sacrificial arena". In Nas ,Peter J. M. *Urban Symbolism*. BRILL. ISBN 90-04-09855-0.

- Wangu, Madhu Bazaz (2003). *Images of Indian Goddesses*. Abhinav Publications. ISBN 81-7017-416-3.

- Woodroffe, Sir John (2001). *The Garland of Letters*. Chennai, India: Ganesh & Co. ISBN 81-85988-12-9.

- Hiltebeitel, Alf. "Goddesses, place, Identity in Nepal". *South Asian Folklore*.

- Jain, Madhu; O. C. Handa (1995). *The Abode of Mahashiva: Cults and Symbology in Jaunsar-Bawar in the Mid – Himalayas*. Indus Publishing. ISBN 81-7387-030-6.

- Banerji, S.C., *Companion to Tantra*, Published 2002, Abhinav Publications, ISBN 81-7017-402-3.

- Harper, Katherine Anne and Brown, Robert L.; *The Roots of Tantra*; Published 2002; SUNY Press; ISBN 0-7914-5305-7

- Pattanaik, Devdutt; *The Goddess in India: The Five Faces of the Eternal Feminine*; Published 2000; Inner Traditions / Bear & Company; 176 pages; ISBN 0-89281-807-7

- Pal, P. *The Mother Goddesses According to the Devipurana* in Singh, Nagendra Kumar, *Encyclopaedia of Hinduism*, Published 1997,Anmol Publications PVT. LTD.,ISBN 81-7488-168-9

- Brooks, Douglas Renfrew. *Auspicious Wisdom: The Texts and Traditions of Srividya Sakta Tantrism*, 1992, SUNY Press, ISBN 0-7914-1145-1.

- Brown, Cheever Mackenzie. *The Devi Gita: The Song of the Goddess: A Translation, Annotation, and Commentary* , 1998, SUNY Press, 404 pages, ISBN 0-7914-3939-9.

- Kalia, Asha (1982). *Art of Osian Temples: Socio-Economic and Religious Life in India, 8th–12th Centuries A.D.* Abhinav Publications. ISBN 0-391-02558-9.

- Schastok, Sara L. (1985). *The Śāmalājī Sculptures and 6th Century Art in Western India.* BRILL. ISBN 90-04-06941-0

- Kiss of the Yogini: "Tantric Sex" in its South Asian Contexts By David Gordon White

- Dehejia, Vidya, *Yogini Cult and Temples.*

2.40.9   External links

- "Matrikas embedded in eight petals of the Kali Yantra: Image"

- "Translation of Devi Mahatmya passages that describe the Sapta matrika and Images"

- Article on "Tantric Hieroglyphics" (*with emphasis on Matrkas*)- Published in Quarterly Journal of Mythic Society by S. Srikanta Sastri

2.41   Menhit

Not to be confused with Mehit.

Menhit /ˈmɛnˌhɪt/ (also spelt Menchit) was originally a Nubian war goddess in Egyptian mythology. Her name depicts a warrior status, as it means *(she who) massacres.*

Due to the aggressive attributes possessed by and hunting methods used by lionesses, most things connected to warfare in Egypt were depicted as leonine, and Menhit was no exception, being depicted as a lioness-goddess.

She also was believed to advance ahead of the Egyptian armies and cut down their enemies with fiery arrows, similar to other war deities[2] She was less known to the people as a crown goddess[3] and was one of the goddesses who represented the protective uraeus on royal crowns.[4]

In the 3rd Nome of Upper Egypt, particularly at Esna, Menhit was said to be the wife of Khnum and the mother of Heka.

She was also worshipped in Lower Egypt, where she was linked with the goddesses Wadjet and Neith.[4]

As the centre of her cult was toward the southern border of Egypt, in Upper Egypt, she became strongly identified with Sekhmet, who was originally the lion-goddess of war for Upper Egypt, after unification of the two Egyptian kingdoms, this goddess began to be considered simply another aspect of Sekhmet.[2]

2.41.1   References

[1] Wörterbuch, II., p.84

Menhit on the left with Khnum on the right, shown on the outside wall of the temple at Esna

[2] Hans Bonnet: *Menhit,* in: *Lexikon der ägyptischen Religionsgeschichte* (English: Lexicon of Egyptian History of Religion) p.451f

[3] Rolf Felde: *Ägyptische Gottheiten* (English: Egyptian Gods) p.34

[4] Wilkinson, Richard H. (2003). *The Complete Gods and Goddesses of Ancient Egypt.* Thames & Hudson. p. 179

2.41.2   Literature

- Rolf Felde: *Ägyptische Gottheiten.* Wiesbaden 1995

- Hans Bonnet: *Lexikon der ägyptischen Religionsgeschichte,* Hamburg 2000; ISBN 3-937872-08-6

2.42   Menrva

Further information: Etruscan mythology

Menrva (also spelled Menerva) was an Etruscan goddess of war, art, wisdom, and health. She contributed much of her character to Roman Minerva.

Though she was seen by Hellenized Etruscans as their counterpart to Greek Athena,[1] Menrva has some unique traits that makes it clear that she was not an import from Greece. Etruscan artists under the influence of Greek culture liked to portray Menrva with Gorgoneion, helmet, spear and shield, and on a mirrorback as born from the head of her father, Tinia.[2] She is also commonly seen as the protector of Hercle (Heracles) and *Pherse* (Perseus).[3] On a bronze mirror found at Praeneste, she attends Perseus, who consults two Graeae,[4] or, on another, holds high the head of Medusa, while she and seated Perseus and Hermes all gaze safely at its reflection in a pool at their feet.[5] These images are more likely to reflect literary sources than any cult practice; however, with Esplace (Asclepius), who bandages Prometheus' chest, she attends a scene of Prometheus unbound on a bronze mirror from Bolsena, ca. 300 BCE.[6] She is often depicted in more essentially Etruscan style as a lightning thrower; Martianus mentions her as one of nine Etruscan lightning gods. Unlike Athena, Menrva seems to have been associated with weather phenomena.[7]

Her name is indigenous to Italy and might even be of Etruscan origin, stemming from an Italic moon goddess *Meneswā* 'She who measures', the Etruscans adopted the inherited Old Latin name, *Menerwā*, thereby calling her Menrva. This has been disputed, however.[8] Carl Becker noted[9] that her name appears to contain the PIE root *men-*, which he notes was linked in Greek primarily to memory words (cf. Greek "mnestis"/μνῆστις 'memory, remembrance, recollection'), but which more generally referred to 'mind' in most Indo-European languages.

She was often depicted in the Judgement of Paris, called Elcsntre (Alexander, his alternative name in Greek) in Etruscan, one of the most popular Greek myths in Etruria.

Menrva was part of a holy triad with Tinia and Uni, later reflected in the Roman Capitoline Triad of Jupiter, Juno, and Minerva.

2.42.1 References

[1] The process, by analogy with *interpretatio graeca*, was termed *interpretatio etrusca* by L.B. van der Meer, *Interpretatio Etrusca': Greek Myths on Etruscan Mirrors*(Amsterdam) 1995.

[2] *E.g.* on a bronze mirrorback, ca. 450–425 BCE, from Praeneste, illustrated in Larissa Bonfante and Judith Swaddling, *Etruscan Myths* (Series The Legendary Past, British Museum/University of Texas), 2006, fig. 28, p. 43.

[3] de Grummond, *Etruscan Myth, Sacred History and Legend,* page 76

[4] Illustrated in Bonfante and Swaddling 2006, fig. 30, p. 45.

[5] Illustrated in Bonfante and Swaddling 2006, fig. 31, p. 46.

[6] Bonfante and Swaddling 2006, fig. 23, page 38.

[7] Nancy Thomson de Grummond, *Etruscan Myth, Sacred History and Legend*, (Philadelphia, 2006) page 71.

[8] de Grummond, *Etruscan Myth, Sacred History and Legend*, page 71

[9] Becker, *A Modern Theory of Language Evolution* 2004, p. 190: mentions *MN preserved in Greek as "Mnemosyne"/μνημοσύνη, and Minerva.

2.43   Minerva

This article is about the Roman goddess. For other uses, see Minerva (disambiguation).

Minerva (/mɪˈnɜr.və/; Latin: [mɪˈnɛr.wa]; Etruscan: *Menrva*) was the Roman goddess of wisdom and sponsor of arts, trade, and strategy. She was born with weapons from the head of Jupiter.[1] After impregnating the titaness Metis Jupiter recalled a prophecy that his own child would overthrow him. Fearing that their child would grow stronger than him and rule the Heavens in his place, Jupiter swallowed Metis whole. The titaness forged weapons and armor for her child while within the father-god, and the constant pounding and ringing gave him a headache. To relieve the pain, Vulcan used a hammer to split Jupiter's head and, from the cleft, Minerva emerged, whole, adult, and bearing her mother's weapons and armor. From the 2nd century BC onwards, the Romans equated her with the Greek goddess Athena.[2] She was the virgin goddess of music, poetry, medicine, wisdom, commerce, weaving, crafts, and magic.[3] She is often depicted with her sacred creature, an owl usually named as the "owl of Minerva",[4] which symbolizes that she is connected to wisdom.

2.43.1   Etruscan Menrva

Main article: Menrva

Stemming from an Italic moon goddess *Meneswā* ('She who measures'), the Etruscans adopted the inherited Old Latin name, *Menerwā*, thereby calling her Menrva. It is assumed that her Roman name, Minerva, is based on this Etruscan mythology. Minerva was the goddess of wisdom, war, art, schools and commerce. She was the Etruscan counterpart to Greek Athena. Like Athena, Minerva was born from the head of her father, Jupiter (Greek Zeus).

By a process of folk etymology, the Romans could have linked her foreign name to the root *men-* in Latin words such as *mens* meaning "mind", perhaps because one of her aspects as goddess pertained to the intellectual. The word *mens* is built from the Proto-Indo-European root **men-* 'mind' (linked with memory as in Greek Mnemosyne/μνημοσύνη and *mnestis*/μνῆστις: memory, remembrance, recollection, *manush* in Sanskrit meaning mind).

2.43.2   Worship in Rome

Raised-relief image of Minerva on a Roman gilt silver bowl, 1st century BC

Temple of Minerva in Sbeitla, Tunisia

The Etruscan Menrva was part of a holy triad with Tinia and Uni, equivalent to the Roman Capitoline Triad of Jupiter-Juno-Minerva. Minerva was the daughter of Jupiter.

As *Minerva Medica*, she was the goddess of medicine and doctors. As *Minerva Achaea*, she was worshipped at Lucera in Apulia where votive gifts and arms said to be those of Diomedes were preserved in her temple.[5][6]

A head of "Sulis-Minerva" found in the ruins of the Roman baths in Bath

In *Fasti* III, Ovid called her the "goddess of a thousand works". Minerva was worshiped throughout Italy, and when she eventually became equated with the Greek goddess Athena, she also became a goddess of war, although in Rome her warlike nature was less emphasized.[7] Her worship was also taken out to the empire—in Britain, for example, she was syncretized with the local goddess Sulis, who was often invoked for restitution for theft.[8]

The Romans celebrated her festival from March 19 to March 23 during the day which is called, in the neuter plural, Quinquatria, the fifth after the Ides of March, the nineteenth, an artisans' holiday . A lesser version, the Minusculae Quinquatria, was held on the Ides of June, June 13, by the flute-players, who were particularly useful to religion. In 207 BC, a guild of poets and actors was formed to meet and make votive offerings at the temple of Minerva on the Aventine Hill. Among others, its members included Livius Andronicus. The Aventine sanctuary of Minerva continued to be an important center of the arts for much of the middle Roman Republic.

Minerva was worshipped on the Capitoline Hill as one of the Capitoline Triad along with Jupiter and Juno, at the Temple of Minerva Medica, and at the "Delubrum Minervae" a temple founded around 50 BC by Pompey on the site now occupied by the church of *Santa Maria sopra Minerva* facing the present-day Piazza della Minerva. When it was founded the emperor himself was present and was applauded and seen to be a god for this act.

2.43.3 Universities and educational establishments

Main article: Minerva in the emblems of educational establishments

As patron goddess of wisdom, Minerva frequently features in statuary, as an image on seals, and in other forms, at educational establishments.

2.43.4 Use by societies and governments

Minerva and owl (right) depicted on Confederate currency (1861).

- The Seal of California depicts the Goddess Minerva. Her having been born fully-grown symbolizes California having become a state without first being a territory.[9]

- In the early 20th century, Manuel José Estrada Cabrera, President of Guatemala, tried to promote a "Worship of Minerva" in his country; this left little legacy other than a few interesting Hellenic style "Temples" in parks around Guatemala.

- According to John Robison's *Proofs of a Conspiracy* (1798), the third degree of the Bavarian Illuminati was called *Minerval* or *Brother of Minerva*, in honour of the goddess of learning. Later, this title was adopted for the first initiation of Aleister Crowley's OTO rituals.

- Minerva is displayed on the Medal of Honor, the highest military decoration awarded by the United States government.

- Minerva is featured in the logo of the Max Planck Society.

- Minerva alongside Mars is displayed on the cap badge of the Artists Rifles Territorial SAS Regiment of the British Army.

- Kingston Upon Hull's oldest Masonic Lodge is named The Minerva Lodge.

- Minerva is the patron goddess of the Theta Delta Chi and Sigma Alpha Epsilon fraternities, and the Kappa Kappa Gamma and Delta Sigma Theta[10] sororities

- Minerva is featured on the Union College seal. The college motto is "We all become brothers under the laws of Minerva."

- Minerva is an Institute for training for SSB Interviews and written examinations like NDA, CDS .It is situated in Sector 120,Mohali,Punjab.It is the first and oldest Armed Forces Preparatory Institute in India and established in 1955.

2.43.5 Public monuments, places and modern culture

- A small Roman shrine to Minerva (the only one still *in situ* in the UK) stands in Handbridge, Chester. It sits in a public park, overlooking the River Dee.

- The Minerva Roundabout in Guadalajara, Mexico, located at the crossing of the López Mateos, Vallarta, López Cotilla, Agustín Yáñez and Golfo de Cortez avenues, features the goddess standing on a pedestal, surrounded by a large fountain, with an inscription which says "Justice, wisdom and strength guard this loyal city".

- A bronze statue of Minerva lies in monument square Portland, Maine. "Our Lady of Victories Monument" dedicated 1891, Richard Morris Hunt and Franklin Simmons.

- A sculpture of Minerva by Andy Scott, known as the Briggate Minerva, stands outside Trinity Leeds shopping centre.

- Minerva is displayed as a statue in Pavia, Italy, near the train station, and is considered as an important landmark in the city.

- Minerva is the name of a supercomputer at the Icahn School of Medicine at Mount Sinai in New York City.

- On the summit of the dome of Liverpool Town Hall in England is a statue, representing Minerva. It is 10 feet (3 m) high and was designed by John Charles Felix Rossi. The present Liverpool Town Hall containing the statue was begun in 1749.

- Minerva is the song title of a single and the third track on the Deftones self-titled album released May 20, 2003.

- Minerva is a reoccurring character in the Assassins Creed franchise as a guide to Desmond and later an antagonist.

- Minerva, along with her Greek counterpart Athena are gods in the Japanese mobile game Puzzle & Dragons

- Minerva is displayed as a cast bronze statue in the Hennepin County Library Central Library, in Minneapolis Minnesota.

- Minerva is displayed as a 7-ft statue in the Science Library at the State University of New York at Albany and is on the official academic seal of the University.[11]

2.43.6 See also

- Celtic mythology

- Second French Empire

- Sulis

2.43.7 References and sources

References

[1] Encarta World English Dictionary 1998-2004 Microsoft Corporation.

[2] *Larousse Desk Reference Encyclopedia*, The Book People, Haydock, 1995, p. 215.

[3] Candau, Francisco J. Cevallos (1994). *Coded Encounters: Writing, Gender, and Ethnicity in Colonial Latin America*. University of Massachusetts Press. p. 215. ISBN 0-87023-886-8.

[4] *Philosophy of Right* (1820), "Preface"

[5] Aristotle *Mirab. Narrat.* 117

[6] Schmitz, Leonhard (1867). "Achaea (2)". In Smith, William. *Dictionary of Greek and Roman Biography and Mythology* **1**. Boston. p. 8.

[7] Mark Cartwright. "Minerva". *Ancient History Encyclopedia*.

[8] R. S. O. Tomlin (1992). "Voices from the Sacred Spring" (PDF). *Bath History* **4**: 8, 10.

[9] http://www.sos.ca.gov/digsig/greatseal.htm

[10] http://www.deltasigmatheta.org/downloads/vendors/list%20of%20registered%20marks.pdf

[11] "University at Albany - SUNY -". *albany.edu*.

Sources

- Origins of English History see Chapter Ten.

- Romans in Britain - Roman religion and beliefs see The Roman gods.

- Old Norse Myths, Literature and Society

- This article incorporates text from a publication now in the public domain: Smith, William, ed. (1870). "article name needed". *Dictionary of Greek and Roman Biography and Mythology*. See page 1090

2.43.8 External links

- Roman Mythology

2.44 Nanaya

The Land grant to Ḫunnubat-Nanaya kudurru *is a stele of King Meli-Shipak II (1186–1172 BCE).* **Nanaya**, *seated on a throne, is being presented the daughter of the king, Ḫunnubat-Nanaya. Kassite period limestone stele, The Louvre.*

This article is about the Mesopotamian goddess; for the Telugu author see Nannayya. For the Tsukihime character, see Shiki Nanaya.

Nanaya (Sumerian 𒀭𒈾𒈾, ᴰNA.NA.A; also transcribed as *"Nanâ", "Nanãy", "Nanaja", "Nanãja", or "'Nanãya"*; in Greek: Ναναια or Νανα; Aramaic: יﬡﬨﬨﬨﬨ) is the canonical name for a goddess worshipped by the Sumerians and Akkadians, a deity who personified "voluptuousness and sensuality".[1] Her cult was large and was spread as far as Syria and Iran. She later became syncretised with the Babylonian Tashmetum.

2.44.1 Notes

[1] Westenholz, 1997

2.44.2 References

- Encyclopedia of Gods, Michael Jordan, Kyle Cathie Limited, 2002

- Mesopotamian Goddess Nanãja, Olga Drewnowska-Rymarz, Agade, 2008

- Westenholz, Joan Goodnick (1997). "Nanya: Lady of Mystery". In I.L. Finkel and M.J. Geller. *Sumerian Gods and their Representations*. Cuneiform Monographs **7**. Groningen: Styx Publications. pp. 57–84. ISBN 90-5693-005-2.

2.44.3 External links

- A *tigi* to Nanaya for Išbi-Erra (Išbi-Erra C), translation at The Electronic Text Corpus of Sumerian Literature

- Nanaja > Antiquity volumes edited by: Hubert Cancik and Helmuth Schneider. Brill Online, 2015, Brill Online Reference Works

2.45 Nane (goddess)

Nane (Armenian: Նանե, *Nanė*; Georgian: ნანა, *Nana*; Bulgarian: Нане, *Nanė*; Russian: Нанэ, *Nanė*, Persian: ننه) was an Armenian pagan mother goddess. She was the goddess of war and wisdom.

Nane looked like a young beautiful woman in the clothing of a warrior, with spear and shield in hand,[1] like the Greek Athena, with whom she identified in the Hellenic period.[2]

She has also been referred to as *Hanea, Hanea, Babylonian Nana, Sumerian Nanai or Sumerian Nanai*.[3]

2.45.1 Early religion

Though originally worshipping nature, Armenia slowly moved to a Zoroastrian like religion, following the path of truth while believing that one must do the right thing, simply because it is the right thing to do. Soon after this new religion, they formed gods of their own around images of everyday hardworking, ambitious and kind people similar to themselves. The created gods quickly grew to be idolized and worship was cult like involving rituals and sacrifices.[4]

2.45.2 Cult

Her cult was closely associated with the cult of the goddess Anahit.

The temple of the goddess Nane was in the town of Thil across from the Lycus River. Her temple was destroyed during the Christianization of Armenia:

> "Then they crossed the Lycus River and demolished the temple of Nane, Aramazd's daughter, in the town of Thil."[5]

> "Gregory then asked the king for permission to overthrow and destroy the pagan shrines and temples. Drtad readily issued an edict entrusting Gregory with this task, and himself set out from the city to destroy shrines along the highways."[6]

According to some authors, Nane was adopted from the Akkadian goddess Nanaya, from the Phrygian goddess Cybele, or was from Elamite origin.[7][8][9][10]

2.45.3 Other influential Gods of her era

- Aramazd was the supreme god and considered to have created Heaven and earth. While providing the earth's fruitfulness, he was comparable to Zues and also happened to be Nane's father. The A-R in his name derives from the Indo-European root for sun, light, and life. His temple was in modern day Kamakh, in Turkey, which then was the center of Armenia.

- Anahit was the goddess of motherhood and fertility. She was the sister of Nane and was one of the most well respected gods. Having the traditional hair of Armenian women, she held a baby in her arms, and many people believed the world continued to exist because of her.

2.45.4   Destruction of Paganism

(Though Christianity was first brought to Armenia by the apostles Bartholomew and Thaddeus of Edessa, it was not accepted nor practiced by most of the people and those who did had to hide their beliefs among Zoroastrian practices.)

After the execution of his father Anak the Parthian, Gregory the Enlightener, escaped Armenia with the help of family friends. He was raised in a christian up bringing and upon growing older he learned that his father had assassinated Khosrov II of Armenia, the king at that time. Obtaining a fake identity, he returned with the hope to evangelize the country to pay for his fathers sins. King Tiridates II of Armenia, was the heir to the throne and became king. He also happened to be the son of Khosrov. After a few years, "Gregory" was admitted onto the kings council where he served for a few years.. [11]

While still practicing a Christian faith, he refused to bring offerings to a pagan Thanksgiving ritual. This and the knowledge of Gregory's true identity infuriated the king. He was tortured yet still would not give in and after increased rage, Tiridates had him thrown into a bottomless pit near modern day Khor Virap. Though he was left to die, he survived for 13 years with the help of a widow who lived in the city. She had dreamt to throw a loaf of bread in the pit every day and did so.

At the time, Armenia had a union with Roman Empire yet tensions were growing tight. After the break of the union, the king went mad. Every cure was tried yet nothing seemed to fully cure him. A woman in the kingdom dreamt that Gregory was still alive and his gods word was the cure. To their awe, he indeed was alive. They brought him to the king and sure enough, he cured him. [12]

After his newly restored health, (around 301 AD) the King declared Christianity as the National religion. (Armenia also happened to be the first Nation to declare Christianity.)[13] He declared that Gregory be the head of the church and quickly the country adapted to christian morals of love and kindness. Together the king and Gregory dismantled and destroyed Pagan temples and worship.

2.45.5   Traditions and symbols

Because the change to Christianity was so forceful, most artifacts, books, and stories were destroyed. As a result, many things are unknown to todays society. [14]

It is however known that in Ancient Armenia, it was traditional for Kings to meet with the oldest woman in their dynasty because she was often seen as the epitome of Nane. Interestingly enough, in Armenia and other countries around the world, the name Nane continues to be used

not only as a personal name, but also as a nickname for the grandmother of the household. *Nanna, Nani, Nannan, etc.*[15]

Am'nor took place on March 21st and is what they called their New Year. It was a celebration of Nane's father, the supreme God. [16]

Before christianity came to Armenia, the cross was important. The Arevkhatch, had four sections, each twisting in a direction of the cross. Eventually it came to represent war and disruption.[17]

2.45.6   See also

- Anahit

- Aramazd

- Nana

2.45.7   Notes

[1] С. Б. Арутюнян. Армянская мифология

[2] http://penelope.uchicago.edu/Thayer/E/Gazetteer/Places/Asia/Armenia/_Texts/KURARM/34*.html

[3] "Armenian Mythology - Mythology Dictionary." Accessed September 15, 2015. http://www.mythologydictionary.com/armenian-mythology.html.

[4] Ananikian, Mardiros Harootioon. Armenian Mythology: Stories of Armenian Gods and Goddesses, Heroes and Heroines, Hells & Heavens, Folklore & Fairy Tales. IndoEuropean Publishing.com, 2010.

[5] A. Carrière. The Eight Sanctuaries of Pagan Armenia according to Agat'angeghos and Movses Xorenats'I [Les huit sanctuaires de l'Arménie payenne]. Paris, 1899, English Translation by Robert Bedrosian, 2009. http://rbedrosian.com/Car1.htm

[6] AGATHANGELOS. History of St. Gregory and the Conversion of Armenia. http://www.vehi.net/istoriya/armenia/agathangelos/en/AGATHANGELOS.html

[7] С. Б. Арутюнян. Армянская мифология S. B. Arutiunyan. The Armenian Mythology (in Russian).

[8] John M. Douglas. The Armenians. New York, 1992, p. 91.

[9] "Armenian Mythology" in The Oxford Companion to World Mythology, by David Leeming, Oxford University Press, 17 Nov 2005, p.29

[10] http://penelope.uchicago.edu/Thayer/E/Gazetteer/Places/Asia/Armenia/_Texts/KURARM/34*.html

[11] Armenian Church. St. Gregory the Enlightener, n.d. http://www.hayastan.com/armenia/religion/history/index2.php.

[12] "The History of the Armenian Church," n.d. http://www.armenianchurch-ed.net/our-church/history-of-the-church/history/.

[13] "Armenian Apostolic Church." Encyclopedia Britannica. Accessed September 16, 2015. http://www.britannica.com/topic/Armenian-Apostolic-Church.

[14] Ananikian, Mardiros Harootioon. Armenian Mythology: Stories of Armenian Gods and Goddesses, Heroes and Heroines, Hells & Heavens, Folklore & Fairy Tales. IndoEuropean Publishing.com, 2010.

[15] "Nane - the Armenian Pagan Mother Goddess." Cradle of Civilization. Accessed September 15, 2015. https://aratta.wordpress.com/2013/08/15/nane-the-armenian-pagan-mother-goddess/.

[16] "Armenian Mythology," n.d. http://www.armenian-history.com/Armenian_mythology.htm.

[17] Armenian Culture, n.d. http://www.armeniapedia.org/wiki/Armenian_pagan_culture.

2.46 Neith

For other uses, see Neith (disambiguation).

Neith (/neɪθ/ or /niːθ/; also spelled **Nit**, **Net**, or **Neit**) was an early goddess in the Egyptian pantheon. She was the patron deity of Sais, where her cult was centered in the Western Nile Delta of Egypt and attested as early as the First Dynasty.[1] The Ancient Egyptian name of this city was Zau.

Neith also was one of the three tutelary deities of the ancient Egyptian southern city of Ta-senet or Iunyt now known as Esna (Arabic: إسنا), Greek: Λατόπολις (Latopolis), or πόλις Λάτων (*polis Laton*), or Λάττων (Laton); Latin: *Lato*), which is located on the west bank of the River Nile, some 55 km south of Luxor, in the modern Qena Governorate.

2.46.1 Symbolism

Neith was a goddess of war and of hunting and had as her symbol, two arrows crossed over a shield. However, she is a far more complex goddess than is generally known, and of whom ancient texts only hint of her true nature. In her usual representations, she is portrayed as a fierce deity, a human female wearing the Red Crown, occasionally holding or using the bow and arrow, in others a harpoon. In fact, the hieroglyphs of her name are usually followed by a determinative containing the archery elements, with the shield symbol of the name being explained as either double

bows (facing one another), intersected by two arrows (usually lashed to the bows), or by other imagery associated with her worship. Her symbol also identified the city of Sais.[2] This symbol was displayed on top of her head in Egyptian art. In her form as a goddess of war, she was said to make the weapons of warriors and to guard their bodies when they died.

As a deity, Neith is normally shown carrying the was scepter (symbol of rule and power) and the ankh (symbol of life). She is also called such cosmic epithets as the "Cow of Heaven," a sky-goddess similar to Nut, and as the Great Flood, Mehet-Weret (MHt wr.t), as a cow who gives birth to the sun daily. In these forms, she is associated with creation of both the primeval time and daily "re-creation." As protectress of the Royal House, she is represented as a uraeus, and functions with the fiery fury of the sun, In time, this led to her being considered as the personification of the primordial waters of creation. She is identified as a great mother goddess in this role as a creator. As a female deity and personification of the primeval waters, Neith encompasses masculine elements which enable her to function as a creator. She is a feminine version of Ptah-Nun, with her feminine nature complemented with masculine attributes symbolized with her association with the bow and arrow. In the same manner, her personification as the primeval waters is Mehetweret (MHt wr.t), the Great Flood, conceptualized as streaming water, related to another use of the verb *sti*, meaning 'to pour'."

Neith is one of the most ancient deities associated with ancient Egyptian culture. Flinders Petrie (*Diopolis Parva*, 1901) noted the earliest depictions of her standards were known in predynastic periods, as can be seen from a representation of a barque bearing her crossed arrow standards in the Predynastic Period, as displayed in the Ashmolean Museum, Oxford.

Her first anthropomorphic representations occur in the early dynastic period, on a diorite vase of King Ny-Netjer of the Second Dynasty, found in the Step Pyramid of Djoser (Third Dynasty) as Saqqara. That her worship predominated the early dynastic periods is shown by a preponderance of theophoric names (personal names which incorporate the name of a deity) within which Neith appears as an element. Predominance of Neith's name in nearly forty percent of early dynastic names, and particularly in the names of four royal women of the First Dynasty, only emphasizes the importance of this goddess in relation to the early society of Egypt, with special emphasis upon the Royal House. In the very early periods of Egyptian history, the main iconographic representations of this goddess appear to have been limited to her hunting and war characteristics, although there is no Egyptian mythological reference to support the concept this was her primary function as a deity. It has been suggested the hunt/war features of Neith's imagery may indicate her origin from Libya, located west and southwest of Egypt, where she was goddess of the combative peoples there.

It has been theorized Neith's primary cult point in the Old Kingdom was established in Saïs (modern Sa el-Hagar) by Hor-Aha of the First Dynasty, in an effort to placate the residents of Lower Egypt by the ruler of the unified country. It appears from textual/iconographic evidence she was something of a national goddess for Old Kingdom Egypt, with her own sanctuary in Memphis indicated the political high regard held for her, where she was known as "North of her Wall," as counterpoise to Ptah's "South of his Wall" epithet. While Neith is generally regarded as a deity of Lower Egypt, her worship was not consistently located in that region. Her cult reached its height in Saïs and apparently in Memphis in the Old Kingdom, and remained important, though to a lesser extent, in the Middle and New Kingdom. However, the cult regained political and religious prominence during the 26th Dynasties when worship at Saïs flourished again, as well as at Esna in Upper Egypt.

Neith's symbol and part of her hieroglyph also bore a resemblance to a loom, and so in later syncretisation of Egyptian myths by the Greek ruling class, she also became goddess of weaving. At this time her role as a creator conflated with that of Athena, as a deity who wove all of the world and existence into being on her loom.

Sometimes Neith was pictured as a woman nursing a baby crocodile, and she was titled "Nurse of Crocodiles", reflecting a provincial mythology that she served as either the mother or the consort of the crocodile god, Sobek. As mother of Ra, in her Mehet-Weret form, she was sometimes described as the "Great Cow who gave birth to Ra". As a maternal figure (beyond being the birth-mother of the sun-god Ra) Neith is associated with Sobek as her son (as far back as the Pyramid Texts), but no male deity is consistently identified with her as a consort. Later triad associations made with her have little or no religious or mythological supporting references, appearing to have been made by political or regional associations only.

This seems to support the contention Neith is an androgynous being, capable of giving birth without a partner and/or creation without sexual imagery, as seen in the myths of Atum and other creator gods. Erik Hornung notes in the Eleventh Hour of the Book of the Amduat, Neith's name appears written with a phallus (*Das Amduat*, **Teil I**: *Text*: 188, No. 800.(Äg. Abh., Band 7, Wiesbaden) 1963). See also Ramadan el-Sayed, *La Déese Neith de Saïs*, **I**:16; 58-60, for both hieroglyphic rendering and discussion of the bisexual nature of Neith as creator/creatress deity, and *Lexikon der Ägyptologie* (**LÄ I**) under *"Götter, androgyne"*: 634-635(W. Westendorf, ed., Harassowitz, Wiesbaden, 1977). In reference to Neith's function as creator with both male

and female characteristics, Peter Kaplony has said in the **Lexikon der Ägyptologie**: "Die Deutung von Neith als *Njt* "Verneinung" ist sekundär. Neith ist die weibliche Entsprechung zu *Nw(w)*, dem Gott der Urflut (Nun and Naunet). (Citing Sethe, *Amun*, § 139)." *LÄ* **II**: 1118 (Harassowitz, Wiesbaden, 1977).

Neith was considered to be eldest of the gods, and was appealed to as an arbiter in the dispute between Horus and Seth. Neith is said to have been "born the first, in the time when as yet there had been no birth." (St. Clair, *Creation Records*: 176). In the Pyramid Texts, Neith is paired with Selket as braces for the sky, which places these two deities as the two supports for the heavens (see PT 1040a-d, following J. Gwyn Griffths, *The Conflict of Horus and Seth*, (London, 1961) p. 1). This ties in with the vignette in the **Contendings of Seth and Horus** when Neith is asked by the gods, as the most ancient of goddesses, to decide who should rule. In her message of reply, Neith selects Horus, and says she will "cause the sky to crash to the earth" if he is not selected.

2.46.2   Attributes

Aegis of Neith, Twenty-sixth dynasty of Egypt. Museum of Fine Arts of Lyon.

An analysis of her attributes shows Neith was a goddess with many roles. From predynastic and early dynasty periods, she was referred to as an "Opener of the Ways" (*wp w3.wt*) which may have referred not only to her leadership in hunting and war, but also as a psychopomp in cosmic and underworld pathways. References to Neith as the "Opener of Paths" occurs in Dynasties 4 through 6, and is seen in the titles of women serving as priestesses of the goddess. Such epithets include: *"Priestess of Neith who opens all the (path)ways," "Priestess of Neith who opens the good pathways," "Priestess of Neith who opens the way in all her places."* (el-Sayed, **I**: 67-69). el-Sayed hypothesizes perhaps Neith should be seen as a feminine doublet of Wepwawet, the ancient jackal-god of Upper Egypt, who was associated with both royalty in victory and as a psychopomp for the dead.

The main imagery of Neith as *wp w3.wt* was as deity of the unseen and limitless sky, as opposed to Nut and Hathor, who represented the manifested night and day skies, respectively. Her epithet as the "Opener of the Sun's paths in all her stations" refers to how the sun is reborn (due to seasonal changes) at various points in the sky, beyond this world, of which only a glimpse is revealed prior to dawn and after sunset. It is at these changing points that Neith reigns as a form of sky goddess, where the sun rises and sets daily, or at its 'first appearance' to the sky above and below. It is at these points, beyond the sky that is seen, that her true power as deity who creates life is manifested. Georges St. Clair (*Creation Records*, 1898) noted that Neith is represented at times as a cow goddess with a line of stars across her back (as opposed to Nut's representations with stars across the belly) [See el-Sayed, II, Doc. 644], and maintained this indicated the ancient goddess represents the full ecliptic circle around the sky (above and below), and is seen iconographically in texts as both the regular and the inverted determinative for the heavenly vault, indicating the cosmos below the horizon. St. Clair maintained it was this realm Neith personified, for she is the complete sky which surrounds the upper (Nut) and lower (Nunet?) sky, and which exists beyond the horizon, and thereby beyond the skies themselves. Neith, then, is that portion of the cosmos which is not seen, and in which the sun is reborn daily, below the horizon (which may reflect the statement assigned to Neith as "I come at dawn and at sunset daily").

Since Neith also was goddess of war, she thus had an additional association with death: in this function, she shot her arrows into the enemies of the dead, and thus she began to be viewed as a protector of the dead, often appearing as a uraeus snake to drive off intruders and those who would harm the deceased (in this form she is represented in the tomb of Tutankhamun). She is also shown as the protectress of one of the Four sons of Horus, specifically, of Duamutef, the deification of the canopic jar storing the stomach, since the abdomen (often mistakenly associated as the stomach) was the most vulnerable portion of the body and a prime target during battle.

Egyptian war goddess Neith wearing the Deshret crown of northern (lower) Egypt, which bears the cobra of Wadjet

2.46.3 Mythology

In some creation myths, she was identified as the mother of Ra and Apep. When she was identified as a water goddess, she was also viewed as the mother of Sobek, the crocodile.[3] It was this association with water, i.e. the Nile, that led to her sometimes being considered the wife of Khnum, and associated with the source of the River Nile. She was associated with the Nile Perch as well as the goddess of the triad in that cult center.

As the goddess of creation and weaving, she was said to reweave the world on her loom daily. An interior wall of the temple at Esna records an account of creation in which Neith brings forth from the primeval waters of the Nun the first land. All that she conceived in her heart comes into being including the thirty gods. Having no known husband she has been described as "Virgin Mother Goddess":

> Unique Goddess, mysterious and great who came to be in the beginning and caused everything to come to be . . . the divine mother of Ra, who shines on the horizon...[4]

Proclus (412–485 AD) wrote that the adyton of the temple of Neith in Sais (of which nothing now remains) carried the following inscription:

> I am the things that are, that will be, and that have been. No one has ever laid open the garment by which I am concealed. The fruit which I brought forth was the sun.[5]

It was said that Neith interceded in the kingly war between Horus and Set, over the Egyptian throne, recommending that Horus rule.

A great festival, called the *Feast of Lamps*, was held annually in her honor and, according to Herodotus, her devotees burned a multitude of lights in the open air all night during the celebration.

2.46.4 Syncretic relationships

Louvre Statuette of Neith

The Greek historian Herodotus (c. 484–425 BC) noted that the Egyptian citizens of Sais in Egypt worshipped Neith and that they identified her with Athena. The *Timaeus*, a dialogue written by Plato, mirrors that identification with Athena, possibly as a result of the identification of both goddesses with war and weaving.[6]

E. A. Wallis Budge argued that the spread of Christianity in Egypt was influenced by the likeness of attributes between the Mother of Christ and goddesses such as Isis and Neith. Parthenogenesis was associated with Neith long before the birth of Christ and other properties belonging to her and Isis were transferred to the Mother of Christ by way of the apocryphal gospels as a mark of honour.[7]

2.46.5 See also

People named after Neith:

- Neithhotep, first recorded Egyptian queen

- Merneith, queen regent

2.46.6 References

[1] Shaw & Nicholson, op, cit., p.250

[2] The Way to Eternity: Egyptian Myth, F. Fleming & A. Lothian, p. 62.

[3] Fleming & Lothian, op. cit.

[4] Lesko, Barbara S. (1999). *The Great Goddesses of Egypt*. University of Oklahoma Press. pp. 60–63. ISBN 0-8061-3202-7.

[5] Proclus (1820). *The Commentaries of Proclus on the Timaeus of Plato, in Five Books*. trans. Thomas Taylor. A.J. Valpy. p. 82.

[6] *Timaeus* 21e

[7] *"The Gods of the Egyptians: Vol 2"*, E. A. Wallis Budge, p. 220-221, Dover ed 1969, org pub 1904, ISBN 0-486-22056-7

2.46.7 Further reading

- el-Sayed, Ramadan (1982). *La déesse Neith de Saïs*. Cairo: Institut Français d'Archéologie Orientale.

- Tower Hollis, Susan (1995). "5 Egyptian Goddesses in the Third Millenium B.C.: Neith, Hathor, Nut, Isis, Nephthys.". **KMT: Journal of Ancient Egypt** 5/4.

- Mallet, Dominique (1888). *Le culte de Neit à Saïs*. Paris : E. Leroux.

2.47 Nemain

In Irish mythology, **Neman** or **Nemain** (modern spelling: **Neamhan**, **Neamhain**) is the spirit-woman or goddess who personifies the frenzied havoc of war. In the ancient texts where The Morrígan appears as a trio of goddesses — the three sisters who make up the *Morrígna*[1][2][3] — one of these sisters is sometimes known as Nemain.[4]

2.47.1 Representation in literature

In the grand Irish epic of the Tain Bo Cuailnge, Neman confounds armies, so that friendly bands fall in mutual slaughter. When the forces of Queen Medb arrive at Magh-Tregham, in the present county of Longford, on the way to Cuailnge, Neman appears amongst them:

> "Then the Neman attacked them, and that was not the most comfortable night with them, from the uproar of the giant Dubtach through his sleep. The bands were immediately startled, and the army confounded, until Medb went to check the confusion." Lebor na hUidhre, fol. 46, b1.

And in another passage, in the episode called "Breslech Maighe Muirthemhne," where a terrible description is given of Cuchullain's fury at seeing the hostile armies of the south and west encamped within the borders of Uladh, we are told (Book of Leinster, fol.54, a2, and b1):Nemain is an Irish goddess who is very powerful. Nemain can kill 100 men with just one single battle cry.

> "He saw from him the ardent sparkling of the bright golden weapons over the heads of the four great provinces of Eriu, before the fall of the cloud of evening. Great fury and indignation seized him on seeing them, at the number of his opponents and at the multitude of his enemies. He seized his two spears, and his shield and his sword, and uttered from his throat a warrior's shout, so that sprites, and satyrs, and maniacs of the valley, and the demons of the air responded, terror-stricken by the shout which he had raised on high. And the Neman confused the army; and the four provinces of Eriu dashed themselves against the points of their own spears and weapons, so that one hundred warriors died of fear and trembling in the middle of the fort and encampment that night."

2.47.2 Kinship

In Cormac's glossary, Nemain is said to have been the wife of Neit, "the god of battle with the pagan Gaeidhel". A poem in the Book of Leinster (fol. 6, a2), couples Badb and Neman as the wives of Neid or Neit:—

> "Neit son of Indu, and his two wives, Badb and Neamin, truly, Were slain in Ailech, without blemish, By Neptur of the Fomorians".

At folio 5, a2, of the same MS., **Fea** and Nemain are said to have been Neit's two wives but in the poem on Ailech printed from the Dinnsenchus in the "Ordinance Memoir of Templemore" (p. 226), Nemain only is mentioned as the wife of Neit. Also, in the Irish books of genealogy, both Fea and Neman are said to have been the two daughters of Elcmar of the Brugh (Newgrange, near the Boyne), who was the son of Delbaeth, son of Ogma, son of Elatan, and the wives of Neid son of Indae. This identical kinship of Fea and Nemain implies that the two are one and the same personality.

She sometimes appears as a bean nighe, the weeping washer by a river, washing the clothes or entrails of a doomed warrior.

2.47.3 Etymology

The variant forms in which her name appears in Irish texts are *Nemon ~ Nemain ~ Neman*. These alternations imply that the Proto-Celtic form of this theonym, if such a theonym existed at that stage, would have been *Nemānjā, *Nemani-s or *Nemoni-s.

The meaning of the name has been various glossed. Squire (2000:45) glossed the name as 'venomous' presumably relating it to the Proto-Celtic *nemi- 'dose of poison' 'something which is dealt out' from the Proto-Indo-European root *nem- 'deal out' (Old Irish nem, pl. neimi 'poison'). However, *nemi- is clearly an *i*-stem noun whereas the stems of the reconstructed forms *Nemā-njā, *Nema-ni-s and *Nemo-ni-s are clearly *a*-stem and *o*-stem nouns respectively.

Equally, the Proto-Celtic *nāmant- 'enemy' (Irish námhaid, genitive namhad 'enemy' from the Old Irish náma, g. námat, pl.n. námait) is too different in form from *Nemānjā, *Nemani-s or *Nemoni-s to be equated with any of them.

The name may plausibly be an extended form of the Proto-Indo-European root of the name is *nem- 'seize, take, deal out' to which is related the Ancient Greek *Némesis* 'wrath, nemesis' and the name *Nemesis*, the personification of retributive justice in Greek mythology. Also related to this Proto-Indo-European root is the Old High German *nâma* 'rapine,' German *nehmen*, 'take,' English *nimble*; Zend *nemanh* 'crime,' Albanian *name* 'a curse' and the Welsh, Cornish, and Breton *nam*, 'blame' . According to this theory, the name would mean something like 'the Great Taker' or the 'Great Allotter.' However, it is just as plausible that the name be related to the Proto-Indo-European root **nem-* 'bend, twist.' Along these lines, the theonym would mean something like the 'Great Twister' or the 'Great Bender.'

2.47.4   References

[1] Sjoestedt, Marie-Louise. *Celtic Gods and Heroes.* Dover Publications. pp. 31–32. ISBN 0-486-41441-8.

[2] O hOgain, Daithi (1991). *Myth, Legend and Romance: An Encyclopedia of the Irish Folk Tradition.* Oxford: Prentice Hall Press. pp. 307–309. ISBN 0-13-275959-4.

[3] Davidson, Hilda Ellis (1988). *Myths and symbols in pagan Europe: early Scandinavian and Celtic religions.* Syracuse: Syracuse University Press. p. 97. ISBN 0-8156-2441-7.

[4] MacKillop, James (1998). *Dictionary of Celtic mythology.* Oxford: Oxford University Press. pp. 335–336. ISBN 0-19-280120-1.

2.47.5   Further reading

- Hennessey, WM. (1870). *The Ancient Irish Goddess of War.* Revue Celtique, Vol 1, pp. 27–57. Available 26 September 2007 online at Sacred-texts.com.

2.48   Nerio

In ancient Roman religion and myth, **Nerio** was an ancient war goddess and the personification of valor. She was the partner of Mars in ancient cult practices, and was sometimes identified with the goddess Bellona, and occasionally with the goddess Minerva. Spoils taken from enemies were sometimes dedicated to Nerio by the Romans. Nerio was later supplanted by mythologized deities appropriated and adapted from other religions.[1]

2.48.1   References

[1] Grimal, p. 308.

2.48.2   Sources

- Grimal, Pierre. *The Dictionary of Classical Mythology.* Oxford: Basil Blackwell, 1986. ISBN 0-631-20102-5

2.49   Nike (mythology)

Nike (/ˈnaɪki/; Greek: Νίκη, "Victory", Ancient Greek: [nǐːkɛː]), in ancient Greek religion, was a goddess who personified victory, also known as the Winged Goddess of Victory. The Roman equivalent was Victoria. Depending upon the time of various myths, she was described as the daughter of the Titan Pallas and the goddess Styx, and the sister of Kratos (Strength), Bia (Force), and Zelus (Zeal).[1]

2.49.1   Etymology

The word νίκη *nike* is of uncertain etymology. R. S. P. Beekes has suggested a Pre-Greek origin.[2]

2.49.2   Ancient references

Nike and her siblings were close companions of Zeus, the dominant deity of the Greek pantheon. According to classical (later) myth, Styx brought them to Zeus when the god was assembling allies for the Titan War against the older deities. Nike assumed the role of the divine charioteer, a role in which she often is portrayed in Classical Greek art. Nike flew around battlefields rewarding the victors with glory and fame, symbolized by a wreath of Laurel leaves (Bay leaves).

Nike is seen with wings in most statues and paintings, one of the most famous being the *Winged Victory of Samothrace*. Most other winged deities in the Greek pantheon had shed their wings by Classical times. Nike is the goddess of strength, speed, and victory. Nike was a very close acquaintance of Athena, and is thought to have stood in Athena's outstretched hand in the statue of Athena located in the Parthenon.[3] Nike is one of the most commonly portrayed figures on Greek coins.[4]

Names stemming from Nike include among others: Nikolaos, Nicholas, Nicola, Nick, Nicolai, Niccolo, Nikolai, Nicolae, Nils, Klaas, Nicole, Ike, Niki, Nikita, Nika, Nieke, Naike, Niketas, Nikki, Nico, and Veronica.

2.49.3   Contemporary usage

- The sports equipment company Nike, Inc. is named after the Greek goddess Nike.

Statuette of goddess Nike found in Vani, Georgia.

Statue of the Goddess Nike on the Titanic Engineers' Memorial, Southampton.

- Project Nike, an American anti-aircraft missile system is named after the goddess Nike.

- A figure of Nike with a vessel was the design of the first FIFA World Cup trophy, known also as the Jules Rimet trophy.

- Since Giuseppe Cassioli's design for the 1928 Summer Olympics, the obverse face of every Olympic medal bears Nike's figure holding a palm frond in her right hand and a winner's laurel crown in her left.[5][6]

- The goddess appears On the emblem of the University of Melbourne.

- The hood ornament used by the automobile manufacturer Rolls-Royce was inspired by Nike.

- The Titanic Engineers' Memorial, Southampton depicts Nike blessing the engineers of the RMS *Titanic* for staying at their post as the ship sank.

- The Honda motorcycle company's logo is inspired by the goddess Nike.[7]

2.49.4 See also

- Winged Victory of Samothrace

- Altar of Victory

- Nike of Paeonius

- Ángel de la Independencia

2.49.5 Notes

[1] Smith, Nice.

[2] R. S. P. Beekes, *Etymological Dictionary of Greek*, Brill, 2009, pp. 1021–2.

[3] "Nike: Greek goddess of victory". Theoi.com. Retrieved 2011-11-15.

[4] Sayles, Wayne G. (2007). *Ancient Coin Collecting II*. Krause Publications. p. 149. ISBN 978-0-89689-516-4.

[5] Winner's medal for the 1948 Olympic Games in London, Olympic.org. Accessed 5 August 2011.

[6] "Picture of 2004 Athens Games Medal". Retrieved 2010-01-28.

[7] http://www.onlytrial.com/1/the_honda_logotype_120282.html

2.49.6 References

- Smith, William; *A Dictionary of Greek and Roman Antiquities*. William Smith, LLD. William Wayte. G. E. Marindin. Albemarle Street, London. John Murray. 1890. Online version at the Perseus Digital Library.

2.49.7   External links

- Media related to Nike at Wikimedia Commons

- The dictionary definition of Nike at Wiktionary

- Theoi Project: Nike

- Goddess Nike

2.50   Oya

For the name, see Oya (name). For the Spanish village, see Oia, Spain.

Oya (known as **Oyá** or **Oiá**; **Yansá** or **Yansã**; and **Iansá**

Iansã Sculpture at the Catacumba Park, Rio de Janeiro, Brazil

or **Iansã** in Latin America) is an Orisha. She is either syncretized with the Virgin of Candelaria or St. Therese of Lisieux.

2.50.1   Name

In Yoruba, the name Oya literally means "She Tore".[1] She is known as **Oya-Iyansan** – the "mother of nine." This is due to the Niger River (known to the Yoruba as the Odo-Oya) traditionally being known for having nine tributaries.[2]

2.50.2   See also

- Egungun-oya

2.50.3   Notes

[1] *Sexuality and the world's religions - David W. Machacek.* Books.google.com. Retrieved 2012-09-24.

[2] A Bahia de Santa Bárbara

2.50.4   References

- OYA, Judith Gleason, Harper, San Francisco, 1992 (Shamballah, 1987), ISBN 0-06-250461-4

- Charles Spencer King.,"Nature's Ancient Religion" ISBN 978-1-4404-1733-7

2.51   Pakhet

In Egyptian mythology, **Pakhet**, Egyptian *Pḥ.t*, meaning *she who scratches* (also spelt **Pachet**, **Pehkhet**, **Phastet**, and **Pasht**) is a lioness goddess of war.

2.51.1   Origin and mythology

Pakhet is likely to be a regional lioness deity, *Goddess of the Mouth of the Wadi*, related to those that hunted in the wadi, near water at the boundary of the desert. Another title is *She Who Opens the Ways of the Stormy Rains*, which probably relates to the flash floods in the narrow valley, that occur from storms in the area. She appeared in the Egyptian pantheon during the Middle Kingdom. As with Bastet and Sekhmet, Pakhet is associated with Hathor and, thereby, is a sun deity as well, wearing the solar disk as part of her crown.

It became said that rather than a simple domestic protector against vermin and venomous creatures or a fierce warrior, she was a huntress, perhaps as a caracal, who wandered the desert alone at night looking for prey, gaining the title *Night huntress with sharp eye and pointed claw*. This desert aspect led to her being associated with desert storms, as was Sekhmet. She also was said to be a protector of motherhood, as was Bastet.

In art, she was depicted as a feline-headed woman or as a feline, often depicted killing snakes with her sharp claws. The exact nature of the feline varied between a desert wildcat, which was more similar to Bastet, or a caracal, resembling Sekhmet.

Hatshepsut and Pakhet. Speos Artemidos.

2.51.2   Temples near al Minya

The rock cut temple of Pakhet by Hatshepsut in Speos Artemidos.

The most famous temple of Pakhet was an underground, cavernous shrine that was built by Hatshepsut near al Minya,[1] among thirty-nine ancient tombs of Middle Kingdom monarchs of the Oryx nome, who governed from Hebenu, in an area where many quarries exist. This is in the middle of Egypt, on the east bank of the Nile. A tomb on the east bank is not traditional (the west was), but the terrain to the west was most difficult. A more ancient temple to this goddess at the location is known but has not survived. Hatshepsut is known to have restored temples in this region that had been damaged by the Hyksos invaders.

Its remarkable catacombs have been excavated. Great numbers of mummified cats have been found buried there. Many are thought to have been brought great distances to be buried ceremonially during rituals at the cult center. Some references associate this goddess as Pakhet-Weret-Hekau, (Weret Hekau meaning *she who has great magic*), implying the association with a goddess such as Hathor or Isis. Another title is *Horus Pakhet*; the presence of many mumified hawks at the site would further the association with Hathor who was the mother of Horus, the hawk, the pharaoh, and the sun.[2]

Her hunting nature led to the Greeks, who later occupied Egypt for three hundred years, identifying Pakhet with Artemis. Consequently, this underground temple became known to them as *Speos Artemidos*, the *Cave of Artemis*, a name that persists even though Artemis is not an Egyptian goddess. The Greeks attempted to align the Egyptian deities with their own, while retaining the traditions of the Egyptian religion. Later, Egypt was conquered by the Romans, just after 30 AD, and they retained many of the Greek place names. Christians and other religious sects occupied some parts of the site during the Roman period. Arabic place names were established after the 7th century.

Hatshepsut and her daughter Neferure have been identified as the builders of a smaller temple dedicated to Pakhet nearby, which was defaced by subsequent pharaohs. It was completed during the reign of Alexander II and is now called *Speos Batn el-Bakarah*.[3]

2.51.3   Coffin text incantation

The Faulkner translation of Ancient Egyptian Coffin Texts, Spell 470 reads,

> O You of the dawn who wake and sleep,
>
> O You who are in limpness, dwelling aforetime in Nedit,
>
> I have appeared as Pakhet the Great,
>
> whose eyes are keen and whose claws are sharp,
>
> the lioness who sees and catches by night....[4]

2.51.4   References

[1] www.maat-ka-ra.de

[2] wwww.ladyoftheflame.co.uk

[3] H.W. Fairman & B. Grdseloff

[4] www.per-bast.org

2.51.5 External links

- *Per-Bast.org*: About Pasht...

2.52 Palioxis

In Greek mythology, **Palioxis** was the personification of backrush in battle (as opposed to Proioxis). She is mentioned together with other personifications having to do with war.[1]

2.52.1 See also

- Makhai

2.52.2 References

[1] *Shield of Heracles* 139 ff

2.52.3 External links

- Theoi Project - Palioxis

2.53 Parvati

"Uma (goddess)" redirects here. For other uses, see Parvati (disambiguation).

Parvati (Devanagari: पार्वती, Tamil: பார்வதி, IAST: Pārvatī) is the Hindu goddess of love, fertility and devotion. She is the goddess of divine strength and power. [1][2][3] She is the gentle and nurturing aspect of the Hindu goddess Shakti. She is the mother goddess in Hinduism and has many attributes and aspects. Each of her aspects is expressed with a different name, giving her over 100 names in regional Hindu mythologies of India.[4] Along with Lakshmi (goddess of wealth and prosperity) and Saraswati (goddess of knowledge and learning), she forms the trinity of Hindu goddesses.[5]

Parvati is the wife of the Hindu deity Shiva - the destroyer, recycler and regenerator of universe and all life.[6] She is the daughter of the mountain king *Himavan* and mother *Mena*.[7] Parvati is the mother of Hindu deities Ganesha and Karttikeya. She is also the mother of Ashokasundari,

whose husband was Nahusha [8] Her elder sister is the goddess Ganges.[9] Some communities also believe her to be the adopted sister of Vishnu.[10]

With Śiva, Pārvatī is a central deity in the Saivism sect of Hinduism. In Hindu belief, she is the recreative energy and power of Śiva, and she is the cause of a bond that connects all beings and a means of their spiritual release.[11][12] In Hindu temples dedicated to her and Śiva, she is symbolically represented as *argha* or *yoni*.[6] She is found extensively in ancient Indian literature, and her statues and iconography grace ancient and medieval era Hindu temples all over South Asia and Southeast Asia.[13][14]

2.53.1 Etymology and nomenclature

Parvati as a two-armed consort goddess of Shiva (left), and as four-armed Lalita with her sons Ganesha and Skanda, Odisha, India. 11th century sculpture from the British Museum. 1872,0701.54 .

Parvata is one of the Sanskrit words for "mountain"; "Parvati" derives her name from being the daughter of king Himavan (also called Himavat, *Parvat*) and mother *Mena*.[6][7] King Parvat is considered lord of the mountains and the personification of the Himalayas; Parvati implies "she of the mountain".[15]

Parvati is known by many names in Hindu literature.[16] Other names which associate her with mountains are *Shailaja* (Daughter of the mountains), *Adrija* or *Nagajaa* or *Shailaputri* (Daughter of Mountains), 'Haimavathi' (Daughter of Himavan) and 'Girija' or 'Girirajaputri' (Daughter of king of the mountains).[17]

The Lalita sahasranama contains a listing of 1,000 names of Parvati (as Lalita).[4] Two of Parvati's most famous epithets are Uma and Aparna.[18] The name Uma is used for Sati (Shiva's first wife, who is reborn as Parvati) in earlier texts, but in the Ramayana, it is used as a synonym for Parvati. In the Harivamsa, Parvati is referred to as Aparna ('One who took no sustenance') and then addressed as Uma, who was dissuaded by her mother from severe austerity by saying u mā ('oh, don't').[19] She is also Ambika ('dear mother'), Shakti (power), Mataji ('revered mother'), Maheshwari ('great goddess'), Durga (invincible), Bhairavi ('ferocious'), Bhavani ('fertility and birthing'), Shivaradni ('Queen of Shiva'), and many hundreds of others. Parvati is also the goddess of love and devotion, or Kamakshi; the goddess of fertility, abundance and food/nourishment, or Annapurna.[20]

The apparent contradiction that Parvati is addressed as the fair one, Gauri, as well as the dark one, Kali or Shyama, has been explained by the following legend: Once, Shiva rebuked Parvati about her dark complexion. An angry Parvati left him and underwent severe austerities to become fair-complexioned as a boon from Brahma.[21] Regional stories of Gauri suggest an alternate origin for Gauri's name and complexion. In parts of India, Gauri's skin color is golden or yellow in honor of her being the goddess of ripened corn/harvest and of fertility.[22][23]

Parvati is sometimes spelled as *Parvathy* or *Parvaty*.

2.53.2 History

Some scholars[24] hold that Parvati does not explicitly appear in Vedic literature, though the Kena Upanishad (3.12) contains a goddess called Uma-Haimavati. Sayana's commentary in *Anuvaka*, however, identifies Parvati in Talavakara Upanishad, suggesting her to be the same as Uma and Ambika in the Upanishad, referring to Parvati is thus an embodiment of divine knowledge and the mother of the world.[16]

She appears as the *shakti*, or essential power, of the Supreme Brahman. Her primary role is as a mediator who reveals the knowledge of Brahman to the Vedic trinity of Agni, Vayu, and Indra, who were boasting about their recent defeat of a group of demons.[25] But Kinsley notes: "it is little more than conjecture to identify her with the later goddess Satī-Pārvatī, although [..] later texts that extol Śiva and Pārvatī retell the episode in such a way to leave no doubt that it was Śiva's spouse.."[24] Sati-Parvati appears in the epic period (400 BC–400 AD), as both the Ramayana and the Mahabharata present Parvati as Shiva's wife.[24] However, it is not until the plays of Kalidasa (5th-6th centuries) and the Puranas (4th through the 13th centuries) that the myths of Sati-Parvati and Shiva acquire more comprehensive details.[26] Kinsley adds that Parvati may have emerged from legends of non-aryan goddesses that lived in mountains.[17] While the word Umā appears in earlier Upanisads, Hopkins notes that the earliest known explicit use of the name Pārvatī occurs in late Haṃsa Upanishad (Yoga / Shukla Yajurveda).[27]

Weber suggests that just like Shiva is a combination of various Vedic gods Rudra and Agni, Parvati in Puranas text is a combination of wives of Rudra and Agni. In other words, the symbolism, legends and characteristics of Parvati evolved over time fusing Uma, Haimavati, Ambika in one aspect and the more ferocious, destructive Kali, Gauri, Nirriti in another aspect.[16][28] Tate suggests Parvati is a mixture of the Vedic goddesses Aditi and Nirriti, and being a mountain goddess herself, was associated with other mountain goddesses like Durga and Kali in later traditions.[29]

2.53.3 Legends

Wall carvings in Ellora Caves- A scene depicting Kalyanasundara *- the wedding of Shiva (four armed figure, right) and Parvati (two armed, left).*

The Puranas tell the tale of Sati's marriage to Shiva against her father Daksha's wishes. Her father Daksha and her husband Shiva do not get along, and ignore the wishes of Sati. The conflict gets to a point where Daksha does not invite Shiva to a major fire ceremony, and Shiva does not come on his own, humiliating Sati. She self-immolates herself at Daksha's yajna ceremony. This shocks Shiva, who is so grief-stricken that he loses interest in worldly affairs, retires and isolates himself in the mountains, in meditation and austerity.[30] Sati is then reborn as Parvati, the second[31] daughter of Himavat and Minavati, and is named Parvati, or "she from the mountains", after her father Himavant who is also called king *Parvat*.[32][33]

According to different versions of her myths, the maiden Parvati resolves to marry Shiva. Her parents learn of her desire, discourage her, but she pursues what she wants. She approaches the god Kama - the Hindu god of desire, erotic love, attraction and affection, and asks him to help her. Kama reaches Shiva and shoots an arrow of desire.[34] Shiva opens his third eye in his forehead and burns the cupid Kama to ashes. Parvati does not lose her hope or her resolve to win over Shiva. She begins to live in mountains like Shiva, engage in the same activities as Shiva, one of asceticism, yogin and tapas. This draws the attention of Shiva and awakens his interest. He meets her in disguised form, tries to discourage her, telling her Shiva's weaknesses and personality problems.[34] Parvati refuses to listen and insists in her resolve. Shiva finally accepts her and they get married.[34][35] Shiva dedicates the following hymn in Parvati's honor,

> I am the sea and you the wave,
> You are Prakṛti, and I Purusha.
> – Translated by Stella Kramrisch[36]

Parvati with Shiva and sons Ganesha (leftmost) and Kartikeya (rightmost). Parvati is depicted with green complexion, denoting dark complexion.

After the marriage, Parvati moves to Mount Kailash, the residence of Shiva. To them are born Kartikeya (also known

as Skanda and Murugan) - the leader of celestial armies, and Ganesha - the god of wisdom that prevents problems and removes obstacles.[6][37]

Alternate stories

There are many alternate Hindu legends about the birth of Parvati and how she got married with Shiva. In the Harivamsa, for example, Parvati has two younger sisters called Ekaparna and Ekapatala.[19] According to Devi Bhagawata Purana and Shiva Purana mount Himalaya and his wife Mena appease goddess Adi Shakti. Pleased, Adi Shakti herself is born as their daughter Parvati. Each major story about Parvati's birth and marriage to Shiva has regional variations, suggesting creative local adaptations. In another version of Shiva Purana, Chapters 17 through 52, cupid Kama is not involved, and instead Shiva appears as a badly behaved, snake wearing, dancing, disheveled beggar who Parvati gets attracted to, but who her parents disapprove of. The stories go through many ups and downs, until Parvati and Shiva are finally married.[38]

Kalidasa's epic *Kumarasambhavam* ("Birth of Kumara") describes the story of the maiden Parvati who has made up her mind to marry Shiva and get him out of his recluse, intellectual, austere world of aloofness. Her devotions aimed at gaining the favor of Shiva, the subsequent annihilation of Kamadeva, the consequent fall of the universe into barren lifelessness, regeneration of life, the subsequent marriage of Parvati and Shiva, the birth of Kartikeya, and the eventual resurrection of Kamadeva after Parvati intercedes for him to Shiva.

2.53.4   Iconography and symbolism

Shivlinga icons are common for Parvati and Shiva. She is symbolically the yoni in the core of a 9th-century Hindu temple of Java, Indonesia temple (left), and in Pashupatinath Temple of Nepal (right).

Parvati, the gentle aspect of Devi Shakti, is usually represented as fair, beautiful and benevolent.[39][40] She typically wears a red dress (often a sari), and may have a head-band.

Uma Maheshvara (Parvati with Shiva), 12th-13th century from India, currently in the British Museum.

When depicted alongside Shiva, she generally appears with two arms, but when alone, she may be depicted having four. These hands may hold a conch, crown, mirror, rosary, bell, dish, farming tool such as goad, sugarcane stalk, or flowers such as lotus.[3] One of her arms in front may be in the Abhaya mudra (hand gesture for 'fear not'), one of her children, typically Ganesha, is on her knee, while her elder son Skanda may be playing near her in her watch. In ancient temples, Parvati's sculpture is often depicted near a calf or cow - a source of food. Bronze has been the chief metal for her sculpture, while stone is next most common material.[3]

A common symbolism for her and her husband Siva is in the form of yoni and linga respectively. In ancient literature, yoni means womb and place of gestation, the yoni-linga metaphor represents "origin, source or regenerative power".[41] The linga-yoni icon is widespread, found in Shaivite Hindu temples of South Asia and Southeast Asia. Often called *Shivalinga*, it almost always has both linga and the yoni.[42] The icon represents the interdependence and union of feminine and masculine energies in recreation and regeneration of all life. In some temples and arts, the iconographic representation of sexuality, fertility and energies of Parvati and Shiva, is more explicit, where they are shown in various stages of their sexual form and union.[42]

In some iconography Parvati's hands may symbolically express many mudras (symbolic hand gestures). For example, Kataka — representing fascination and enchantment, Hirana — representing the antelope, the symbolism for nature and the elusive, Tarjani by the left hand — representing gesture of menace, and Chandrakal — representing the moon, a symbol of intelligence. Kataka is expressed by hands closer to the devotee; Tarjani mudra with the left hand, but far from devotee.

If Parvati is depicted with two hands, Kataka mudra — also called Katyavalambita or Katisamsthita hasta — is common, as well as Abhaya (fearlessness, fear not) and Varada (beneficence) are representational in Parvati's iconography. Parvati's right hand in Abhaya mudra symbolizes "do not fear anyone or anything", while her Varada mudra symbolizes "wish fulfilling".[43] In Indian dance, *Parvatimudra* is dedicated to her, symbolizing divine mother. It is a joint hand gesture, and is one of sixteen *Deva Hastas*, denoting most important deities described in *Abhinaya Darpana*. The hands mimic motherly gesture, and when included in a dance, the dancer symbolically expresses Parvati.[44] Alternatively, if both hands of the dancer are in *Ardhachandra* mudra, it symbolizes an alternate aspect of Parvati.[45]

Parvati is sometimes shown with golden or yellow colour skin, particularly as goddess Gauri, symbolizing her as the goddess of ripened harvests.[46]

In some manifestations, particularly as angry, ferocious aspects of Shakti such as Durga or Kali, she has eight or ten arms, and is astride on a tiger or lion. In benevolent manifestation such as Kamakshi or Meenakshi, a parrot sits near her right shoulder symbolizing cheerful love talk, seeds and fertility. A parrot is found with Parvati's form as Kamakshi - the goddess of love, as well as Kama - the cupid god of desire who shoots arrows to trigger infatuation.[47] A crescent moon is sometimes included near the head of Parvati particularly the Kamakshi icons, for her being half of Shiva. In South Indian legends, her association with the parrot began when she won a bet with her husband and asked for his loin cloth as victory payment; Shiva keeps his word but first transforms her into a parrot. She flies off and takes refuge in the mountain ranges of south India, appearing as Meenakshi (also spelled Minakshi).[48]

Symbolism of many aspects for the same goddess

Parvati is expressed in many roles, moods, epithets and aspects. In Hindu mythology, she is an active agent of the universe, the power of Shiva. She is expressed in nurturing and benevolent aspects, as well as destructive and ferocious aspects.[49] She is the voice of encouragement, reason, freedom and strength, as well as of resistance, power, action and retributive justice. This paradox symbolizes her willingness to realign to *Pratima* (reality) and adapt to needs of circumstances in her role as the universal mother.[49] She identifies and destroys evil to protect (Durga), as well as creates food and abundance to nourish (Annapurna).

2.53.5 Manifestations and aspects of Parvati

Parvati is expressed in many different aspects. As Annapurna she feeds, as Durga (shown above) she is ferocious.

Several myths present alternate aspects of Parvati, such as the ferocious, violent aspect as Shakti and related forms. Shakti is pure energy, untamed, unchecked and chaotic. Her wrath crystallizes into a dark, blood-thirsty, tangled-hair Goddess with an open mouth and a drooping tongue. This goddess is usually identified as the terrible *Mahakali* or Kali (time).[50] In Linga Purana, Parvati metamorphoses into Kali, on the request of Shiva, to destroy a female asura (demoness) Daruka. Even after destroying the demoness, Kali's wrath could not be controlled. To lower Kali's rage, Shiva appeared as a crying baby. The cries of the baby raised the maternal instinct of Kali who resorts back to her benign form as Parvati.[51]

In Skanda Purana, Parvati assumes the form of a warrior-goddess and defeats a demon called *Durg* who assumes the form of a buffalo. In this aspect, she is known by the name Durga.[52] Although Parvati is considered another aspect of Sakti, just like Kali, Durga, Kamakshi, Meenakshi, Gauri and many others in modern day Hinduism, many of these "forms" or aspects originated from regional legends and traditions, and the distinctions from Parvati are pertinent.[53]

In Devi Bhagwata Purana, Parvati is the lineal progenitor of all other goddesses. She is the one who is the source of all forms of goddesses. She is worshiped as one with many forms and names. Her different moods bring different forms or incarnation. For example,

- Durga is a demon-fighting form of Parvati, and some texts suggest Parvati took the form of Durga to kill the

demon Durgamasur.

- Kali is another ferocious form of Parvati, as goddess of time and change, with mythological origins in the deity Nirriti.

- Chandi is the epithet of Durga, considered to be the power of Parvati; she is black in color and rides on a lion, slayer of the demon Mahishasura.

- Ten Mahavidyas are the ten aspects of Shakti. In tantra, all have importance and all are different aspects of Parvati.

- 52 Shakti Peethas suggests all goddesses are expansions of the goddess Parvati.

- Navadurga nine forms of the goddess Parvati

- Meenakshi, goddess with eyes shaped like a fish.

- Kamakshi, goddess of love and devotion.

- Lalita, the playful Goddess of the Universe, she is a form of the Devi Parvati.

- Akhilandeshwari, found in coastal regions of India, is the goddess associated with water.[54]

- Annapurna is the representation of all that is complete and of food.

2.53.6 Story of The Attainment of The Name Durga

A demon named Durgasur has undertook severe austerities to please Lord Brahma. Being pleased with his penances, as his blessing, he cannot be killed by any man, demon, God or male deity. He gathered his large demonic forces and declared war against the Gods. Durgasur and Indra's forces engage in a severe war. In the end, Durgasur defeats Indra and he, with the help of his fellow demons take over the three worlds, and the heavens. Durgasur, full of pride and arrogance started tormenting and torturing innocent common people like villagers, wrecking down the religious schools and students and teachers, molesting other sages' wives and wreaking atrocities on the sages also. All the Gods, sages, their wives, the common people, teachers and students, united all together went to Kailash to seek the refuge of Lord Shiva but he was not there. They turned to his wife, Goddess Parvati, the full form of the Adi Parashakti and requested her to kill Durgasur and put an end to his every bad deed and atrocity. Parvati, hearing the atrocities of Durgasur, felt compassionate for them and she promised to stop Durgasur. She invokes Kaalratri, in the form of a damsel and requested her to go to Durgasur and ordered him to stop his atrocities on vulnerable people and Gods. Kaalratri went to Durgasur's territory and she requested him to cease his every atrocity on the Gods and common people and to hand over their respective abodes by going back to where he came from or get slayed at the hands of Parvati. Hearing this, Durgasur becomes very annoyed and he refuses to stop his atrocities on the world and ordered his demons to catch hold of the female messenger. Kaalratri turns furious and so she grew massive in her original form. She tells him to make preparations for his death. Durgasur becomes angry and commands his army to attack Kailash. Kaalratri returns to Parvati and conveyed the complete message to her. Parvati, on hearing this, she tells Durgasur that his last wish is to fight and his wish would be fulfilled by her. Parvati infuses Kaalratri in her body. Then, she, along with the Gods and common people approach the battlefield, waiting for Durgasur. Parvati creates a luminous circle around them as their own safety shield. Durgasur and his corps reach the battleground. Seeing them, Parvati sprouted a thousand hands holding all types of weapons. Seeing this thousand-armed form of Parvati, the Gods and common people express their gratitude awhile Durgasur and his army corps are terrified. At her call, all her Shaktis, of female forms, having a number of arms, weapons, wearing different garments, ornaments and apparels, riding on all kinds of animal vehicles, some of them were fierce and some of them were beneficial, they were of different names and incarnations and/or forms of Adi Parashakti. The war began. The fierce forms of Parvati managed to destroy the entire demon army of Durgasur. A severe duel erupted between Parvati and Durgasur. In the end, Parvati kills Durgasur with her trident. Seeing this end or Durgasur, the Gods and common people's joy knew no bounds and started worshipping her. She was instantly pleased. The Gods gave Parvati the name Durga as she killed demon Durgasur. Parvati restored all the worlds and abodes of the Gods and common people and the worlds were at peace again.

2.53.7 Legends

Parvati's legends are intrinsically related to Shiva. In the goddess-oriented Shakta texts, that she is said to transcend even Shiva, and is identified as the Supreme Being.[17] Just as Shiva is at once the presiding deity of destruction and regeneration, the couple jointly symbolise at once both the power of renunciation and asceticism and the blessings of marital felicity.

Parvati thus symbolises many different virtues esteemed by Hindu tradition: fertility, marital felicity, devotion to the spouse, asceticism, and power. Parvati represents the householder ideal in the perennial tension in Hinduism in the household ideal and the ascetic ideal, the later represented by Shiva.[50] Renunciation and asceticism is highly valued in Hinduism, as is householder's life - both feature as

Shiva with Parvati, 12th Century Chola sculpture, Tamil Nadu, India.

Ashramas of an ethical and proper life. Shiva is portrayed in Hindu legends as the ideal ascetic withdrawn in his personal pursuit in the mountains with no interest in social life, while Parvati is portrayed as the ideal householder keen about the nurturing worldly life and society.[34] Numerous chapters, stories and legends revolve around their mutual devotion as well as disagreements, their debates on Hindu philosophy as well as the proper life.

Parvati tames Shiva, the "great unpredictable madman" with her presence.[50] When Shiva does his violent, destructive Tandava dance, Parvati is described as calming him or complementing his violence by slow, creative steps of her own Lasya dance.[55] In many myths, Parvati is not as much his complement as his rival, tricking, seducing, or luring him away from his ascetic practices.[55]

Three images are central to the mythology, iconography and philosophy of Parvati: the image of Shiva-Shakti, the image of Shiva as Ardhanarishvara (the Lord who is half-woman), and the image of the linga and the yoni. These images that combine the masculine and feminine energies, Shiva and Parvati, yield a vision of reconciliation, interdependence and harmony between the way of the ascetic and that of a householder.[56]

The couple is often depicted in the Puranas as engaged in

"dalliance" or seated on Mount Kailash debating concepts in Hindu theology. They are also depicted as quarreling.[21] In stories of the birth of Kartikeya, the couple is described as love-making; generating the seed of Shiva. Parvati's union with Shiva symbolises the union of a male and female in "ecstasy and sexual bliss".[57] In art, Parvati is depicted seated on Shiva's knee or standing beside him (together the couple is referred to as *Uma-Maheshvara* or *Hara-Gauri*) or as *Annapurna* (the goddess of grain) giving alms to Shiva.[58]

Shaiva approaches tend to look upon Parvati as the Shiva's submissive and obedient wife. However, Shaktas focus on Parvati's equality or even superiority to her consort. The story of the birth of the ten Mahavidyas (Wisdom Goddesses) of Shakta Tantrism. This event occurs while Shiva is living with Parvati in her father's house. Following an argument, he attempts to walk out on her. Her rage at Shiva's attempt to walk out, manifests in the form of ten terrifying goddesses who block Shiva's every exit.

David Kinsley states,

Ardhanarishvara - the Hindu concept of an ideal couple as complementing union, inspired by Siva-Parvati. Ardhanarishvara in Elephanta Caves (left), and as an androgynous painting with one half Shiva, the other Parvati.[60]

> The fact that [Parvati] is able to physically restrain Shiva dramatically makes the point that she is superior in power. The theme of the superiority of the goddess over male deities is common in Shakta texts, [and] so the story is stressing a central Shakta theological principle. ... The fact that Shiva and Parvati are living in her father's house in itself makes this point, as it is traditional in many parts of India for the wife to leave her father's home upon marriage and become a part of her husband's lineage and live in his home among his relatives. That Shiva dwells in Parvati's house thus implies Her priority in their relationship. Her priority is also demonstrated in her ability, through the Mahavidyas, to thwart Shiva's will and assert her own.[59]

Ardhanarisvara

Parvati is portrayed as the ideal wife, mother and householder in Indian legends.[61] In Indian art, this vision of ideal couple is derived from Shiva and Parvati as being half of the other, represented as *Ardhanarisvara*.[62] This concept is represented as an androgynous image that is half man and half woman, Siva and Parvati respectively.[60][63]

Ideal wife, mother and more

In Hindu Epic the Mahabharata, she as Umā suggests that

the duties of wife and mother are as follows - being of a good disposition, endued with sweet speech, sweet conduct, and sweet features. Her husband is her friend, refuge, and god.[64] She finds happiness in physical, emotional nourishment and development of her husband and her children. Their happiness is her happiness. She is positive and cheerful even when her husband or her children are angry, she's with them in adversity or sickness.[64] She takes interest in worldly affairs, beyond her husband and family. She is cheerful and humble before family, friends, and relatives; helps them if she can. She welcomes guests, feeds them and encourages righteous social life. Her family life and her home is her heaven, Parvati declares in Book 13 of the Mahabharata.[64]

Rita Gross states,[42] that the view of Parvati only as ideal wife and mother is incomplete symbolism of the power of the feminine in mythology of India. Parvati, along with other goddesses, are involved with the broad range of culturally valued goals and activities.[42] Her connection with motherhood and female sexuality does not confine the feminine or exhaust their significance and activities in Hindu literature. She is balanced by Durga, who is strong and capable without compromising her femaleness. She manifests in every activity, from water to mountains, from arts to inspiring warriors, from agriculture to dance. Parvati's numerous aspects, states Gross,[42] reflects the Hindu belief that the feminine has universal range of activities, and her gender is not a limiting condition.

Ganesha

Hindu literature, including the Matsya Purana, Shiva Purana, and Skanda Purana, dedicates many stories to Parvati and Shiva and their children.[65] For example, one about Ganesha is:

> Once, while Parvati wanted to take a bath, there were no attendants around to guard her and stop anyone from accidentally entering the house. Hence she created an image of a boy out of turmeric paste which she prepared to cleanse her body, and infused life into it, and thus Ganesha was born. Parvati ordered Ganesha not to allow anyone to enter the house, and Ganesha obediently followed his mother's orders. After a while Shiva returned and tried to enter the house, Ganesha stopped him. Shiva was infuriated, lost his temper and severed the boy's head with his trident. When Parvati came out and saw her son's lifeless body, she was very angry. She demanded that Shiva restore Ganesha's life at once. Shiva did so by attaching an elephant's head to Ganesha's body, thus giving rise to the elephant headed deity.[66][67]

Parvati nursing Ganesha

2.53.8 Parvati in culture

Festivals

Teej is a significant festival for Hindu women, particularly in northern and western states of India. Parvati is the primary deity of the festival, and it ritually celebrates married life and family ties.[68] It also celebrates the monsoon. The festival is marked with swings hung from trees, girls playing on these swings typically in green dress (seasonal color of crop planting season), while singing regional songs.[69] Historically, unmarried maidens prayed to Parvati for a good mate, while married women prayed for the well-being of their husbands and visited their relatives. In Nepal, Teej is a three-day festival marked with visits to Shiva-Parvati temples and offerings to linga.[68] Teej is celebrated as Teeyan in Punjab.[70]

The Gowri Habba, or Gauri Festival, is celebrated on the seventh, eighth, and ninth of Bhadrapada (Shukla paksha). Parvati is worshipped as the goddess of harvest and protectress of women. Her festival, chiefly observed by women, is closely associated with the festival of her son Ganesha

Haryali Teej is a festival for girls and women, marking goddess Parvati.

(Ganesh Chaturthi). The festival is popular in Maharashtra and Karnataka.[71]

Parvati being celebrated at Gauri Festival, Rajasthan.

In Rajasthan the worship of Gauri happens during the Gangaur festival. The festival starts on the first day of Chaitra the day after Holi and continues for 18 days. Images of Issar and Gauri are made from Clay for the festival.

Another popular festival in reverence of Parvati is Navratri,

in which all her manifestations are worshiped over nine days. Popular in eastern India, particularly in Bengal, Odisha, Jharkhand and Assam, as well as several other parts of India such as Gujarat, this is associated with Durga, with her nine forms i.e. Shailaputri, Brahmacharini, Chandraghanta, Kushmanda, Skandamata, Katyayini, Kaalratri, Mahagauri, Siddhidatri.[72]

Another festival *Gauri tritiya* is celebrated from Chaitra shukla third to Vaishakha shukla third. This festival is popular in Maharashtra and Karnataka, less observed in North India and unknown in Bengal. The unwidowed women of the household erect a series of platforms in a pyramidal shape with the image of the goddess at the top and a collection of ornaments, images of other Hindu deities, pictures, shells etc. below. Neighbours are invited and presented with turmeric, fruits, flowers etc. as gifts. At night, prayers are held by singing and dancing. In south Indian states such as Tamil Nadu and Andhra Pradesh, the Kethara Gauri Vritham festival is celebrated on the new moon day of Diwali and married women fast for the day, prepare sweets and worship Parvati for the well-being of the family.[73]

Arts

From sculpture to dance, many Indian arts explore and express the stories of Parvati and Shiva as themes. For example, *Daksha Yagam* of Kathakali, a form of dance-drama choreography, adapts the romantic episodes of Parvati and Shiva.[74]

The Gauri-Shankar bead is a part of religious adornment rooted in the belief of Parvati and Shiva as the ideal equal complementing halves of the other. Gauri-Shankar is a particular *rudraksha* (bead) formed naturally from the seed of a tree found in India. Two seeds of this tree sometimes naturally grow as fused, and considered to symbolic of Parvati and Shiva. These seeds are strung into garlands and worn, or used in *malas* (rosaries) for meditation in Saivism.[75]

Numismatics

Ancient coins from Bactria (Central Asia) of Kushan Empire era, and those of king Harsha (North India) feature Uma. These were issued sometime between 3rd- and 7th-century AD. In Bactria, Uma is spelled *Ommo*, and she appears on coins holding a flower.[76][77] On her coin is also shown Shiva, who is sometimes shown in ithyphallic state holding a trident and standing near Nandi (his *vahana*). On coins issued by king Harsha, Parvati and Shiva are seated on a bull, and the reverse of the coin has Brahmi script.[78]

Major temples

See also: Shakti Peetha

Parvati is often present with Shiva in Saivite Hindu temples

Meenakshi Amman temple in Madurai, Tamil Nadu is a major temple dedicated to Meenakshi, an aspect of Hindu goddess Parvati.

all over South Asia and southeast Asia.

Some locations (*Pithas* or *Shaktipeeths*) are considered special because of their historical importance and legends about their origins in the ancient texts of Hinduism. Other locations celebrate major events in Parvati's life. For example, the World Heritage Site at Khajuraho is one such site where Parvati temple is found.[79] It is one of the four major sites associated with Parvati, along with Kedarnath, Kashi and Gaya. The temple's origin in Khajuraho has been traced to the Hindu mythology in which Khajuraho is the place where Parvati and Shiva got married.[80][81]

> One interpretation of the (Khajuraho) temples is that they were built to celebrate the mythic marriage of Shiva and his consort. At Mahashivratri in Khajuraho, they celebrate the marriage of Shiva and Parvati. (...) The erotic sculptures are a metaphor of the union of Shiva and Parvati, the marriage of two cosmic forces, of light and darkness, sky and earth, spirit and matter.[81]

Each major Parvati-Shiva temple is a pilgrimage site that has an ancient legend associated with it, which is typically a part of a larger story that links these Hindu temples across South Asia with each other.

Some temples where Parvati can be found include Annapurneshwari temple, Attukal Bhagavathy temple, Chengannur Mahadeva temple, Oorpazhachi Kavu, Valiya Kavu Sree Parvathi Devi temple, Sri Kiratha Parvathi Temple Paramelpadi, Korechal Kirathaparvathi temple, Sree Bhavaneeswara Temple Palluruthy, Irumkulangara Durga Devi Temple, Chakkulathukavu Temple, Nedukavu Parvathy Devi temple, Karthyayani Devi temple, Varanad Devi Temple, Veluthattu Vadakkan Chowa temple, Thiruvairanikulam Mahadeva temple, Ardhanariswara temple and Kadampuzha Devi Temple in Kerala, Meenakshi Amman Temple in Tamil Nadu, Kamakshi Amman Temple in Tamil Nadu, Sri Siva Durga Temple , Mandaikadu Bhagavathi Temple and Devi Kanya Kumari in Tamil Nadu, Mookambika Devi Temple and Banashankari Temple in Karnataka, Maanikyambika Bhimeswara temple in Andhra pradesh, Vishalakshi Temple, Vishalakshi Gauri temple and Annapurna devi temple in Uttar Pradesh, Parvati Temple in Madhya Pradesh, Tulja Bhavani Temple in Maharashtra, Nartiang Durga Temple in Meghalaya, Tripura Sundari Temple in Tripura.

2.53.9 Outside India

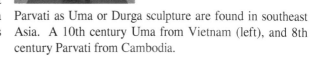

Parvati as Uma or Durga sculpture are found in southeast Asia. A 10th century Uma from Vietnam (left), and 8th century Parvati from Cambodia.

Sculpture and iconography of Parvati, in one of her many manifestations, have been found in temples and literature of southeast Asia. For example, early Saivite inscriptions of the Khmer in Cambodia, dated as early as the fifth century AD, mention Parvati (Uma) and Siva.[82] Many ancient and medieval era Cambodian temples, rock arts and river bed carvings such as the Kbal Spean are dedicated to Parvati and Shiva.[83][84]

Boisselier has identified Uma in a Champa era temple in Vietnam.[85]

Dozens of ancient temples dedicated to Parvati as Uma, with Siva, have been found in the islands of Indonesia and Malaysia. Her manifestation as Durga has also been found in southeast Asia.[86] Many of the temples in Java dedicated to Siva-Parvati are from second half of 1st millennium AD, and some from later centuries.[87] Durga icons and worship have been dated to be from the 10th- to 13th-century.[88]

Pillar temple with offerings to Dewi Sri (Uma) in Bali.

In Nakhorn Si Thammarat province of Thailand, excavations at Dev Sathan has yielded a Hindu Temple dedicated to Vishnu (Na Pra Narai), a lingam in yoni, a Shiva temple (San Pra Isuan). The sculpture of Parvati found at this excavation site reflect the South Indian style.[89][90]

Bali, Indonesia

Parvati, locally spelled as *Parwati*, is a principal goddess in modern day Hinduism of Bali. She is more often called *Uma*, and sometimes referred to as *Giriputri* (daughter of the mountains).[91] She is the goddess of mountain Gunung Agung.[92] Like Hinduism of India, Uma has many manifestations in Bali, Indonesia. She is the wife of deity *Siwa*. Uma or Parwati is considered as the mother goddess that nurtures, nourishes, grants fertility to crop and all life. As *Dewi Danu*, she presides over waters, lake Batur and Gunung Batur, a major volcano in Bali. Unlike India where Sri refers to Lakshmi, Sri is another name of Uma in Bali;[91] her icons and pillar temples grace terraced rice fields (*sawahs*). Parwati's small pillar temples in rice fields is to seek her blessings of abundance and a good crop.[93] Her ferocious form in Bali is *Dewi Durga*.[94] As *Rangda*, she is wrathful and presides cemeteries.[92] As *Ibu Petri*, Parwati of Balinese Hinduism is the goddess of earth.[92] The legends about various manifestations of Parwati, and how she changes from one form to another, are in Balinese literature, such as the palm-leaf (*lontar*) manuscript *Andabhuana*.[95]

2.53.10 Related goddesses

Buddhism

Tara found in some sects of Buddhism, particularly Tibetan and Nepalese, is related to Parvati.[96][97] Tara too appears in many manifestations. In tantric sects of Buddhism, as well as Hinduism, intricate symmetrical art forms of yantra or mandala are dedicated to different aspects of Tara and Parvati.[98][99]

Ancient civilizations

Parvati is closely related in symbolism and powers as Cybele of Greek and Roman mythology and as Vesta the guardian goddess of children.[6][100] In her manifestation as *Durga*, Parvati parallels Mater Montana.[6] She is the equivalent of *Magna Mater* (Universal Mother).[15] As *Kali* and punisher of all evil, she corresponds to Proserpine and Diana Taurica.[101]

As *Bhawani* and goddess of fertility and birthing, she is the symbolic equivalent of Ephesian *Diana*.[101] In Crete, *Rhea* is the mythological figure, goddess of the mountains, paralleling Parvati; while in some mythologies from islands of Greece, the terrifying goddess mirroring Parvati is *Diktynna* (also called Britomartis).[102] At Ephesus, Cybele is shown with lions, just like iconography of Parvati is sometimes shown with a lion.[102]

Carl Jung, in *Mysterium Coniunctionis*, states that aspects of Parvati belong to the same category of black goddesses as Artemis, Isis and Mary.[103][104] Edmund Leach equates Parvati in her relationship with Shiva, with that of Greek goddess Aphrodite - a symbol of sexual love.[105]

2.53.11   108 names of Parvati

Parvati is known by 108 different names. Following are the name along with it meaning.[106]

1. **Aadya**: The meaning of this name is initial reality.

2. **Aarya**: It is the name of the Goddess

3. **Abhavya**: Signifies fear

4. **Aeindri**: The power of Lord Indra.

5. **Agnijwala**: Signifies fire

6. **Ahankaara**: Indicates pride.

7. **Ameyaa**: The name signifies beyond measure.

8. **Ananta**: Signifies one who is infinite.

9. **Ananta**: The Infinite

10. **Anekashastrahasta**: It means the possessor of many hand weapons

11. **AnekastraDhaarini**: It means the possessor of many weapons

12. **Anekavarna**: Person with multiple complexions.

13. **Aparna**: Signifies a person who does not eat anything during fasting

14. **Apraudha**: Signifies a person who does not age

15. **Bahula**: Various forms

16. **Bahulaprema**: Loved by everyone

17. **Balaprada**: Signifies the giver of strength

18. **Bhaavini**: The Beautiful Woman

19. **Bhavya**: Future

20. **Bhadrakaali**: One of the forms of Goddess Kali

21. **Bhavani**: The abode of the universe

22. **Bhavamochani**: The absolver of the universe

23. **Bhavaprita**: Loved by everyone in the universe

24. **Bhavya**: Indicates magnificence

25. **Braahmi**: God Brahma's power

26. **Brahmavaadini**: Present everywhere

27. **Buddhi**: Intelligence

28. **Buddhida**: The bestower of wisdom

29. **Chamunda**: Name of Goddess who killed the demons Chanda and Munda

30. **Chandaghanta**: Mighty bells

31. **ChandaMundaVinashini**: Goddess who killed asuras Chanda and Munda

32. **Chinta**: Tension

33. **Chita**: Death-bed

34. **Chiti**: The thinking mind

35. **Chitra**: The Picturesque

36. **Chittarupa**: Thinking or thoughtful state.

37. **Dakshakanya**: It is the name of daughter of Daksha

38. **Dakshayajnavinaashini**: Interrupter of the sacrifice of Daksha

39. **Devamata**: Mother Goddess

40. **Durga**: The Invincible

41. **Ekakanya**: The girl child

42. **Ghorarupa**: Fierce outlook

43. **Gyaana**: Knowledge

44. **Jalodari**: Abode of the ethereal universe

45. **Jaya**: The Victorious

46. **Kaalaratri**: Goddess who is black and is similar to the night.

47. **Kaishori**: The adolescent

48. **Kalamanjiiraranjini**: Musical anklet

49. **Karaali**: Violent

50. **Katyayani**: Sage Katyanan worships this name

51. **Kaumaari**: Adolescent

52. **Komaari**: Beautiful adolescent

53. **Kriya**: Action

54. **Krrooraa**: Brutal

55. **Lakshmi**: Goddess of Wealth

56. **Maaheshvari**: Power of Lord Shiva

57. **Maatangi**: Goddess of Matanga

58. **MadhuKaitabhaHantri**: Goddess that killed the demons Madhu and Kaitabha

59. **Mahaabala**: Strength

60. **Mahatapa**: Penance

61. **Mahodari**: Keeping the universe in a huge belly

62. **Manah**: Mind

63. **Matangamunipujita**: Worshipped by Sage Matanga

64. **Muktakesha**: Open tresses

65. **Narayani**: Lord Narayana destructive attributes

66. **NishumbhaShumbhaHanani**: Goddess who killed brothers Shumbha Nishumbha

67. **Mahishasura Mardini**: Goddess who killed demon Mahishasura

68. **Nitya**: Eternal one

69. **Paatala**: The color red

70. **Paatalavati**: Wearing the color red and white

71. **Parameshvari**: Ultimate Goddess

72. **Pattaambaraparidhaana**: Dress made of leather

73. **Pinaakadharini**: Trident of Shiva

74. **Pratyaksha**: Real

75. **Praudha**: Old

76. **Purushaakriti**: Taking the form of a man

77. **Ratnapriya**: Adorned

78. **Raudramukhi**: Fierce face like destroyer Rudra

79. **Saadhvi**: Sanguine

80. **Sadagati**: Bestowing Moksha

81. **Sarvaastradhaarini**: Possessor of missile weapons

82. **Sarvadaanavaghaatini**: Ability to kill all the demons

83. **Sarvamantramayi**: Instruments of thought

84. **Sarvashaastramayi**: Deft in all theories

85. **Sarvavahanavahana**: Rides all vehicles

86. **Sarvavidya**: Knowledgeable

87. **Sati**: Women who burned on the pyre of her husband

88. **Satta**: Above all

89. **Satya**: Truth

90. **Satyanandasvarupini**: Eternal bliss

91. **Savitri**: Daughter of the Sun God Savitr

92. **Shaambhavi**: Consort of Shambhu

93. **Shivadooti**: Ambassador of Lord Shiva

94. **Shooldharini**: Person who holds a monodent

95. **Sundari**: Gorgeous

96. **Sursundari**: Very Beautiful

97. **Tapasvini**: Engaged in penance

98. **Trinetra**: Person with three eyes.

99. **Vaarahi**: Person who rides on Varaah

100. **Vaishnavi**: Invincible

101. **Vandurga**: Goddess of forests

102. **Vikrama**: Violent

103. **Vimalauttkarshini**: Providing joy

104. **Vishnumaya**: The spells of Lord Vishnu

105. **Vriddhamaata**: Mother who is old

106. **Yati**: Person one who renounces the world

107. **Yuvati**: Woman

2.53.12   See also

2.53.13   Notes

[1] H.V. Dehejia, Parvati: Goddess of Love, Mapin, ISBN 978-8185822594

[2] James Hendershot, Penance, Trafford, ISBN 978-1490716749, pp 78

[3] Suresh Chandra (1998), Encyclopaedia of Hindu Gods and Goddesses, ISBN 978-8176250399, pp 245-246

[4] Keller and Ruether (2006), Encyclopedia of Women and Religion in North America, Indiana University Press, ISBN 978-0253346858, pp 663

[5] Frithjof Schuon (2003), Roots of the Human Condition, ISBN 978-0941532372, pp 32

[6] Edward Balfour, *Parvati*, p. 153, at Google Books, The Encyclopaedia of India and of Eastern and Southern Asia, pp 153

[7] H.V. Dehejia, Parvati: Goddess of Love, Mapin, ISBN 978-8185822594, pp 11

[8] James W. Haag et al (2013), The Routledge Companion to Religion and Science, Routledge, ISBN 978-0415742207, pp 491-496

[9] William J. Wilkins, Uma - Parvati, Hindu Mythology - Vedic and Puranic, Thacker Spink London, pp 295

[10] Edward Washburn Hopkins, *Epic Mythology*, p. 224, at Google Books, pp. 224-226

[11] Ananda Coomaraswamy, Saiva Sculptures, Museum of Fine Arts Bulletin, Vol. 20, No. 118 (Apr., 1922), pp 17

[12] Stella Kramrisch (1975), The Indian Great Goddess, History of Religions, Vol. 14, No. 4, pp. 261

[13] Hariani Santiko, The Goddess Durgā in the East-Javanese Period, Asian Folklore Studies, Vol. 56, No. 2 (1997), pp. 209-226

[14] Ananda Coomaraswamy, Saiva Sculptures, Museum of Fine Arts Bulletin, Vol. 20, No. 118 (Apr., 1922), pp 15-24

[15] Alain Daniélou (1992), Gods of Love and Ecstasy: The Traditions of Shiva and Dionysus, ISBN 978-0892813742, pp 77-80

[16] John Muir, *Original Sanskrit Texts on the Origin and History of the People of India*, p. 422, at Google Books, pp 422-436

[17] Kinsley p.41

[18] Gopal, Madan (1990). K.S. Gautam, ed. *India through the ages*. Publication Division, Ministry of Information and Broadcasting, Government of India. p. 68.

[19] Wilkins pp.240-1

[20] Kinsley pp. 142-143

[21] Kennedy p.334

[22] Edward Balfour, *Parvati*, p. 381, at Google Books, The Encyclopaedia of India and of Eastern and Southern Asia, pp 381

[23] Ernest Payne (1997), The Saktas: An Introductory and Comparative Study, Dover, ISBN 978-0486298665, pp 7-8, 13-14

[24] Kinsley p.36

[25] *Kena Upanisad*, III.1--IV.3, cited in Müller and in Sarma, pp. *xxix-xxx*.

[26] Kinsley p.37

[27] Edward Washburn Hopkins, *Epic Mythology*, p. 224, at Google Books, pp. 224-225

[28] Weber in Hindu Mythology, Vedic and Purbnic By William J. Wilkins p.239

[29] Tate p.176

[30] Wilkins p.243

[31] In the Ramayana, the river goddess Ganga is the first daughter and the elder sister of Parvati; William J. Wilkins, Uma - Parvati, Hindu Mythology - Vedic and Puranic, Thacker Spink London

[32] Kinsley p.42

[33] William J. Wilkins, Uma - Parvati, Hindu Mythology - Vedic and Puranic, Thacker Spink London, pp 300-301

[34] James Lochtefeld (2005), "Parvati" in The Illustrated Encyclopedia of Hinduism, Vol. 2: N–Z, pp. 503-505, Rosen Publishing, ISBN 0-8239-2287-1

[35] Kinsley p.43

[36] Stella Kramrisch (1975), The Indian Great Goddess, History of Religions, Vol. 14, No. 4, pp. 235-265

[37] Ganesa: Unravelling an Enigma By Yuvraj Krishan p.6

[38] Alain Daniélou (1992), Gods of Love and Ecstasy: The Traditions of Shiva and Dionysus, ISBN 978-0892813742, pp 82-87

[39] Wilkins pp.247

[40] Harry Judge (1993), *Devi*, Oxford Illustrated Encyclopedia, Oxford University Press, pp 10

[41] James Lochtefeld (2005), "Yoni" in The Illustrated Encyclopedia of Hinduism, Vol. 2: N–Z, pp. 784, Rosen Publishing, ISBN 0-8239-2287-1

[42] Rita M. Gross (1978), Hindu Female Deities as a Resource for the Contemporary Rediscovery of the Goddess, Journal of the American Academy of Religion, Vol. 46, No. 3 (Sep., 1978), pp. 269-291

[43] Caroll and Caroll (2013), Mudras of India, ISBN 978-1848191099, pp 34, 266

[44] Caroll and Caroll (2013), Mudras of India, ISBN 978-1848191099, pp 184

[45] Caroll and Caroll (2013), Mudras of India, ISBN 978-1848191099, pp 303, 48

[46] *The Shaktas: an introductory comparative study* Payne A.E. 1933 pp. 7, 83

[47] Devdutt Pattanaik (2014), Pashu: Animal Tales from Hindu Mythology, Penguin, ISBN 978-0143332473, pp 40-42

[48] Sally Kempton (2013), Awakening Shakti: The Transformative Power of the Goddesses of Yoga, ISBN 978-1604078916, pp 165-167

[49] Ellen Goldberg (2002), The Lord Who Is Half Woman: Ardhanarisvara in Indian and Feminist Perspective, State University of New York Press, ISBN 978-0791453254, pp 133-153

[50] Kinsley p.46

[51] Kennedy p.338

[52] Kinsley p.96

[53] Kinsley pp. 4

[54] Subhash C Biswas, India the Land of Gods, ISBN 978-1482836554, pp 331-332

[55] Kinsley p.48

[56] Kinsley p.49

[57] Tate, p.383

[58] Coleman p.65

[59] Kinsley, p. 26.

[60] MB Wangu (2003), Images of Indian Goddesses: Myths, Meanings, and Models, ISBN 978-8170174165, Chapter 4 and pp 86-89

[61] Wojciech Maria Zalewski (2012), The Crucible of Religion: Culture, Civilization, and Affirmation of Life, ISBN 978-1610978286, pp 136

[62] Betty Seid (2004), The Lord Who Is Half Woman (Ardhanarishvara), Art Institute of Chicago Museum Studies, Vol. 30, No. 1, Notable Acquisitions at The Art Institute of Chicago, pp. 48-49

[63] A Pande (2004), Ardhanarishvara, the Androgyne: Probing the Gender Within, ISBN 9788129104649, pp 20-27

[64] Anucasana Parva The Mahabharata, pp 670-672

[65] Kennedy p.353-4

[66] Paul Courtright (1978), Ganesa: Lord of Obstacles, Lord of Beginnings, Oxford University Press, ISBN 9780195057423

[67] Robert Brown (1991), Ganesh: Studies of an Asian God, SUNY Press, ISBN 978-0791406564

[68] Constance Jones (2011), Religious Celebrations: An Encyclopedia of Holidays (Editor - J. Gordon Melton), ISBN 978-1598842050, pp 847-848

[69] Devotion, mirth mark 'Hariyali Teej' The Hindu (August 10, 2013)

[70] Gurnam Singh Sidhu Brard (2007), East of Indus: My Memories of Old Punjab, ISBN 978-8170103608, pp 325

[71] The Hindu Religious Year By Muriel Marion Underhill p.50 Published 1991 Asian Educational Services ISBN 81-206-0523-3

[72] S Gupta (2002), Festivals of India, ISBN 978-8124108697, pp 68-71

[73] The Hindu Religious Year By Muriel Marion Underhill p.100

[74] Ragini Devi (2002), Dance Dialects of India, Motilal Banarsidass, ISBN 978-8120806740, pp 201-202

[75] James Lochtefeld (2005), "Gauri-Shankar" in The Illustrated Encyclopedia of Hinduism, Vol. 1: A-M, pp. 244, Rosen Publishing, ISBN 0-8239-2287-1

[76] John M. Rosenfield (1967), The Dynastic Arts of the Kushans, University of California Press, Reprinted in 1993 as ISBN 978-8121505796, pp 94-95

[77] AH Dani et al, History of Civilizations of Central Asia, Vol. 2, Editors: Harmatta et al, UNESCO, ISBN 978-9231028465, pp 326-327

[78] Arthur L. Friedberg and Ira S. Friedberg (2009), Gold Coins of the World: From Ancient Times to the Present, ISBN 978-0871843081, pp 462

[79] Shobita Punja (1992), Divine Ecstasy - The Story of Khajuraho, Viking, New Delhi, ISBN 978-0670840274

[80] Devangana Desai, Khajuraho, Oxford University Press, ISBN 9780195653915, pp 42-51, 80-82

[81] Steven Leuthold (2011), Cross-Cultural Issues in Art: Frames for Understanding, Routledge, ISBN 978-0415578004, pp 142-143

[82] Sanderson, Alexis (2004), "The Saiva Religion among the Khmers, Part I.", Bulletin de Ecole frangaise d'Etreme-Orient, 90-91, pp 349-462

[83] Michael Tawa (2001), At Kbal Spean, Architectural Theory Review, Volume 6, Issue 1, pp 134-137

[84] Helen Jessup (2008), The rock shelter of Peuong Kumnu and Visnu Images on Phnom Kulen, Vol. 2, National University of Singapore Press, ISBN 978-9971694050, pp. 184-192

[85] Jean Boisselier (2002), "The Art of Champa", in Emmanuel Guillon (Editor) - Hindu-Buddhist Art in Vietnam: Treasures from Champa, Trumbull, p. 39

[86] Hariani Santiko (1997), The Goddess Durgā in the East-Javanese Period, Asian Folklore Studies, Vol. 56, No. 2 (1997), pp. 209-226

[87] R Ghose (1966), Saivism in Indonesia during the Hindu-Javanese period, Thesis, Department of History, University of Hong Kong

[88] Peter Levenda (2011), Tantric Temples: Eros and Magic in Java, ISBN 978-0892541690, pp 274

[89] R. Agarwal (2008), "Cultural Collusion: South Asia and the construction of the Modern Thai Identities", Mahidol University International College (Thailand)

[90] Gutman, P. (2008), Siva in Burma, In Selected Papers from the 10th International Conference of the European Association of Southeast Asian Archaeologists: the British Museum, London, 14th-17th September 2004: Interpreting Southeast Asia's past, monument, image, and text (Vol. 10, p. 135), National University of Singapore Press

[91] Reinhold Rost, *Miscellaneous Papers Relating to Indo-China and the Indian Archipelago*, p. 105, at Google Books, Volume 2, pp 105

[92] Jones and Ryan, Encyclopedia of Hinduism, ISBN 978-0816054589, pp 67-68

[93] Wouter Cool and EJ Taylor, *With the Dutch in the East*, p. 86, at Google Books, pp 86

[94] Michele Stephen (2005), Desire Divine & Demonic: Balinese Mysticism in the Paintings, University of Hawaii Press, ISBN 978-0824828592, pp 119-120, 90

[95] J Stephen Lansing (2012), *Perfect Order: Recognizing Complexity in Bali,* Princeton University Press, ISBN 978-0691156262, pp 138-139

[96] David Leeming (2005), The Oxford Companion to World Mythology, Oxford University Press, ISBN 978-0195156690, pp 374-375

[97] Monier Williams, *Buddhism: In Its Connexion with Brāhmanism and Hindūism*, p. 216, at Google Books, pp 200-219

[98] David Frawley (1994), Tantric Yoga and the Wisdom Goddesses: Spiritual Secrets of Ayurveda, ISBN 978-1878423177, pp 57-85

[99] Rebeca French, The Golden Yoke: The Legal Cosmology of Buddhist Tibet, ISBN 978-1559391719, pp 185-188

[100] George Stanley Faber, *The Origin of Pagan Idolatry*, p. 488, at Google Books, pp 260-261, 404-419, 488

[101] Maria Callcott, *Letters on India*, p. 345, at Google Books, pp 345-346

[102] Alain Daniélou (1992), Gods of Love and Ecstasy: The Traditions of Shiva and Dionysus, ISBN 978-0892813742, pp 79-80

[103] Joel Ryce-Menuhin (1994), Jung and the Monotheisms, Routledge, ISBN 978-0415104142, pp 64

[104] Ann Casement (2001), Carl Gustav Jung, SAGE Publications, ISBN 978-0761962373, pp 56

[105] Edmund Ronald Leach, The Essential Edmund Leach: Culture and human nature, Yale University Press, ISBN 978-0300085082, pp 85

[106] "Goddess Parvati names". Goddess Parvati website. Retrieved Sep 2015.

2.53.14 References

- David Kinsley, *Hindu Goddesses: Vision of the Divine Feminine in the Hindu Religious Traditions* (ISBN 81-208-0379-5)

- Vans Kennedy, *Researches Into the Nature and Affinity of Ancient and Hindu Mythology*; Published 1831; Printed for Longman, Rees, Orme, Brown, and Green; 494 pages; Original from Harvard University; Digitized Jul 11, 2005

- William J. Wilkins, Uma - Parvati, *Hindu Mythology, Vedic and Puranic*; Republished 2001 (first published 1882); Adamant Media Corporation; 463 pages; ISBN 1-4021-9308-4

- Wendy Doniger O'Flaherty, *Śiva, the Erotic Ascetic*

- Charles Coleman, *Mythology of the Hindus*

- Karen Tate, *Sacred Places of Goddess: 108 Destinations*

2.53.15 External links

- Parvati Encyclopædia Britannica

- Devotional hymns and eulogies on Parvati

2.54 Pele (deity)

For other uses, see Pele (disambiguation).

In the Hawaiian religion, **Pele** (/ˈpeɪleɪ/ Pel-a; [ˈpɛlɛ]),

According to legend, Pele lives in the Halemaʻumaʻu crater Kīlauea

the Fire Goddess, is the goddess of fire, lightning, wind and volcanoes and the creator of the Hawaiian Islands. Often referred to as "Madame Pele" or "Tūtū Pele" as a sign of respect, she is a well-known deity within Hawaiian mythology, and is notable for her contemporary presence and cultural influence as an enduring figure from ancient Hawaii.[1] Epithets of the goddess include *Pele-honua-mea* ("Pele of the sacred land") and *Ka wahine 'ai honua* ("The earth-eating woman").[2]

2.54.1 Legends

Arthur Johnsen's Pele

There are several traditional legends associated with Pele in Hawaiian mythology. In addition to being recognized as the goddess of volcanoes, Pele is also known for her power, passion, jealousy, and capriciousness.

She has numerous siblings, including Kāne Milohai, Kamohoali'i, Nāmaka and numerous sisters named Hi'iaka, the most famous being Hi'iakaikapoliopele (Hi'iaka in the bosom of Pele). They are usually considered to be the offspring of Haumea. Pele's siblings include deities of various types of wind, rain, fire, ocean wave forms, and cloud forms. Her home is believed to be the fire pit called Halema'uma'u crater, at the summit caldera of Kīlauea, one of the Earth's most active volcanoes; but her domain encompasses all volcanic activity on the Big Island of Hawai'i.[3]

Pele shares features similar to other malignant deities inhabitants of volcanoes, as in the case of the devil Guayota

of Guanche Mythology in Canary Islands (Spain), living on the volcano Teide and was considered by the aboriginal Guanches as responsible for the eruptions of the volcano.[4]

Expulsion version

In one version of the story, Pele is daughter of Kanehoalani and Haumea in the mystical land of Kuaihelani, a floating free land like Fata Morgana. Kuaihelani was in the region of Kahiki (*Kukulu o Kahiki*). She stays so close to her mother's fireplace with the fire-keeper Lono-makua. Her older sister Nā-maka-o-Kaha'i, a sea goddess, fears that Pele's ambition would smother the home-land and drives Pele away. Kamohoali'i drives Pele south in a canoe called Honua-i-a-kea with her younger sister Hi'iaka and with her brothers Kamohoali'i, Kanemilohai, Kaneapua, and arrives at the islets above Hawaii. There Kane-milo-hai is left on Mokupapapa, just a reef, to build it up in fitness for human residence. On Nihoa, 800 feet above the ocean she leaves Kane-apua after her visit to Lehua and crowning a wreath of kau-no'a. Pele feels sorry for her younger brother and picks him up again. Pele used the divining rod, Pa'oa to pick a new home. A group of chants tells of a pursuit by Namakaokaha'i and Pele is torn apart. Her bones, Kai-wioPele form a hill on Kahikinui, while her spirit escaped to the island of Hawai'i.[5]:157 (Pele & Hi'iaka A myth from Hawaii by Nathaniel B. Emerson)

Flood version

In another version, Pele comes from a land said to be "close to the clouds," with parents Kane-hoa-lani and Ka-hina-li'i, and brothers Ka-moho-ali'i and Kahuila-o-ka-lani. From her husband Wahieloa (also called Wahialoa) she has a daughter Laka and a son Menehune. Pele-kumu-honua entices her husband and Pele travels in search of him. The sea pours from her head over the land of Kanaloa (perhaps the island now known as Kaho'olawe) and her brothers say:

O the sea, the great sea!
Forth bursts the sea:
Behold, it bursts on Kanaloa!

The sea floods the land, then recedes; this flooding is called Kai a Kahhinalii ("The sea of Ka-hina-li'i"), as Pele's connection to the sea was passed down from her mother Kahinalii.[5]:158[6][7]

Pele and Poli'ahu

Pele was considered to be a rival of the Hawaiian goddess of snow, Poli'ahu, and her sisters Lilinoe (a goddess of fine rain), Waiau (goddess of Lake Waiau), and Kahoupokane (a kapa maker whose kapa making activities create thunder, rain, and lightning). All except Kahoupokane reside on Mauna Kea. The kapa maker lives on Hualalai.

One myth tells that Poliʻahu had come from Mauna Kea with her friends to attend sled races down the grassy hills south of Hamakua. Pele came disguised as a beautiful stranger and was greeted by Poliʻahu. However, Pele became jealously enraged at the goddess of Mauna Kea. She opened the subterranean caverns of Mauna Kea and threw fire from them towards Poliʻahu, with the snow goddess fleeing towards the summit. Poliʻahu was finally able to grab her now-burning snow mantle and throw it over the mountain. Earthquakes shook the island as the snow mantle unfolded until it reached the fire fountains, chilling and hardening the lava. The rivers of lava were driven back to Mauna Loa and Kīlauea. Later battles also led to the defeat of Pele and confirmed the supremacy of the snow goddesses in the northern portion of the island and of Pele in the southern portion.[8]

Historical times

Pele belief continued after the old religion was officially abolished in 1819. In the summer of 1823 English missionary William Ellis toured the island to determine locations for mission stations.[9]:236 After a long journey to the volcano Kīlauea with little food, Ellis eagerly ate the wild berries he found growing there.[9]:128 The berries of the ʻōhelo (*Vaccinium reticulatum*) plant were considered sacred to Pele. Traditionally prayers and offerings to Pele were always made before eating the berries. The volcano crater was an active lava lake, which the natives feared was a sign that Pele was not pleased with the violation.[9]:143 Although wood carvings and thatched temples were easily destroyed, the volcano was a natural monument to the goddess.

In December 1824 the High Chiefess Kapiʻolani descended into the Halemaʻumaʻu crater after reciting a Christian prayer instead of the traditional one to Pele. She was not killed as predicted, and this story was often told by missionaries to show the superiority of their faith.[10] Alfred, Lord Tennyson (1809–1892) wrote a poem about the incident in 1892.[11]

When businessman George Lycurgus ran a hotel at the rim of Kīlauea, called the Volcano House, he would often "pray" to Pele for the sake of the tourists. Park officials took a dim view of his habit of tossing items such as gin bottles (after drinking their contents) into the crater.[12]

Plantation owner William Hyde Rice published a version of the story in his collection of legends.[13] In 2003 the Volcano Art Center had a special competition for Pele paintings to replace one done in the early 20th century by D. Howard Hitchcock displayed in the Hawaii Volcanoes National Park visitors center. Some criticized what looked like a blond caucasian as the Hawaiian goddess.[14] Over 140 paintings were submitted, and finalists were displayed at sites within the park.[15] The winner of the contest was Pahoa, Hawaii artist Arthur Johnsen. This version shows the goddess in shades of red, with a digging stick in her left hand (the ʻōʻō, for which the currently erupting vent was named), and an embryonic form of Hiʻiaka-i-ka-poli-o-Pele in her right hand. The painting is now on display at the Kīlauea Visitor Center on the edge of the Kīlauea crater.[16]

2.54.2 Relatives

Pele's other prominent relatives are:

- Hiʻiaka, spirit of the dance

- Kā-moho-aliʻi, a shark god and the keeper of the water of life

- Kaʻōhelo, a mortal sister

- Kapo, a goddess of fertility

- Ka-poho-i-kahi-ola, spirit of explosions

- Kane-Hekili, spirit of the thunder (a hunchback)

- Ke-ō-ahi-kama-kaua, the spirit of lava fountains (a hunchback)

- Ke-ua-a-ke-pō, spirit of the rain and fire

- Kane-hoa-lani, father and division with fire

- Hina-alii,mother and takes place of different forms

2.54.3 Science

Pele's hair, a volcanic glass in strands

Several phenomena connected to volcanism have been named after her, including Pele's hair, Pele's tears, and Limu o Pele (Pele's seaweed). A volcano on the Jovian moon Io is also named Pele.[17]

2.54.4　Pop culture references

- The musician Tori Amos named an album *Boys for Pele* in her honor. A single lyrical excerpt from the song "Muhammad My Friend" makes the only outright connection, "You've never seen fire until you've seen Pele blow." However, the entire record deals with the ideas usually associated with Pele, such as feminine "fire," or power. Amos claims the title reflects the idea of boys being devoured by Pele, or alternatively, as boys worshipping Pele.

- Simon Winchester, in his book *Krakatoa*, stated about the Pele myth: "Like many legends, this old yarn has its basis in fact. The sea attacks volcanoes – the waters and the waves erode the fresh laid rocks. And this is why Pele herself moved, shifting always to the younger and newer volcanoes, and relentlessly away from the older and worn-out islands of the northwest."

- In 2004, American composer Brian Balmages composed a piece entitled "Pele for Solo Horn and Wind Ensemble" on commission by Jerry Peel, professor of French Horn at the University of Miami Frost School of Music. It was premiered by the University of Miami Wind Ensemble under the direction of Gary Green, with Jerry Peel on Horn.

- Pele is mentioned in the song "Hot Lava" by Perry Farrell on the South Park Album:

    And after the eruption, we lay dormant for a while

    Let's just hold each other and talk,

    For now, Pele sleeps

- Steven Reineke created a musical composition called "Goddess of Fire" which was inspired by the story and life of Pele.

- In the 1990s a character claiming to be the goddess Pele appeared as a villainess in the DC Comics comic book *Superboy*. Pele later reappeared in the comic book *Wonder Woman* where she sought revenge against Wonder Woman for the murder of Kāne Milohai, who in that story was her father, at the hands of the Greek god Zeus.[18]

- In Marvel Comics's *Chaos War* event, Pele appears as an ally to Hercules and the daughter of Gaea.

- An eight-woman world-beat band (featuring djimbe drums, steel drums, and saxophone) called Pele Juju was based in Santa Cruz, California.

- Pele appears on Sabrina the Teenage Witch in the episode "The good, the bad and the luau", as Sabrina's relative, who gives her the final clue to the family secret. This version of her has a slight tendency to unwittingly set things on fire.

- In Borderlands and its sequel, Pele is referenced in the rare weapon named "Volcano", which the ammunition can explode causing fire damage on impact. The descriptions reads "Pele demands a sacrifice!" in the first game and "Pele humbly requests a sacrifice, if it's not too much trouble." in the second.

- In the Wildefire book series written by Karsten Knight, Pele is one of many deities that are reincarnated in teenagers along the centuries. Ashline Wilde and her two sisters (Evelyn and Rose) represent the spirit of the goddess (the Flame, the Spark and the Fuse), which was divided in three by the Cloak because of the (self)destructiveness of hers.

- Pele appears in a 1969 'Hawaii Five-0 episode' 'The Big Kahuna' in which her appearance is faked by a couple of crooks intent on frightening their uncle into selling his property to them.

- Pele was also referenced in an episode of "Raven", entitled Heat, in which she is alluded to as the cause of a severe heat wave, as well as being a mysterious woman who leads Jonathan to causing an explosion.

- Pele appears as a demon in the video game *Shin Megami Tensei IV* along with several other deities.

- The song Budding Trees by Nahko and Medicine for the People references the Hawaiian goddess Pele.[19]

2.54.5　See also

- Painting of Pele

2.54.6　References

[1] 'Iolana, Patricia (2006). "TuTu Pele: The Living Goddess of Hawaii's Volcanoes". *Sacred History*.

[2] H. Arlo Nimmo (2011). *Pele, Volcano Goddess of Hawai'i: A History*. McFarland. p. 208. ISBN 0-7864-6347-3.

[3] William Westervelt (1999). *Hawaiian Legends of Volcanoes*. Mutual Publishing, originally published 1916 by Ellis Press.

[4] Ethnografia y anales de la conquista de las Islas Canarias

[5] Martha Warren Beckwith (1940). *Hawaiian Mythology*. Forgotten Books. ISBN 978-1-60506-957-9.

[6] Nicholson, Henry Whalley (1881). *From Sword to Share; Or, A Fortune in Five Years at Hawaii*. London, England: W.H. Allen and Co. p. 39.

[7] "Pele and the Deluge," Access Genealogy *Hawaiian Folk Tales A Collection of Native Legends* , 1907, Retrieved on 24 October 2012.

[8] W. D. Westervelt, *Hawaiian legends of volcanoes*. Boston, G.H. Ellis Press, 1916.

[9] William Ellis (1823). "A journal of a tour around Hawai'i, the largest of the Sandwidch Islands". Crocker and Brewster, New York, republished 2004, Mutual Publishing, Honolulu. ISBN 1-56647-605-4.

[10] Penrose C. Morris (1920). "Kapiolani". *All about Hawaii: Thrum's Hawaiian annual and standard guide* (Thomas G. Thrum, Honolulu): 40–53.

[11] Alfred Lord Tennyson (1899). Hallam Tennyson, ed. *The life and works of Alfred Lord Tennyson* **8**. Macmillan. pp. 261–263. ISBN 0-665-79092-9.

[12] "The Volcano House". *Hawaii Nature Notes* (National Park Service) **5** (2). 1953.

[13] William Hyde Rice, preface by Edith J. K. Rice (1923). "Hawaiian Legends" (PDF). *Bulletin 3*. Bernice P. Bishop Museum, Honolulu,. Retrieved 2010-01-08.

[14] Rod Thompson (July 13, 2003). "Rendering Pele: Artists gather paints and canvas in effort to be chosen as Pele's portrait maker". *Honolulu Star-Bulletin*. Retrieved 2010-01-08.

[15] "Visions of Pele, the Hawaiian Volcano Deity" (PDF). *Press release on Volcano Art Center Gallery web site*. August 2003. Retrieved 2010-01-08.

[16] "Arthur Johnsen: Painter". *Arthur Johnsen Gallery web site*. Retrieved 2010-04-28.

[17] Radebaugh, J.; et al. (2004). "Observations and temperatures of Io's Pele Patera from Cassini and Galileo spacecraft images". *Icarus* **169**: 65–79. Bibcode:2004Icar..169...65R. doi:10.1016/j.icarus.2003.10.019.

[18] *Wonder Woman* (vol. 3) #35-36

[19] https://www.youtube.com/watch?v=1LsabQV0Yjk

2.54.7 External links

- Mythical Realm: Pele, Goddess of Fire

- MP3 sample by native speaker Ka'upena Wong: Legend of Pele, Goddess of Fire

2.55 Proioxis

In Greek mythology, **Proioxis** was the personification of onrush in battle (as opposed to Palioxis). She is mentioned together with other personifications having to do with war.[1]

2.55.1 See also

- Makhai

2.55.2 References

[1] *Shield of Heracles* 139 ff

2.55.3 External links

- Theoi Project - Proioxis

2.56 Qamaits

Qamaits is a warrior goddess of the indigenous Nuxalk (sometimes called Bella Coola) people of the central coast of British Columbia in Canada.

Qamaits is also the Goddess of the death and the beginning. At the dawn of Time, Qamaits did battle against the giants of the mountains, which were so high that nothing could survive on them. Qamaits, being a ferocious warrior, defeated legions of giants and turned them into the mountain landscapes of today, knocking them down to the size they are today. After that she grew bored of Earth and left for residence elsewhere. Her assistant Senx tends to look after the daily tasks of creation.

She doesn't think much of humans and rarely visits the earth, but when she does, she causes earthquakes, forest fires, and sickness. Sometimes she visits to take her pet snake Sisiutl and to attack a few humans about and cause disasters. Her snake is a sign that she is coming.

She is also referred to as Our Woman and Afraid-of-Nothing.

2.56.1 References

http://www.godchecker.com/pantheon/native-american-mythology.php?deity=QAMAITS Retrieved: 19 May 2015

http://www.goddessaday.com/native-american/qamaits Retrieved: 19 May 2015

2.57 Sekhmet

For other uses, see Sekhmet (disambiguation).

In Egyptian mythology, **Sekhmet** /ˈsɛkˌmɛt/[1] or **Sachmis** (/ˈsækmɪs/; also spelled Sakhmet, Sekhet, or Sakhet, among other spellings) was originally the warrior goddess as well as goddess of healing for Upper Egypt, when the kingdom of Egypt was divided. She is depicted as a lioness, the fiercest hunter known to the Egyptians. It was said that her breath formed the desert. She was seen as the protector of the pharaohs and led them in warfare.

Her cult was so dominant in the culture that when the first pharaoh of the twelfth dynasty, Amenemhat I, moved the capital of Egypt to Itjtawy, the centre for her cult was moved as well. Religion, the royal lineage, and the authority to govern were intrinsically interwoven in Ancient Egypt during its approximately three millennia of existence.

Sekhmet also is a Solar deity, sometimes called the daughter of the sun god Ra and often associated with the goddesses Hathor and Bast. She bears the Solar disk and the uraeus which associates her with Wadjet and royalty. With these associations she can be construed as being a divine arbiter of the goddess Ma'at (Justice, or Order) in the Judgment Hall of Osiris, associating her with the Wadjet (later the Eye of Ra), and connecting her with Tefnut as well.

2.57.1 Etymology

This golden cultic object is called an aegis. It is devoted to Sekhmet, highlighting her solar attributes. Walters Art Museum, Baltimore.

Sekhmet's name comes from the Ancient Egyptian word "sekhem" which means "power or might". Sekhmet's name

suits her function and means "the (one who is) powerful". She also was given titles such as the "(One) Before Whom Evil Trembles", "Mistress of Dread", "Lady of Slaughter" and "She Who Mauls".

2.57.2 History

Sekhmet from the temple of Mut at Luxor, granite, 1403–1365 B.C., in the National Museum, Copenhagen

In order to placate Sekhmet's wrath, her priestesses performed a ritual before a different statue of the goddess on each day of the year. This practice resulted in many images of the goddess being preserved. Most of her statuettes were rigidly crafted and do not exhibit any expression of movements or dynamism; this design was made to make them last a long time rather than to express any form of functions or actions she is associated with. It is estimated that more than seven hundred statues of Sekhmet once stood in one funerary temple alone, that of Amenhotep III, on the west bank of the Nile.

She was envisioned as a fierce lioness, and in art, was depicted as such, or as a woman with the head of a lioness, who was dressed in red, the color of blood. Sometimes the dress she wears exhibits a rosetta pattern over each breast, an ancient leonine motif, which can be traced to observation of the shoulder-knot hairs on lions. Occasionally, Sekhmet was also portrayed in her statuettes and engravings with minimal clothing or naked. Tame lions were kept

Image from a ritual Menat necklace, depicting a ritual being performed before a statue of Sekhmet on her throne, she also is flanked by the goddess Wadjet as the cobra and the goddess Nekhbet as the white vulture, symbols of lower and upper Egypt respectively who always were depicted on the crown of Egypt and referred to as the two ladies, and the supplicant holds a complete menat and a sistrum for the ritual, circa 870 B.C. (Berlin, Altes Museum, catalogue number 23733)

in temples dedicated to Sekhmet at Leontopolis.

Festivals and evolution

To pacify Sekhmet, festivals were celebrated at the end of battle, so that the destruction would come to an end. During an annual festival held at the beginning of the year, a festival of intoxication, the Egyptians danced and played music to soothe the wildness of the goddess and drank great quantities of wine ritually to imitate the extreme drunkenness that stopped the wrath of the goddess—when she almost destroyed humanity. This may relate to averting excessive flooding during the inundation at the beginning of each year as well, when the Nile ran blood-red with the silt from upstream and Sekhmet had to swallow the overflow to save humankind.

In 2006, Betsy Bryan, an archaeologist with Johns Hopkins University excavating at the temple of Mut presented her findings about the festival that included illustrations of the priestesses being served to excess and its adverse effects being ministered to by temple attendants.[2] Participation in the festival was great, including the priestesses and the population. Historical records of tens of thousands attending the festival exist. These findings were made in the temple of Mut because when Thebes rose to greater prominence, Mut absorbed some characteristics of Sekhmet. These temple excavations at Luxor discovered a "porch of drunkenness" built onto the temple by the Pharaoh Hatshepsut, during the height of her twenty-year reign.

Bust of the Goddess Sakhmet, ca. 1390-1352 B.C.E. Granodiorite, Brooklyn Museum

In a myth about the end of Ra's rule on the earth, Ra sends Hathor or Sekhmet to destroy mortals who conspired against him. In the myth, Sekhmet's blood-lust was not quelled at the end of battle and led to her destroying almost all of humanity, so Ra poured out beer dyed with red ochre or hematite so that it resembled blood. Mistaking the beer for blood, she became so drunk that she gave up the slaughter and returned peacefully to Ra.[3]

Sekhmet later was considered to be the mother of Maahes, a deity who appeared during the New Kingdom period. He was seen as a lion prince, the son of the goddess. The late origin of Maahes in the Egyptian pantheon may be the incorporation of a Nubian deity of ancient origin in that cul-

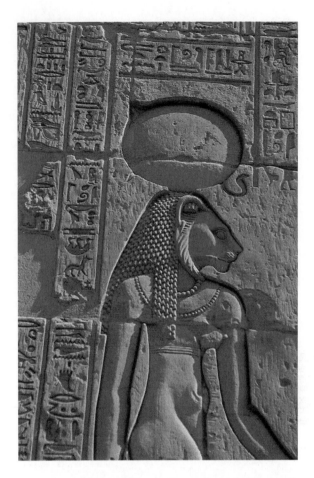

The warrior goddess Sekhmet, shown with her sun disk and cobra crown from a relief at the Temple of Kom Ombo.

Upper torso and head of the goddess Sekhmet, Kelvingrove Art Gallery and Museum, Glasgow.

ture, arriving during trade and warfare or even, during a period of domination by Nubia. During the Greek dominance in Egypt, note was made of a temple for Maahes that was an auxiliary facility to a large temple to Sekhmet at Taremu in the delta region (likely a temple for Bast originally), a city which the Greeks called Leontopolis, where by that time, an enclosure was provided to house lions.

2.57.3   In popular culture

- Death metal band Nile referenced Sekhmet in the title track of their album "Ithyphallic", and in "The Eye Of Ra" on their album *Those Whom the Gods Detest*.

- Death metal band Behemoth referenced Sekhmet in the song "Christgrinding Avenue" on their album *The Apostasy*.

- Sekhmet is one of the evil female trinity of demigod vampires in author Kevin Given's "*Last Rites: The Return of Sebastian Vasilis*" which is the first novel in the

"*Karl Vincent: Vampire Hunter*" series the other two being the Hebrew Lilith and the Hindu Kali. She is also seen in the same author's comic book "*Karl Vincent: Vampire Hunter*" issues 1-6 which adapts the novel.

- Sekhmet is used in *The 39 Clues* book *Beyond the Grave* and is the reason why the characters travel to Cairo.

- Sekhmet is also featured in *The Red Pyramid* written by Rick Riordan as a minor antagonist.

- Sekhmet is the subject of "Lionheart" a song about the goddess by the symphonic power metal band, Amberian Dawn from their *The Clouds of Northland Thunder* album.

- Sekhmet is the focus of "Resurrection", an episode of *Stargate SG-1*. The plot centers around a young girl named Anna who was created by a German doctor,

Head and upper body of the goddess Sekhmet, Kelvingrove Art Gallery and Museum, Glasgow.

who is the son of a Nazi. Sam, Daniel and Teal'c find artifacts belonging to the Goa'uld Sekhmet in the doctor's compound and realize that Anna was cloned using genetic material from the original Sekhmet, who was the executioner of Ra, the villain from the original film. A (possibly different) Sekhmet is also featured in the *Stargate SG-1* game *Stargate SG-1 Unleashed*.

- In *Tutenstein*, an animated TV series about Ancient Egypt, Sekhmet is featured in one of the episodes. She goes on a rampage in the museum and the building site to make people build a pyramid for Tut.

- The space vessel "Sekhmet" is a level in the video game *Jet Force Gemini*, a third person shooter developed by Rare in 1999.

- Sekhmet is also the name of an alien Aragami in the PlayStation Portable game, *God Eater*.

- In the video game *Skullgirls*, Sekhmet is the name of the cat-like skeleton parasite bonded to the Egypt themed character Eliza.

- In the BBC TV series *Sherlock* episode "The Great Game", John Watson believes a cat named Sekhmet is responsible for the death of her owner.

- Sekhmet is the main character in Author S.K. Whiteside's *World of the Guardians* book series. Set in modern day New Orleans, Sekhmet goes by the name of Syn.

- Sekhmet appears in the Big Finish Doctor Who audio drama, The Bride of Peladon. She is an Osiran.

- Temple of Goddess Spirituality in Southern Nevada that is dedicated to the Goddess Sekhmet.

- The subject of Margaret Atwood's poem titled "Sekhmet, the Lion-headed Goddess of War."

- In the comic *The Wicked + The Divine*, Sekhmet (spelled *Sakhmet*) is one of twelve gods who reincarnate every 90 years only to die within two years. In the current incarnation, she is a popstar modelled on Rihanna.

- In Elizabeth Peters' Amelia Peabody series of books, Sekhmet is the name of one of the Emersons' cats.

- Sekhmet appears in the comic *Beasts of Burden: The Unfamiliar* after being summoned by a gathering of witches and familiars.

2.57.4   See also

- Lion and Sun#Other (non-Iranian) variants

- Prathyangira

- Narasimha

- Durga

2.57.5   References

[1] "Sekhmet". *Dictionary.com*. Random House. 2012.

[2] "Sex and booze figured in Egyptian rites", archaeologists find evidence for ancient version of 'Girls Gone Wild'. From MSNBC, October 30, 2006

[3] Lichtheim, Miriam (2006) [1976]. *Ancient Egyptian Literature, Volume Two: The New Kingdom*. University of California Press. pp. 197–199

2.57.6   Further reading

- Germond, Philippe (1981). *Sekhmet et la protection du monde* (in French). Editions de Belles-Lettres.

- Hoenes, Sigrid-Eike (1978). *Untersuchungen zu Wesen und Kult der Göttin Sachmet* (in German). R. Habelt Verlag.

- von Känel, Frédérique (1984). *Les prêtres-ouâb de Sekhmet et les conjurateurs de Serket* (in French). Presses Universitaires de France.

2.57.7   External links

- Ancient Egypt: the Mythology - Sekhmet

- "Ancient war goddess statues unearthed in Egypt", archaeologists unearth six statues of the lion-headed war goddess Sekhmet in temple of pharaoh Amenhotep III. 2006-03-06

- "Karl Vincent: Vampire Hunter" series

2.58   Seonangsin

Seonangshin (Hangul: 서낭신) is the patron deity of the village in Korean mythology. As the goddess of villages, boundaries, and war, the deity is one of the better-known Korean deities.

2.58.1   Worship

Main article: Seonangdang

The goddess was believed to embody the Seonangdang, a stone tower, large stone, house, or holy tree where people prayed to Seonangshin. Travelers built Seonangdangs on trails, and other travelers added three stones to the Seonangdang. After adding three stones, the travelers prayed for safety on their journey. Other travelers left an object that he (or she) owned, or spat on the Seonangdang, before praying. She was regarded to defend against disease and misfortune and bring luck and plenty to the travelers or village.

Most Seonangshin are female; however, a few are a pair of female and male deities. In the Golmaegi Seonangdang, a Seonangdang in Gangwon Province, it is believed that two Seonangshin, a god and a goddess, reside as a family within one Seonangdang. The Seonangshins of the Golmaegi Seonangdang are also the gods of plenty.[1]

In fishing villages, there is a deity called Baeseonang, the Seonangshin of boats. She is believed to defend the boats from sinking.[2]

Certain records show the Malseonang, a characteristic male form of Seonangshin. The Malseonang is a war deity, with a large sword in one hand and reining a flying horse in the other. He is dressed in full armor from hear to toe, with a bow and quiver on his back and a helmet on his head. He was believed to kill Gwishin, or evil spirits, with his blade.[3]

The Gut (ritual) dedicated to Seonangshin was done every three years; however, smaller rites were given to her annually. The Seonanggut was the second Gut in the Jeseok Bonpuli ritual (First: Bujeonggut, *cleansing Gut*, Second: Seonanggut, *Gut of Seonang*, Third: Josanggut, *Ancestor Gut*, Fourth: Seongjugut, *Gut of Seongju*, Fifth: Jishingut, *Gut of Jishin*, Sixth: Shijungut, *Gut of Dangeum Agi*, Seventh: Sanshingut, *Gut of the Sanshin*, Eighth: Yongwanggut, *Gut of the Dragon King*, Ninth: Chukwongut, *Praying Gut*, Tenth: Georipuli, *Gut of the Gwishin*)[4]

2.58.2   In Mythology

According to the *Seongjugut*, the Seonangshin are the children of the evil Sojinhang. The patron of the house, the deity Seongjushin, made the children of Sojinhang turn into Seonangshin, who had to feed on salivia. This origin of Seonangshin shows that in Korean mythology, Seonangshin were considered to be one of the weaker deities, especially as the *Seongjugut* mentions that Seonangshin are 'lowly soldiers'.[5]

2.58.3   References

[1] http://terms.naver.com/entry.nhn?docId=574112& mobile&categoryId=1627

[2] http://terms.naver.com/entry.nhn?docId=574112& mobile&categoryId=1627

[3] Alive Korean Mythology, page 180

[4] http://terms.naver.com/entry.nhn?docId=1010219& mobile&categoryId=97

[5] Alive Korean Mythology, page 265

2.59   Shailaputri

Shailputri is the first form amongst the Navadurga or the nine forms of Hindu goddess Durga or (Shakti), worshipped on first day during the Navratri celebrations – the nine divine nights.[1] She is the first among Navadurgas and the first day of Navratri pooja is dedicated to Durga Shailaputri. Variously known as Sati, Bhavani, Parvati or Hemavati. Maa Shailaputri is the absolute form of Mother Nature. She is also known as Goddess Parvati the consort of Lord Shiva and mother of Ganesha and Kartikeya. In the Navratra festival the worshiping Mother Goddess has a half moon in her forehead & she is holding a trident in her right hand & lotus flower in her left hand. she rides on mount Nandi (bull).

2.59.1 Mythology

She is a daughter of Himalaya and first among nine Durgas. Shailaputri literally means the daughter (putri) of the mountains (shaila). Goddess Durga was born in the house of King of Mountains "Parvat Raj Himalaya", so she is called "Shailaputri" means the daughter of mountain. Variously known as Sati Bhavani, Parvati or Hemavati, the daughter of Hemavana - the king of the Himalayas.[2]

The embodiment of the power of Brahma, Vishnu and Shiva, she rides a bull and carries a trident and a lotus in her two hands. In previous birth she was the daughter of Daksha. Her name was Sati - Bhavani. i.e. the wife of Lord Shiva. Once Daksha had organized a big Yagna and did not invite Shiva. But Sati being obstinate, reached there. Thereupon Daksha insulted Shiva. Sati could not tolerate the insult of husband and burnt herself in the fire of Yagna. In other birth she became the daughter of Himalaya in the name of Parvati - Hemavati and got married with Shiva. As per Upanishad she had torn and the egotism of Indra, etc. Devtas. Being ashamed they bowed and prayed that, "In fact, thou are Shakti, we all - Brahma, Vishnu and Shiva are capable by getting Shakti from you."

In some scriptures like Shiva Purana & Devi-Bhagavata Purana the story of Mother Goddess is written as follow: Maa Bhagwati in her earlier birth was born as a daughter of Daksha Prajapati. Then her name was 'Sati' and she was married to Lord Shiva. But in a sacrificial ceremony organized by her father Prajapati Daksha, she got her body burnt in the yogic fire, because she could not bear the insult of her husband Lord Shiva by her father Prajapati Daksha in the sacrificial ceremony.

In her next birth she incarnated her as Goddess Parvati, the daughter of Parvat Raj Himalaya and among Nava Durgas she has been referred to as Shailaputri who was again known as Hemavati. In her Hemavati aspect she defeated all prominent gods. Like her previous birth in this life also Maa Shailaputri (Parvati) got married with Lord Shiva. The first and the most prominent among Nava Durgas, Shailaputri is of immense importance and her glories are endless. On the first day of Navratri worship it is she who is worshipped.

She is the Devi of the root chakra, who, upon awakening, begins Her journey upwards. Sitting on Nandi, and making her first journey from the Muladhara chakra. As from her father to her husband – the awakening Shakti, beginning Her search for Lord Shiva or making a move towards her Shiva. So that, In Navratri pooja the first day Yogi's keep their mind concentrated on Muladhara. This is the starting point of their spiritual discipline. They started their Yogasadha from here. Shailaputri is the Muladhara Shakti to be realized within Self and sought for higher depths, in the yogic meditation.

Shailaputri means the daughter of the Himalaya. *SHAILA* is the derivative of the word *SHILA*. Shila means a rock, a stone. It is the rock of spiritual standing and the whole world gets strength from the Shailaputri aspect of Purna Prakriti DURGA.

From the Yogic point of view, the First Navratri is considered to be very auspicious day. This is the Yogic start for being in tune with the Divine Mother Durga. Those who want to have any kind of initiation in the Shakti Mantras, can have it on the First of Shukla Pratipada.

The aspiration of a devotee is to reach higher and further higher, for spiritual evolution, and for the attainment of Siddhi, which is perfection associated with Ananda (bliss). Verily, Shailaputri is the Muladhara Shakti to be realized within Self and sought for higher depths, in the YOGA-maditation. This is an experience in the soul-searching of Immutable within human existence. Shailaputri is the physical consciousness of the Divine Mother Durga. She is truly PARVATI, daughter of the King Hemavana, as described in the Shiva Purana. Shailaputri is the manifestation of this earth planet, which includes what is apparent on this earth, and within the globe. Shailaputri covers all the hills, vales, water resources, seas and oceans, including atmosphere.

Therefore, Shailaputri is the essence of the earthly existence. Her abode is in the Muladhara Chakra. The divine Energy is latent in every human being. It is to be realized. Its color is crimson. The Tattva (element) is Earth, with the Guna (quality) of coherence, and with the Bheda (distinct) characteristics of Ghraana (the smell).

Prayers

Its Mantra is La+Ma, i.e.Lama, of the Sanskrit Varṇamālā (Sanskrit, n., वर्णमाला). Its focus is on the tip of the tongue, and lips.

Dhyana Mantra Of Shailaputri:

VANDE VAANCHHIT LAABHAAYA CHANDRARDHA KRITA SHEKHARAAM,

VRISHAARUDHAAM SHULAD-HARAAM SHAILA- PUTRIM YASHASVINIIM

"I pay my VANDANA/ obeisance to the DIVINE MOTHER SHAILA-PUTRI, who bestows upon the choicest boons to the devotees. The moon in the crescent form is adorned as the crown on Her forehead. She is mounted on the bullock. She holds a lance in her hand. She is Yashasvini -the CELEBRATED MOTHER DURGA."

2.59.2 Temples

- Shailputri Temple is located at A-40/11, Marhia Ghat, Varanasi, Uttar Pradesh -INDIA.

- Hedavde Mahalaxmi is located at Hedavde Village, On Mumbai Ahemdabad Highway, Vasai Virar region, Maharastra -INDIA.

2.59.3 References

[1] "Article on Hindu Deities & Mantra -Shailaputri". Retrieved 13 December 2012.

[2] "Article on Navadurga: The Nine Forms of Goddess Durga". Retrieved 13 December 2012.

2.60 Shala

For other uses, see Shala (disambiguation).

Shala was an ancient Sumerian goddess of grain and the emotion of compassion. The symbols of grain and compassion combine to reflect the importance of agriculture in the mythology of Sumer, and the belief that an abundant harvest was an act of compassion from the Gods.[1] Traditions identify Shala as wife of the fertility god Dagon, or consort of the storm god Adad also called Ishkur.[2] In ancient depictions, he carries a double-headed mace-scimitar embellished with lion heads.[3]

2.60.1 References

[1] Stewart and Janet Farrar (1987). The Witches' Goddess: The Feminine Principle of Divinity. Phoenix Publishing. ISBN 978-0919345911.

[2] Jeremy Black and Anthony Green (1992). Gods, Demons and Symbols of Ancient Mesopotamia. University of Texas Press. ISBN 978-0-292-70794-8.

[3] Michael Jordan (2002). Encyclopedia of Gods. Kyle Cathie Limited. ISBN 978-1-85626-131-9.

2.60.2 External links

- Ancient Mesopotamian Gods and Goddesses: Šala (goddess)

2.61 Shivadooti

Shivaduti is a powerful manifestation of Mother Goddess Shakti. Shivaduti means one who has Shiva as her messenger. Goddess Shivaduti made her appearance in the battle against demons Shumbha and Nishumbha. She symbolically represents the unfathomable power of Mother Goddess Shakti. As per Devi Mahatmyam, in the battle against the forces of Shumbh and Nishumbh, Mother Goddess took the manifestation of the Saptamatrikas. They were Shaktis of the male gods. After this appeared Shivaduti, the Shakti of Mother Goddess. This form is not associated with any male form. Devi Mahatmyam states that she appeared from the body of Mother Goddess in the most gruesome form – yelping like a hundred jackals. She then asked Lord Shiva to carry the message to Shumbha and Nishumbha that if they desire to battle against her out of arrogance and false belief in their strength, then they and their forces be ready to be devoured by her jackals. It must be noted here that Goddess Shivaduti is a symbolic representation of what form Goddess Shakti can take to put down Adharma. She is depicted as a woman armed with a trident and rosary, the right lower hand is in the gesture of fear-dispellings and she seated on a lion.

2.62 Tanit

See also: Religion in Carthage

Tanit[1] was a Punic and Phoenician goddess, the chief deity of Carthage alongside her consort Ba`al Hammon.[2][3] She was also adopted by the Punic Berber people.

Tanit is also called **Tinnit**, **Tannou** or **Tangou**. The name appears to have originated in Carthage (modern day Tunisia), though it does not appear in local theophorous names.[4] She was equivalent to the moon-goddess Astarte, and later worshipped in Roman Carthage in her Romanized form as Dea Caelestis, Juno Caelestis or simply Caelestis.

In modern-day Tunisian Arabic, it is customary to invoke "Omek Tannou" or "Oumouk Tangou" (Mother Tannou or Tangou depending on the region), the years of drought to

Stele with Tanit's symbol in Carthage's Tophet, including a crescent moon over the figure

A Punic coin featuring Tanit, minted in Punic Carthage between 215-205 BC.

bring rain; just as we speak of "Ba`li" farming, for non-irrigated farming, to say that it only depends on god Ba`al Hammon.[5]

2.62.1 Worship

Tanit was worshiped in Punic contexts in the Western Mediterranean, from Malta to Gades into Hellenistic times. From the fifth century BCE onwards, Tanit's worship is associated with that of Ba`al Hammon. She is given the epithet *pene baal* ("face of Baal") and the title *rabat*, the female form of *rab* (chief).[6] In North Africa, where the inscriptions and material remains are more plentiful, she was, as well as a consort of Baal Hammon, a heavenly goddess of war, a virginal (not married) mother goddess and nurse, and, less specifically, a symbol of fertility, as are most female forms. Several of the major Greek goddesses were identified with Tanit by the syncretic *interpretatio graeca*, which recognized as Greek deities in foreign guise the gods of most of the surrounding non-Hellene cultures.

Tanit with a lion's head

Her shrine excavated at Sarepta in southern Phoenicia revealed an inscription that identified her for the first time in her homeland and related her securely to the Phoenician goddess Astarte (Ishtar).[7] One site where Tanit is uncovered is at Kerkouane, in the Cap Bon peninsula in Tunisia.

2.62.2 Child sacrifice

The origins of Tanit are to be found in the pantheon of Ugarit, especially in the Ugaritic goddess Anat (Hvidberg-Hansen 1982), a consumer of blood and flesh. There is significant, albeit disputed, evidence, both archaeological and within ancient written sources, pointing towards child sacrifice forming part of the worship of Tanit and Baal Hammon.[8]

Some archaeologists theorised that infant sacrifices have occurred. Lawrence E. Stager, who directed the excavations of the Carthage Tophet in the 1970s, believes that infant sacrifice was practiced there. Paolo Xella of the National Research Council in Rome summarized the textual, epigraphical, and archaeological evidence for Carthaginian infant sacrifice.[9] Modern scholars argue that evidence of Carthaginian child sacrifice is sketchy at best and that these reports are more likely to have been a Roman blood libel against the Carthaginians to justify their conquest and destruction.

Archaeological evidence

Stelae in the Tophet of Salammbó covered by a vault built in the Roman period

"Tophet" is a term derived from the Bible, used to refer to a site near Jerusalem at which Canaanites and Israelites who strayed from Judaism by practicing Canaanite idolatry would sacrifice children. It is now used as a general term for all such sites with cremated human and animal remains. The Hebrew Bible does not specify that the Israelite victims were buried, only burned, although the "place of burning" was probably adjacent to the place of burial. We have no idea how the Phoenicians themselves referred to the places of burning or burial, or to the practice itself.

Several apparent "Tophets" have been identified, chiefly a large one in Carthage, dubbed the "Tophet of Salammbó", after the neighbourhood where it was unearthed in 1921.[10] Soil in the Tophet of Salammbó was found to be full of olive wood charcoal, probably from the sacrificial pyres. It was the location of the temple of the goddess Tanit and the necropolis. Animal remains, mostly sheep and goats, found inside some of the Tophet urns, strongly suggest that this was not a burial ground for children who died prematurely. The animals were sacrificed to the gods, presumably in place of children (one surviving inscription refers to the animal as "a substitute"). It is conjectured that the children unlucky enough not to have substitutes were also sacrificed and then buried in the Tophet. The remains include the bodies of both very young children and small animals, and those who argue in favor of child sacrifice have argued that if the animals were sacrificed then so too were the children.[11] The area covered by the Tophet in Carthage was probably over an acre and a half by the fourth century BCE,[12] with nine different levels of burials. About 20,000 urns were deposited between 400 BCE and 200 BCE,[12] with the practice continuing until the early years of the Christian period. The urns contained the charred bones of newborns and in some cases the bones of fetuses and two-year-olds. These double remains have been interpreted to mean that in the cases of stillborn babies, the parents would sacrifice their youngest child.[13]

A detailed breakdown of the age of the buried children includes pre-natal individuals – that is, still births. It is also argued that the age distribution of remains at this site is consistent with the burial of children who died of natural causes, shortly before or after birth.[11][14] Sergio Ribichini has argued that the Tophet was "a child necropolis designed to receive the remains of infants who had died prematurely of sickness or other natural causes, and who for this reason were "offered" to specific deities and buried in a place different from the one reserved for the ordinary dead". He adds that this was probably part of "an effort to ensure the benevolent protection of the same deities for the survivors."[15] However, this analysis is disputed; Patricia Smith and colleagues from the Hebrew University and Harvard University show from the teeth and skeletal analysis at the Carthage Tophet that infant ages at death (about two months) do not correlate with the expected ages of natural mortality (perinatal).[16]

2.62.3 Other usage

Long after the fall of Carthage, Tanit was still venerated in North Africa under the Latin name of *Juno Caelestis*, for her identification with the Roman goddess Juno.[17] The ancient Berber people of North Africa also adopted the Punic cult of Tanit.[18] In Egyptian, her name means *Land of Neith*, Neith being a war goddess. Her symbol, found on many ancient stone carvings, appears as a trapezium (trapezoid) closed by a horizontal line at the top and surmounted in the middle by a circle: the horizontal arm is often terminated either by two short upright lines at right angles to it or by hooks. Later, the trapezium is frequently replaced by an isosceles triangle. The symbol is interpreted by Hvidberg-Hansen as a woman raising her hands. Hvidberg-Hansen (Danish professor of Semitic philology), notes that Tanit is sometimes depicted with a lion's head, showing her warrior quality.[19]

In modern times the name, with the spelling "Tanith", has been used as a female given name, both for real people, Tanit Phoenix and, more frequently, in occult fiction.

2.62.4 Cultural references

In Gustave Flaubert's historical novel *Salammbô* (1862), the title character is a priestess of Tanit. Mâtho, the chief male protagonist, a Libyan mercenary rebel at war with Carthage, breaks into the goddess' temple and steals her veil.[20]

In Kate Elliot's Spiritwalker Trilogy, Tanit is one of many deities commonly worshiped in a polytheistic Europa. The narrator, Catherine, frequently appeals to "Blessed Tanit, Protector of Women", and the goddess occasionally appears to her.

In Margaret Atwood's The Blind Assassin there is an epigraph on a Carthaginian funerary urn that reads, "I swam, the sea was boundless, I saw no shore./Tanit was merciless, my prayers were answered./O you who drown in love, remember me."

2.62.5 See also

- Ishtar

- Isis

2.62.6 Notes

[1] 'TNT in Phoenician and Punic inscriptions.

[2] Richard Miles *Carthage Must Be Destroyed* (Penguin, 2011), p.68

[3] F. O. Hvidberg-Hansen, *La déesse TNT: une Etude sur la réligion canaanéo-punique* (Copenhagen: Gad) 1982, is the standard survey. An extensive critical review by G. W.

Ahlström appeared in *Journal of Near Eastern Studies* **45**.4 (October 1986), pp. 311–314.

[4] Claas Jouco Bleeker; Geo Widengren (1988). *Historia Religionum, Volume 1 Religions of the Past*. BRILL. pp. 209– . ISBN 90-04-08928-4. At Carthage the great goddess is called Tinnit (formerly read Tanit) ... It would seem that Tinnit is the specific Carthaginian form of Astarte, but strangely enough there are no theophorous names containing the element Tinnit, while there are a few with Astarte. The name seems to have originated in Carthage ...

[5] Ottavo contributo alla storia degli studi classici e del mondo antico Arnaldo Momigliano - 1987 p240.

[6] Markoe 2000:130.

[7] James B. Pritchard, *Recovering Sarepta, a Phoenician City* (Princeton: Princeton University Press) 1978.; see Sarepta. The inscription reads TNT TTRT and could identify Tanit as an epithet of Astarte at Sarepta, for the TNT element does not appear in theophoric names in Punic contexts (Ahlström 1986 review, p 314).

[8] Markoe, p. 136

[9] Paolo Xella, Josephine Quinn, Valentina Melchiorri and Peter van Dommelen. Phoenician bones of contention. Volume: 87 Number: 338 Page: 1199–1207. http://antiquity.ac.uk/ant/087/ant0871199.htm accessed 17 February 2014

[10] Briand-Ponsart, Claude and Crogiez, Sylvie (2002). *L'Afrique du nord antique et médievale: mémoire, identité et imaginaire*. Publication Univ Rouen Havre, p. 13. ISBN 2-87775-325-5. (French)

[11] Skeletal Remains from Punic Carthage Do Not Support Systematic Sacrifice of Infants http://www.plosone.org/article/info:doi/10.1371/journal.pone.0009177

[12] Stager 1980, p. 3.

[13] Stager 1980, p. 6.

[14] Jeffrey H. Schwartz, Frank Houghton, Roberto Macchiarelli, Luca Bondioli. Skeletal Remains from Punic Carthage Do Not Support Systematic Sacrifice of Infants. PLOS One. Published: 17 February 2010. DOI: 10.1371/journal.pone.0009177 http://www.plosone.org/article/info:doi/10.1371/journal.pone.0009177 accessed 23 January 2014

[15] Ribichini 1988, p. 141.

[16] Patricia Smith, Lawrence E. Stager, Joseph A. Greene and Gal Avishai. Archaeology. Volume: 87 Number: 338 Page: 1191–1199. Age estimations attest to infant sacrifice at the Carthage Tophet. http://antiquity.ac.uk/ant/087/ant0871191.htm accessed 23 January 2014

[17] Tate, Karen (2008). *Sacred Places of Goddess*. CCC Publishing, p. 137. ISBN 1-888729-11-2

[18] Michael Brett and Elizabeth Fentress *The Berbers* (Blackwell, 1997), p.269

[19] *The Phoenician solar theology* by Joseph Azize, page 177.

[20] Laurence M. Porter *Gustave Flaubert's "Madame Bovary":
A Reference Guide* (Greenwood, 2002), p.xxxi

2.62.7   References

- Markoe, Glenn E. (2000). *Phoenicians*. Peoples of the
  Past. Berkeley, Calif.: University of California Press.
  ISBN 9780520226142. OCLC 45096924.

2.62.8   External links

- Limestone stela with images of the goddess Tanit

2.63   The Morrígan

"Morrigan" redirects here. For other uses, see Morrigan
(disambiguation).

The Morrígan ("phantom queen") or **Mórrígan** ("great
queen"), also written as **Morrígu** or in the plural as
Morrígna, and spelled **Morríghan** or **Mór-ríoghain** in
Modern Irish, is a figure from Irish mythology.

The primary themes associated with the Morrígan are battle, strife, and sovereignty. She most frequently appears in
the form of a crow, flying above the warriors, and in the
Ulster Cycle she also takes the forms of an eel, a wolf and a
cow. Most popular, however, is her embodiment as a crow
where her representation as the goddess of death is most
complete with crows/ravens frequent appearances on battlefield and birds eye view from above to view the world from
below. [1]She is generally considered a war deity comparable with the Germanic Valkyries, although her association
with a cow may also suggest a role connected with wealth
and the land.

She is often depicted as a trio of individuals, all
sisters.[2][3][4] Although membership of the triad varies, the
most common combination in modern sources is Badb,
Macha and Nemain.[5] However the primary sources indicate a more likely triad of Badb, Macha and Anand; Anand
is also given as an alternate name for Morrigu.[6] Other accounts name Fea and others.[5]

2.63.1   Etymology

There is some disagreement over the meaning of the Morrígan's name. *Mor* may derive from an Indo-European
root connoting terror or monstrousness, cognate with the
Old English *maere* (which survives in the modern English

word "nightmare") and the Scandinavian *mara* and the
Old Russian "mara" ("nightmare");[7] while *rígan* translates
as 'queen'.[8] This can be reconstructed in Proto-Celtic as
*Moro-rīganī-s.[9] Accordingly, *Morrígan* is often translated as "Phantom Queen". This is the derivation generally
favoured in current scholarship.[10]

In the Middle Irish period the name is often spelled *Mórrígan* with a lengthening diacritic over the 'o', seemingly
intended to mean "Great Queen" (Old Irish *mór*, 'great';[11]
this would derive from a hypothetical Proto-Celtic **Māra
Rīganī-s*).[12] Whitley Stokes believed this latter spelling
was due to a false etymology popular at the time.[13] There
have also been attempts by modern writers to link the Morrígan with the Welsh literary figure Morgan le Fay from
Arthurian romance, in whose name 'mor' may derive from
a Welsh word for 'sea', but the names are derived from different cultures and branches of the Celtic linguistic tree.[14]

2.63.2   Sources

Glosses and glossaries

The earliest sources for the Morrígan are glosses in Latin
manuscripts, and glossaries (collections of glosses). In a
9th-century manuscript containing the Latin Vulgate translation of the Book of Isaiah, the word *Lamia* is used
to translate the Hebrew *Lilith*.[15] A gloss explains this
as "a monster in female form, that is, a *morrígan*".[16]
Cormac's Glossary (also 9th century), and a gloss in the later
manuscript H.3.18, both explain the plural word *gudemain*
("spectres")[17] with the plural form *morrígna*.[16] The 8th
century *O'Mulconry's Glossary* says that Macha is one of
the three *morrígna*.[16]

Ulster Cycle

The Morrígan's earliest narrative appearances, in which she
is depicted as an individual,[18] are in stories of the Ulster
Cycle, where she has an ambiguous relationship with the
hero Cú Chulainn. In *Táin Bó Regamna* (*The Cattle Raid of
Regamain*), Cúchulainn encounters the Morrígan, but does
not recognise her, as she drives a heifer from his territory.
In response to this perceived challenge, and his ignorance of
her role as a sovereignty figure, he insults her. But before he
can attack her she becomes a black bird on a nearby branch.
Cúchulainn now knows who she is, and tells her that had he
known before, they would not have parted in enmity. She
notes that whatever he had done would have brought him ill
luck. To his response that she cannot harm him, she delivers
a series of warnings, foretelling a coming battle in which he
will be killed. She tells him, "it is at the guarding of thy
death that I am; and I shall be."[19]

In the *Táin Bó Cuailnge* queen Medb of Connacht launches an invasion of Ulster to steal the bull Donn Cuailnge; the Morrígan, like Alecto of the Greek Furies, appears to the bull in the form of a crow and warns him to flee.[20] Cúchulainn defends Ulster by fighting a series of single combats at fords against Medb's champions. In between combats the Morrígan appears to him as a young woman and offers him her love, and her aid in the battle, but he rejects her offer. In response she intervenes in his next combat, first in the form of an eel who trips him, then as a wolf who stampedes cattle across the ford, and finally as a white, red-eared heifer leading the stampede, just as she had warned in their previous encounter. However Cúchulainn wounds her in each form and defeats his opponent despite her interference. Later she appears to him as an old woman bearing the same three wounds that her animal forms sustained, milking a cow. She gives Cúchulainn three drinks of milk. He blesses her with each drink, and her wounds are healed.[21] He regrets blessing her for the three drinks of milk which is apparent in the exchange between the Morrígan and Cúchulainn, "She gave him milk from the third teat, and her leg was healed. 'You told me once,' she said, 'that you would never heal me.' 'Had I known it was you,' said Cúchulainn, 'I never would have.'"[22] As the armies gather for the final battle, she prophesies the bloodshed to come.[23]

In one version of Cúchulainn's death-tale, as Cúchulainn rides to meet his enemies, he encounters the Morrígan as a hag washing his bloody armour in a ford, an omen of his death. Later in the story, mortally wounded, Cúchulainn ties himself to a standing stone with his own entrails so he can die upright, and it is only when a crow lands on his shoulder that his enemies believe he is dead.[24]

Mythological Cycle

The Morrígan also appears in texts of the Mythological Cycle. In the 12th century pseudohistorical compilation *Lebor Gabála Érenn* she is listed among the Tuatha Dé Danann as one of the daughters of Ernmas, granddaughter of Nuada.[6]

The first three daughters of Ernmas are given as Ériu, Banba, and Fódla. Their names are synonyms for Ireland, and they were married to Mac Cuill, Mac Cécht, and Mac Gréine, the last three Tuatha Dé Danann kings of Ireland. Associated with the land and kingship, they probably represent a triple goddess of sovereignty. Next come Ernmas's other three daughters: Badb, Macha, and the Morrígan. A quatrain describes the three as wealthy, "springs of craftiness" and "sources of bitter fighting". The Morrígu's name is also said to be Anand,[6] and she had three sons, Glon, Gaim, and Coscar. According to Geoffrey Keating's 17th century *History of Ireland*, Ériu, Banba, and Fódla worshipped Badb, Macha, and the Morrígan respectively.[25]

The Morrígan also appears in *Cath Maige Tuireadh* (*The Battle of Mag Tuired*).[26] On Samhain she keeps a tryst with the Dagda before the battle against the Fomorians. When he meets her she is washing herself, standing with one foot on either side of the river Unius. In some sources she is believed to have created the river. After they have sex, the Morrígan promises to summon the magicians of Ireland to cast spells on behalf of the Tuatha Dé, and to destroy Indech, the Fomorian king, taking from him "the blood of his heart and the kidneys of his valour". Later, we are told, she would bring two handfuls of his blood and deposit them in the same river (however, we are also told later in the text that Indech was killed by Ogma).

As battle is about to be joined, the Tuatha Dé leader, Lug, asks each what power they bring to the battle. The Morrígan's reply is difficult to interpret, but involves pursuing, destroying and subduing. When she comes to the battlefield she chants a poem, and immediately the battle breaks and the Fomorians are driven into the sea. After the battle she chants another poem celebrating the victory and prophesying the end of the world.[27][28]

In another story she lures away the bull of a woman named Odras. Odras then follows the Morrígan to the Otherworld, via the cave of Cruachan. When Odras falls asleep, the Morrígan turns her into a pool of water.[29]

2.63.3 Nature and functions

The Morrígan is often considered a triple goddess, but this triple nature is ambiguous and inconsistent. These triple appearances are partially due to the Celtic significance of threeness. [1] Sometimes she appears as one of three sisters, the daughters of Ernmas: Morrígan, Badb and Macha.[30] Sometimes the trinity consists of Badb, Macha and Anand, collectively known as the Morrígna. Occasionally Nemain or Fea appear in the various combinations. However, the Morrígan can also appear alone,[18] and her name is sometimes used interchangeably with Badb.[27]

The Morrígan is usually interpreted as a "war goddess": W. M. Hennessy's "The Ancient Irish Goddess of War", written in 1870, was influential in establishing this interpretation.[31] Her role often involves premonitions of a particular warrior's violent death, suggesting a link with the Banshee of later folklore. This connection is further noted by Patricia Lysaght: "In certain areas of Ireland this supernatural being is, in addition to the name banshee, also called the *badhb*".[32] Her role was to not only be a symbol of imminent death, but to also influence the outcome of war. Most often she did this by appearing as a crow flying overhead and would either inspire fear or courage in the hearts of the warriors. In some cases, she is written to have appeared in visions to those who are destined to die in battle by washing their bloody armor. In this specific role, she is also given the role of foretelling imminent death with a particular emphasis on the individual. [33]There are also a few rare accounts where she would join in the battle itself as a warrior and show her favouritism in a more direct manner.[34]

It has also been suggested that she was closely tied to Irish *männerbund* groups[35] (described as "bands of youthful warrior-hunters, living on the borders of civilized society and indulging in lawless activities for a time before inheriting property and taking their places as members of settled, landed communities")[36] and that these groups may have been in some way dedicated to her. If true, her worship may have resembled that of Perchta groups in Germanic areas.[37]

However, Máire Herbert has argued that "war *per se* is not a primary aspect of the role of the goddess",[38] and that her association with cattle suggests her role was connected to the earth, fertility and sovereignty; she suggests that her association with war is a result of a confusion between her and the Badb, who she argues was originally a separate figure. She can be interpreted as providing political or military aid, or protection to the king—acting as a goddess of sovereignty, not necessarily a war goddess. There have been many cases where, after having been a cause of strife, the Morrigan has in turn become one of great help when a certain level of respect has been shown.

There is a burnt mound site in County Tipperary known as Fulacht na Mór Ríoghna ('cooking pit of the Mórrígan'). The fulachtaí sites are found in wild areas, and usually associated with outsiders such as the Fianna and the above-mentioned *männerbund* groups, as well as with the hunting of deer. The cooking connection also suggests to some a connection with the three mythical hags who cook the meal of dogflesh that brings the hero Cúchulainn to his doom. The Dá Chich na Morrigna ('two breasts of the Mórrígan'), a pair of hills in County Meath, suggest to some a role as a tutelary goddess, comparable to Anu, who has her own hills, Dá Chích Anann ('the breasts of Anu') in County Kerry. Other goddesses known to have similar hills are Áine and Grian of County Limerick who, in addition to a tutelary function, also have solar attributes.

2.63.4 Arthurian legend

There have been attempts by some modern authors of fiction to link the Arthurian character Morgan le Fay with the Morrígan. Morgan first appears in Geoffrey of Monmouth's *Vita Merlini* (*The Life of Merlin*) in the 12th century. In these Arthurian legends, such as Sir Gawaine and the Green Knight, Morgan is portrayed as an evil hag whose actions set into motion a bloody trail of events that lead the hero into numerous instances of danger. Morgan is also depicted as a seductress, much like the older legends of the goddess and has numerous sexual encounters with Merlin. The character is frequently depicted of wielding power over others to achieve her own purposes, allowing those actions to play out over time, to either the benefit or detriment of other characters. [39]

However, while the creators of the literary character of Morgan may have been somewhat inspired by the much older tales of the goddess, the relationship ends there. Scholars such as Rosalind Clark hold that the names are unrelated, the Welsh "Morgan" (Wales being the source of Arthurian legend) being derived from root words associated with the sea, while the Irish "Morrígan" has its roots either in a word for "terror" or a word for "greatness".[40]

2.63.5 Modern depictions

See: Irish mythology in popular culture: The Morrígan

2.63.6 See also

- Bean Nighe
- Clídna
- Mongfind

2.63.7 Notes

[1] Aldhouse-Green, Miranda (2015). *The Celtic Myths: A Guide To The Ancient Gods And Legends*. New York: Thames & Hudson. p. 125. ISBN 978-0-500-25209-3.

[2] Sjoestedt, Marie-Louise. *Celtic Gods and Heroes*. Dover Publications. pp. 31–32. ISBN 0-486-41441-8.

[3] O hOgain, Daithi (1991). *Myth, Legend and Romance: An Encyclopedia of the Irish Folk Tradition*. Oxford: Prentice Hall Press. pp. 307–309. ISBN 0-13-275959-4.

[4] Davidson, Hilda Ellis (1988). *Myths and symbols in pagan Europe: early Scandinavian and Celtic religions*. Syracuse: Syracuse University Press. p. 97. ISBN 0-8156-2441-7.

[5] MacKillop, James (1998). *Dictionary of Celtic mythology*. Oxford: Oxford University Press. pp. 335–336. ISBN 0-19-280120-1.

[6] *Lebor Gabála Érenn §62, 64: "Badb and Macha and Anand... were the three daughters of Ernmas the she-farmer." "Badb and Morrigu, whose name was Anand."*

[7] *Dictionary of the Irish Language* p. 468.

[8] DIL p. 507.

[9] Proto-Celtic – English wordlist; EtymologyOnline: "nightmare"

[10] Rosalind Clark (1990) *The Great Queens: Irish Goddesses from the Morrígan to Cathleen Ní Houlihan* (Irish Literary Studies, Book 34) ISBN 0-389-20928-7

[11] *Dictionary of the Irish Language* (DIL), Compact Edition, Royal Irish Academy, 1990, pp. 467–468

[12] Alexander McBain, *An Etymological Dictionary of the Gaelic Language*, 1911: *mór, ribhinn*

[13] Stokes, Whitley (1891) Notes to "The Second Battle of Moytura" in *Revue Celtique* xii, p. 128.

[14] *Dictionary of the Irish Language*, "Morrígan".

[15] Isaiah 34:14 "And wild beasts shall meet with hyenas, the satyr shall cry to his fellow; yea, there shall the *night hag* alight, and find for herself a resting place." (Revised Standard Version, emphasis added)

[16] Angelique Gulermovich Epstein, *War Goddess: The Morrígan and her Germano-Celtic Counterparts*, electronic version, #148, (September 1998), pp. 45–51.

[17] DIL p. 372

[18] *Táin Bó Regamna*, Corpus of Electronic Texts Edition, p.33, Author: Unknown

[19] "The Cattle Raid of Regamna", translated by A. H. Leahy, from *Heroic Romances of Ireland* Vol II, 1906

[20] Cecile O'Rahilly (ed & trans), *Táin Bó Cuailnge* Recension 1, 1976, p. 152

[21] Cecile O'Rahilly (ed & trans), *Táin Bó Cuailnge* Recension 1, 1976, pp. 176–177, 180–182; Cecile O'Rahilly (ed & trans), *Táin Bó Cualnge* from the Book of Leinster, 1967, pp. 193–197

[22] Ciaran Carson, "The Táin: A New Translation of the Táin Bó Cúlailnge, 2007, pp. 96

[23] Cecile O'Rahilly (ed & trans), *Táin Bó Cuailnge* Recension 1, 1976, pp. 229–230

[24] "The Death of Cú Chulainn"

[25] Geoffrey Keating, *The History of Ireland* Book 2 Section 11

[26] 'The Second Battle of Moytura, translated by Whitley Stokes

[27] *Cath Maige Tuired*: The Second Battle of Mag Tuired, Text 166, Author: Unknown

[28] Elizabeth A. Gray (ed. & trans.), *Cath Maige Tuired: The Second Battle of Mag Tuired*, section 167, 1982

[29] "Odras", from *The Metrical Dindshenchas* Vol 4, translated by E. Gwynn

[30] Macalister, R.A.S. (trans.) (1941). *Lebor Gabála Érenn: Book of the Taking of Ireland Part 1-5*. Dublin: Irish Texts Society.

[31] W. M. Hennessy, "The Ancient Irish Goddess of War", *Revue Celtique* 1, 1870–72, pp. 32–37

[32] Patricia Lysaght, *The Banshee: The Irish Death Messenger*, 1986, ISBN 1-57098-138-8, p. 15

[33] Rolleston, T. W. (1911). *Celtic Myths And Legends*. New York: Barnes and Noble. ISBN 978-0-7607-8335-1.

[34] Arthur Cotterell, "The Encyclopedia of Mythology", 2010, pp. 102, pp. 152

[35] Angelique Gulermovich Epstein, "War Goddess: The Morrígan and her Germano-Celtic Counterparts", electronic version, #148 (September 1998)

[36] Maire West, "Aspects of *díberg* in the tale *Togail Bruidne Da Derga*", *Zeitschrift für Celtische Philologie* vol. 49–50, p. 950

[37] Carlo Ginzburg, *Ecstasies: Deciphering the Witches' Sabbath*, New York, Pantheon Books, 1991, ISBN 0-394-58163-6, pp. 6–7, 91, 101–2, 115 (note 47), 146 (note 62), 193, 182–204, 262, as well as numerous related references throughout Parts Two and Three

[38] Máire Herbert, "Transmutations of an Irish Goddess", in Miranda Green & Sandra Billington (ed.), *The Concept of the Goddess*, 1996

[39] *Morgan le Fay in Sir Gawain and the Green Knight*.

[40] Clark (1990) pp. 21–23, 208n.5

2.63.8 References

- Rosalind Clark, *The Great Queens: Irish Goddesses from the Morrígan to Cathleen Ní Houlihan* (Irish Literary Studies, Book 34)

- Barry Cunliffe, *The Ancient Celts*

- Miriam Robbins Dexter, *Whence the Goddesses: A Source Book*

- James MacKillop, *Dictionary of Celtic Mythology*

- Daithi O hOgain, *Myth, Legend and Romance: An Encyclopedia of the Irish Folk Tradition* Prentice Hall Press, (1991) : ISBN 0-13-275959-4

- Anne Ross, *Pagan Celtic Britain: Studies in Iconography*

- Anne Ross, "The Divine Hag of the Pagan Celts", in V. Newall (ed.), *The Witch Figure*.

2.63.9   External links

- War Goddess: the Morrígan and her Germano-Celtic Counterparts thesis by Angelique Gulermovich Epstein (ZIP format)

2.64   Toci

For Ţoci village in Alba County, Romania, see Sohodol.
Toci (Nahuatl pronunciation: [ˈtosi] "Our grandmother")[1]

Statue of Toci (Tlazolteotl) from Mexico, 900-1521 CE (British Museum, id:Am1989,Q.3)

is a deity figuring prominently in the religion and mythology of the pre-Columbian Aztec civilization of Mesoamerica. In Aztec mythology she is attributed as the "Mother of the Gods" (**Teteo Innan**[2] or *Teteoinnan*), and associated as a Mother goddess (also called **Tlalli Iyollo**, "Heart of the Earth").

2.64.1   Characteristics and associations

Although considered to be an aged deity, Toci is not always shown with specific markers of great age. Toci is frequently depicted with black markings around the mouth and nose, wearing a headdress with cotton spools (Miller and Taube 1993, p. 170). These are also characteristic motifs for Tlazolteotl, a central Mesoamerican goddess of both purification and filth (*tlazolli* in Nahuatl), and the two deities are closely identified with one another.

Toci was also associated with healing, and venerated by curers of ailments and midwives. In the 16th century *Florentine Codex* compiled by Bernardino de Sahagún Toci is identified with *temazcalli* or sweatbaths, in which aspect she is sometimes termed **Temazcalteci**, or "Grandmother of sweatbaths". Tlazolteotl also has an association with *temazcalli* as the "eater of filth", and such bathhouses are likely to have been dedicated to either Tlazolteotl or Toci/Temazcalteci.[3]

Toci also had an identification with war, and had also the epithet "Woman of Discord".

2.64.2   Traditions in mythology

By one Mexica-Aztec legendary tradition, at some point during their long peregrinations after leaving the mythical homeland Aztlan, the Mexica served as mercenaries to the Culhua at their capital of Culhuacan. The Culhua ruler bestowed his daughter upon the Mexica for an intended marriage with one of the Mexica nobility; however the Mexica's guiding and chief deity Huitzilopochtli intervened and ordered that she be flayed and sacrificed, instead. When this was done she transformed into Toci. The Mexica were expelled from Culhuacan by the Culhua ruler for the act, and the Mexica were pressed on towards Lake Texcoco. It was here that shortly thereafter they founded their capital Tenochtitlan, from which base they would later grow in power to form the Aztec Empire and exert their dominion over the Valley of Mexico (Miller and Taube 1993).

2.64.3   Festivals and rites

During the *veintena* of Ochpaniztli in the Aztec calendar, harvest-time festival rites were held to honor Toci, in her aspect as "Heart of the Earth" (Miller and Taube 1993) were held, associated with the time of harvest.

2.64.4   See also

- Tlazolteotl

- Coatlicue

2.64.5   Notes

[1] From *to-*, first person plural possessive, and *cihtli*, "grandmother" (the absolutive suffix *-tli* is dropped). See also

Campbell (1997).

[2] *Lit.* "gods, their mother". Campbell, *op. cit.*

[3] Sections of the Codex Magliabechiano indicate that the god Tezcatlipoca served as tutelary god for *temazcalli*, however its illustrations also clearly show the face of Tlazolteotl above the doorway; see discussion in Miller and Taube (1993, p.159).

2.64.6 References

- Campbell, R. Joe (1997). "Florentine Codex Vocabulary". Archived from the original on 2006-04-28. Retrieved 2006-07-17.

- Miller, Mary; Karl Taube (1993). *The Gods and Symbols of Ancient Mexico and the Maya*. London: Thames and Hudson. ISBN 0-500-05068-6.

2.65 Trebaruna

Trebaruna, also *Treborunnis* and possibly **Trebarunu* was a Lusitanian deity, probably a goddess.

Trebaruna's cult was located in the cultural area of Gallaecia and Lusitania (in the territory of modern Galicia (Spain) and Portugal). Her name could be derived from the Celtic **trebo* (home) and **runa* (secret, mystery), suggesting a protector or protectress of property, home and families.[1]

Two small altars dedicated to this goddess were found in Portugal, one in Roman-Lusitanian Egitania (current Proença-a-Velha) and another in Lardosa. The Tavares Proença Regional Museum in Castelo Branco now contains the altar from Lardosa. It was located in an area where the people from a Castro settlement founded a Roman-Lusitanian villa. This altar used to hold a statue of the goddess which has since been lost. Nevertheless, it still preserves these inscriptions: TREBARONNE V(otum) S(Olvit) OCONUS OCONIS f(ilius). Which translate as: *Oconus, son of Oco, has fulfilled the vow to Trebaruna.*[2] A name *Trebarune* (probably in the dative case) also appears on the inscription of Cabeço das Fráguas as a divinity receiving a sacrifice of a sheep.

Following the announcement in 1895 by José Leite de Vasconcelos of the discovery of *Trebaruna* as a new theonym, a poem celebrating this was published which likened Trebaruna to the Roman Victoria.[3] She has recently[4] become among neo-Pagans, a goddess of battles and alliances.[5] The Portuguese metal-band Moonspell composed a song called "Trebaruna" which is a celebration of the goddess.

2.65.1 See also

- List of Lusitanian deities

- Lusitanian mythology

2.65.2 References

[1] *O Archeologo Português*, 1/29, 1933, p.163

[2] ibid, pp. 165-166

[3] *Trebaruna, deusa Lusitana, ode heroica*, José Leite de Vasconcelos, Barcelos : Typographia da Aurora do Cavado (1895)

[4] O que é a Pagan Federation?

[5] Pagan Federation Portugal

2.66 Varahi

For the river, see Varahi River.

Varahi (Sanskrit: वाराही, Vārāhī)[note 1] is one of the Matrikas, a group of seven or eight mother goddesses in the Hindu religion. With the head of a sow, Varahi is the shakti (feminine energy, or sometimes, consort) of Varaha, the boar Avatar of the god Vishnu. In Nepal, she is called **Barahi**.

Varahi is worshipped by all the three major schools of Hinduism: Shaktism (goddess worship); Shaivism (followers of the god Shiva); and Vaishnavism (devotion to Vishnu). She is usually worshipped at night, and according to secretive Vamamarga Tantric practices. The Buddhist goddesses Vajravarahi and Marichi are believed to have their origins in the Hindu goddess Varahi.

2.66.1 Hindu legends

According to the Shumbha-Nishumbha myth of the *Devi Mahatmya* from the *Markandeya Purana* religious texts, the Matrikas goddesses appear as *shakti*s (feminine powers) from the bodies of the gods. The scriptures say that Varahi was created from Varaha. She has a boar form, wields a chakra (discus), and fights with a sword.[1][2] After the battle described in the myth, the Matrikas dance – drunk on their victim's blood.[3]

According to a latter episode of the *Devi Mahatmya* that deals with the killing of the demon Raktabija, the warrior-goddess Durga creates the Matrikas from herself and with their help slaughters the demon army. When the demon

The goddess Durga leads the eight Matrikas in battle against the demon Raktabija. The red-skinned Varahi (bottom row, leftmost) rides a buffalo and holds a sword, shield, and goad. Folio from a Devi Mahatmya

Devi Varahi Ambika at Parashakthi Temple in Pontiac, USA

Shumbha challenges Durga to single combat, she absorbs the Matrikas into herself.[4] In the *Vamana Purana*, the Matrikas arise from different parts of the Divine Mother Chandika; Varahi arises from Chandika's back.[2][5]

The *Markendeya Purana* praises Varahi as a granter of boons and the regent of the northern direction, in a hymn where the Matrikas are declared as the protectors of the directions. In another instance in the same Purana, she is described as riding a buffalo.[6] The *Devi Bhagavata Purana* says Varahi, with the other Matrikas, is created by the Supreme Mother. The Mother promises the gods that the Matrikas will fight demons when needed. In the Raktabija episode, Varahi is described as having a boar form, fighting demons with her tusks while seated on a preta (corpse).[7]

In the *Varaha Purana*, the story of Raktabija is retold, but here each of Matrikas appears from the body of another Matrika. Varahi appears seated on Shesha-nāga (the serpent on which the god Vishnu sleeps) from the posterior of Vaishnavi, the Shakti of Vishnu.[8] Varahi is said to represent the vice of envy (*asuya*) in the same Purana.[9][10]

The *Matsya Purana* tells a different story of the origin of Varahi. Varahi, with other Matrikas, is created by Shiva to help him kill the demon Andhakasura, who has the ability – like Raktabija – to regenerate from his dripping blood.[8]

2.66.2   Associations

The *Devi Purana* paradoxically calls Varahi the mother of Varaha (*Varahajanani*) as well as *Kritantatanusambhava*, who emerges from Kritantatanu. Kritantatanu means "death personified" and could be an attribute of Varaha or a direct reference to Yama, the god of death.[11] Elsewhere in the scripture, she is called *Vaivasvati* and described as engrossed in drinking from a skull-cup. Pal theorizes that the name "Vaivasvati" means that Varahi is clearly identi-

fied with Yami, the shakti of Yama, who is also known as Vivasvan. Moreover, Varahi holds a staff and rides a buffalo, both of which are attributes of Yama; all Matrikas are described as assuming the form of their creator-gods.[12]

In the context of the Matrikas' association to the Sanskrit alphabet, Varahi is said to govern the *pa varga* of consonants, namely *pa, pha, ba, bha, ma*.[13] The *Lalita Sahasranama*, a collection of 1,000 names of the Divine Mother, calls Varahi the destroyer of demon Visukaran.[14] In another context, Varahi, as *Panchami*, is identified with the wife of Sadashiva, the fifth *Brahma*, responsible for the regeneration of the Universe. The other *Panch Brahmas* ("five Brahmas") are the gods Brahma, Govinda, Rudra, and Isvara, who are in charge of creation, protection, destruction, and dissolution respectively.[10] In yet another context, Varahi is called *Kaivalyarupini*, the bestower of Kaivalya ("detachment of the soul from matter or further transmigrations") – the final form of mukti (salvation).[10] The Matrikas are also believed to reside in a person's body. Varahi is described as residing in a person's navel, and governs the manipura, svadhisthana, and muladhara chakras.[15]

Haripriya Rangarajan, in her book *Images of Varahi—An Iconographic Study*, suggests that Varahi is none other than Vak devi, the goddess of speech.[16]

2.66.3   Iconography

Varahi's iconography is described in the *Matsya Purana* and agamas like the *Purva-karnagama* and the *Rupamandana*.[17] The Tantric text *Varahi Tantra* mentions that Varahi has five forms of Varahi: Svapna Varahi, Canda Varahi, Mahi Varahi (Bhairavi), Krcca Varahi, and Mat-

A chlorite statue of Varahi, 1000–1100 CE, from eastern Bihar state, India. Currently housed in Asian Art Museum of San Francisco

trikas – except Chamunda – are depicted as slender and beautiful.[19][21] One belief suggests that since Varahi is identified with the Yoganidra of Vishnu, who holds the universe in her womb (*Bhugarbha Paranmesvari Jagaddhatri*), that she should be shown as pot-bellied.[10][16] Another theory suggests that the pot-belly reflects a "maternal aspect", which Donaldson describes as "curious" because Varahi and Chamunda "best exemplify" the terrible aspect of the Divine Mother.[19] A notable exception is the depiction of Varahi as human-faced and slender at the sixth-century Rameshvara cave (Cave 21), the Ellora Caves. She is depicted here as part of the group of seven Matrikas.[22] A third eye and/or a crescent moon is described to be on her forehead.[2][10]

Varahi may be two, four, or six-armed.[10][17] The *Matsya Purana*, the *Purva-karnagama*, and the *Rupamandana* mention a four-armed form. The *Rupamandana* says she carries a ghanta (bell), a chamara (a yak's tail), a chakra (discus), and a gada (mace). The *Matsya Purana* omits the ghanta and does not mention the fourth weapon.[2][17][23] The *Purva-Karanagama* mentions that she holds the Sharanga (the bow of Vishnu), the *hala* (plough), and the *musula* (pestle). The fourth hand is held in the Abhaya ("protection gesture") or the Varada Mudra ("blessing gesture").[8][17] The *Devi Purana* mentions her attributes as being sword, iron club, and noose. Another description says her hair is adorned with a garland with red flowers. She holds a staff and drinking skull-cup (kapala).[12][20] The *Varahini-nigrahastaka-stotra* describes her attributes as a plough, a pestle, a skull-cup, and the abhaya mudra.[24] The *Vamana Purana* describes her seated on Shesha while holding a chakra and a mace.[2] The *Agni Purana* describes her holding the gada, shankha, sword, and ankusha (goad).[2] The *Mantramahodadhi* mentions she carries a sword, shield, noose, and goad.[2] In Vaishnava images, since she is associated with Vishnu, Varahi may be depicted holding all four attributes of Vishnu — Shankha (conch), chakra, Gada, and Padma (lotus).[16] The *Aparajitapriccha* describes her holding a rosary, a khatvanga (a club with a skull), a bell, and a kamandalu (water-pot).[24]

The *Vishnudharmottara Purana* describes a six-armed Varahi, holding a danda (staff of punishment), khetaka (shield), khadga (sword), and pasha (noose) in four hands and the two remaining hands being held in Abhaya and Varada Mudra ("blessing gesture").[8] She also holds a *shakti* and *hala* (plough). Such a Varahi sculpture is found at Abanesi, depicted with the dancing Shiva.[8] She may also be depicted holding a child sitting on her lap, like Matrikas are often depicted.[16][22]

Matsya Varahi is depicted as two-armed, with spiral-coiled hair and holding a fish (*matsya*) and a kapala. The fish and wine-cup kapala are special characteristics of Tantric Shakta images of Varahi, the fish being exclusive to Tantric

sya Varahi.[10][18] The Matrikas, as shaktis of gods, are described to resemble those gods in form, jewellery, and mount, but Varahi inherits only the boar-face of Varaha.[19]

Varahi is usually depicted with her characteristic sow face on a human body with a black complexion comparable to a storm cloud.[8][20] The scholar Donaldson informs us that the association of a sow and a woman is seen derogatory for the latter, but the association is also used in curses to protect "land from invaders, new rulers, and trespassers".[19] Rarely, she is described as holding the Earth on her tusks, similar to Varaha.[2] She wears the *karaṇḍa mukuṭa*, a conical basket-shaped crown.[8][17] Varahi can be depicted as standing, seated, or dancing.[16] Varahi is often depicted pot-bellied and with full breasts, while most all other Ma-

Vaishanava images often depict Varahi holding all four attributes of Vishnu.

Barahi temple, Phewa lake, Nepal

descriptions.[10][18]

The vahana (vehicle) of Varahi is usually described as a buffalo (*Mahisha*). In Vaishnava and Shakta images, she is depicted as either standing or seated on a lotus pitha (pedestral) or on her vahana (a buffalo) or on its head, or on a boar, the serpent Shesha, a lion, or on Garuda (the eagle-man vahana of Vishnu). In Tantric Shakta images, the vahana may be specifically a she-buffalo or a corpse (*pretasana*).[10][16][17][20][24] An elephant may be depicted as her vahana.[8] The goddess is also described as riding on her horse, Jambini.[25] Garuda may be depicted as her attendant.[21] She may also be depicted seated under a *kalpaka* tree.[8]

When depicted as part of the Sapta-Matrika group ("seven mothers"), Varahi is always in the fifth position in the row of Matrikas, and thus is called **Panchami** ("fifth"). The goddesses are flanked by Virabhadra (Shiva's fierce form) and Ganesha (Shiva's elephant-headed son and wisdom god).[10]

2.66.4   Worship

For worship and temples of Varahi as part of the Sapta-Matrika group, see Matrika Worship

Varahi is worshipped by Shaivas, Vaishnavas, and Shaktas.[16] Varahi is worshipped in the Sapta-Matrikas group ("seven mothers"), which are venerated in Shaktism, as well as associated with Shiva.

Varahi is a *ratri devata* (night goddess) and is sometimes called Dhruma Varahi ("dark Varahi") and Dhumavati ("goddess of darkness"). According to Tantra, Varahi should be worshipped after sunset and before sunrise. *Parsurama Kalpasutra* explicitly states that the time of worship is the middle of the night.[10] Shaktas worship Varahi by secretive Vamamarga Tantric practices,[16] which are particularly associated with worship by panchamakara – wine, fish, grain, meat, and ritual copulation. These practices are observed in the Kalaratri temple on the bank of the Ganges, where worship is offered to Varahi only in the night; the shrine is closed during the day.[16] Shaktas consider Varahi to be a manifestation of the goddess Lalita Tripurasundari or as "Dandanayika" or "Dandanatha" – the commander-general of Lalita's army.[16] The Sri Vidya tradition of Shaktism elevates Varahi to the status of Para Vidya ("transcendental knowledge").[16] The Devi mahatmya suggests evoking Varahi for longevity.[10] Thirty yantras and thirty mantras are prescribed for the worship of Varahi and to acquire siddhis by her favour. This, according to the scholar Rath, indicates her power. Some texts detailing her iconography compare her to the Supreme Shakti.[10]

Prayers dedicated to Varahi include Varahi Anugrahashtakam, for her blessing, and Varahi Nigrahashtakam, for destruction of enemies; both are composed in Tamil.[26][27]

Temples

Apart from the temples in which Varahi is worshipped as part of the Sapta-Matrika, there are notable temples where Varahi is worshipped as the chief deity.

Central icon of Varahi Chaurasi temple

India

A 9th-century Varahi temple exists at Chaurasi about 14 km from Konark, Orissa, where Varahi is installed as Matysa Varahi and is worshipped by Tantric rites.[10][28] The famous Jaganath temple, Puri, is associated with and sends offerings to a Barahi temple, which is a centre of Tantric activities. In Varanasi, Varahi is worshipped as Patala Bhairavi. In Chennai, there is a Varahi temple in Mylapore, while a bigger temple is being built near Vedanthangal.[25] Ashadha Navaratri, in the Hindu month of Ashadha (June/July), is celebrated as a nine-day festival in honour of Varahi at the Varahi shrine at Brihadeeswarar temple (a Shaiva temple), Thanjavur. The goddess is decorated with different types of *alankaram*s (ornaments) every day.[14] Full moon days are considered sacred to Varahi.[14] An ancient Varahi devi temple worshipped as Uttari Bhawani is situated in Gonda District. In Gujarat, there is a Varahi temple in a village named Dadhana where the goddess is venerated as the Gotra-devi of a surname "Dadhaniya" Another temple in Gujarat is located in Talaja town of Bhavnagar district where idol of goddess was brought from hathasani village near palitana The idol of goddess was found by digging in shetrunji river in that area.

Maha Varahi temple is located in peelamedu(118,sowripalayam pirivu),coimbatore, Tamil Nadu. This temple has both Maha varahi and Goddess Dhandanatha(Varthali) - The commander in chief of Goddess Lalitha(Sri Raja rajeshwari's) army. This temple is run by Sri Varahi mantralayam trust. Varahi homam happens here on every panchami. This temple performs Dasamahavidhya homam(the 10 cosmic forms of goddess). Homa for Goddess bagalamukhi and Goddess Dhumavathi(Dhumra Varahi) are done on amavasai(new moon) and pournami(full moon).[29]

Nepal

A Barahi temple is situated in the middle of Phewa Lake, Nepal. Here, Barahi, as she is known as in Nepal, is worshipped in the Matysa Varahi form as an incarnation of Durga and an Ajima ("grandmother") goddess. Devotees usually sacrifice male animals to the goddess on Saturdays.[30] Jaya Barahi Mandir, Bhaktapur, is also dedicated to Barahi.[31]

Other countries

Devi Varahi Ambika Homam is done at the Parashakthi temple in Pontiac, Michigan, USA on every Amavaasya(New moon) night. Devi Varahi was installed at the Temple in February 2005 by Yanthra Prana prateeshta.[32] Varahi was installed in Sri Maha Muthu Mariamman temple Lunas, Kedah on 21 February 2014. That is the only Varahi Amman temple in the Malaysia.

Vajravarahi, with a sow's head on her right side

2.66.5   In Buddhism

Vajravarahi ("vajra-hog" or Buddhist Varahi), the most common form of the Buddhist goddess Vajrayogini, originated from the Hindu Varahi. Vajravarahi is also known as Varahi in Buddhism. Vajravarahi inherits the fierce character and wrath of Varahi. Both are invoked to destroy enemies. The sow head of Varahi is also seen as the right-side head attached to the main head in one of Vajravarahi's most common forms. The hog head is described in Tibetan scriptures to represent the sublimation of ignorance ("moha"). According to Elizabeth English, Varahi enters the Buddhist pantheon through the yogatantras. In the *Sarvatathagatatattvasamgaraha*, Varahi is described initially as a Shaiva *sarvamatr* ("all-mother") located in hell, who is converted to the Buddhist mandala by Vajrapani, assuming the name Vajramukhi ("vajra-face"). Varahi also enters the Heruka-mandala as an attendant goddess. Varahi, along with Varttali (another form of Varahi), appears as the hog-faced attendant of Marichi, who also has a sow face – which may be an effect of the Hindu Varahi.[16][33]

2.66.6   See also

Varaha

2.66.7   Notes

Footnotes

[1]   Varahi is also used as the name of the consort of Varaha, who is identified with Lakshmi (Vishnu's wife). This consort is depicted in a human form.

2.There are 12 names of varahi which are beneficial to everyone. They are Panchami, Dandhanatha, Sangyetha, Samayeshwari, Samaya sangyetha, Varahi, Varthali, Bothrini, Arikni, Mahasena, Agnachakreshwari, Shiva.

Citations

[1]   Kinsley p. 156, Devi Mahatmya verses 8.11–20

[2]   Donaldson p. 158

[3]   Kinsley p. 156, Devi Mahatmya verses 8.62

[4]   Kinsley p. 158, Devi Mahatmya verses 10.2–5

[5]   Kinsley p. 158,verses 30.3–9

[6]   Moor, Edward (2003). "Sacti: Consorts or Energies of Male Deities". *Hindu Pantheon*. Whitefish, MT: Kessinger Publishing. pp. 25, 116–120. ISBN 978-0-7661-8113-7.

[7]   Swami Vijnanananda (1923). *The Sri Mad Devi Bhagavatam: Books One Through Twelve*. Allahabad: The Panini Office. pp. 121, 138, 197, 452–7. OCLC 312989920.

[8]   Goswami, Meghali; Gupta, Dr. Ila; Jha, Dr. P. of IIT, Roorkee (March 2005). "Sapta Matrikas in Indian Art and Their Significance in Indian Sculpture and Ethos: A Critical Study" (PDF). *Anistoriton Journal*. Anistoriton. Retrieved 2008-01-08. Anistoriton is an electronic Journal of History, Archaeology and Art History. It publishes scholarly papers since 1997 and it is freely available on the Internet. All papers and images since vol. 1 (1997) are available on line as well as on the free Anistorion CD-ROM edition.

[9]   Kinsley p. 159, Varaha Purana verses 17.33–37

[10]   Rath, Jayanti (September–October 2007). "The Varahi Temple of Caurasi". *Orissa Review* (Government of Orissa): 37–9.

[11]   Pal pp. 1844–5

[12]   Pal p.1849

[13]   Padoux, André (1990). *Vāc: the Concept of the Word in Selected Hindu Tantras*. Albany: SUNY Press. p. 155. ISBN 978-0-7914-0257-3.

[14]   G. Srinivasan (24 July 2007). "Regaling Varahi with Different 'Alankarams in 'Ashada Navaratri'". *The Hindu*. Retrieved 22 January 2010.

[15] Sri Chinmoy (1992). *Kundalini: the Mother-Power*. Jamaica, NY: Aum Publications. p. 18.

[16] Nagaswamy, R (8 June 2004). "Iconography of Varahi". The Hindu. Retrieved 16 January 2010.

[17] Kalia, Asha (1982). *Art of Osian Temples: Socio-Economic and Religious Life in India, 8th–12th Centuries A.D.* New Delhi: Abhinav Publications. pp. 108–10. ISBN 0-391-02558-9.

[18] Donaldson p. 160

[19] Donaldson p. 155

[20] Pal p. 1846

[21] Bandyopandhay p. 232

[22] Images at Berkson, Carmel (1992). *Ellora, Concept and Style*. New Delhi: Abhinav Publications. pp. 144–5, 186. ISBN 81-7017-277-2.

[23] Rupamandana 5.67-8, Matsya Purana 261.30

[24] Donaldson p. 159

[25] Swaminathan, Chaitra (1 December 2009). "Presentation on Varahi". The Hindu. Retrieved 23 January 2010.

[26] P. R. Ramachander (Translation) (2002–2010). "Varahi Anugrahashtakam". *Vedanta Spiritual Library*. Celextel Enterprises Pvt. Ltd. Retrieved 24 January 2010.

[27] P. R. Ramachander (Translation) (2002–2010). "Varahi Nigrahashtakam (The Octet of Death Addressed to Varahi)". *Vedanta Spiritual Library*. Celextel Enterprises Pvt. Ltd. Retrieved 24 January 2010.

[28] "Destinations: Konark". Tourism Department, Government of Orissa. Retrieved 24 January 2010.

[29] http://varahi.org/

[30] "Barahi Temple on Phewa Lake". *Channel Nepal site*. Paley Media, Inc. 1995–2010. Retrieved 24 January 2010.

[31] Reed, David; McConnachie, James (2002). "The Kathmandu Valley: Bhaktapur". *The Rough Guide to Nepal*. Rough Guides. London: Rough Guides. p. 230. ISBN 978-1-85828-899-4.

[32] http://www.parashakthitemple.org/vaarahi.aspx

[33] English, Elizabeth (2002). "The Emergence of Vajrayogini". *Vajrayoginī: Her Visualizations, Rituals, and Forms*. Boston: Wisdom Publications. pp. 47–9, 66. ISBN 978-0-86171-329-5.

2.66.8 References

- Bandyopandhay, Sudipa (1999). "Two Rare Matrka Images from Lower Bengal". In Mishra, P. K. *Studies in Hindu and Buddhist Art*. New Delhi: Abhinav Publications. ISBN 978-81-7017-368-7.

- Donaldson, Thomas Eugene (1995). "Orissan Images of Vārāhī, Oḍḍiyāna Mārīcī, and Related Sow-Faced Goddesses". *Artibus Asiae* (Artibus Asiae Publishers) **55** (1/2): 155–182. OCLC 483899737.

- Kinsley, David (1988). *Hindu Goddesses: Vision of the Divine Feminine in the Hindu Religious Traditions*. Delhi: Motilal Banarsidass. ISBN 81-208-0394-9.

- Pal, P. (1997). "The Mother Goddesses According to the Devipurana". In Singh, Nagendra Kumar. *Encyclopaedia of Hinduism*. New Delhi: Anmol Publications. ISBN 81-7488-168-9.

2.66.9 External Links

- Varahi by Dr Haripriya Rangarajan at the National Museum Symposium: The Return of the Yogini, New Delhi, October 2013.

2.67 Victoria (mythology)

Victoria, in ancient Roman religion, was the personified goddess of victory.[2] She is the Roman equivalent of the Greek goddess Nike, and was associated with Bellona. She was adapted from the Sabine agricultural goddess Vacuna and had a temple on the Palatine Hill. The goddess Vica Pota was also sometimes identified with Victoria. Victoria is often described as a daughter of Pallas and Styx, and as a sister of Zelus, Kratos, and Bia.[3]

Unlike the Greek *Nike*, the goddess Victoria (Latin for "victory") was a major part of Roman society. Multiple temples were erected in her honor. When her statue was removed in 382 CE by Emperor Gratianus there was much anger in Rome.[4][5] She was normally worshiped by triumphant generals returning from war.[2]

Also unlike the Greek Nike, who was known for success in athletic games such as chariot races, Victoria was a symbol of victory over death and determined who would be successful during war.[2]

Victoria appears widely on Roman coins,[6] jewelry, architecture, and other arts. She is often seen with or in a chariot, as in the late 18th-century sculpture representing Victory in a quadriga on the Brandenburg Gate in Berlin, Germany; "Il Vittoriano" in Rome has two. Nike or Victoria was the

*Victoria on top of the Berlin Victory Column
(cast by Gladenbeck, Berlin)[1]*

charioteer for Zeus in his battle to over take Mount Olympus.

2.67.1 Winged victories

Winged figures, very often in pairs, representing victory and referred to as "victories", were common in Roman official iconography, typically hovering high in a composition, and often filling spaces in spandrels or other gaps in architecture.[7] These represent the spirit of victory rather than the goddess herself. They continued to appear after Christianization of the Empire, and slowly mutated into Christian angels.

2.67.2 Gallery

- Gold coin of Constantine II depicting Victoria on the reverse

2.67.3 References

[1] "Oscar Gladenbeck (1850-1921)". *ISSUU.com*. Retrieved 18 June 2015.

[2] "Victoria". *talesbeyondbelief.com*. Retrieved 5 August 2015.

[3] "Nike". *theoi.com*. Retrieved 5 August 2015.

[4] Sheridan, J.J., "The Altar of Victory – Paganism's Last Battle." L'Antiquite Classique 35 (1966): 187.

[5] Ambrose Epistles 17–18; Symmachus Relationes 1–3.

[6] "All About Gold". *numismaclub.com*. Retrieved 5 August 2015.

[7] "Winged Victoria Spandrels". *google.com*. Retrieved 5 August 2015.

2.67.4 See also

- 12 Victoria

2.67.5 External links

- Media related to Victoria (goddess) at Wikimedia Commons

2.68 Virtus (deity)

See Virtus (disambiguation) for other meanings.

In Roman mythology, **Virtus** was the deity of bravery and military strength, the personification of the Roman virtue of virtus.[1] The Greek equivalent deity was Arete.[1]

He/she was identified with the Roman god Honos (personification of honour), and was often honoured together with him. As reported in Valerius Maximus,[2] this joint cult led to plans in 210 BC by Marcus Claudius Marcellus to erect a joint temple for them both.[3] This led to objections from the pontifical college that, if a miracle should occur in such a temple, the priests would not know to which of the two gods to offer the sacrifice in thanks for it. Marcellus therefore erected a temple for Virtus alone which was the only way in to a separate temple of Honos, financing them both with the loot from his sacking of Syracuse and defeats of

Gallic coin featuring Virtus.

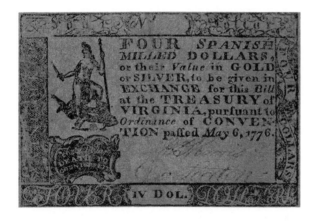

U.S. Continental currency Virginia Four-Dollar Note of 1776 (obverse) with Virtus at the left.

the Gauls. This temple was at the Porta Capena, and later renovated by Vespasian.

This deity was represented in a variety of ways - for example, on the coins of Tetricus, it can appear as a matron, an old man, or a young man, with a javelin or only clothed in a cape. Within the realm of funerary reliefs Virtus is never shown without a male companion.[4] Often her presence within this realm of art is to compliment and provide assistance to the protagonist of the relief during a scene of intense masculinity or bravery.[5]

2.68.1 Modern era

In 1776, Virtus was made the central figure in Seal of Virginia and the subsequent state's flag which features the seal. The Virginia Four-Dollar Note, a Continental currency, had a similar Virtus pictured on its obverse.

2.68.2 References

[1] J. Rufus Fears, "The Theology of Victory at Rome: Approaches and Problem," *Aufstieg und Niedergang der römischen Welt* II.17.2 (1981), pp. 747–748, 776 (note 201).

[2] "Honos et Virtus". *A Topographical Dictionary of Ancient Rome*. 15 June 2007. Retrieved 28 June 2007. External link in |work= (help)

[3] "Valeri Maximi". *Factorum et Dictorum Memorabilium*. 22 April 2007. Retrieved 28 June 2007.

[4] Hansen, L (2008). *MUSES as models : learning and the complicity of authority*. The University of Michigan. p. 280.

[5] Hansen, L (2008). *MUSES as models : learning and the complicity of authority*. The University of Michigan. p. 281.

2.69 Vishva Shakti Durga Mandir

Vishva Shakti Durga Mandir Association वश्वि शक्त्ति दुर्गा मन्दरि(VSDMA) was incorporated in 1997 as a nonprofit organization to promote the religious, social, and cultural activities of Indo-Canadians in Ottawa and Eastern Ontario. **Vishva Shakti Durga Mandir** is the newest temple in the National Capital Region of Canada. It is located in The Glebe neighborhood off Bank Street. Devi Durga and other Pujas are held each evening, and special services are held each Sunday starting at 11:00 AM. **Durga Temple** promotes and practice ideals of Hindu and Hindu based religions through worship, education and teaching. It also strives for spiritual richness and human excellence through assimilation of values in Hindu scriptures into daily lives and we recognize and respect other religions and belief systems in their proper context.

2.69.1 Temple operations

The temple serves both as a religious and a cultural centre for the Hindus in the area. Major events that are routinely held at the temple or performed by the Pandit Ravindra Narain Panday ji are the engagement ceremony, marriages, Namakaran, Annaprashana, Mundan Sanskar, Havan, Bhoomi Pooja, Vastu Shanti/Graha Pravesh, Satyanarayan Pooja, Navagraha Pooja, and Maata Ki Chowki.

History

Devi Durga devotees Leena Shukla and the late Rama Juneja originally conceived the idea of having a Durga Mandir in the National Capital Region of Canada, and they were the founding members of the temple. Inspired by their efforts, Surinder Sumra joined them as co-founder a few months later. The name Vishva Shakti Durga Mandir Association (VSDMA) for the temple was suggested by Maharaj Ji of India.

Pandit Ravindra Narain Panday Ji accepted the reins of the temple's priesthood in mid-December 1997. These included regular Sunday services, other required services, and services at devotee's homes. The Community Center at Bellman Street served as the temple's temporary location until May 1998. With expanding membership, the temple moved to the Community Center at the corner of Bank Street and Riverside Drive in June 1998. The temple later moved once again to another Community Center on Somerset Street East. The temple's present location on Clary Avenue became its permanent home in September 2005.

With the tremendous efforts of previous President, Mr. Nityanand Varma and the great support of our devotees, we finally succeeded in finding a permanent home for the temple at its present location, 55 Clary Avenue, where the devotees reshaped an old church into a vibrant temple in September 2005 and started the regular prayers on a daily basis. Our past President, late Mr. Gopal Verma planned the auspicious Sthapana of the Moorties of Maa Durga, Rama Parivar, Radha Krishna, Shiva Parivar, Lord Ganesha, Lord Vishnu and Lakshmi, Hanuman and Shiva Lingam and turn that building into a vibrant temple. Our last president, Mr. Pramod Sood ji and Parmod Chhabra, PRO and other Board Members worked very hard to make **Durga Temple**, one of the best places to worship in Ottawa.

Main deities

- Ganesha

- Rama Parivar

- Radha Krishna

- Maa Durga

- Shiva Parivar

- Hanuman

- Vishnu and Lakshmi

- Shiva Lingam

Major festivals

- Navratra: Vasant Navaratras (March–April) and Sharana Navratras (September–October) are celebrated for nine days at the temple. There is Mata Ki Chowki on Saturdays during that week.

- Krishna Janmashtami

- Diwali: Diwali is celebrated with Laxmi Pooja on the day of Diwali. The temple also organises a Diwali dinner and dance night in October or November every year.

- Maha Shivratri

- Holi

- Karva Chauth

Goals

The main purpose of the temple is to promote Hinduism in Ottawa, Eastern Ontario, and Canada.

- Religious goal: To cater to the religious needs of the community in accordance with traditional Hindu philosophy

- Cultural goal: To cultivate a better understanding of Indian culture and heritage for the coming generation

- Social goal: To promote social activities leading to social cohesion and human betterment

- Educational goal: To promote the learning of Indian languages, leading to a better understanding of the Indian literature and philosophies

2.69.2   See also

- World Hinduism

- Hinduism by country

- Hindu calendar

- List of Hindu temples

- Hindu deities

- List of Hindu deities

- List of Hinduism-related articles

- History of India

- Hindu scriptures

2.69.3 References

2.69.4 External links

- Canadian Desi

- 108 names of Durga from the Durgāsaptaśatī

Coordinates: 45°24′03″N 75°41′11″W / 45.400898°N 75.686521°W

2.70 Wadjet

This article is about the Egyptian goddess. For the ancient Egyptian symbol, see Eye of Horus.

Wadjet (/ˈwɑːˌdʒɛt/ or /ˈwædˌdʒɛt/; Egyptian *w?dyt*,

Two images of Wadjet appear on this carved wall in the Hatshepsut Temple at Luxor

"green one"),[1] known to the Greek world as **Uto** (/ˈjuːtoʊ/ or **Buto** /ˈbjuːtoʊ/) among other names, was originally the ancient local goddess of the city of Dep (Buto),[2] which became part of the city that the Egyptians named **Per-Wadjet**, *House of Wadjet*, and the Greeks called Buto (Desouk

now),[3] a city that was an important site in the Predynastic era of Ancient Egypt and the cultural developments of the Paleolithic. She was said to be the patron and protector of Lower Egypt and upon unification with Upper Egypt, the joint protector and patron of all of Egypt with the "goddess" of Upper Egypt. The image of Wadjet with the sun disk is called the uraeus, and it was the emblem on the crown of the rulers of Lower Egypt. She was also the protector of kings and of women in childbirth.

As the patron goddess, she was associated with the land and depicted as a snake-headed woman or a snake—usually an Egyptian cobra, a venomous snake common to the region; sometimes she was depicted as a woman with two snake heads and, at other times, a snake with a woman's head. Her oracle was in the renowned temple in Per-Wadjet that was dedicated to her worship and gave the city its name. This oracle may have been the source for the oracular tradition that spread to Greece from Egypt.[4]

The *Going Forth of Wadjet* was celebrated on December 25 with chants and songs. An annual festival held in the city celebrated Wadjet on April 21. Other important dates for special worship of her were June 21, the Summer Solstice, and March 14. She also was assigned the fifth hour of the fifth day of the moon.

Wadjet was closely associated in the Egyptian pantheon with the Eye of Ra, a powerful protective deity. The hieroglyph for her eye is shown below; sometimes two are shown in the sky of religious images. Per-Wadjet also contained a sanctuary of Horus, the child of the sun deity who would be interpreted to represent the pharaoh. Much later, Wadjet became associated with Isis as well as with many other deities.

In the relief shown to the right, which is on the wall of the Hatshepsut Temple at Luxor, there are two images of Wadjet: one of her as the uraeus sun disk with her head through an ankh and another where she precedes a Horus hawk wearing the double crown of united Egypt, representing the pharaoh whom she protects.

2.70.1 Etymology

The name Wadjet[5] is derived from the term for the symbol of her domain, Lower Egypt, the *papyrus*.[6]

Her name means "papyrus-colored one",[7] as *wadj* is the ancient Egyptian word for the color green (in reference to the color of the papyrus plant) and the *et* is an indication of her gender. Its hieroglyphs differ from those of the Green Crown (Red Crown) of Lower Egypt only by the determinative, which in the case of the crown was a picture of the Green Crown[8] and, in the case of the goddess, a rearing cobra.

2.70.2 Protector of country, pharaohs, and other deities

Eventually, Wadjet was claimed as the patron goddess and protector of the whole of Lower Egypt and became associated with Nekhbet, depicted as a white vulture, who held unified Egypt. After the unification the image of Nekhbet joined Wadjet on the crown, thereafter shown as part of the uraeus.

The ancient Egyptian word *Wadj* signifies blue and green. It is also the name for the well known *Eye of the Moon*.[9] Indeed, in later times, she was often depicted simply as a woman with a snake's head, or as a woman wearing the uraeus. The uraeus originally had been her body alone, which wrapped around or was coiled upon the head of the pharaoh or another deity

Wadjet was depicted as a cobra. As patron and protector, later Wadjet often was shown coiled upon the head of Ra; in order to act as his protection, this image of her became the uraeus symbol used on the royal crowns as well.

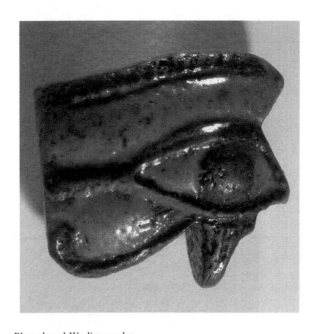

Blue-glazed Wadjet amulet

Another early depiction of Wadjet is as a cobra entwined around a papyrus stem, beginning in the Predynastic era (prior to 3100 B.C.) and it is thought to be the first image that shows a snake entwined around a staff symbol. This is a sacred image that appeared repeatedly in the later images and myths of cultures surrounding the Mediterranean Sea, called the caduceus, which may have had separate origins.

Her image also rears up from the staff of the "flag" poles that are used to indicate deities, as seen in the hieroglyph for *uraeus* above and for *goddess* in other places.

2.70.3 Associations with other deities

Wadjet as Wadjet-Bast, *depicted as the body of a woman with a lioness head, wearing the uraeus*

An interpretation of the Milky Way was that it was the primal snake, Wadjet, the protector of Egypt. In this interpretation she was closely associated with Hathor and other early deities among the various aspects of the great mother goddess, including Mut and Naunet. The association with Hathor brought her son Horus into association also. The cult of Ra absorbed most of Horus's traits and included the protective eye of Wadjet that had shown her association with Hathor.

When identified as the protector of Ra, who was also a sun deity associated with heat and fire, she was sometimes said to be able to send fire onto those who might attack, just as the cobra spits poison into the eyes of its enemies.[10] In this role she was called the *Lady of Flame*.

She later became identified with the war goddess of Lower Egypt, Bast, who acted as another figure symbolic of the nation, consequently becoming ***Wadjet-Bast***. In this role, since Bast was a lioness, Wadjet-Bast was often depicted with a lioness head.

After Lower Egypt had been conquered by Upper Egypt and they were unified, the lioness goddess of Upper Egypt, Sekhmet, was seen as the more powerful of the two warrior goddesses. It was Sekhmet who was seen as the *Avenger of Wrongs*, and *the Scarlet Lady*, a reference to blood, as the one with bloodlust. She is depicted with the solar disk and Wadjet, however.

Eventually, Wadjet's position as patron led to her being identified as the more powerful goddess Mut, whose cult had come to the fore in conjunction with rise of the cult of Amun, and eventually being absorbed into her as the *Mut-Wadjet-Bast* triad.

When the pairing of deities occurred in later Egyptian myths, since she was linked to the land, after the unification of Lower and Upper Egypt she came to be thought of as the wife of Hapy, a deity of the Nile, which flowed through the land.[11]

Wadjet, as the goddess of Lower Egypt, had a big temple at the ancient Imet (now Tell Nebesha) in the Nile Delta. She was worshipped in the area as the 'Lady of Imet'. Later she was joined by Min and Horus to form a triad of deities. This was based on an Osiriac model identified elsewhere in Egypt.[12]

Wadjet is not to be confused with the Egyptian demon Apep, who is also represented as a snake in Egyptian mythology.

2.70.4   See also

- Ethnoherpetology

- Eye of Horus

- Mehen

- Serpent (symbolism)

- Snake goddess

- Snakes in mythology

- Unut

- Uraeus

2.70.5   Footnotes

[1] Also spelled **Wadjit**, **Wedjet**, **Uadjet** or **Ua Zit**

[2] Wilkinson, *Early Dynastic Egypt*, p.297

[3] *Wörterbuch der ägyptischen Sprache*, 1, 268.18

[4] Herodotus ii. 55 and vii. 134

[5] *Wörterbuch der ägyptischen Sprache*, 1, 268.17

[6] *Wörterbuch der ägyptischen Sprache*, 1, 263.7–264.4

[7] J. A. Coleman, *The Dictionary of Mythology: A–Z Reference of Legends and Heroes*

[8] *Wörterbuch der ägyptischen Sprache*, 1, 268.16;

[9] *Wörterbuch der ägyptischen Sprache* 1, 268.13

[10] Curl, *The Egyptian Revival*, p.469

[11] Ana Ruiz, *The Spirit of Ancient Egypt*, p.119

[12] Vincent Razanajao, D'Imet à Tell Farâoun : recherches sur la géographie, les cultes et l'histoire d'une localité de Basse-Égypte orientale. (English synopsis)

2.70.6   References

- James Stevens Curl, *The Egyptian Revival: Ancient Egypt as the Inspiration for Design Motifs in the West*, Routledge 2005

- Adolf Erman, Hermann Grapow, *Wörterbuch der ägyptischen Sprache*, Berlin 1963

- Ana Ruiz, *The Spirit of Ancient Egypt*, Algora Publishing 2001

- Toby A. H. Wilkinson, *Early Dynastic Egypt*, Routledge 1999

2.70.7   External links

2.71   Šauška

Šauška or **Shaushka** (Hittite: *Šauša*, & later *Šawuška*[1]) was a Hurrian goddess who was also adopted into the Hittite pantheon. She is known in detail because she became the patron goddess of the Hittite king Hattusili III (1420–1400 BC) following his marriage to Puduhepa, the daughter of the goddess' high priest. Her cultic center was Lawazantiya in Kizzuwatna.[2]

Shaushka is a goddess of fertility, war and healing. She is depicted in human form with wings, standing with a lion and accompanied by two attendants. She was considered equivalent to the Mesopotamian goddess Ishtar and is sometimes identified using Ishtar's name in Hittite cuneiform.[3]

Shaushka is interesting in that she uses her authority in matters of sexuality to mess around a little where she saw fit. Texts describe Shaushka as similar to Ishtar, as an ambiguous goddess who supervised conjugal love and harmonious relationships but, unpredictably, could turn love into a dangerous endeavor. Reliefs at Yazilikaya show the goddess twice: in one relief she is depicted with male gods and in another with the goddesses. According to Hittite texts about Shaushka of Lawazantiya: she is clothed like a man and like a woman, and has male attributes such as an axe and weapons. Sometimes this has been taken as a sign of her bisexual or androgynous character.[4]

2.71.1 Amarna letters "*Šauška*"

In the 1350-1335 BC Amarna letters correspondence, (written mostly to the Ancient Egyptian pharaoh), one letter EA 23, (EA for 'el Amarna'), written to the pharaoh, has as its topic, the *Loaning of a Statue* to Egypt. It is presumed that it's due to the health of the Egyptian king, but there are other theories or explanations.

The title of the letter is: *"A goddess travels to Egypt".*

It is a short, 32-line letter, from Tushratta, (letter no. 7 of 13), and the 2nd half of the letter states:

> *"Now, in the time, too, of my father ... ..went to this country, and just as earlier she dwelt there and they honored her, may my brother now honor her 10 times more than before. May my brother honor her, –(then) at (his) pleasure let her go so that she may come back.*
>
> *May Šauška, the mistress of heaven, protect us, my brother and me, 100,000 years, and may our mistress grant both of us great joy. And let us act as friends.*
>
> *Is Šauška for me alone my god(dess), and for my brother not his god(dess)?"*

Black Egyptian script is also written on the reverse side of this letter, (in the open space remaining).

2.71.2 See also

- Hittite mythology
- Hurrian mythology
- Amarna letter EA 19

2.71.3 References

- Moran, William L. *The Amarna Letters.* Johns Hopkins University Press, 1987, 1992. (softcover, ISBN 0-8018-6715-0)

2.71.4 References

[1] Beckman, Gary. "Ištar of Nineveh Reconsidered." JCS 50 (1998).

[2] *Sirkeli Höyük – Exploring an Ancient Hittite City in Cilicia.* Accessed 11 Dec 2010.

[3] Beckman, Gary. "Ištar of Nineveh Reconsidered." JCS 50 (1998).

[4] Karel van der Toorn; Bob Becking; Pieter Willem van der Horst (1999). *Dictionary of Deities and Demons in the Bible.* Brill. pp. 758–759. ISBN 90-04-11119-0.

2.71.5 External links

- EA 23-(Reverse), with **Black** *Hieratic*; Article-(British Museum)

- For a collection of Amarna letters photographs, see: Pirissi and Tulubri links, (Tushratta letters, and others).

Chapter 3

Text and image sources, contributors, and licenses

3.1 Text

- **Women warriors in literature and culture** *Source:* https://en.wikipedia.org/wiki/Women_warriors_in_literature_and_culture?oldid= 679973279 *Contributors:* Ant, Lquilter, N-true, Haryo, Scott Sanchez, DocWatson42, Fergananim, Kaldari, Mike Rosoft, Rich Farmbrough, Pmsyyz, Dbachmann, Thu, 23skidoo, Viriditas, Anthony Appleyard, Scarecroe, Mike riversdale, Simoncursitor, AnmaFinotera, Stefanomione, Sjö, Rjwilmsi, Phileas, Vegaswikian, Maurog, Satanael, Hairy Dude, RussBot, Pigman, Yamara, Bloodofox, Welsh, Nanten, Zythe, Asarelah, CKarnstein, Pawyilee, NYArtsnWords, Aquaviann, Bibliomaniac15, SmackBot, Uthanc, Classicfilms, Malkinann, Jagged 85, Kintetsubuffalo, Lyta79, Pwjb, Lcarscad, NickPenguin, Blaze33541, BrownHairedGirl, Bookwench, Evolutionselene, Armyrifle9, Robofish, Kransky, Kyoko, Intranetusa, Sandry25, Koweja, Iridescent, Colonel Warden, RekishiEJ, WolfgangFaber, SkyWalker, Adam Keller, Gotheek, SamSandy, Pro bug catcher, Schmorgluck, Metacosm, Hebrides, Doug Weller, Kalinmoor, Moonshadow Rogue, Missvain, Modgamers, JustAGal, Ludde23, Noclevername, Masamage, Ronja Addams-Moring, Fayenatic london, Killerman2, Legionaireb, Lord Crayak, MegX, Bazzalisk, R'n'B, CommonsDelinker, Dinoguy1000, Eliz81, A Nobody, Johnbod, Infinitysend, Astropixie, Johnnyswitchblade, Davecrosby uk, Deor, CWii, Hersfold, Indubitably, PhoenixVTam, Relover, H. Carver, Mzmadmike, Bllasae, Nights1stStar, Squaretex, Regemet, Purplefire, WizzieBlue, Qworty, Newmoonnight, Norman728, BaconManAtWork, Flare13, Noveltyghost, Yintan, Jc-S0CO, Shakko, Fratrep, Dravecky, Spartan198, RobynHarris, Lyddiechu, Brian Tjoe-Nij, Foofbun, BlueAmethyst, Ronaldloui, Pinkpicnic, Coralmizu, Dr. Stantz, Manushyan1, FaithLehaneTheVampireSlayer, Mediadimension, TheRedPenOfDoom, Sunecao, Mlaffs, Rds865, Kingdom2, Lx 121, DumZiBoT, Lostfaction, Not050, XLinkBot, Ticklemepink127, Sakura22222, Dthomsen8, Aelfgiva, Addbot, Nyalyn, Heavenlyblue, Werewolfking, Tomato Jr., Yobmod, Stingyedra, USchick, Maple50, Download, Ccacsmss, Silverbead, Astadourian, Polhymnia, Smitsy159, Terwilliger44, Westrim, Yobot, Granpuff, Darkangel788, JWAbrams, AnomieBOT, Anne McDermott, Rubinbot, Mintrick, Sourbagel, Materialscientist, Akiradilandau, Jmundo, Omnipaedista, Albert347, Paine Ellsworth, Tobby72, Xttina.Garnet, Steve Quinn, Slivicon, FriscoKnight, Phlyaristis, Degen Earthfast, Woowoowikiwoo, Fulldate unlinking bot, Scareepete, Katerenka, TheGrimReaper NS, Nicolahh, GoingBatty, MikeyMouse10, Aftesk, Wikiraj121, Guilins, NTox, AgentSniff, Ptdtch, Chisme, Quick and Dirty User Account, Helpful Pixie Bot, Iamthecheese44, LoneWolf1992, The Vintage Feminist, F karlo, Prince of Strings, OldFishHouse, Beag maclir and Anonymous: 309

- **List of women warriors in folklore** *Source:* https://en.wikipedia.org/wiki/List_of_women_warriors_in_folklore?oldid=686580471 *Contributors:* William Avery, Hyacinth, Joy, Jsonitsac, Evertype, Discospinster, Florian Blaschke, Xezbeth, Dbachmann, Avatarum, Alansohn, Carbon Caryatid, Ghirlandajo, Woohookitty, Dmol, Paxsimius, BD2412, Rjwilmsi, Angusmclellan, RussBot, Yamara, Bloodofox, Ospalh, Zythe, Rwalker, CorbieVreccan, Asarelah, Pawyilee, Open2universe, SmackBot, Classicfilms, Nightbat, Kintetsubuffalo, HeartofaDog, Hmains, Colonies Chris, OrphanBot, Huon, Fuhghettaboutit, Valenciano, GuillaumeTell, Osteck, Ceplm, Fredwords, Newone, CmdrObot, Doug Weller, Biruitorul, Missvain, Egwess, Froid, Pavel Jelínek, R'n'B, CommonsDelinker, Adavidb, KylieTastic, KellyPhD, Redtigerxyz, Cnilep, Thanatos666, StAnselm, Oldag07, Trigaranus, Zalktis, Wcris, Tejuspratap, Wikievil666, Drmies, TheOldJacobite, Niceguyedc, Onlyeightfingers, DarkerStar, Johnuniq, Bilsonius, JigsyQ, Tiggywinkle25, Manjunath Doddamani Gajendragad, Fyrael, USchick, Polhymnia, Tassedethe, Peridon, Jarble, Yobot, Darx9url, Serpasas, AnomieBOT, Lecen, Prasadksap, Gatorgirl7563, FrescoBot, Neptunekh2, Phlyaristis, I dream of horses, Dazedbythebell, Skyerise, Mozartfan14, Heinrich krebs, Cnwilliams, Dustynyfeathers, Reaper Eternal, Mukogodo, John of Reading, Gigi2020, Bahramm 2, Lunagoth, GrindtXX, Vuhoangsonhn, Jasonz2z, FurrySings, ClueBot NG, Asb227, Poojones1969, Corusant, Uion, Helpful Pixie Bot, Drsimonz, BrookISU, Pacerier, Mysterytrey, Fillthemill, Iamthecheese44, Palbrattberg, Conew~enwiki, Glacialfox, Darangsc, Khazar2, Kunogi, Mogism, Twilus, Epicgenius, Nerezine, Lakshmiprasadj, I am One of Many, Hansmuller, OliviaSp, Saectar, Krishnaprasad120543, Beag maclir, Filedelinkerbot, RobertBDurham, ChamithN, Loraof, TD712, Lmichelsen, Maggiejcd and Anonymous: 144

- **Agasaya** *Source:* https://en.wikipedia.org/wiki/Agasaya?oldid=614960757 *Contributors:* SimonP, RussBot, Ugur Basak, Asarelah, SmackBot, Arbadihist, Castanea dentata, Axem Titanium, Goldenrowley, T@nn, VolkovBot, Addbot, Yobot, Erik9bot, TjBot, SFK2, Ponyfan58425, George7890 and Anonymous: 2

- **Agrona** *Source:* https://en.wikipedia.org/wiki/Agrona?oldid=655723304 *Contributors:* Dori, TUF-KAT, Gtrmp, Jossi, YUL89YYZ, QuartierLatin1968, Nicknack009, Cuchullain, Vegaswikian, Eburaconos, Ugur Basak, Asarelah, SmackBot, Unschool, Bluebot, Cydebot, Erin Navan, Scotia Scotia, Legobot, SassoBot, Skyerise, Krakkos and Anonymous: 6

N3philim, Axosman, ClueBot NG, ClaretAsh, PT05Benni, Micpop, Rossetti29, Riley Huntley, Jagerwhoodie, Bksatyanarayana, Hmainsbot1, Mogism, Bibehilú, Brewerypub55, Rosetta Stele, Kethrus, KasparBot and Anonymous: 107

- **Athena** *Source:* https://en.wikipedia.org/wiki/Athena?oldid=686866743 *Contributors:* Kpjas, The Epopt, Vicki Rosenzweig, Bryan Derksen, Andre Engels, Josh Grosse, Christian List, William Avery, Shii, Heron, Rsabbatini, Zimriel, Montrealais, Hephaestos, Tucci528, Frecklefoot, Edward, JohnOwens, Michael Hardy, Paul Barlow, Fred Bauder, Dante Alighieri, Liftarn, Wapcaplet, Sannse, Karl Stas, Loooix~enwiki, Ahoerstemeier, Jimfbleak, Docu, Typhoon, TUF-KAT, Angela, Darkwind, Potatoscone, Mnementh, Agtx, Adam Bishop, Jallan, Andrewman327, WhisperToMe, CBDunkerson, Tpbradbury, Furrykef, Head, Bevo, Renato Caniatti~enwiki, Optim, Wetman, Adam Carr, Frazzydee, Francs2000, Jni, Aenar, Robbot, Astronautics~enwiki, ChrisO~enwiki, Moriori, Chris 73, ZimZalaBim, Altenmann, Yelyos, Naddy, Securiger, Bmcdaniel, Chris Roy, UtherSRG, Delpino, Wikibot, Mandel, Tsavage, Xanzzibar, DocWatson42, Gtrmp, Jyril, Drunkasian, Inter, Meursault2004, Michael Devore, Wikiwikifast, Beardo, Gilgamesh~enwiki, Per Honor et Gloria, Eequor, Macrakis, Bobblewik, Golbez, RivGuySC, Bacchiad, Knutux, Academician, Slowking Man, Antandrus, OverlordQ, Andux, Jossi, Vina, Rdsmith4, Oneiros, ScottyBoy900Q, Tail, Zfr, Bepp, Neutrality, Neale Monks, Klemen Kocjancic, Hillel, Chmod007, Lacrimosus, Aziri, Mike Rosoft, D6, Perey, Freakofnurture, CALR, DanielCD, Ultratomio, Discospinster, Brianhe, Rich Farmbrough, Ffirehorse, Silence, Dbachmann, Paul August, Bender235, ESkog, Kjoonlee, Pedant, Brian0918, Aranel, El C, DS1953, Mwanner, Kross, Sietse Snel, Art LaPella, Markussep, Adambro, Sole Soul, Bobo192, Martey, Feitclub, Smalljim, Elipongo, JW1805, ParticleMan, TheProject, Americist, Sam Korn, C-squared, Batneil, Merope, Ranveig, Jumbuck, Danski14, Alansohn, Christopher-Willis, Voyelles, Borisblue, Jeltz, Riana, Lectonar, Viridian, GavinSharp, DanD, TomH, Cdc, DreamGuy, Wtmitchell, Kanodin, Knowledge Seeker, Suruena, Sciurinæ, Gene Nygaard, Netkinetic, Megan1967, Nuno Tavares, Kelly Martin, Reinoutr, OwenX, TarmoK, Yansa, Rocastelo, Miaow Miaow, ZZz, MONGO, Prashanthns, Stefanomione, Dysepsion, Mandarax, Graham87, WBardwin, Magister Mathematicae, Cuchullain, FreplySpang, Sjö, Tabercil, Sjakkalle, Rjwilmsi, Coemgenus, Koavf, Саша Стефановић, Gryffindor, Bruce1ee, MZMcBride, Salanth, Akzennay, The wub, Bhadani, MarnetteD, Sango123, Ev, Yamamoto Ichiro, Titoxd, Miskin, RobertG, Ysangkok, Crazycomputers, Nivix, Kerowyn, RexNL, Gurch, TeaDrinker, Kaisershrout, Codex Sinaiticus, Ben Babcock, Gareth E Kegg, Butros, Chobot, Shauni, Todd@waze, Sharkface217, DVdm, Hitokirishinji, Sasoriza, Bgwhite, Gwernol, The Rambling Man, Satanael, Borgx, RobotE, TheSPY, Hairy Dude, Mahahahaneapneap, Kafziel, Phantomsteve, Longbow4u, Pigman, Chaser, Stephenb, Gaius Cornelius, Eleassar, Theelf29, Rsrikanth05, Wimt, Ravenous, Anomalocaris, Marcus Cyron, Megistias, Odysses, NawlinWiki, Wiki alf, Grafen, Jaxl, Welsh, Korny O'Near, Thiseye, Bmdavll, Apokryltaros, Nick, Larry laptop, Jpai235, Raven4x4x, Moe Epsilon, Mlouns, DeadEyeArrow, Kewp, Tomisti, Nlu, N. Harmonik, Ms2ger, AnnaKucsma, Sandstein, Donbert, Iamvered, Ninly, Italian boy, Arthur Rubin, JQF, GraemeL, Ipstenu, NielsenGW, Contaldo80, Emc2, Lando242, David Biddulph, Argos'Dad, PMHauge, GMan552, Katieh5584, Moomoomoo, NeilN, GrinBot~enwiki, Bibliomaniac15, Luk, Crystallina, Qoqnous, SmackBot, Rohitk89, Krychek, Tarret, Psythor, Olorin28, Hydrogen Iodide, Lagalag, Kimon, Pgk, Bomac, Thunderboltz, WookieInHeat, Bradtcordeiro, Jab843, Silverhand, Kintetsubuffalo, HalfShadow, Alsandro, Gilliam, Ohnoitsjamie, Hmains, Skizzik, Fetofs, Chris the speller, Bluebot, Persian Poet Gal, JDCMAN, MalafayaBot, SchfiftyThree, Ted87, Baa, DHN-bot~enwiki, Sbharris, IMFromKathlene, Rlevse, Can't sleep, clown will eat me, Egsan Bacon, Skoglund, Akhilleus, Nerrolken, Rrburke, Addshore, SundarBot, Huon, Krich, BehemothCat, Valenciano, John D. Croft, Dreadstar, Mistress Selina Kyle, Rramir16, JoannaJMHicks, Antipode, Salamurai, Schgooda, SashatoBot, Dane Sorensen, Harryboyles, Sixtimes, Kuru, Paladinwannabe2, Minna Sora no Shita, Goodnightmush, NongBot~enwiki, IronGargoyle, The Man in Question, Beatrix.knight, A. Parrot, Nanodeath, Mr Stephen, Optakeover, Waggers, Astrolog~enwiki, Michael Greiner, Neddyseagoon, Funnybunny, Midnightblueowl, Citicat, Sifaka, PigInZen, BranStark, Joey-Merl, Iridescent, Wjejskenewr, Chika11, Shoshonna, Quodfui, Womaningreen, Ewulp, Courcelles, Scarlet Lioness, FairuseBot, Tawkerbot2, Pi, JForget, Ollie, Planktonbot, CmdrObot, Sir Vicious, Dexileos~enwiki, Jwhale9382, Banedon, GHe, Reahad, Strike Chaos, Dgw, Neelix, Fordmadoxfraud, Bettyejmiller, Learned Sam, Sopoforic, Cydebot, Treybien, Goldfritha, The Great Honker, Gogo Dodo, Frosty0814snowman, Corpx, Llort, JamesLucas, Tectar, Tawkerbot4, Christian75, Codetiger, DumbBOT, Smileybone, Paddles, Ameliorate!, After Midnight, Po132, Dehoqu, DLBerek, Casliber, JamesAM, Thijs!bot, Epbr123, Anita13, Atenea26, N5iln, Antinate, Mojo Hand, Marek69, Missvain, Tapir Terrific, A3RO, Folantin, SomeStranger, James086, Corwin MacGregor, AgentPeppermint, Bkinn214, Lunamaria, Nick Number, Ollymay, Sean William, Dawnseeker2000, Sensemaker, AntiVandalBot, Luna Santin, Why My Fleece?, Seaphoto, Xuchilbara, NeilEvans, 1927 Orchestra, Chantamutka, Madbehemoth, Fayenatic london, Bakabaka, Tarana, North Shoreman, Pichote, Gdo01, Blacksun1942, AubreyEllenShomo, Wahabijaz, Ingolfson, Golgofrinchian, JAnDbot, WANAX, Deflective, Husond, Al Damjo, Dsp13, Nyerguds, Midnightdreary, Peachey88, Andonic, Snowolfd4, PhilKnight, Cynwolfe, Bencherlite, Plamoa, ΚΕΚΡΩΨ, Bibi Saint-Pol, Magioladitis, Bongwarrior, VoABot II, T@nn, JNW, Khalidkhoso, Doug Coldwell, Korenyuk, Tedickey, Anonymousphrase, Iainsona, Aa35te, Avicennasis, Vanished user dkjsdfkljeritekk4, Ciaccona, Estan williams, DerHexer, Edward321, Simon Peter Hughes, BaldClarke, Valerius Tygart, Textorus, Patstuart, Simpaticos4343, NatureA16, AliaGemma, Nina Smith, Riccardobot, MartinBot, CliffC, GoldenMeadows, Nehwyn, El Krem, Naohiro19, Feijuada, R'n'B, Kateshortforbob, Cr0uch, CommonsDelinker, AlexiusHoratius, LedgendGamer, Chrishy man, Danerz34, Tgeairn, Artaxiad, Kaoak, Huzzlet the bot, J.delanoy, Nev1, Trusilver, Greatone1234567, Hyphen25, The hyphenator, Uncle Dick, Maurice Carbonaro, Jonpro, Extransit, WarthogDemon, Gzkn, Marcusmax, Acalamari, IdLoveOne, Penguinwithin, McSly, ChanceTheGardener, Bailo26, Monkeyknife, Robertson-Glasgow, Cyclocifra, Belovedfreak, NewEnglandYankee, Molly-in-md, Saltysailor, 83d40m, Zuracech lordum, BrettAllen, SSSN, Atropos235, KylieTastic, AED1111, Arctic sunrise, Boa05zs, Sarregouset, AnastasiaPeru, Martial75, Urheimat, RJASE1, Redtigerxyz, Spekkio~enwiki, Echosmoke, Deor, VolkovBot, TreasuryTag, Macedonian, Mrh30, Shinju, Irish Pearl, Philip Trueman, Dchmelik, Spurius Furius Fusus, TXiKiBoT, Erik the Red 2, Davehi1, JJ the Crusader, Thesugarbear, GcSwRhIc, Coltonmarkham, Aymatth2, Qxz, Mark Miller, Lradrama, Garhuckle.caprice, Clarince63, Markisgreen, Tprtpr, Varoon Arya, Ilyushka88, Datakukri, Tu est stupid, Jamiemm, Jmcfarlan, Entrinzikyl, Crested Penguin, Falcon8765, True ozzy, Enviroboy, Bunnyhugger, Edwards0013, Marcmello, Thanatos666, HiDrNick, Sue Rangell, Kehrbykid, Logan, NHRHS2010, EmxBot, Austriacus, Drecool12, Vanessa 132, LovelyLillith, Randommelon, Sonicology, Heyhockeytownx11, Picasso&Lotion, Mungo Kitsch, Dawn Bard, Caltas, Rafnles, Smsarmad, The Real Hobbes15, Vanessa 132 delgado, Arda Xi, Breawycker, Flyer22 Reborn, AragornSonOfArathorn, Hxhbot, Ferret, Aruton, Bguest, Hello71, KoshVorlon, Lightmouse, Miguel.mateo, Macy, Sunrise, Tetraktys-English, Dimboukas, Denisarona, Explicit, ImageRemovalBot, Atif.t2, Martarius, Elassint, Jokerpainter, ClueBot, Adgjladgjl, GorillaWarfare, Nielspeterqm, Ideal gas equation, Kafka Liz, Plastikspork, Drmies, Mild Bill Hiccup, Shinpah1, Ifnkovhg, SuperHamster, Skäpperöd, Edwardcb, Niceguyedc, MARKELLOS, CPXB, Puchiko, Tiroth, Auntof6, PMDrive1061, Athang1504, Excirial, Alexbot, Jusdafax, PixelBot, Tcob44, BobKawanaka, Gtstricky, ILDB, YDaniel7, Cenarium, Eustress, Rphb, SchreiberBike, BOTarate, Renrut1993, Catalographer, Thingg, Aitias, BVBede, Scalhotrod, Kevdav63, Johnuniq, Marontia, Tdslk, MasterOfHisOwnDomain, DumZiBoT, Chris1834, Oskar71, BarretB, Spitfire, Gnowor, DaL33T, Avoided, Skarebo, NellieBly, Kaiwhakahaere, Addbot, Pyfan, Some jerk on the Internet, Takamachi5039, Ronhjones, CanadianLinuxUser, Datinamou5, Hendrecoed, Htrace521, Mentisock, Download, Ccacsmss, Glane23, Chzz, Debresser, AnnaFrance, Favonian, Tupelocase, LemmeyBOT, LinkFA-Bot, West.andrew.g, 5 albert square, Ghwood, Xev lexx, AgadaUrbanit, Bob991, Timeu, Tide rolls, Malwinder25, LuK3, Borg2008, Legobot, Luckas-bot, TheSuave, Yobot, Worldbruce, Ptbotgourou, Fraggle81, Legobot II, Oilstone, Victoriaearle, Guy1890, Jimasripper~enwiki, South Bay, AnomieBOT, Anne McDermott, DemocraticLuntz, Alex contributing, Coopkev2, JackieBot, Neptune5000, 9258fahsflkh917fas, AdjustShift, LlywelynII, Bluerasberry, Ashleymtisdalefank, Materialscientist, Citation bot, E2eamon, Edrowland, Grossmünster, Dodo, Xqbot, The Fiddly Leprechaun, Addihockey10, Aaronappaswamy, Millahnna, Jackiestud, Ddmar99, Sellyme, Gilo1969, NFD9001, Anna Frodesiak, Quintus314, Almabot, Susannah Dingley, Jdsteakley, Ute in DC, Ashumaloz, Omnipaedista, RibotBOT, Queen Rhana, Enceladusgeysers, Shadowjams, Sadbuttrue92, Bezaaum, Fkitselis, Elemesh, A.amitkumar, Thehelpfulbot, Prari, Ochitofu, Paine Ellsworth, InspectorSands, HJ Mitchell, BenzolBot, Jamesooders, Egmontbot, A little insignificant, DivineAlpha, Klubbit, Venividiwplwiki, ShadowRangerRIT, I dream of horses, Elockid, HRoestBot, Notedgrant, Arctic Night, LittleWink, Padme22, Mayormaynot, LinDrug, Onthegogo, Calmer Waters, Hamtechperson, A8UDI, Moonraker, RedBot, Pikiwyn, Serols, Philly boy92, Kevintampa5, RandomStringOfCharacters, Fumitol, RazielZero, Kibi78704, Reconsider the static, IJBall, Jauhienij, Tim1357, Tsunamus, Orenburg1, FoxBot, Greco22, Jade Harley, Jan11989, Notpietru, Pederz, LogAntiLog, Callanecc, Javierito92, Fox Wilson, Dinamik-bot, Xeuorux, Vrenator, Defender of torch, Ithink713, Joesilver72, Glorioussandwich, TheGrimReaper NS, Specs112, Magiczlol, Suffusion of Yellow, PleaseStand, Simple123456, Tbhotch, SCS100, DARTH SIDIOUS 2, Andrea105, AXRL, Bluenerfs, Mean as custard, Wartoy99, Bento00, Alph Bot, VernoWhitney, DRAGON BOOSTER, Ichimpy, Hajatvrc, BCtl, Salvio giuliano, Bigpapi6292, CalicoCatLover, LcawteHuggle, Maplekins13, DASHBot, EmausBot, Pruthvish, Alagos, Sunuraju, Ajraddatz, Wildcaat, Golfandme, Bua333, Twilightgirl18, RA0808, Babnolan, The Sharminator, RenamedUser01302013, Viti12345, Athena's messanger, Popdogg, Tommy2010, Winner 42, Merrikin, Wikipelli, GuttormsenE, Wickednitesade, Malcolm77, Werieth, Doggymaster1, Fatnuts100, John Cline, 123456pies, Fæ, Josve05a, Traxs7, SupaG114, Alpha Quadrant, Yiosie2356, I Will Conquer All 69, Bwise5, Christina Silverman, Wayne Slam, Tolly4bolly, Coasterlover1994, L Kensington, Philafrenzy, Palosirkka, Donner60, Odysseus1479, Jbergste, Sailsbystars, Someone1215, Orange Suede Sofa, Bill william compton, Tot12, ChuispastonBot, VictorianMutant, EdoBot, E. Fokker, Sonicyouth86, JessicaPenguin, Subrette, ClueBot NG, Christinneee, Jordyn1456321, Loocool1, Athena2106, Mjanja, CocuBot, MrLiambegiam, SMM03H, Chester Markel, Millermk, Yakyback, Hazhk, ScottSteiner, AlienXescape, Dream of Nyx, Smirkybec, Marechal Ney, Mannanan51, Mossey0801, Widr, Wisegirl01, Carlspizza, Crazymonkey1123, SquidSupreme, Helpful Pixie Bot, Fantage11236, Titodutta, WNYY98, Lowercase sigmabot, BG19bot, Flax5, Michelle0624, Sirbaby, Riggioc738, ChessBOT, Leonxlin, Random0000, Wiki13, Amp71, Pinkchick45, Lieutenant Waaxe, Davidiad, Dan653, Piguy101, Mark Arsten, Michael Barera, Cncmaster, Awesome597, P-Twist, Coralia(lia), Insidiae, Nscrunch, BBCatport, Jonadin93, Jakebarrington, Emilia-Romagna, Srowell13, Teammm, Mutos124, Mdann52, Fraulein451, Cigaro Pizarro, Haymouse, Cyberbot II, ChrisGualtieri, GoShow, Khazar2, EuroCarGT, Hawveand000, 2Flows, MadGuy7023, Dexbot, Webclient101, Interlude65, Mogism, Craigory.T, TwoTwoHello, Lugia2453, Frosty, Lequenne Gwendoline, Hladio, King jakob c, Athomeinkobe, Catimari, Kcwcat, Cadillac000, Maniesansdelire, VanishedUser 2313214sad1, Ekips39, Sambmaryl, Epicgenius, NightWolf52, Chaoyangopterus, WalkingKebab, Coonbat, AmaryllisGardener, Eyesnore, Harlem Baker Hughes, Thedoob, PhantomTech, Averilove07, EvergreenFir, Idekidec, Tetradracma, ElHef, DavidLeighEllis, Snickers2686, Manavatha, Jestmoon, Mmay2, BadKittieKat76, The Herald, Don B. Cilly, Noyster, TruthSeekerJC, Philroc, JaconaFrere, Skr15081997, Howunusual, Tyranosopher, Keith14hall, Vieque, Nathaniel360, Ydanay, Сяра, Robbert4849, Biblioworm, Picapicacuckoo, Lau1104, Mollymyers2003, Sidbad, Unician, Kiana jones, Zion123458, Swaggedout14, Charles938, Jameerocks, Karl's Wagon, Crystallizedcarbon, Kanyeweston, Liance, Tacolover75, TheCoffeeAddict, Rhadamantheus, AthenaAliceMajied, AthenaAliceMaji, Helpful person 2, Jhe fernandez, Skip2MyLulu, Pyrotle, GreekLover2004, Gargotteebong, LavaBaron, Smarty123patrickypbossgf, Dlf452, Wikimanpowi, AustinLover32, Hey im sarah, Minecraft work, Nøkkenbuer, Idunnoyou123, KasparBot, Eihpos11, JJMC89, Jesus-hernandez224, KianaJames123, Ss624, Farmgirl12, Spcmessick, Zmh99055 and Anonymous: 1663

- **Ayao** *Source:* https://en.wikipedia.org/wiki/Ayao?oldid=634497632 *Contributors:* Crystallina, Premjs, Colonies Chris, Doug Weller, M-le-mot-dit, Pomba Gira, Addbot, Xqbot, Cubaking, Lorynote, Omo Obatalá and Anonymous: 6

- **Badb** *Source:* https://en.wikipedia.org/wiki/Badb?oldid=686619641 *Contributors:* PierreAbbat, Heron, Olivier, TUF-KAT, TUF-KAT, Charles Matthews, Wetman, Gtrmp, Eequor, Critto~enwiki, Bookcat, Fergananim, Xezbeth, Aecis, Kwamikagami, QuartierLatin1968, Anthony Appleyard, Nicknack009, Mogmios, MarkusHagenlocher, Rjwilmsi, Whateley23, YurikBot, RobotE, RussBot, Pigman, GeeJo, CorbieVreccan, Orioane, SMcCandlish, JAn Dudík, Ohconfucius, Switchercat, Juhachi, Warhorus, Thijs!bot, Michael A. White, Goldenrowley, JAnDbot, 83d40m, Asaralaí, Jalo, VVVBot, Roidhrigh, PipepBot, Shoemoney2night, TheOldJacobite, SexyEnglishGayLad, DumZiBoT, Felix Folio Secundus, Addbot, Cowgod14, Yobot, Anypodetos, AnomieBOT, Mintrick, Anoderate1, Cavila, Tanngnost, HRoestBot, Megaman62889, Kargandarr, Lairbhan, Helpful Pixie Bot, BattyBot, TricksterBacon and Anonymous: 20

- **Banba** *Source:* https://en.wikipedia.org/wiki/Banba?oldid=651333898 *Contributors:* SGBailey, TUF-KAT, TUF-KAT, The Warlock, Decumanus, Critto~enwiki, Fergananim, Evertype, Neutrality, Jnestorius, Aecis, Kwamikagami, QuartierLatin1968, Nicknack009, Embryomystic, DePiep, FlaBot, Eubot, YurikBot, Pigman, GeeJo, Asarelah, Superp, Ollamh (fr), Cerdic, Cydebot, Kariteh, T@nn, Taibhdhearc, Hockadori, VolkovBot, GeoffreyGleadall, Asarlaí, Francvs, Addbot, Yobot, The Emperor's New Spy, Unknownnaming, LCS check and Anonymous: 9

- **Bastet** *Source:* https://en.wikipedia.org/wiki/Bastet?oldid=686468248 *Contributors:* Mav, Llywrch, Ixfd64, Looxix~enwiki, TUF-KAT, TUF-KAT, Andres, Hashar, RodC, RickK, Andrewman327, Maximus Rex, Dyrwen, דוד, Wetman, Hajor, Robbot, Yosri, Modeha, Lzur, David Gerard, Gtrmp, Cronos~enwiki, Alensha, Mboverload, Alvestrand, Keith Edkins, Slowking Man, Lockeownzj00, Onco p53, Clarknova, Gscshoyru, Urhixidur, Baghaii, Eyrian, Larrybob, SoM, Discospinster, Rama, Vsmith, Dbachmann, Aecis, Kwamikagami, Svdmolen, Mairi, Bobo192, Viriditas, Nsaa, HasharBot~enwiki, Ranveig, Alansohn, Jic, Jeltz, DreamGuy, Ffbond, Alai, Finsternis, Reikku, Siafu, FeanorStar7, Nefertum17, WadeSimMiser, -Ril-, Scm83x, Jergen, Fishface, Enzo Aquarius, Josh Parris, Gryffindor, Vegaswikian, The wub, Yamamoto Ichiro, FlaBot, Old Moonraker, Overand, WriterHound, Algebraist, YurikBot, RussBot, Hede2000, Limulus, Joel7687, Dureo, Thiseye, Asarelah, Elkman, TransUtopian, Wikilackey, Sandstein, DasBrose~enwiki, Lt-wiki-bot, Nikkimaria, Closedmouth, Allens, NeilN, GrinBot~enwiki, Nekura, That Guy, From That Show!, Sardanaphalus, SmackBot, InverseHypercube, RobotJcb, Kintetsubuffalo, Gilliam, Jprg1966, Thumperward, OrangeDog, Pebasti, VMS Mosaic, Leoboudv, Addshore, Seduisant, Artemisboy, Queer Scout, Risssa, Thor Dockweiler, DIEGO RICARDO PEREIRA, A. Parrot, Ryulong, Dodo bird, Iridescent, Dionysia, JoeBot, Mh29255, Majora4, Scarlet Lioness, Piepie, Ozbrithian, Switchercat, CmdrObot, FlyingToaster, WeggeBot, MC10, ST47, Doug Weller, Calluna~enwiki, Mount Terror, Editor at Large, Thijs!bot, Skb8721, Dogaroon, Memty Bot, Mojo Hand, Philippe, Dawnseeker2000, Seaphoto, Pinkleboo, Nimmo27, Ingolfson, WANAX, JonnyBrokenBones, Kuzosake, Struthious Bandersnatch, Andonic, .anacondabot, Magioladitis, Jeff Dahl, T@nn, Simon Peter Hughes, Cat Boy, DGG, MartinBot, Jim.henderson, Gunkarta, Dennymeta, J.delanoy, Bogey97, Pirene Rei, Ian.thomson, Acalamari, EthicsGradient, Paris1127, Clerks, Nwbeeson, Cobi, 83d40m, Toon05, STBotD, Trypika, Kotofeij K. Bajun, Lights, VolkovBot, TXiKiBoT, Davehi1, Apepch7, Rei-bot, SteveStrummer, JhsBot, Sandorman, Jackfork, Isis4563, Fishhook, AnnekeBart, Turgan, Ottarvendel, SheepNotGoats, Zephyrus67, VVVBot, Merotoker1, Mimihitam, Goustien, Alex.muller, Estiv, Mighty Nut, Mr. Stradivarius, Sodfactor, Martarius, Beeblebrox, ClueBot, Arakunem, UserDoe, Arunsingh16, DragonBot, Excirial, Leonard^Bloom, Miyamoto Hachimaro, Zuzzerack, BOTarate, Thingg, 1ForTheMoney, Aitias, Illustrious

One, Life of Riley, JRWoodwardMSW, XLinkBot, Bradv, RyanCross, Thebestofall007, Addbot, Wp1226, Some jerk on the Internet, Fluffernutter, Noikaf, BabelStone, SomeUsr, Favonian, SpBot, Alpinwolf, Tide rolls, Iune, Jarble, Leovizza, CAJonesProductions, Legobot, Luckasbot, Yobot, Donfbreed, Amirobot, Russneavey, AnomieBOT, Rubinbot, Jim1138, Somewhere Out There, Taam, Materialscientist, ArthurBot, TinucherianBot II, Cureden, Cavila, Pmlineditor, Backpackadam, FrescoBot, Anna Roy, Bast the cat god, D'ohBot, Pinethicket, I dream of horses, Tahir mq, Jauhienij, Dmthoth, Veron, Raidon Kane, Reaper Eternal, Sideways713, Onel5969, RjwilmsiBot, Ripchip Bot, EmausBot, WikitanvirBot, Bradrothman, RA0808, Noctilca, Tommy2010, Johnoakgrove, FinalRapture, Donner60, Crheiser, Wcarey6, Manytexts, Rides, ClueBot NG, Cmcalpine, Conveyance, Braskute, Nisha.G.Mohan, Andrew Kurish, Agelarakis, Rezabot, Widr, Oddbodz, Helpful Pixie Bot, GuitarDudeness, HMSSolent, BG19bot, Midknight616, Reynolis, MusikAnimal, AvocatoBot, ChloeKing, Mark Arsten, Mottengott, BattyBot, GamingWithStatoke, Teammm, W.D., Haymouse, Iry-Hor, JYBot, Dexbot, Webclient101, Greencoracle, Lugia2453, Frosty, Kayax012, Vanamonde93, Joe Ziegler, Deanan, WGA Bishop, Everymorning, Pixelmage, DavidLeighEllis, Glaisher, Reyolis, Rosetta Stele, Jevonignasius, Earthbasedstar, Lorda12, Monkbot, Nathaniel360, Chandra,Eye of Ma'at, Isis edelen, Flower daisyl, KasparBot, Blake.simpson 2, Plummyplum, IRONFIRE6, Creamiluvs and Anonymous: 430

- **Bellona (goddess)** *Source:* https://en.wikipedia.org/wiki/Bellona_(goddess)?oldid=684495054 *Contributors:* Robbot, Wereon, DocWatson42, Rpyle731, Robdumas, Deror avi, Quuxplusone, Gdrbot, Alma Pater, Pigman, Rwalker, Crisco 1492, Bill, Attilios, SmackBot, Omnivore, Neddyseagoon, Wjejskenewr, Charvex, Treviboy, Gogo Dodo, Doug Weller, Thijs!bot, Missvain, Cynwolfe, BJpoet719, T@nn, Sue Gardner, Bogey97, USN1977, Rodolph, VolkovBot, Bewtros, WarddrBOT, TXiKiBoT, AlleborgoBot, SieBot, Flyer22 Reborn, Martarius, Amovrvs, Pjurdeczka, SchreiberBike, Kwjbot, Alansplodge, Surtsicna, Addbot, BepBot, Tassedethe, مانع, Luckas-bot, Jan Arkesteijn, Lavallen, Xqbot, RibotBOT, Erik9bot, FrescoBot, Rayshade, ItsZippy, GregKaye, Neferkare, Cowlibob, Lucyluthien, EmausBot, Peter Karlsen, Terraflorin, ClueBot NG, MerlIwBot, Keving2011, Lautensack, Tentinator, 226fideii, Library Guy, Msto282, Raghuvardhanan, ComicsAreJustAllRight, RoadWarrior445 and Anonymous: 58

- **Bia (mythology)** *Source:* https://en.wikipedia.org/wiki/Bia_(mythology)?oldid=662542684 *Contributors:* Hephaestos, Tucci528, Mrwojo, Ellywa, TUF-KAT, Emperor, LittleDan, Slawojarek, Robbot, UtherSRG, Hansjorn, Bacchiad, The Singing Badger, Didactohedron, Paul August, Woohookitty, Isnow, Paxsimius, Mandarax, Umberto Petrocelli, YurikBot, Cissi, RussBot, Qwertzy2, Yamara, Stephenb, Ravenous, Deucalionite, BOT-Superzerocool, Asarelah, Lt-wiki-bot, SmackBot, Cralize, Adamantios, Jedai~enwiki, Arctic-Editor, Big Smooth, Dr.K., MTSbot~enwiki, Kazubon~enwiki, Thijs!bot, JAnDbot, Waacstats, Captain panda, Belovedfreak, Smitty, DorganBot, TXiKiBoT, BotKung, Bsayusd, AlleborgoBot, SieBot, Iwfi, BenoniBot~enwiki, DragonBot, PixelBot, Chronicler~enwiki, Addbot, Vatrena ptica, AndersBot, ירו55, Aviados, Luckas-bot, Erud, GrouchoBot, Omnipaedista, Erik9bot, LucienBOT, Lesath, Mys 721tx, GregKaye, Sentōkisei, LoveWaffle, Sven Manguard, ClueBot NG, Iiii I I I, BG19bot, Davidiad, Haymouse, ChrisGualtieri and Anonymous: 38

- **Brigantia (goddess)** *Source:* https://en.wikipedia.org/wiki/Brigantia_(goddess)?oldid=655723429 *Contributors:* Paul Barlow, Bearcat, Jossi, Dbachmann, QuartierLatin1968, MatthiasKabel, Deror avi, NantonosAedui, Woohookitty, Cuchullain, FlaBot, Aspro, CJLL Wright, RussBot, Pigman, CorbieVreccan, SmackBot, Bejnar, JHunterJ, Richard Keatinge, Cydebot, Doug Weller, Walgamanus, Malleus Fatuorum, Nick Number, Goldenrowley, Erin Navan, Cynwolfe, T@nn, R'n'B, Scotia Scotia, VolkovBot, TXiKiBoT, Niceguyedc, Alexbot, Xchange, Addbot, Shjfebv, Luckas-bot, LlywelynII, GregKaye, EmausBot, Finn Bjørklid, Mentibot, Xoancarlos, Sowlos, Krakkos and Anonymous: 15

- **Cathubodua** *Source:* https://en.wikipedia.org/wiki/Cathubodua?oldid=664435833 *Contributors:* QuartierLatin1968, Nicknack009, Deror avi, Cuchullain, Josh Parris, RussBot, Euraconos, GeeJo, Veledan, Zwobot, SmackBot, Hmains, The Man in Question, Ollamh (fr), Thijs!bot, T@nn, Addbot, EmausBot, Krakkos and Anonymous: 8

- **Chamunda** *Source:* https://en.wikipedia.org/wiki/Chamunda?oldid=685599610 *Contributors:* SimonP, TUF-KAT, Carlossuarez46, Michael Devore, Utcursch, Sharavanabhava, Ma'ame Michu, Alren, Ogress, HasharBot~enwiki, Wiki-uk, Dangerous-Boy, Rjwilmsi, Bhadani, YurikBot, Pigman, Dysmorodrepanis~enwiki, CorbieVreccan, Asarelah, BorgQueen, SmackBot, Shivap, Laura Anglin, BostonMA, Skinsmoke, Rnb, NickW557, Ramitmahajan, Gimmetrow, Epbr123, E. Ripley, Dr. Blofeld, Darklilac, Sluzzelin, Magioladitis, Ling.Nut, Bksharma, Arjun01, Pruthvi.Vallabh, Balajijagadesh, Redtigerxyz, TreasuryTag, Chaos5023, Philip Trueman, TXiKiBoT, Snehilsharma, Mohonu, Sfan00 IMG, Ssriram mt, Niceguyedc, Putonghua, Tripping Nambiar, DumZiBoT, Cminard, Ism schism, Addbot, Arnold40, Jonoikobangali, Martin-vogel, Jim1138, Materialscientist, Vimaljain1974, J04n, Sambya, Omnipaedista, SassoBot, FrescoBot, Hasiru, Mjs1991, Trappist the monk, Ndkartik, Jethwarp, Orphan Wiki, H3llBot, Idlyforbfast, Nayansatya, TYelliot, ClueBot NG, Sanshlistha m, Frietjes, MKar, Fraulein451, Unnikris094, Mrt3366, Indicologist, The Rahul Jain, Monkbot, BudChrSch and Anonymous: 56

- **Chandraghanta** *Source:* https://en.wikipedia.org/wiki/Chandraghanta?oldid=685830474 *Contributors:* SummerPhD, Lfstevens, Ekabhishek, Redtigerxyz, Dthomsen8, Yobot, Donner60, Giso6150, Lk56835, SJ Defender, Fresh1face19, Kev8927, Nachiketa barve, Annalingy, LiKaren, MormonJoel, Funnybunny4488, Sunaj Sh. Ajdini, Terrerojo, Lushii, Devontavious and Anonymous: 2

- **Cihuateteo** *Source:* https://en.wikipedia.org/wiki/Cihuateteo?oldid=684734866 *Contributors:* TUF-KAT, Hajor, Robbot, GreatWhiteNortherner, Gtrmp, Dystopos, Ogress, Sburke, CJLL Wright, Ptcamn, Asarelah, Maunus, SmackBot, Radagast83, Steipe, Thijs!bot, Alphachimpbot, T@nn, Alleborgo, Simon Peter Hughes, TommieDrash, Murderbike, Jagun, MystBot, Addbot, Luckas-bot, Erik9bot, NSH002, EmausBot, Alagos, Aztlshamb, RichardMills65, Hundr and Anonymous: 8

- **Durga** *Source:* https://en.wikipedia.org/wiki/Durga?oldid=687013521 *Contributors:* Graft, Ihcoyc, TUF-KAT, TUF-KAT, Gokul madhavan, Topbanana, Joy, Johnleemk, Carlossuarez46, RedWolf, Goethean, Altenmann, Alan Liefting, Jwinters, Crculver, DocWatson42, Nichalp, Meursault2004, Ragib, Wmahan, Utcursch, Fuzzybunn, Mukerjee, Sam Hocevar, Dyanne Nova, Anirvan, Master Of Ninja, RossPatterson, Discospinster, Rich Farmbrough, Murtasa, ESkog, El C, Kwamikagami, QuartierLatin1968, Shanes, Cmdrjameson, Nicke Lilltroll~enwiki, Giraffedata, Pearle, Jonathunder, Ogress, Anthony Appleyard, Arthena, Wiki-uk, Marie Rowley, Snowolf, Cromwellt, Sfacets, Ringbang, Dodiad, Shmitra, Dangerous-Boy, John Hill, Tydaj, BloodyRoses, BD2412, Dwaipayanc, Koavf, Hgkamath, TheRingess, Bhadani, FlaBot, Swami Vimokshananda, Hottentot, TeaDrinker, DaGizza, Mordicai, DVdm, Bgwhite, Guptadeepak, YurikBot, Shimirel, RussBot, Pigman, Gaius Cornelius, CambridgeBayWeather, Lemon-s, Douglasfrankfort~enwiki, Veledan, Thiseye, Rwalker, Jessemerriman, Asarelah, Tachs, Seemagoel, FF2010, Sandstein, Pbwelch, GraemeL, Aamrun, Anclation~enwiki, ArielGold, Sassisch, SmackBot, Classicfilms, Hydrogen Iodide, Manjunathbhatt, Iph, Typhoonchaser, Sushant gaur, Aksi great, JFHJr, Gilliam, Ohnoitsjamie, Chris the speller, Bluebot, MartinPoulter, Miquonranger03, Aerol, Darth Panda, Shivap, OrphanBot, Pnkrao, RandomP, Mistress Selina Kyle, Ryan Roos, WoodElf, GourangaUK, Ged UK, Ohconfucius, Festivalsindex, Snowgrouse, Lambiam, Thesmothete, Rigadoun, Heimstern, Armyrifle9, Breno, Tktktk, Shyamsunder, Deepraj, Beetstra, Dr.K., Qualihost, Skinsmoke, Kvng, Akiyama, Dl2000, Hu12, Sameboat, Revera, TheDrinkNinja, Ksoileau, Mariici~enwiki, JessBr, Gogo Dodo,

ST47, Mattisse, Marek69, John254, Rajaramraok, Natalie Erin, Devanshi.shah, Dhruvtanna, Wahabijaz, Liveindia, Sanatan1, Ekabhishek, Magioladitis, VoABot II, T@nn, Hekerui, Cgingold, Priti12, Philg88, Teardrop onthefire, Ashisranjan, B9 hummingbird hovering, Jackson Peebles, NAHID, Anaxial, Gunkarta, Fconaway, J.delanoy, Abecedare, Dkonwar, R powers, Sramana18, Ian.thomson, Paris1127, Jigesh, Chiswick Chap, Jmcw37, KellyPhD, Sachinbhinge, Pratap Singh Rajawat, Makira 101, Akut, Leopart, Idioma-bot, Sbharti, Redtigerxyz, Thisisborin9, Indubitably, Bovineboy2008, Barneca, Mcewan, TXiKiBoT, NayakDeepti, Conjoiner, IPSOS, Snehilsharma, Buddhipriya, Jera89, Nazar, SwordSmurf, B4upradeep, Rangestudy1, AlleborgoBot, Isis07, Drdey, Fanatix, Copana2002, GoonerDP, SieBot, Sarangu 001, Oldag07, Yintan, ChloeD, Flyer22 Reborn, Mankar Camoran, Prakashsubbarao, Databasex, UncleMartin, Lotussculpture, Gireeshelemec, Onvnamboodiri, Randy Kryn, RegentsPark, MBK004, ClueBot, Ssriram mt, Niceguyedc, Rayabhari, Canis Lupus, Alexbot, Relata refero, Exact~enwiki, Naleh, Muhandes, Isthisthingworking, Abhilekhagarwal, Apparition11, Wnt, Barmank, XLinkBot, Cminard, Qgr, Dthomsen8, WikHead, Ism schism, Ambient Transient, Addbot, Harishaluru, Goddessaday, Queenmomcat, Opus88888, Debnatha, Diablokrom, Underwaterbuffalo, Debresser, Madana161, Amajumder, Tide rolls, Luckas-bot, Yobot, Legobot II, THEN WHO WAS PHONE?, Durgasubburaman, Boolyme, AnomieBOT, ThaddeusB, Kingpin13, Materialscientist, ادری فاتح, ArthurBot, TinucherianBot II, Dhananjay Aditya, 1500sampark, Gilo1969, Vasishtha33, Omnipaedista, Leandroii, AdalCobos, Graidan, FrescoBot, Dollarsterling, Vivpradhan, Tubai1983, Hasiru, BenzolBot, Samskriti5, Redrose64, XxTimberlakexx, Pinethicket, Elockid, Dazedbythebell, M for Molecule, Raj misra deep, Ganjamorissa, Trulytito, Tea with toast, FoxBot, TobeBot, Poitrine, Sizzle Flambé, Tbhotch, World8115, Woken Wanderer, Rakeshmallick27, Letdemsay, EmausBot, Super48paul, Niru786, SteveM123, Stiatent, Badri kannan, Tommy2010, Wikipelli, Dcirovic, Arunabhsaikia, Melakavijay, Kkm010, ZéroBot, Trinanjon, Akerans, Soumit ban, Jay-Sebastos, Vanished user qwqwijr8hwrkjdnvkanfoh4, ChuispastonBot, Nayansatya, Abhisingla87, Pernoctator, Helpsome, ClueBot NG, Ramtulsi0, Peter James, MelbourneStar, Chester Markel, Frietjes, Dream of Nyx, Sephalon1, Helpful Pixie Bot, Thisthat2011, Titodutta, Paglakahinka, Vikram.muttineni, BG19bot, Durga drishti007, Saxafrax, Viresh Raj Sah, Mark Arsten, Anil 666, Sreeshetty, Dswaroop100, DrPhen, PaintedCarpet, Sungmin23, Joydeep, JaQueeta, Rynsaha, Meatsgains, Bvmdpjtk, Risingstar12, Onceshook1, Glacialfox, MattMauler, Aisteco, Aristotys, Babaidmun, Tamravidhir, Justincheng12345-bot, Garconlevis, Valleyforge2012, Jagdishsarva, Mrt3366, Cyberbot II, Kay rishma, Khazar2, Durga Prasad Dash, JYBot, Umadbro2479, Aditya Mahar, Hotmuru, Mogism, Ritik18, Lugia2453, Lkharb, MrMorphism, Poipoise, Soulsdone3, Anand0408ib, Harshad dewari, Rupert loup, Jhavikram, Royroydeb, KD-Singhania, I am One of Many, Eshwar.om, Prince.Google, Jodosma, Ananya.h07, CensoredScribe, Badbuu1000, Nambbus, Deepak Singh11, বিজয় চক্রবর্তী, Guidance63, Lk56835, Sam Sailor, Kafkette, Deepankar Mukherjee 11, Poshk3343, Alayambo, Xgamer2013, Monkbot, Sm041188, Pumanis, DeepaprakashSuramani, Blobbysad, Wayoyo, ForrestLyle, Macofe, Feelingfancyfree, Akifumii, Shadow.daemon, KH-1, Mouryan, Brahmadutta, Chamunda Mundamalini, Saivinodhini, Aymym, Minordeity, Swami tusharananda, Joshua50231, Seervims, Devisharnam, Kev8927, Ankush 89, KasparBot, Ajiqubic, Dongar Kathorekar, Ravnishdayal, ThaneFreedomScholar, Kartiktiwary and Anonymous: 478

- **Enyo** *Source:* https://en.wikipedia.org/wiki/Enyo?oldid=684597680 *Contributors:* Tucci528, Olivier, Frecklefoot, Menchi, Publius~enwiki, Stormie, Renato Caniatti~enwiki, Wetman, Dimadick, GreatWhiteNortherner, DocWatson42, Aranel, Kwamikagami, Jonsafari, Zachlipton, Poromenos, Snowolf, GlaucusAtlanticus, FlaBot, Ayla, Chobot, YurikBot, Rtkat3, RussBot, Xihr, Pigman, RazorICE, Zwobot, Deucalionite, Asarelah, Olympic god, Sandstein, Lt-wiki-bot, Flamarande, Tamfang, BehemothCat, Neddyseagoon, MTSbot~enwiki, Galo1969X, WeggeBot, Neelix, Iokseng, Besieged, JamesAM, Missvain, JAnDbot, .anacondabot, T@nn, ZackTheJack, NERV~enwiki, R'n'B, Patar knight, M-le-mot-dit, VolkovBot, TreasuryTag, Yone, Vahagn Petrosyan, Yorozu, Iwfi, Gerakibot, Underme, Metodicar, Addbot, Omnipedian, Luckas-bot, Yobot, Rubinbot, Omnipaedista, Andromeas, Dger, Ghrei, Phlyaristis, Trec'hlid mitonet, Pinkbeast, EmausBot, J1812, ClueBot NG, Cntras, Twfos, Davidiad, Derschueler, ByronVargas, Maelrys, ChrisGualtieri, YFdyh-bot, Tahc, Makecat-bot, AmaryllisGardener, PhantomTech, Tortie tude, Zeusencinia, Hermes120, Filedelinkerbot, 18JohnM, Raghuvardhanan and Anonymous: 42

- **Eris (mythology)** *Source:* https://en.wikipedia.org/wiki/Eris_(mythology)?oldid=685173853 *Contributors:* Kpjas, Archibald Fitzchesterfield, Vicki Rosenzweig, Bryan Derksen, The Anome, Andre Engels, Josh Grosse, Shii, Ben-Zin~enwiki, LapoLuchini, Marknau, Tucci528, Zocky, Nixdorf, Menchi, Sannse, Lament, TUF-KAT, Ugen64, Glenn, Andres, The Tom, Jallan, Morwen, Elwoz, Renato Caniatti~enwiki, Wetman, SinatraFonzarelli, Hadal, Scooter~enwiki, Jpbrenna, Jor, GreatWhiteNortherner, DocWatson42, Gtrmp, Curps, Digital infinity, Leonard G., Daibhid C, Eequor, Bacchiad, The Singing Badger, Jeshii, Kuralyov, DenisMoskowitz, El-Ahrairah, Crazyeddie, Urhixidur, Didactohedron, Adashiel, Cosh, Paul August, Zanderredux, Art LaPella, 23skidoo, Marblespire, Angie Y., Jumbuck, Gunter.krebs, Mac Davis, Fourthgeek, Kdau, Maqs, RainbowOfLight, Harvestdancer, Hijiri88, Zntrip, Woohookitty, Bjones, GregorB, Graham87, Cuchullain, BD2412, Rjwilmsi, Voretus, MarnetteD, Fish and karate, Crazycomputers, Mathiastck, MikeyChalupa, Kenmayer, Chobot, Satanael, YurikBot, Rtkat3, Pigman, Cougarwalk, Gaius Cornelius, CambridgeBayWeather, Eleassar, Akhristov, Odysses, Merman, Ngorongoro, D. F. Schmidt, Bota47, Asarelah, Lt-wiki-bot, Scriber~enwiki, ColinMcMillen, LeonardoRob0t, Exvicious, Curpsbot-unicodify, Garion96, Nixer, Ilmari Karonen, Banus, GrinBot~enwiki, TJF588, Kyaa the Catlord, Mike Teavee, SmackBot, AndreniW, Reedy, Bigbluefish, Roofus, UrsaFoot, Alsandro, Tasogare, Macduff, Bluebot, Egsan Bacon, TKB, Akhilleus, Writtenright, OrphanBot, WinstonSmith, Phaedriel, Artemisboy, Murdoch, BehemothCat, Hateless, BryanG, Jiminy pop, Vasiliy Faronov, JamesFox, Shadowlynk, JoshuaZ, DIEGO RICARDO PEREIRA, Ckatz, RandomCritic, Comicist, MarkSutton, Redeagle688, Ryulong, Sijo Ripa, Thatcher, Justinwerden, Chris Stangl, Yodin, WonderbreadUSA, Ewulp, Misa J., Tigrahawk, Bighominid, Neenerjay, Betaeleven, Kwinston, Neodammerung, Binky The WonderSkull, Fordmadoxfraud, Omglazers, Qrc2006, Cydebot, Nbound, Agne27, Synergy, Christian75, Refuteku, Gimmetrow, JamesAM, IamthatIam, Thijs!bot, Paulthemime, Thor2000, Bigwyrm, LietKynes, Sobreira, Marek69, Nimakha, Danielfowl, Cattona, WinBot, Tchoutoye, Fayenatic london, Nipisiquit, Storkk, Bailmoney27, Hayesgm, Something14, TAnthony, LittleOldMe, That Jason, Bibi Saint-Pol, VoABot II, T@nn, Connor Kent, Theranos, Ferconex, Glen, Wikianon, Gwern, MartinBot, Jim.henderson, Rettetast, R'n'B, J.delanoy, Shawn in Montreal, DarkFalls, M-le-mot-dit, Phirazo, Equazcion, Squids and Chips, BierHerr, Midasminus, VolkovBot, TreasuryTag, Jeff G., JohnBlackburne, Abyca, Vipinhari, A4bot, Rei-bot, Wikidemon, Cool pokemon trainer, Maxim, Osho-Jabbe, Graymornings, Burntsauce, PGWG, MrChupon, Adthebad12, SieBot, Weeliljimmy, Gerakibot, Caltas, Zelchenko, Ms2150, Android Mouse Bot 3, RSStockdale, BenoniBet~enwiki, Halcionne, OKBot, Evilbunnie, Kutera Genesis, Randy Kryn, Kanonkas, Martarius, ClueBot, Dant328, Plastikspork, Chisner, TheOldJacobite, PicketyFence, Auntof6, Luke4545, Kitsunegami, Alexbot, JohnEMcClure, Elizium23, Manco Capac, Versus22, Phynicen, DumZiBoT, Akjtia, Basilicofresco, CZ2, Willking1979, C6541, LatitudeBot, Wælgæst wæfre, PranksterTurtle, Omnipedian, Legobot, Luckas-bot, Yobot, Nocturnalsleeper, Jim1138, IRP, Mintrick, Flewis, The High Fin Sperm Whale, Phluid61, Obersachsenxbot, Xqbot, Russki516, Mario777Zelda, Omnipaedista, RibotBOT, Andersenman, SD5, ChiMama, FrescoBot, LucienBOT, Wil 9156SPR, Pepper, Dger, Trewal, Wireless Keyboard, Kuneshka, Full-date unlinking bot, Lotje, GregKaye, No One of Consequence, Diannaa, Alph Bot, Jeff540, Superk1a, EmausBot, AmericanLeMans, ZéroBot, PBS-AWB, Susfele, Ὁ οἶστρος, L Kensington, ClueBot NG, Koolio225, Widr, Thirdleg32, Muddbrixx, Infolover123, Helpful Pixie Bot, Curb Chain, BG19bot, Lieutenant Waaxe, Davidiad, ChrisGualtieri, DavidLeighEllis, Mpszafir, BadKittieKat76, ThatGuyInDaCorner, Semeiya, Sapphire-101-2002, Amortias, Karl's Wagon, Nøkkenbuer, KasparBot, FRUIT and Anonymous: 274

- **Erzulie** *Source:* https://en.wikipedia.org/wiki/Erzulie?oldid=666695070 *Contributors:* TUF-KAT, Ugen64, Amcaja, Johnathan, DocWatson42, Jurema Oliveira, Sonjaaa, Bender235, Flammifer, Cuchullain, Koavf, Vidkun, Rwalker, SmackBot, Jwillbur, Ser Amantio di Nicolao, Hotspur23, Qyd, Cydebot, I do not exist, E. Ripley, Goldenrowley, .anacondabot, T@nn, Frellingfahrb0t, Rocinante9x, Captain panda, Paris1127, Random Passer-by, INXS-Girl, Orestek, Phe-bot, Fuddle, Excirial, MauriceRoman, Addbot, Fieldday-sunday, Freerainbowhugs, Yobot, Arthur-Bot, DirlBot, LilHelpa, Obersachsebot, Lonet, GrouchoBot, FrescoBot, Fortdj33, SpaceFlight89, L'Alessandrino, Veronica delacroix, Dick Grune, RustyMorr, Splashen, ClueBot NG, DavidAnstiss, BG19bot, Josvebot, Agathenon, Epicgenius, Ntb612, Savvyjack23, Johnsoniensis and Anonymous: 67

- **Freyja** *Source:* https://en.wikipedia.org/wiki/Freyja?oldid=685410402 *Contributors:* Mav, Bryan Derksen, Sjc, Christian List, PierreAbbat, Ben-Zin~enwiki, Hephaestos, JohnOwens, Nixdorf, Liftarn, Egil, Ihcoyc, TUF-KAT, Jallan, Haukurth, Wetman, Robbot, PBS, Sam Spade, Ashley Y, Henrygb, Puckly, Desmay, Mulukhiyya, Xanzzibar, Fabiform, DocWatson42, Gtrmp, Nunh-huh, Wiglaf, Eequor, Critto~enwiki, Chameleon, Latitudinarian, Mr d logan, Sonjaaa, Danny Rathjens, Antandrus, Bumm13, Tail, Remino, Io usurped, Warfieldian, اﺣﻤ, Rich Farmbrough, Bishonen, Triskaideka, Dbachmann, El C, PhilHibbs, Peter Greenwell, Bobo192, Key45, Johnkarp, Maxdillon, SpeedyGonsales, Aquillion, Eritain, Vanished user 19794758563875, Jumbuck, Rh~enwiki, Svartalf, DreamGuy, Hijiri88, Waldir, Dpv, Rjwilmsi, Salleman, Nandesuka, Matt Deres, Yamamoto Ichiro, FlaBot, Eubot, Stoph, Mathiastck, Snarkibartfast, M7bot, Chobot, DaGizza, Sharkface217, Tone, The Rambling Man, Satanael, YurikBot, Wavelength, Borgx, Muchness, Pigman, Gaius Cornelius, Theelf29, Pseudomonas, Bloodofox, Welsh, Brad Eleven, Thiseye, Retired username, Asarelah, Lucky number 49, Dylankidwell, AdamFunk, Orioane, Canley, Sarefo, Tevildo, Katieh5584, NeilN, Esthanya, Sardanaphalus, SmackBot, Classicfilms, Tom Lougheed, Wakuran, TharkunColl, Gaff, Habasi, Donama, Chris the speller, H2ppyme, Rex Germanus, Enkyklios, Hibernian, Sadads, WeniWidiWiki, Theilert, Springeragh, Grhabyt, Lpgeffen, Snowgrouse, SashatoBot, Kuru, RandomCritic, Neddyseagoon, Midnightblueowl, MTSbot~enwiki, Caiaffa, Brianbarrtt, GDallimore, Martin Kozák, CmdrObot, Cerdic, Khatru2, ST47, Tkynerd, Sigo, Gnfnrf, PamD, Mbrutus, Missvain, Eilev G. Myhren~enwiki, Escarbot, Oreo Priest, AntiVandalBot, Flibjib8, Figma, Sluzzelin, JAnDbot, Barek, Dsp13, BeastmasterGeneral, Sigurd Dragon Slayer, MegX, Xact, Bongwarrior, T@nn, Singularity, Jvhertum, Berig, Simon Peter Hughes, WLU, Frazzzle, CommonsDelinker, J.delanoy, Pharaoh of the Wizards, R powers, Blacklazarus, Neotribal42, Jasper33, Cmbankester, Thorgis, P4k, Chiswick Chap, Rosenknospe, 83d40m, Bonadea, Idioma-bot, Deor, Enubis, RuneStorm, TXiKiBoT, GroveGuy, Godingo, Bass fishing physicist, Pigslookfunny, Nedrutland, Thefirstfirefox, AlleborgoBot, Archwyrm, SieBot, Anyep, YonaBot, Cameron1992, Momo san, AngelOfSadness, Jokeaccount, Lightmouse, KathrynLybarger, Freya Worshiper, Alatari, Lucky number 47, Myth Researcher, Shrine Maiden, ACookie, Escape Orbit, Caspiax, Keinstein, SlackerMom, ClueBot, Neko Mimi Mode, Deanlaw, Knepflerle, Saddhiyama, Evighet~enwiki, Mild Bill Hiccup, DiasJuturna, DragonBot, Leontios, NuclearWarfare, Kit Berg, Cameronia, Jpdaelin, XLinkBot, BodhisattvaBot, WikHead, Gts phl, Willking1979, AVand, Tcncv, Atethnekos, Holt, Diablokrom, CanadianLinuxUser, BabelStone, Nordisk varg, LemmeyBOT, Elen of the Roads, Tassedethe, Tide rolls, Krano, Thebiggnome, Legobot, Luckas-bot, Yobot, Bunnyhop11, Sprachpfleger, Yngvadottir, Victoriaearle, Anypodetos, Eric-Wester, AnomieBOT, JackieBot, Nighty22, Materialscientist, Maxis ftw, Randomguy54321, LilHelpa, Olscaife, Omnipaedista, RibotBOT, Philip72, Kenchikuka~enwiki, Freycram, LucienBOT, Cyberwitchy, Freyja1331, HRoestBot, BigDwiki, Kibi78704, Lotje, Andraste315, Aoidh, EmausBot, ZéroBot, Brothernight, Obotlig, Sahimrobot, ChuispastonBot, AgentSniff, Titania79, Eclectic Angel, ClueBot NG, CocuBot, KarmicCharlie, Helpful Pixie Bot, Tblissing79, Häxa-gudinna, Plantdrew, Lambant, Whencrazybee, Shyguy76767, 4msuperstars, United States Man, Klilidiplomus, Illumimason, GamingWithStatoke, Thelivingparadox, Magicwoman415, Super sailr, Smilerreborn, Ande315, Baugrzip, Geordiehorse, Nitpicking polish, Jodosma, Ringler.dk, Mushroommunch, Hazelares, Perksdice, Csemerick, Ginsuloft, Spurofatonement, Jackmcbarn, ThormodMorrisson, Freyjajaja478, TonyaCole99, Freyjathepoo, Spoderman.sweg, Cartmen23, Fasolt2112, KasparBot, Paraminacardinal, Platestrunk345, Gonermimes and Anonymous: 339

- **Hysminai** *Source:* https://en.wikipedia.org/wiki/Hysminai?oldid=599873167 *Contributors:* Moonriddengirl, Addbot, Yobot, Omnipaedista, Phlyaristis, Trappist the monk, Alagos and Davidiad

- **Inanna** *Source:* https://en.wikipedia.org/wiki/Inanna?oldid=684072037 *Contributors:* Hephaestos, AnonMoos, UninvitedCompany, Sam Spade, Pablo-flores, Unfree, Michael Devore, Ezod, SWAdair, Sysy, Dbachmann, SamEV, Bender235, Summer Song, Mairi, Raverdrew, Oop, Anthony Appleyard, Jeltz, Adkins, Adam Dray, DreamGuy, Kober, Redvers, Sburke, Tydaj, Ashmoo, Cuchullain, BD2412, FreplySpang, Miq, Rjwilmsi, Gabrielsimon, PinchasC, AKeckarov, CiaPan, Chobot, Bgwhite, RussBot, Zafiroblue05, Pigman, Ksyrie, Thiseye, Tony1, Igiffin, Nikkimaria, Thamis, Tadorne, KnightRider~enwiki, SmackBot, UrbanTerrorist, Edgar181, Chris the speller, RDBrown, Egsan Bacon, Skoglund, Light in Water, Glengordon01, Castanea dentata, Thegingerone, John D. Croft, Thegraham, Gurdjieff, Axem Titanium, Enelson, The Man in Question, RandomCritic, A. Parrot, NJMauthor, Brianbarrtt, Jetman, LadyofShalott, CmdrObot, Dycedarg, Reahad, ONUnicorn, Ntsimp, ArgentTurquoise, Batobalani, The Great Honker, Anonymous44, Thijs!bot, DL77, Xuchilbara, DagosNavy, JAnDbot, WANAX, Deflective, Xact, T@nn, Sarahj2107, Nyttend, Tonyfaull, TheCormac, R'n'B, R powers, Whitestarlion, Tty63, Dakirw8, Katalaveno, Framhein, 83d40m, Dkudler, Idioma-bot, VolkovBot, Thewolf37, Tunnels of Set, Jeff G., Harbar1232, TXiKiBoT, Utgard Loki, IPSOS, Sun shine 545, Adapa Atra-Hasis, Eve Teschlemacher, FinnWiki, SieBot, StAnselm, Ivan Štambuk, WereSpielChequers, Gerakibot, Rob.bastholm, Njmessmer01, Ganna24, Til Eulenspiegel, Typritc, Keilana, Timelesseyes, Kateorman, WikipedianMarlith, ClueBot, Dubsarmah, Zlerman, A plague of rainbows, Sumerophile, SilvonenBot, Ploversegg, Tar-ba-gan, Addbot, Holt, USchick, Download, Proxima Centauri, Favonian, SpBot, Dacaria, Tide rolls, Verbal, Legobot, Luckas-bot, Yobot, AnomieBOT, VanishedUser sdu9aya9fasdsopa, Pequod76, Mann jess, Materialscientist, Maxmay, LilHelpa, American9agir, Omnipaedista, Little Flower Eagle, FrescoBot, Ionutzmovie, Izzedine, Enki B., Enki H., Vajragarlic, Skyerise, Pmokeefe, Praxia, Genkai Shinigami, Zoeperkoe, Diannaa, Kittyxcaterina, EmausBot, John of Reading, Schauschgamuwa, Wikipelli, ZéroBot, Cherri777, Arubafirina, 11 Arlington, Donner60, MimmiDingirInanna, TheHigherLevelEntity, ChuispastonBot, Pandeist, Imorthodox23, ClueBot NG, Hawa-Ave, Chester Markel, FluffyBunnyX, Iamthecheese44, Julien Jean, Glacialfox, BattyBot, Skepp, Several Pending, Khazar2, Jdcraton, Wikicorrects123, Epicgenius, Captainalliswell, Cary828Grant, DavidLeighEllis, CensoredScribe, Dutch30001, Ssrich1953, Jooojay, Noyster, The Last Archivist, Prestigiouzman, Calken934, Ponyfan58425, Сяра, Kiro Vermaas, Inanna Lust, Venusexu, Thorsf999, H.dhayal5, Whalestate, KasparBot and Anonymous: 150

- **Ioke (mythology)** *Source:* https://en.wikipedia.org/wiki/Ioke_(mythology)?oldid=596578400 *Contributors:* Yobot, Phlyaristis, Davidiad and MrLinkinPark333

- **Ishtar** *Source:* https://en.wikipedia.org/wiki/Ishtar?oldid=685937443 *Contributors:* Brion VIBBER, Bryan Derksen, Andre Engels, Zoe, Isis~enwiki, Hephaestos, Chris~enwiki, Menchi, Zeno Gantner, Looxix~enwiki, TUF-KAT, Andres, Hashar, Jallan, VeryVerily, Chidoll, Anon-Moos, DavidA, Astronautics~enwiki, Jmabel, Modulatum, Lowellian, Mirv, Rursus, Wereon, Widsith, DocWatson42, Marnanel, Gtrmp, Ryz,

Eequor, Zeimusu, Antandrus, Kaldari, Gauss, Elektron, Zfr, Fratley, Mschlindwein, Mike Rosoft, Kathar, Discospinster, 4pq1injbok, Rich Farmbrough, Dbachmann, Mani1, Paul August, Ntennis, Aranel, JoeHenzi, Summer Song, Duk, .:Ajvol:., Oop, TheProject, Naturenet, Haham hanuka, Storm Rider, Anthony Appleyard, Atlant, MarkGallagher, Kdau, ReyBrujo, Woodstone, La la land, Chemical Halo, Jackhynes, Darked~enwiki, Nuno Tavares, Angr, Richard Arthur Norton (1958-), Woohookitty, Saggiga, Jonathanbishop, Briangotts, Tydaj, Marcg106, BD2412, Island, Miq, Dpv, Tabercil, Guyd, Gryffindor, Wikibofh, Sargonious, FlaBot, Str1977, Codex Sinaiticus, Proserpine, ToucheGnome, Chobot, Utaking, Gwernol, YurikBot, 999~enwiki, RussBot, Pigman, Gardar Rurak, Yamara, RadioFan, Gaius Cornelius, DBPhil, Tastemyhouse, Thiseye, Asarelah, Darc, KateH, Calvin08, JuJube, HopperUK, Tsiaojian lee, Curpsbot-unicodify, Minnesota1, SmackBot, Maelwys, Pomerangolarst, Stepa, Webwarlock, Kabong2000, Donquixote, Metalbladex4, Ado, Mahanchian, WinstonSmith, Castanea dentata, Japeo, Thegingerone, Adrigon, Lisasmall, Kunal c, Ripe, RandomCritic, A. Parrot, Eivind F Øyangen, Zmmz, Brianbarrtt, Derella, Christian Peralta, CmdrObot, Cydebot, The Great Honker, Hebrides, Doug Weller, Ssilvers, Plaasjaapie, Thijs!bot, Mojo Hand, Martin Rizzo, Missvain, Escarbot, Brianmarkhahn, Ermeyers, Sophie means wisdom, Braindog, .anacondabot, VoABot II, StudierMalMarburg, Mjw65, T@nn, JNW, TheCormac, Edward321, Green i, Rettetast, R'n'B, Gunkarta, Wiki Raja, Maurice Carbonaro, Ian.thomson, J.A.McCoy, DadaNeem, 83d40m, Phatius McBluff, Sfwarptour23, Idioma-bot, Gothbag, Melchizedekjesus, Tunnels of Set, AlnoktaBOT, Evil-mer0dach, Mediocredave, Hellie Hut, Burpen, IPSOS, Kljenni, SteinAlive, AlleborgoBot, BotMultichill, Mlgrillo, Ganna24, Xenophon777, Fishtar, Lagrange613, TX55, ClueBot, Deanlaw, Drmies, Bagworm, Rock zap11, Highheater93, SchreiberBike, Muro Bot, DumZiBoT, Addbot, LaaknorBot, Ccacsmss, Numbo3-bot, Tide rolls, Jarble, Luckas-bot, Yobot, Piffloman, Ptbotgourou, Nallimbot, KamikazeBot, Hinio, Iroony, AnomieBOT, Materialscientist, Xqbot, TheAMmollusc, Vanoi71, Jackiestud, DSisyphBot, GrouchoBot, Omnipaedista, Omar77, Verbum Veritas, A.amitkumar, FrescoBot, Belmut, Vicharam, Izzedine, Enver62, Enki H., Lilaac, I dream of horses, LittleWink, Diomedea Exulans, MastiBot, Tahir mq, KlingsorOfOz, Desibouy, Lotje, John of Reading, Jokekiller92, Lutrina, Camocon, Johnoakgrove, Arubafirina, Donner60, Manytexts, ClueBot NG, Tanbircdq, Dream of Nyx, BlindMic, Titodutta, Wikih101, TheRedOwl, Scialex~enwiki, Tutelary, Saturnia Regna, JYBot, Jeremy49917, Mogism, WilliamDigiCol, Faizan, Epicgenius, Alexwho314, Genther, Supercrediblesourcelol, Kitttyb, Dutch30001, Jooojay, Rosetta Stele, Ponyfan58425, Imamazingfrick, 11r010fkme, Ninjabit, 92slim, Whalestate, Zach Plotkin, KasparBot, Syed bukhari34, Ordo de Essentia and Anonymous: 245

- **Kaalratri** *Source:* https://en.wikipedia.org/wiki/Kaalratri?oldid=686480869 *Contributors:* Racklever, Courcelles, Woodshed, Ekabhishek, Snehilsharma, Eeekster, Queenmomcat, Yobot, Helpsome, ClueBot NG, Frietjes, Shire Reeve, MrNiceGuy1113, Hotmuru, Pratik12951, Samuel waikiki, Srivatsan kumar, Kev8927 and Anonymous: 11

- **Katyayini** *Source:* https://en.wikipedia.org/wiki/Katyayini?oldid=686570745 *Contributors:* Utcursch, RJFJR, Kosher Fan, Dangerous-Boy, DaGizza, Priyanath, SmackBot, Hmains, Chris the speller, Colonies Chris, Katyayanita, Skinsmoke, Ekabhishek, T@nn, Captain panda, R powers, RedChinaForever, Oldag07, Yintan, Gireeshelemec, XLinkBot, Indu, Addbot, Jonoikobangali, Vyom25, Luckas-bot, Yobot, AnomieBOT, J04n, FrescoBot, Dazedbythebell, Skyerise, Arnab Sarkar, BCtl, GoingBatty, ZéroBot, JanetteDoe, Dvellakat, Frietjes, Helpful Pixie Bot, BG19bot, Prasadspshetty, JaQueeta, ChrisGualtieri, Hotmuru, Mogism, Arjuncm3, WBRSin, Pratik12951, JustBerry, Ilango adikal chera, Filedelinkerbot, Bordwall, Srivatsan kumar and Anonymous: 23

- **Kaumari** *Source:* https://en.wikipedia.org/wiki/Kaumari?oldid=685030677 *Contributors:* Rathfelder, AnomieBOT, Jbhunley, Kev8927 and Anonymous: 3

- **Korravai** *Source:* https://en.wikipedia.org/wiki/Korravai?oldid=640266396 *Contributors:* Alan Liefting, Rjwilmsi, Alastair Haines, Redtigerxyz, Citation bot, LilHelpa, CitationCleanerBot and Anonymous: 3

- **Lua (goddess)** *Source:* https://en.wikipedia.org/wiki/Lua_(goddess)?oldid=651899700 *Contributors:* Manuel Anastácio, Aecis, Ross Burgess, Gaius Cornelius, GeeJo, Ck lostsword, Attys, Magioladitis, T@nn, Btumpak, Aseld, DumZiBoT, Addbot, AnomieBOT, Paine Ellsworth, Phlyaristis, GregKaye, ZéroBot, Wbm1058, Davidiad and Anonymous: 3

- **Macha** *Source:* https://en.wikipedia.org/wiki/Macha?oldid=681439986 *Contributors:* Bryan Derksen, Jpatokal, TUF-KAT, Reddi, RedWolf, Bkell, Eequor, Critto~enwiki, Fergananim, RedDragon, Dbachmann, Kwamikagami, QuartierLatin1968, Anthony Appleyard, Stevegiacomelli, Nicknack009, HollyI, Dysepsion, Cuchullain, FlaBot, RexNL, Pigman, Cordie Vreccan, Asarelah, Limetom, Ohconfucius, Yms, OS2Warp, Dgw, JAnDbot, TheEditrix2, Cynwolfe, T@nn, Vox Rationis, Asarlaí, Cantiorix, AlleborgoBot, Kayopos~enwiki, Dairukou, Vanished user ewfisn2348tui2f8n2fio2utjfeoi210r39jf, Mr. Stradivarius, SexyEnglishGayLad, WikHead, Alexius08, Aashrithh, Addbot, Legobot, Luckas-bot, Yobot, AnomieBOT, Citation bot, Jayarathina, Cavila, Unknownnaming, HRoestBot, TobeBot, Sizzle Flambé, RjwilmsiBot, Life in General, K kisses, Lairbhan, Ancatmara, Cyberbot II, ChrisGualtieri, Khazar2, Claíomh Solais, Moony22, 302ET, GeneralizationsAreBad and Anonymous: 24

- **Maheshvari** *Source:* https://en.wikipedia.org/wiki/Maheshvari?oldid=648391022 *Contributors:* Kev8927

- **Matrikas** *Source:* https://en.wikipedia.org/wiki/Matrikas?oldid=679699634 *Contributors:* Mahaabaala, Imc, Carlossuarez46, Luis Dantas, Michael Devore, Sharavanabhava, Rosarino, El C, Giraffedata, Hanuman Das, Wiki-uk, Hoary, Woohookitty, Dangerous-Boy, BD2412, Rjwilmsi, Koavf, Jake Wartenberg, TheRingess, Bhadani, DaGizza, DanMS, Aamrun, SmackBot, Dineshkannambadi, Skinsmoke, Iridescent, Tarchon, Nick Ottery, DBaba, Srath, Epbr123, Joy1963, Ekabhishek, MER-C, Steven Walling, JaGa, B9 hummingbird hovering, R'n'B, Captain panda, Zerokitsune, SriMesh, Redtigerxyz, A Ramachandran, IPSOS, Snehilsharma, Mohonu, WereSpielChequers, Gabrieli, Yintan, Fratrep, Sitush, Randy Kryn, Martarius, Sfan00 IMG, Foxj, IceUnshattered, Tamil33, SchreiberBike, Flutterman, Cminard, WikHead, Addbot, Rejectwater, More random musing, Luckas-bot, Yobot, Browndog72, Materialscientist, Citation bot, LilHelpa, The Banner, AdalCobos, Aditya soni, OgreBot, PigFlu Oink, HRoestBot, Jonesey95, Sizzle Flambé, Jethwarp, H3llBot, Spicemix, Sanshlistha m, Benjamín Preciado, Frietjes, CEAA-India, Helpful Pixie Bot, MKar, Noopur28, Solomon7968, DPL bot, All Worlds, Natuur12, Arjuncm3, IndianBio, Irisbox, Ugog Nizdast, Monkbot, Sunil kumar sadh, BudChrSch, Grathmy, Kev8927, KasparBot and Anonymous: 34

- **Menhit** *Source:* https://en.wikipedia.org/wiki/Menhit?oldid=673205736 *Contributors:* TUF-KAT, Robbot, Gtrmp, Cronos~enwiki, Alensha, Aranel, Drbreznjev, Sburke, Briangotts, -Ril-, FlaBot, Gurch, Fram, SmackBot, Mira, Merlin-UK, The Man in Question, A. Parrot, Sobreira, "D", JAnDbot, Deflective, 83d40m, STBotD, Henrykus, FinnWiki, Ptolemy Caesarion, PipepBot, PixelBot, Addbot, AnnaFrance, Luckas-bot, Yobot, ArthurBot, Erik9bot, Tahir mq, Dmthoth, Dudy001, GoingBatty, AvicAWB, YFdyh-bot, Dexbot and Anonymous: 10

- **Menrva** *Source:* https://en.wikipedia.org/wiki/Menrva?oldid=679583497 *Contributors:* Eurleif, TUF-KAT, Wetman, DocWatson42, Gtrmp, Eequor, Icairns, Seancdaug, YurikBot, GeeJo, Dysmorodrepanis~enwiki, SmackBot, Dr. Elwin Ransom, Glengordon01, Xiaphias, Neddyseagoon, Laurent paris, CmdrObot, Karenjc, Atomaton, Thijs!bot, Epbr123, Sluzzelin, T@nn, Pax:Vobiscum, Kateshortforbob, Medellia, R powers,

VolkovBot, TXiKiBoT, Daufer, Sanya3, Badgernet, Addbot, Numbo3-bot, Yobot, Tonyrex, Carlomenon, EmausBot, Finn Bjørklid, AvicAWB, Lieutenant Waaxe, ChrisGualtieri, JaconaFrere, Nøkkenbuer and Anonymous: 23

- **Minerva** *Source:* https://en.wikipedia.org/wiki/Minerva?oldid=678042077 *Contributors:* Bryan Derksen, Zundark, Andre Engels, Tucci528, Olivier, Infrogmation, Michael Hardy, Gabbe, Looxix~enwiki, Angela, Raven in Orbit, Agtx, Furrykef, VeryVerily, Head, Renato Caniatti~enwiki, Wetman, Robbot, Wereon, Mushroom, Gtrmp, Netartnet, Eequor, AaronW, Bacchiad, Gdr, LiDaobing, Slowking Man, The Singing Badger, Andux, Karl-Henner, Chmod007, Moverton, Discospinster, Rich Farmbrough, Vague Rant, Randee15, Vsmith, Silence, Smyth, Furius, Aranel, QuartierLatin1968, Aude, Bobo192, HiddenInPlainSight, Smalljim, Man vyi, Haham hanuka, Foeke~enwiki, Hu, Vengeful Cynic, Dave.Dunford, Redvers, Ttownfeen, Woohookitty, ScottDavis, Timo Laine, Tripodics, MONGO, Essjay, MassGalactusUniversum, Chris Weimer, BD2412, Dpv, Саша Стефановић, Biederman, FlaBot, Naraht, Margosbot~enwiki, MGSpiller, Chobot, DaGizza, EamonnPKeane, YurikBot, Retodon8, Adam1213, Conscious, Pigman, Amitembedded, Yamara, Van der Hoorn, Stephenb, Gaius Cornelius, NawlinWiki, Wiki alf, Grafen, RL0919, DeadEyeArrow, Asarelah, Botteville, Igiffin, AnnaKucsma, Johndburger, Lt-wiki-bot, Italian boy, Ketsuekigata, E Wing, Josh3580, Rredwell, Katieh5584, SmackBot, Tom Lougheed, KnowledgeOfSelf, Pgk, Dr. Elwin Ransom, Hmains, Rearden Metal, Brettpeace, Gorwell, Sbharris, Hongooi, Can't sleep, clown will eat me, Akhilleus, Glengordon01, Ofthehudson, JNIBERT, BehemothCat, Mistress Selina Kyle, Freedom to share, Niera, SashatoBot, Pizzahut2, Kuru, Butko, Onlim, Lisapollison, SMasters, MarkSutton, Samfreed, Xiaphias, Neddyseagoon, Midnightblueowl, Iridescent, Red 81, Joseph Solis in Australia, Zekigal, Matanariel, Namiba, Anakata, Zureks, Fordmadoxfraud, Gregbard, Rmallins, Atomaton, Bellerophon5685, Doug Weller, SiN~enwiki, Wexcan, Thijs!bot, Andyjsmith, Waveformula, Vertium, Missvain, Crzycheetah, Itsmejudith, VaneWimsey, Dfrg.msc, AntiVandalBot, MoogleDan, Luna Santin, JAnDbot, Deflective, Instinct, Andonic, Ahrarara, Cynwolfe, .anacondabot, Magioladitis, Freedomlinux, Frankyboy5, VoABot II, AuburnPilot, T@nn, Fordsfords, Andykoom, Doug Coldwell, Papoise, Animum, Heliac, Simon Peter Hughes, Ironicon, Sibak, Jonomacdrones, MartinBot, Nehwyn, Anaxial, Jay Litman, Kateshortforbob, CommonsDelinker, PrestonH, Tgeairn, Nev1, Tilla, TheTrojanHought, Thetravellinggourmet, SSSN, Darkfrog24, Frankpeters, Marlodge, Redtigerxyz, Cobwall, VolkovBot, Jeff G., Ecclesiastical, Philip Trueman, TXiKiBoT, Erik the Red 2, Davehi1, Pjm4474, Rei-bot, Captain Wikify, Clarince63, Eubulides, Dark Tea, Spinningspark, Thanatos666, Pjoef, Stonecherub, Okelliot, PericlesofAthens, Xalexjx, NHRHS2010, Chmarlyblob, SieBot, Euryalus, ToePeu.bot, Caltas, Seally13, Socal gal at heart, Lesssthan, Oxymoron83, Jm2gm, Jerrymanderhonk, Wiki-BT, Denisarona, Nature's Mistake, Jvwieringen, Joanna.Licata, ClueBot, GorillaWarfare, DFRussia, Agaddis, Kashunda, Xioxox, Fotpegis, ChandlerMapBot, Excirial, Jena123, Sun Creator, 7&6=thirteen, A classicist, SchreiberBike, Alexyo50, Natyayl, Cataloguer, Thingg, Bkwrmgrl1, Versus22, Egmontaz, Jjvs, Editor2020, Zxly, Coccionos, Frood, Bgag, Addbot, Allynwalters, Thrutheseasons, Mac Dreamstate, Ccacsmss, Favonian, Udugunit, Jsmtty11, Numbo3-bot, Lightbot, Bartledan, Drpickem, Luckas-bot, Victoriaearle, THEN WHO WAS PHONE?, AnomieBOT, Jim1138, Tom87020, OllieFury, Cheeseynips, LilHelpa, Xqbot, Ekwos, Narthring, Elshitsa, Nautaparata, Gris379, Omnipaedista, Mattis, Gator13, Mithrandir, Citation bot 1, SuperJew, Cubs197, Subirendra, Iblackie, FoxBot, TobeBot, Lotje, Seanoneal, Extra999, Jethwarp, Schulz47, RjwilmsiBot, VernoWhitney, Bradyf01, Teogarno, Deagle AP, EmausBot, WikitanvirBot, Ghostofnemo, Britannic124, Kagemusha77, Lolsaywhaat, Alpha Quadrant, Yiosie2356, Aeonx, Suslindisambiguator, Philafrenzy, Bobbythemazarin, Donner60, DASHBotAV, ClueBot NG, Cwmhiraeth, HauserF, Iiii I I I, A520, Mottenen, Yakyback, Kevin Gorman, Widr, Robberto1986, Helpful Pixie Bot, HMSSolent, Vagobot, Zanyfire, AhMedRMaaty, Davidiad, Mark Arsten, Rembrandt 1976, Luvhpc, TreboniusArtorius, Bethechangeyouhopetosee, Loupiotte, Intelligent 1000, MythBuffer, Hmainsbot1, TwoTwoHello, Jamesx12345, Rainbow Shifter, Deoxys12, Godot13, Minerva1976, Ldfkumjyfg, Ginsuloft, Lakun.patra, Jemmabluemoon, Indianasean, Сяра, CamelCase, StarGuerra, Angeldimaria2807, Sleath56, Smarterasapigfeet, KasparBot, Vicinca, LamarRobin and Anonymous: 513

- **Nanaya** *Source:* https://en.wikipedia.org/wiki/Nanaya?oldid=670150309 *Contributors:* SamEV, RussBot, Asarelah, Sadads, Nishkid64, Ntsimp, Doug Weller, Goldenrowley, T@nn, Niceguyedc, Sumerophile, Addbot, Historicpastime, Sisyph, Xqbot, Enki H., DrilBot, RjwilmsiBot, EmausBot, GoingBatty, ZéroBot, FinalRapture, MarcusLeDain, Helpful Pixie Bot, BigEars42, Vagobot, Ponyfan58425 and Anonymous: 5

- **Nane (goddess)** *Source:* https://en.wikipedia.org/wiki/Nane_(goddess)?oldid=683515091 *Contributors:* Woohookitty, Mandarax, The Man in Question, Woodshed, Future Perfect at Sunrise, Magioladitis, R'n'B, Ian.thomson, MF-Warburg, Karim Ali, Addbot, Tassedethe, Konstantinos~enwiki, AnomieBOT, Materialscientist, Nima Farid, BRUTE, GregKaye, EmausBot, Werieth, Bamyers99, Simba22, Lemnaminor, Simosel22, Bursting Red, Ateel93 and Anonymous: 11

- **Neith** *Source:* https://en.wikipedia.org/wiki/Neith?oldid=686067818 *Contributors:* Bryan Derksen, Llywrch, Menchi, Looxix~enwiki, Snoyes, TUF-KAT, TUF-KAT, Angela, Cyan, Andres, Silverfish, Schneelocke, RickK, Eugene van der Pijll, Robbot, Yosri, Premeditated Chaos, Wikibot, Eliashedberg, Cronos~enwiki, Eequor, Mustafaa, Mud, Eisnel, Aziri, Rich Farmbrough, Rama, JohnLynch, Aranel, SS~enwiki, Bobo192, Deacon of Pndapetzim, Notcarlos, Megan1967, Isfisk, Sburke, ZZz, Nefertum17, -Ril-, Tutmosis, Cuchullain, JamesBurns, Kinu, FlaBot, Nihiltres, Str1977, YurikBot, RussBot, Pigman, Asarelah, Kramden, Mmcannis, That Guy, From That Show!, Sardanaphalus, SmackBot, Hydrogen Iodide, Zerida, Kkhemet, Salmar, Leoboudv, Artemisboy, John D. Croft, Pmei, Rodsan18, The Man in Question, A. Parrot, MTSbot~enwiki, Missionary, KyraVixen, WeggeBot, Cydebot, Michael C Price, Doug Weller, JamesAM, Thijs!bot, JAnDbot, WANAX, Deflective, Jeff Dahl, T@nn, Simon Peter Hughes, Afterthewar~enwiki, B9 hummingbird hovering, J.delanoy, R powers, Skumarlabot, Ian.thomson, Belovedfreak, Rosenknospe, 83d40m, Lanternix, Idioma-bot, Deor, VolkovBot, Atari500, TXiKiBoT, Apepch7, Jamelan, AlleborgoBot, SieBot, BotMultichill, Fidelia, Mimihitam, Ptolemy Caesarion, BenoniBot~enwiki, Escape Orbit, PipepBot, Abu America, Amovrvs, Cataloguer, Adwija, WikHead, Thatguyflint, Addbot, Vatrena ptica, Eivindbot, ChenzwBot, Xel-Hassodin, Wikkidd, Kgriffisgreenberg, Yobot, Ptbotgourou, Taam, Materialscientist, ArthurBot, Omnipaedista, YurilowellPS3, Pinethicket, Skyerise, Tahir mq, Dmthoth, RjwilmsiBot, RA0808, ClueBot NG, MusikAnimal, Mark Arsten, CitationCleanerBot, Jaybear, GamingWithStatoke, Dexbot, Rakz234, Eyesnore, DavidLeighEllis, Artemis Vee, Chandra,Eye of Ma'at, Thendlove, RNGeebus and Anonymous: 87

- **Nemain** *Source:* https://en.wikipedia.org/wiki/Nemain?oldid=686926434 *Contributors:* Hephaestos, Ahoerstemeier, The Warlock, Merovingian, Gtrmp, Eequor, Critto~enwiki, Fergananim, D6, QuartierLatin1968, Nicknack009, SteinbDJ, YurikBot, RussBot, Eburaconos, Pigman, Neilbeach, GeeJo, CorbieVreccan, Ohconfucius, Ollamh (fr), Thijs!bot, Michael A. White, Captain panda, Cú Faoil, Asarlaí, Jalo, Muro Bot, SexyEnglishGayLad, Dthomsen8, Addbot, CarsracBot, AnomieBOT, HRoestBot, Reimmichl-212, Helpful Pixie Bot, Aisteco and Anonymous: 13

- **Nerio** *Source:* https://en.wikipedia.org/wiki/Nerio?oldid=681637687 *Contributors:* Zoe, Tucci528, Minesweeper, Emperorbma, GreatWhiteNortherner, SimonMayer, Silence, Aecis, GeeJo, Bloodofox, Zwobot, Deucalionite, Asarelah, SmackBot, Blah3, Cynwolfe, T@nn, TXiKiBoT, MystBot, Addbot, Tony Esopi, ChrisGualtieri, AK456 and Anonymous: 6

- **Nike (mythology)** *Source:* https://en.wikipedia.org/wiki/Nike_(mythology)?oldid=686289796 *Contributors:* Mark, Youssefsan, Tucci528, D, Gdarin, Gabbe, Collabi, Menchi, Sannse, Todd, CatherineMunro, TUF-KAT, Julesd, Glenn, Adam Bishop, Morwen, Renato Caniatti~enwiki, AnonMoos, Wetman, Adam Carr, Mrdice, Opponent, ChrisO~enwiki, Halibutt, UtherSRG, Fuzzzone, Gtrmp, Gilgamesh~enwiki, Eequor, Matthead, Chameleon, Christopherlin, Bacchiad, OldakQuill, Gauss, Didactohedron, Chmod007, Adashiel, Shotwell, Jiy, Discospinster, Dbachmann, Paul August, ESkog, Violetriga, Brian0918, Kwamikagami, Shanes, Robotje, Smalljim, Zwilson, Obradovic Goran, Nsaa, Orangemarlin, Alansohn, SnowFire, Mr Adequate, Riana, Calton, DreamGuy, Wtmitchell, Bsadowski1, Redvers, RyanGerbil10, Reikku, Scjessey, SeventyThree, FreplySpang, Mendaliv, Vary, Mike s, SMC, Ghepeu, Matt Deres, Ev, Jamesmusik, FlaBot, Nivix, RexNL, Aikakone, Krun, Gurubrahma, Chobot, P0per, Jared Preston, Sasoriza, Gwernol, Cornellrockey, YurikBot, Sceptre, Brandmeister (old), Gaius Cornelius, Ravenous, RazorICE, Maxfield, Apeman, Deucalionite, AdelaMae, Asarelah, Kelovy, Jkelly, Lt-wiki-bot, Denisutku, Dspradau, Allens, DearPrudence, DVD R W, Luk, SmackBot, MyrddinEmrys, KnowledgeOfSelf, NaiPiak, Kimon, Alsandro, Peter Isotalo, Gilliam, Skizzik, Amatulic, Bluebot, Persian Poet Gal, Fuzzform, MalafayaBot, SchfiftyThree, Kungming2, Rrburke, Greenshed, Cybercobra, Mackintyre, Freedom to share, SashatoBot, TheStripèdOne, Gobonobo, Gigamaligabyte, Linnell, IronGargoyle, DIEGO RICARDO PEREIRA, Bilby, CPAScott, A. Parrot, Valepert, Dammit, Doczilla, Big Smooth, MTSbot~enwiki, Hipnip, MrDolomite, MikeWazowski, Bigplankton, LeyteWolfer, Igoldste, Bob diablo, Courcelles, Tawkerbot2, Georgejmyersjr, BertieB, J Milburn, CmdrObot, ShelfSkewed, MetaruKoneko, Xhsfootball27, Cydebot, Gogo Dodo, B, Christian75, Sp, Epbr123, Jaxsonjo, HappyInGeneral, Callmarcus, Mojo Hand, Marek69, Escarbot, Igorwindsor~enwiki, Oreo Priest, Mentifisto, WinBot, MoogleDan, NeilEvans, EarthPerson, JAnDbot, MER-C, Cassius335, Smith Jones, MirkMeister, Cynwolfe, Acroterion, Freedomlinux, Bongwarrior, VoABot II, T@nn, Theranos, Daibot~enwiki, Catgut, Ben Ram, Wanderer~enwiki, People.are.watching, Fang 23, DerHexer, Patstuart, MartinBot, Pupster21, Rettetast, Jay Litman, CommonsDelinker, AlexiusHoratius, Lifeisagame247, Nevakee11, J.delanoy, Pharaoh of the Wizards, Nev1, Altes, Dmitri Yuriev, Lalalaabc123, Gombang, Amoscare, Dcs315, 83d40m, Sm91, Juliancolton, DorganBot, Peter Clark, Ja 62, Dorftrottel, Deor, VolkovBot, ABF, Macedonian, ICE77, Echochernik, Jeff G., Indubitably, Philip Trueman, TXiKiBoT, Taeho, Crohnie, Sean D Martin, JayC, Bobdylan06.1, Martin451, JhsBot, Chokolada, LeaveSleaves, Meters, Falcon8765, Enviroboy, Thanatos666, Brianga, NHRHS2010, EmxBot, SieBot, Zenlax, Gopher292, Tiddly Tom, Krawi, YourEyesOnly, Caltas, Yintan, MatthewMillican, Jan Winnicki, Keilana, Flyer22 Reborn, Socopsycho, Alex.muller, BenoniBot~enwiki, IdreamofJeanie, Spartan-James, StaticGull, Wiki-BT, Atif.t2, Loren.wilton, ClueBot, LAX, NickCT, GorillaWarfare, The Thing That Should Not Be, Plastikspork, Mx3, Amovrvs, Drmies, Cenhinen, Uncle Milty, DragonBot, Excirial, Pumpmeup, -Midorihana-, Jusdafax, Estirabot, Stealth500, Kakofonous, Sparrowgoose, Catalographer, Thingg, Aitias, 7, SoxBot III, DumZiBoT, Hotcrocodile, BodhisattvaBot, Prosperosity, Avoided, WikHead, SilvonenBot, Addbot, Euterpe the Muse, Guoguo12, Tcncv, Non-dropframe, Queenmomcat, 1Dominic1, Fluffernutter, Cst17, Classicsnerd, Glane23, Favonian, SpBot, Bluerockstar95, Tide rolls, Bfigura's puppy, הורה55, Luckas Blade, Ochib, Ben Ben, Math Champion, Luckas-bot, Wurth Skidder, Victoriaearle, THEN WHO WAS PHONE?, Mydoctor93, Eric-Wester, Tempodivalse, AnomieBOT, Galoubet, Materialscientist, Dendlai, Citation bot, Wikichickey, RealDoctor, Shadowmaster13, Xqbot, Capricorn42, Raganaut, Esc861, Omnipaedista, RibotBOT, 78.26, Bezaaum, Žiedas, Epp, Smartpants101, Cheeks101, Meishern, Pinethicket, ShadowRangerRIT, HRoestBot, Adlerbot, Georgemalcomthomsom, Tinton5, MastiBot, Fui in terra aliena, MJ, Reconsider the static, GregKaye, Xplod348, Goalie344, Suffusion of Yellow, Lotusfield2, Tbhotch, Jesse V., Hornlitz, Onel5969, Superxemilis, Ilovehector, Spike35031, Bento00, Phlegat, 20091207chen, BagOfMostlyH20, CalicoCatLover, Skamecrazy123, 2009mbtmvp, Yellow1500, EmausBot, AmericanLeMans, Racerx11, NotAnonymous0, Koolkid875, Smappy, Slightsmile, Tommy2010, Wikipelli, K6ka, Evanh2008, Wikitoov, Unclebigcats, ZéroBot, Daay zaay, Susfele, Fæ, Pelagaios, Thine Antique Pen, L Kensington, Tot12, Rocketrod1960, ClueBot NG, Jnorton7558, NapoleonX, The Master of Mayhem, Widr, Mattgardner4, Mightymights, Helpful Pixie Bot, Etradenike, Calabe1992, Wiki13, MusikAnimal, Mondria, AvocatoBot, Davidiad, The little green pig, Stgnwiki, Georgethesexy, Goddessnike, W.D., Haymouse, Makalathomas22, Tacolover22, Benchevy, Webclient101, Frosty, Wywin, Melonkelon, Eyesnore, 19be, DavidLeighEllis, Origamite, Ginsuloft, Noyster, JaconaFrere, Crystallizedcarbon, Black ninjag, RegistryKey, Lord Cupid, ToonLucas22, GREEKgal123, KasparBot, Mistermcsquiggles, Fghvg123:);,$$)((, Mr Potto, Heelezed, Man of me and Anonymous: 624

- **Oya** *Source:* https://en.wikipedia.org/wiki/Oya?oldid=683563842 *Contributors:* Wapcaplet, TUF-KAT, Phil Boswell, RedWolf, Romanm, Liotier, RoyBoy, Reinyday, Mark Dingemanse, Reikku, Graham87, Bhadani, Semisomna, RussBot, Pigman, Leutha, Grafen, AKeen, CaliforniaAliBaba, CorbieVreccan, Asarelah, Closedmouth, Allens, Bill, SmackBot, Classicfilms, Srnec, Colonies Chris, Nixeagle, Qyd, HRH, Doug Weller, Gus andrews, Thijs!bot, Goldenrowley, OloObatala, T@nn, Coppertwig, Belovedfreak, Gallador, STBotD, Bwjsmartdude, Indubitably, TXiKiBoT, Rei-bot, Haikon, AlleborgoBot, SieBot, Ogun7, Pomba Gira, Sanya3, StewieK, Addbot, Glane23, SpBot, Yobot, Gongshow, AnomieBOT, TheAMmollusc, Lily20, Cubaking, Oyaschild99, Ellenois, Lotje, Aoidh, EmausBot, JohnCengiz77, Tolly4bolly, 28bot, Frietjes, Otelemuyen, Helpful Pixie Bot, Jneimark, GOAL08, Stevengravel, Cyberbot II, ChrisGualtieri, GoShow, Hello020020202020202020, Sacred-Labyrinth, Vieque, Omo Obatalá, KasparBot and Anonymous: 57

- **Pakhet** *Source:* https://en.wikipedia.org/wiki/Pakhet?oldid=685153766 *Contributors:* Alensha, SWAdair, Grm wnr, Discospinster, Meggar, Iustinus, -Ril-, Tutmosis, Josh Parris, YurikBot, Zwobot, BL Lacertae, Sardanaphalus, SmackBot, Hmains, Leoboudv, A. Parrot, Nehrams2020, Switchercat, TheTito, Synergy, KonstableBot, T@nn, Twsx, Simon Peter Hughes, Captain panda, Naniwako, 83d40m, VolkovBot, Jalo, FinnWiki, Work permit, Ptolemy Caesarion, Pinkadelica, PipepBot, The Thing That Should Not Be, Place Clichy, Muro Bot, Katanada, Addbot, Souljapenguin11, Chamal N, Xel-Hassodin, Ben Pirard, Ulric1313, ArthurBot, Khruner, SassoBot, JMCC1, Tahir mq, Dmthoth, Mandolinface, ZéroBot, Haymouse, ChrisGualtieri, Iry-Hor, Dexbot and Anonymous: 18

- **Palioxis** *Source:* https://en.wikipedia.org/wiki/Palioxis?oldid=541257975 *Contributors:* Addbot, Yobot, Amirobot, Phlyaristis, ZéroBot and Davidiad

- **Parvati** *Source:* https://en.wikipedia.org/wiki/Parvati?oldid=686011327 *Contributors:* Shii, DopefishJustin, Dominus, Mkweise, TUF-KAT, Charles Matthews, Imc, Carlossuarez46, Goethean, Sam Spade, Mboverload, Utcursch, LordSimonofShropshire, Jaycia, Brother Dysk~enwiki, Xezbeth, Bender235, Kwamikagami, QuartierLatin1968, Balajiviswanathan, Hintha, Pearle, Jakew, Mdd, Anthony Appleyard, Wiki-uk, Andrew Gray, Grenavitar, Hijiri88, Anusuya, Shmitra, Bkwillwm, Dangerous-Boy, RxS, Rjwilmsi, Wikirao, Bhadani, Yamamoto Ichiro, FlaBot, Swami Vimokshananda, Gnikhil, Windharp, Chobot, DaGizza, Bgwhite, YurikBot, CambridgeBayWeather, Rsrikanth05, Srini81, Douglasfrankfort~enwiki, Badagnani, Priyanath, Varano, IceCreamAntisocial, Seemagoel, N-Bot, Lt-wiki-bot, Sanyarajan, Aeon1006, Ethan Mitchell, SmackBot, Errarel, Bjelleklang, Aksi great, Ohnoitsjamie, Aaadddaaammm, Bluebot, MartinPoulter, Deli nk, ImpuMozhi, Can't sleep, clown will eat me, Egsan Bacon, Shivap, MilitaryTarget, Pilotguy, Snowgrouse, RandomCritic, 2T, Sharnak, MTSbot~enwiki, Skinsmoke, Hu12, Iridescent, Sameboat, Laurens-af, Sinaloa, Wjejskenewr, Courcelles, Tawkerbot2, Danberbro, Subravenkat, Doug Weller, Thijs!bot, Epbr123, Anupam, Marek69, James086, E. Ripley, Nick Number, Escarbot, AntiVandalBot, RobotG, Widefox, Devi bhakta, Oubliette, Wahabijaz, Sluzzelin, Ekabhishek, Hut 8.5, Exairetos, Magioladitis, VoABot II, Soulbot, Abhilashrana, Froid, KConWiki, Tuncrypt, Edward321, Teardrop onthefire, Draken3314, Ravichandar84, R'n'B, CommonsDelinker, Fconaway, Abecedare, MercuryBlue, Benscripps, Clerks, Jigesh, Skier Dude, Chiswick Chap, Achika54, Morinae, Cometstyles, STBotD, KellyPhD, Idioma-bot, Redtigerxyz, DanBealeCocks, VolkovBot, Netito777, Philip Trueman, TXiKiBoT, T.sujatha, Sankalpdravid, IPSOS, Snehilsharma, Robert1947, Rumiton, B4upradeep, AlleborgoBot, Smurali49, SieBot, Flyer22 Reborn, Jothilingam, Le Pied-bot~enwiki, 0rrAvenger, Techman224, Lotussculpture, OKBot, TX55, Dust Filter, Gireeshelemec, Randy Kryn, ImageRemovalBot, Invertzoo, ClueBot, Foxj, The Thing That Should Not Be, B1atv, Subramanianvb, Blogeswar, Mild Bill Hiccup, The-OldJacobite, Ssriram mt, Niceguyedc, DragonBot, Alexbot, Exact~enwiki, Primalmoon, TheRedPenOfDoom, Navvis, Versus22, Θ, AaronCarson, Ism schism, Good Olfactory, Addbot, Goddessaday, Willking1979, Debnatha, Diablokrom, SpBot, Krano, Yobot, Hinio, Anand.Hegde, AnomieBOT, Cantanchorus, حفاتس ىردا, DAFMM, E2eamon, ArthurBot, LilHelpa, Xqbot, Vanoi71, GrouchoBot, RibotBOT, The Interior, Trusha Desai, AdalCobos, Graidan, FrescoBot, LucienBOT, Skaranam, All knowledge is free for all, DrilBot, Biker Biker, VikasJain, Elockid, HRoestBot, Skyerise, Truth only truth, VenomousConcept, Cmahale, Vprashanth87, Vrenator, Sizzle Flambé, Cowlibob, Going-Batty, K6ka, Melakavijay, Kkm010, Fæ, Kind creation, Infinte loop, Empty Buffer, Saint91, Johnoakgrove, Mayur, Himanshu2212, Chuis-pastonBot, Nayansatya, Mahmoudalrawi, ClueBot NG, Jack Greenmaven, LogX, Chester Markel, Benjamín Preciado, Frietjes, Dream of Nyx, Helpful Pixie Bot, IrishStephen, Ruhimartin, BG19bot, MKar, Vagobot, Ganesh24, Arjunkanagal, PhnomPencil, Bonnie13J, RikkiAaron, Ubhashan, JaQueeta, Joshua Jonathan, Glacialfox, Ambikanandan, Mrt3366, Cyberbot II, Aniha990, Hridith Sudev Nambiar, Cwobeel, Aditya Mahar, Pritha1997, Mogism, Vrisakapi, Arunshankar1234, Nicolas ANCEAU, Mumumusic, Soulsdone3, Khushu480001, Nzkiwi37, Faizan, EvHoof, Consider42, KD-Singhania, Eshwar.om, Dr Saurav Deka, Prabaharan p.Pacchaiappan, Lk56835, Modsiv, Raghav Sharman, Girishkumar19, Arjunkrishna90, JaconaFrere, Proloyb, Abbey kershaw, Xgamer2013, MythoEditor, Reitea, AKS.9955, Filedelinkerbot, Abyshree, Animesh.mishr, Greecoroman, PotatoNinja, Ashwin2345, Shrofshrs, Saivinodhini, Vikneshraj 108, Alee243, Abdulgoswami, Swami tusharananda, Sumedh Tayade, Kev8927, KasparBot, AnadiDoD, Crazybals and Anonymous: 285

- **Pele (deity)** *Source:* https://en.wikipedia.org/wiki/Pele_(deity)?oldid=680799199 *Contributors:* Ixfd64, Mkweise, Ntnon, Bearcat, Gentgeen, Robbot, Nurg, Blainster, Xanzzibar, Lythic, Daibhid C, Yugure, FrYGuY, Solipsist, Quadell, Beland, DenisMoskowitz, Gachet, Ilikea, Kwamikagami, Bobo192, Smalljim, Viriditas, Caeruleancentaur, Bkdelong, Anthony Appleyard, Mysdaao, Avenue, Gpvos, Lee-Anne, Paradiver, De-Piep, Akubhai, Rjwilmsi, Gryffindor, Vegaswikian, Chekaz, Rtkat3, Muchness, King Zeal, Gaius Cornelius, EmpressChang, Astral, Nut-meg, Evmore, Asarelah, JereKrischel, Wsiegmund, NeilN, SmackBot, McGeddon, Bluebot, Ctrlfreak13, Darth Panda, Egsan Bacon, Maande10, Red-Hillian, Artemisboy, Makana Chai, Salamurai, Kahuroa, Polihale, Hey Teacher, PSeibert~enwiki, Sera404, KarlM, Ckatz, Rkmlai, Doczilla, Ryulong, Iridescent, 293.xx.xxx.xx, Tenbergen, Thijs!bot, Komdori, Mercury~enwiki, I do not exist, The Obento Musubi, Masamage, Deflective, Barek, Californian Treehugger, Hut 8.5, T@nn, KConWiki, Ali'i, Hula Rider, MartinBot, Viralxtreme14, Bancho~enwiki, Wowaconia, Slash, Pechette, Eskimospy, Chriswiki, NewEnglandYankee, Shaloha, KylieTastic, Gemini1980, ELLusKa 86, Squids and Chips, Signalhead, Seattle Skier, TXiKiBoT, Baileypalblue, ErikWarmelink, Seresin, Mbz1, Radon210, Wmpearl, Lightmouse, Sanya3, Sitush, ImageRemovalBot, York60, ClueBot, EBY3221, 0XQ, Promethean, Iohannes Animosus, SoxBot III, Trulystand700, XLinkBot, Roxy the dog, ErgoSum88, AndreNatas, Skarebo, Billwhittaker, KAVEBEAR, Hunymonte, SpockMonkey, Addbot, Willking1979, Gsullsc, LaaknorBot, Ben Ben, Luckasbot, Yobot, Citation bot, Lomahuh, C.M.Cottrell, Chris.urs-o, Hiart, W Nowicki, Wikiunicorn, Redrose64, DrilBot, Pinethicket, Pmcgurn, Vicenarian, ImageTagBot, Rangi Sky Father, RjwilmsiBot, EmausBot, Winner 42, Bombalabomba, ZéroBot, Namoroka, Donner60, ClueBot NG, Helpful Pixie Bot, Charne808, Kinaro, BG19bot, Gravitydude2011, Wiki13, RobertaCM, Avuncular58, Alicekim53, Kanani1970, Dexbot, Dwight Hawai, Lugia2453, Kelcourt, Ugog Nizdast, Jackmcbarn, Monkbot, SantiLak, Kobe32143, KasparBot and Anonymous: 179

- **Proioxis** *Source:* https://en.wikipedia.org/wiki/Proioxis?oldid=541258111 *Contributors:* Addbot, Yobot, Amirobot, Phlyaristis, ZéroBot and Davidiad

- **Qamaits** *Source:* https://en.wikipedia.org/wiki/Qamaits?oldid=678457122 *Contributors:* Dpv, Ketiltrout, Salix alba, SmackBot, Themightyquill, Cydebot, MarshBot, Goldenrowley, T@nn, Avicennasis, Addbot, QueenCake, Erik9bot, D'ohBot, A little insignificant, Kibi78704, Listmeister and Anonymous: 4

- **Sekhmet** *Source:* https://en.wikipedia.org/wiki/Sekhmet?oldid=681812731 *Contributors:* Magnus Manske, Dan~enwiki, Rmhermen, Vik-Thor, Looxix~enwiki, TUF-KAT, TUF-KAT, RickK, JorgeGG, Jmabel, Yosri, Dehumanizer, Lzur, DocWatson42, Gtrmp, No Guru, Alensha, Yekrats, Dmmaus, Eequor, The Singing Badger, Onco p53, PhotoBox, Discospinster, Rich Farmbrough, Stbalbach, Semper distans, Stesmo, FoekeNoppert, Duk, Jic, Keenan Pepper, DreamGuy, RainbowOfLight, Capecodeph, The JPS, Sburke, -Ril-, FlaBot, HS Yuna, Bgwhite, Roygbiv666, YurikBot, JustSomeKid, Gaius Cornelius, Pseudomonas, Stassats, Fabulous Creature, Bota47, Kelovy, Niankhsekhmet, Emijrp, Lt-wiki-bot, Spawn Man, Eeee, Spliffy, Pred, Sardanaphalus, SmackBot, Classicfilms, Unyoyega, Eskimbot, Bluebot, Leoni2, Aquatico, Can't sleep, clown will eat me, Zentuk~enwiki, Glengordon01, Leoboudv, Egg-Emperor, Snowgrouse, The Man in Question, A. Parrot, Rkmlai, Redeagle688, Neddyseagoon, Dr.K., Fannyfae, Polymerbringer, CmdrObot, No11akersfan, Funnyfarmofdoom, Tkircher, Amunptah777, Tbird1965, Phobospyros, Doug Weller, MerytMaat, JohnInDC, Thijs!bot, Epbr123, Mojo Hand, Prolog, JAnDbot, Deflective, Vultur~enwiki, Jaysweet, Jeff Dahl, T@nn, JamesBWatson, DerHexer, Simon Peter Hughes, Future-ms-haskell, MartinBot, Katjamoonwind, Tgeairn, Ian.thomson, M-le-mot-dit, Belovedfreak, 83d40m, KylieTastic, STBotD, DorganBot, Idioma-bot, VolkovBot, Teledildonix314, Philip Trueman, Apepch7, AnnekeBart, FinnWiki, Burntsauce, BillBrent, Sonicology, Caltas, France3470, Flyer22 Reborn, Ptolemy Caesarion, Mojoworker, Almufasa, Mighty Nut, Jmcclare, Martarius, ClueBot, Adamsmith2311, The Thing That Should Not Be, Simunescu, Adamox06, Lsilva~enwiki, Excirial, Thingg, Lockmaynard, Bluemoons123456, XLinkBot, Bilsonius, Jovianeye, Kwjbot, SchwarzeHerz, Addbot, Landon1980, Vatrena ptica, Diablokrom, LaaknorBot, Thetasashhatap, Favonian, Tide rolls, OlEnglish, WikiDreamer Bot, Contributor777, Suwa, Luckas-bot, Yobot, تارامإ1971, Pink!Teen, Pt-botgourou, Fraggle81, AnomieBOT, Jim1138, Materialscientist, Lily20, Gospodar svemira, NFD9001, Griffinofwales, Mmcasetti, FrescoBot, Wikiy2k, Smuckola, MastiBot, Tahir mq, Tim1357, Dmthoth, DARTH SIDIOUS 2, Noraft, Andrea105, Derek-william-rose, TjBot, Alagos, Ajraddatz, GoingBatty, Bitter Chivalry, The Mysterious El Willstro, Tommy2010, Wikipelli, RusudanGulaziani, Bollyjeff, LionFosset, Alliecat500, Fatale001, ClueBot NG, Conveyance, Bryanbaird84, Widr, Newyorkadam, Vibhijain, GloriaChoi0329, GMatrix, DBigXray, PhnomPencil, Frze, Necro Shea mo, Fdgert, Neuroforever, Plunderbegcurse, Haymouse, Picklesquidly, Dexbot, Mogism, DavidLeighEllis, Tracield, KierraF, Brian McInnis, Sophistakation, JaconaFrere, BethNaught, Purpleconeflower, Crystallizedcarbon, Kevinrgiven, KasparBot, IRON-FIRE6, Darknsinth and Anonymous: 227

- **Seonangsin** *Source:* https://en.wikipedia.org/wiki/Seonangsin?oldid=646918346 *Contributors:* Bgwhite, Nick Number, Shirt58, R'n'B, Hahc21, AnomieBOT, Wingtipvortex, Sawol and Seonookim

- **Shailaputri** *Source:* https://en.wikipedia.org/wiki/Shailaputri?oldid=686054102 *Contributors:* Redtigerxyz, Yobot, LilHelpa, EmausBot, Helpsome, Frietjes, Jeraphine Gryphon, Anastomoses, Hotmuru, Arjuncm3, Samuel waikiki, Srivatsan kumar and Anonymous: 4

Malleus Fatuorum, Thijs!bot, Country Wife~enwiki, Marek69, Escarbot, Goldenrowley, Darklilac, JAnDbot, WANAX, Deflective, T@nn, Andi d, Simon Peter Hughes, R'n'B, J.delanoy, Euku, 83d40m, Redtigerxyz, VolkovBot, Shinju, Moon wolff, AnnekeBart, FinnWiki, Ottarvendel, SieBot, Ptolemy Caesarion, ClueBot, Vegas Bleeds Neon, SilvonenBot, Addbot, LaaknorBot, Kisbesbot, Tide rolls, Xel-Hassodin, Yobot, Sziwbot, DirlBot, Khruner, Queen Rhana, Ionutzmovie, Zach7775, Tahir mq, VenomousConcept, TobeBot, MrArifnajafov, TjBot, EmausBot, Faris knight, Wayne Slam, Y-barton, ChuispastonBot, Lorynote, ClueBot NG, Jack Greenmaven, Mondigomo, Haleybaby14, Dream of Nyx, PatHadley, Haymouse, MMMMEEEE, Buttholeus, Fionalouiiise3110 and Anonymous: 45

- **Šauška** *Source:* https://en.wikipedia.org/wiki/%C5%A0au%C5%A1ka?oldid=673253568 *Contributors:* FlaBot, Dobromila, Mmcannis, SmackBot, Milton Stanley, Guy0307, Magioladitis, T@nn, Boneyard90, Muhandes, Addbot, Twofistedcoffeedrinker, Yobot, LlywelynII, ZéroBot, Frietjes, Alphasinus, Epicgenius, Lushess, KasparBot and Anonymous: 4

3.2 Images

- **File:2005_Austria_10_Euro_60_Years_Second_Republic_front.jpg** *Source:* https://upload.wikimedia.org/wikipedia/en/c/c3/2005_ Austria_10_Euro_60_Years_Second_Republic_front.jpg *License:* Fair use *Contributors:* http://austrian-mint.at *Original artist:* ?

- **File:3-Maa_Chandraghantaa_(Vaishno_Devi_Maa_Chhatikra-Vrindaban).png** *Source:* https://upload.wikimedia.org/wikipedia/ commons/c/c4/3-Maa_Chandraghantaa_%28Vaishno_Devi_Maa_Chhatikra-Vrindaban%29.png *License:* CC BY-SA 3.0 *Contributors:* Own work *Original artist:* Loveonce

- **File:332_Durga-alone.png** *Source:* https://upload.wikimedia.org/wikipedia/commons/1/1e/332_Durga-alone.png *License:* Public domain *Contributors:* English Wikipedia *Original artist:* Mukerjee

- **File:7mothers56.jpg** *Source:* https://upload.wikimedia.org/wikipedia/commons/f/f7/7mothers56.jpg *License:* Public domain *Contributors:* Transferred from en.wikipedia to Commons by User:Baccy. *Original artist:* Mohonu at en.wikipedia

- **File:AUM_symbol,_the_primary_(highest)_name_of_the_God_as_per_the_Vedas.svg** *Source:* https://upload.wikimedia.org/wikipedia/ commons/b/b7/Om_symbol.svg *License:* Public domain *Contributors:* ? *Original artist:* ?

- **File:Ac.parthenon5.jpg** *Source:* https://upload.wikimedia.org/wikipedia/commons/3/35/Ac.parthenon5.jpg *License:* Public domain *Contributors:* ? *Original artist:* ?

- **File:Aegis_of_Neith-H1550-IMG_0172.jpg** *Source:* https://upload.wikimedia.org/wikipedia/commons/b/b3/Aegis_of_Neith-H1550-IMG_ 0172.jpg *License:* CC BY-SA 2.0 fr *Contributors:* Rama Own work *Original artist:* ?

- **File:Ah,_what_a_lovely_maid_it_is!_by_Elmer_Boyd_Smith.jpg** *Source:* https://upload.wikimedia.org/wikipedia/commons/2/2b/Ah% 2C_what_a_lovely_maid_it_is%21_by_Elmer_Boyd_Smith.jpg *License:* Public domain *Contributors:* Page 122 of Brown, Abbie Farwell (1902). "In the Days of Giants: A Book of Norse Tales" Illustrations by E. Boyd Smith. Houghton, Mifflin & Co. *Original artist:* Elmer Boyd Smith

- **File:Aker.svg** *Source:* https://upload.wikimedia.org/wikipedia/commons/1/1c/Aker.svg *License:* GFDL *Contributors:* Own work *Original artist:* Jeff Dahl

- **File:All_Gizah_Pyramids.jpg** *Source:* https://upload.wikimedia.org/wikipedia/commons/a/af/All_Gizah_Pyramids.jpg *License:* CC BY-SA 2.0 *Contributors:* All Gizah Pyramids *Original artist:* Ricardo Liberato

- **File:Altes_Museum_-_Antikensammlung_058.JPG** *Source:* https://upload.wikimedia.org/wikipedia/commons/3/33/Altes_Museum_-_ Antikensammlung_058.JPG *License:* CC-BY-SA-3.0 *Contributors:* Own work *Original artist:* Marcus Cyron

- **File:Amazon_preparing_for_the_battle_(Queen_Antiope_or_Armed_Venus)_-_Pierre-Eugene-Emile_Hebert_1860_-_NG_of_ Arts_Wash_DC_rotated_and_cropped.jpg** *Source:* https://upload.wikimedia.org/wikipedia/commons/f/fb/Amazon_preparing_for_the_ battle_%28Queen_Antiope_or_Armed_Venus%29_-_Pierre-Eugene-Emile_Hebert_1860_-_NG_of_Arts_Wash_DC_rotated_and_cropped. jpg *License:* Public domain *Contributors:* http://commons.wikimedia.org/wiki/File:Amazon_preparing_for_the_battle_(Queen_Antiope_or_ Armed_Venus)_-_Pierre-Eugene-Emile_Hebert_1860_-_NG_of_Arts_Wash_DC.jpg *Original artist:* RsAzevedo

- **File:Ambox_important.svg** *Source:* https://upload.wikimedia.org/wikipedia/commons/b/b4/Ambox_important.svg *License:* Public domain *Contributors:* Own work, based off of Image:Ambox scales.svg *Original artist:* Dsmurat (talk · contribs)

- **File:Ambox_question.svg** *Source:* https://upload.wikimedia.org/wikipedia/commons/1/1b/Ambox_question.svg *License:* Public domain *Contributors:* Based on Image:Ambox important.svg *Original artist:* Mysid, Dsmurat, penubag

- **File:Amphora_birth_Athena_Louvre_F32.jpg** *Source:* https://upload.wikimedia.org/wikipedia/commons/4/42/Amphora_birth_Athena_ Louvre_F32.jpg *License:* Public domain *Contributors:* Own work *Original artist:* User:Bibi Saint-Pol

- **File:An_array_of_Lingam_at_Pashupatinath_Nepal.jpg** *Source:* https://upload.wikimedia.org/wikipedia/commons/2/25/An_array_of_ Lingam_at_Pashupatinath_Nepal.jpg *License:* CC BY 2.0 *Contributors:* Lingam *Original artist:* momo from Hong Kong

- **File:Anahit_Stamp.jpg** *Source:* https://upload.wikimedia.org/wikipedia/commons/5/5c/Anahit_Stamp.jpg *License:* Public domain *Contributors:* Transferred from ru.wikipedia *Original artist:* дизайн марки Эдуарда Кургиняна. Original uploader was Zara-arush at ru.wikipedia

- **File:Anahita_Vessel,_300-500_AD,_Sasanian,_Iran,_silver_and_gilt_-_Cleveland_Museum_of_Art_-_DSC08130.JPG** *Source:* https://upload.wikimedia.org/wikipedia/commons/b/b4/Anahita_Vessel%2C_300-500_AD%2C_Sasanian%2C_Iran%2C_silver_and_gilt_-_ Cleveland_Museum_of_Art_-_DSC08130.JPG *License:* CC0 *Contributors:* Daderot *Original artist:* Daderot

- **File:Anahitcoin.jpg** *Source:* https://upload.wikimedia.org/wikipedia/commons/b/b9/Anahitcoin.jpg *License:* Public domain *Contributors:* English Wikipedia, originally from Central Bank of Armenia *Original artist:* Eupator

- **File:Anat_(Anath).png** *Source:* https://upload.wikimedia.org/wikipedia/commons/5/50/Anat_%28Anath%29.png *License:* CC0 *Contributors:* Own work *Original artist:* Camocon

- **File:Ancient_Egypt_Wings.svg** *Source:* https://upload.wikimedia.org/wikipedia/commons/9/9e/Ancient_Egypt_Wings.svg *License:* GFDL *Contributors:* This vector image was created with Inkscape by Jeff Dahl. *Original artist:* Jeff Dahl

- **File:Ardhanari.jpg** *Source:* https://upload.wikimedia.org/wikipedia/commons/7/73/Ardhanari.jpg *License:* CC BY-SA 3.0 *Contributors:* English Wikipedia *Original artist:* User:Pratheepps

- **File:As-Julia_Maesa-Sidon_AE30_BMC_300.jpg** *Source:* https://upload.wikimedia.org/wikipedia/commons/a/a0/As-Julia_Maesa-Sidon_AE30_BMC_300.jpg *License:* CC-BY-SA-3.0 *Contributors:* ? *Original artist:* ?

- **File:Ashta-Matrika.jpg** *Source:* https://upload.wikimedia.org/wikipedia/commons/d/da/Ashta-Matrika.jpg *License:* Public domain *Contributors:* Source: LACMA[1]. Transfered from en.wikipedia. Original uploader was Redtigerxyz at en.wikipedia Transfer was stated to be made by User:Giggy. 2007-07-11 (original upload date) *Original artist:* Unknown Nepali

- **File:Atena_farnese,_copia_romana_da_orig._greco_della_cerchia_fidiaca,_forse_Pyrrhos_nel_430_ac_ca.,_6024,_01.JPG** *Source:* https://upload.wikimedia.org/wikipedia/commons/1/12/Atena_farnese%2C_copia_romana_da_orig._greco_della_cerchia_fidiaca%2C_forse_Pyrrhos_nel_430_ac_ca.%2C_6024%2C_01.JPG *License:* CC BY 3.0 *Contributors:* Own work *Original artist:* Sailko

- **File:Atene_-_Partenone.jpg** *Source:* https://upload.wikimedia.org/wikipedia/commons/5/5d/Atene_-_Partenone.jpg *License:* CC BY 2.5 *Contributors:* ? *Original artist:* ?

- **File:Athena-Schale_Hildesheimer_Silberfund.jpg** *Source:* https://upload.wikimedia.org/wikipedia/commons/8/87/Athena-Schale_Hildesheimer_Silberfund.jpg *License:* Public domain *Contributors:* Own work (own photograph) *Original artist:* Photo: Andreas Praefcke

- **File:Athena_Carpegna_Massimo.jpg** *Source:* https://upload.wikimedia.org/wikipedia/commons/2/2d/Athena_Carpegna_Massimo.jpg *License:* Public domain *Contributors:* Jastrow (2006) *Original artist:* ?

- **File:Athena_Giustiniani.jpg** *Source:* https://upload.wikimedia.org/wikipedia/commons/1/1a/Athena_Giustiniani.jpg *License:* Public domain *Contributors:* photo-engraving from 1899 book. Taken from en:Image:PallasGiustiniani.jpg; found, scanned, and uploaded to en:Wikipedia by Infrogmation 01:17, 1 May 2004. *Original artist:* Unknown

- **File:Athena_Herakles_Staatliche_Antikensammlungen_2648.jpg** *Source:* https://upload.wikimedia.org/wikipedia/commons/4/4f/Athena_Herakles_Staatliche_Antikensammlungen_2648.jpg *License:* Public domain *Contributors:* User:Bibi Saint-Pol, own work, 2007-02-13 *Original artist:* Python (potter) and Douris (painter)

- **File:Athena_Parthenos_Altemps_Inv8622.jpg** *Source:* https://upload.wikimedia.org/wikipedia/commons/d/db/Athena_Parthenos_Altemps_Inv8622.jpg *License:* Public domain *Contributors:* Marie-Lan Nguyen (September 2006) *Original artist:* **English:** Antiochos (signed), copy of Phidias

- **File:AttalusICorrected.jpg** *Source:* https://upload.wikimedia.org/wikipedia/commons/9/9a/AttalusICorrected.jpg *License:* Public domain *Contributors:* ? *Original artist:* ?

- **File:Aum_red.svg** *Source:* https://upload.wikimedia.org/wikipedia/commons/8/81/Aum_red.svg *License:* Public domain *Contributors:* Author *Original artist:* DoSiDo

- **File:Aztec_serpent_sculpture.JPG** *Source:* https://upload.wikimedia.org/wikipedia/commons/b/bb/Aztec_serpent_sculpture.JPG *License:* CC BY 2.0 *Contributors:* Own work *Original artist:* Rosemania

- **File:B010ellst.png** *Source:* https://upload.wikimedia.org/wikipedia/commons/3/38/B010ellst.png *License:* Public domain *Contributors:* own work, see Friedrich Ellermeier und Margret Studt, Handbuch Assur 2003 *Original artist:* Margret Studt

- **File:B153ellst.png** *Source:* https://upload.wikimedia.org/wikipedia/commons/1/17/B153ellst.png *License:* CC BY-SA 2.5 *Contributors:* own work; see Friedrich Ellermeier - Margret Studt, Handbuch Assur 2003 *Original artist:* Margret Studt

- **File:BAPS_Shri_Swaminarayan_Mandir,_Toronto.jpg** *Source:* https://upload.wikimedia.org/wikipedia/commons/0/0a/BAPS_Shri_Swaminarayan_Mandir%2C_Toronto.jpg *License:* CC BY-SA 2.0 *Contributors:* Flickr *Original artist:* Ian Muttoo

- **File:Baal_epic_mp3h8973.jpg** *Source:* https://upload.wikimedia.org/wikipedia/commons/e/ec/Baal_epic_mp3h8973.jpg *License:* CC BY-SA 2.0 fr *Contributors:* Own work *Original artist:* Rama

- **File:Babylonlion.JPG** *Source:* https://upload.wikimedia.org/wikipedia/commons/8/88/Babylonlion.JPG *License:* Public domain *Contributors:* ? *Original artist:* ?

- **File:Bagbazar_Sarbojanin_Arnab_Dutta_2010.JPG** *Source:* https://upload.wikimedia.org/wikipedia/commons/3/3e/Bagbazar_Sarbojanin_Arnab_Dutta_2010.JPG *License:* CC BY-SA 3.0 *Contributors:* Own work *Original artist:* Jonoikobangali

- **File:Barahi_temple,_Phewa_lake,_Pokhara.jpg** *Source:* https://upload.wikimedia.org/wikipedia/commons/6/6b/Barahi_temple%2C_Phewa_lake%2C_Pokhara.jpg *License:* CC BY 2.0 *Contributors:* originally posted to **Flickr** as Phewa lake, Pokhara *Original artist:* Tom Booth

- **File:Bardo_National_Museum_tanit.jpg** *Source:* https://upload.wikimedia.org/wikipedia/commons/a/a2/Bardo_National_Museum_tanit.jpg *License:* CC BY-SA 2.0 *Contributors:* originally posted to **Flickr** as 3270 *Original artist:* Sarah Murray

- **File:Bas_relief_from_Arch_of_Marcus_Aurelius_showing_sacrifice.jpg** *Source:* https://upload.wikimedia.org/wikipedia/commons/7/78/Bas_relief_from_Arch_of_Marcus_Aurelius_showing_sacrifice.jpg *License:* CC BY-SA 3.0 *Contributors:* Own work *Original artist:* User: MatthiasKabel

- **File:Bastet_Istanbul_museum.JPG** *Source:* https://upload.wikimedia.org/wikipedia/commons/9/90/Bastet_Istanbul_museum.JPG *License:* GFDL *Contributors:* Own work *Original artist:* Gryffindor

- **File:Batakaru6.JPG** *Source:* https://upload.wikimedia.org/wikipedia/commons/7/76/Batakaru6.JPG *License:* CC BY-SA 3.0 *Contributors:* Own work *Original artist:* Arabsalam

- **File:Bellona,_&_count'{}s_coronet,_C19th_floor_tile,_in_a_Wiltshire_church,_UK_(i-phone_photo_2014).jpg** *Source:* https://upload.wikimedia.org/wikipedia/commons/e/e2/Bellona%2C_%26_count%27s_coronet%2C_C19th_floor_tile%2C_in_a_Wiltshire_church%2C_UK_%28i-phone_photo_2014%29.jpg *License:* CC BY-SA 3.0 *Contributors:* photo of ceramic tile in church floor. **Previously published:** 1870-1900. *Original artist:* Rodolph

- **File:Berlin_-_Siegessäule_Spitze.jpg** *Source:* https://upload.wikimedia.org/wikipedia/commons/7/7e/Berlin_-_Siegess%C3%A4ule_Spitze.jpg *License:* FAL *Contributors:* Own work *Original artist:* Taxiarchos228

- **File:Birth_of_Venus_detail.jpg** *Source:* https://upload.wikimedia.org/wikipedia/commons/0/0f/Birth_of_Venus_detail.jpg *License:* Public domain *Contributors:* Web Gallery of Art: <a href='http://www.wga.hu/art/b/botticel/5allegor/32birth.jpg' data-x-rel='nofollow'><img alt='Inkscape.svg' src='https://upload.wikimedia.org/wikipedia/commons/thumb/6/6f/Inkscape.svg/20px-Inkscape.svg.png' width='20' height='20' srcset='https://upload.wikimedia.org/wikipedia/commons/thumb/6/6f/Inkscape.svg/30px-Inkscape.svg.png 1.5x, https://upload.wikimedia.org/wikipedia/commons/thumb/6/6f/Inkscape.svg/40px-Inkscape.svg.png 2x' data-file-width='60' data-file-height='60' /></a> Image <a href='http://www.wga.hu/html/b/botticel/5allegor/32birth.html' data-x-rel='nofollow'><img alt='Information icon.svg' src='https://upload.wikimedia.org/wikipedia/commons/thumb/3/35/Information_icon.svg/20px-Information_icon.svg.png' width='20' height='20' srcset='https://upload.wikimedia.org/wikipedia/commons/thumb/3/35/Information_icon.svg/30px-Information_icon.svg.png 1.5x, https://upload.wikimedia.org/wikipedia/commons/thumb/3/35/Information_icon.svg/40px-Information_icon.svg.png 2x' data-file-width='620' data-file-height='620' /></a> Info about artwork *Original artist:* Sandro Botticelli

- **File:Bishnuvi_(Bhairab_Naach_mask).jpg** *Source:* https://upload.wikimedia.org/wikipedia/commons/f/fa/Bishnuvi_%28Bhairab_Naach_mask%29.jpg *License:* Public domain *Contributors:* Own work *Original artist:* Shakeelstha (talk) (Uploads)

- **File:Blenda_uppmanar_-_August_Malmström_1860.jpg** *Source:* https://upload.wikimedia.org/wikipedia/commons/b/bf/Blenda_uppmanar_-_August_Malmstr%C3%B6m_1860.jpg *License:* Public domain *Contributors:* Unknown *Original artist:* August Malmström

- **File:Blue_eye-shaped_amulet_HARGM3762.JPG** *Source:* https://upload.wikimedia.org/wikipedia/commons/b/b1/Blue_eye-shaped_amulet_HARGM3762.JPG *License:* CC BY-SA 4.0 *Contributors:* This file was donated by Harrogate Museums and Arts service as part of the Yorkshire Network GLAMwiki. The service operates Royal Pump Room, the Mercer Art Gallery and Knaresbrough Castle. You can find out more about their GLAMwiki work on their directory page: Harrogate Museums *Original artist:* Staff or representatives of Harrogate Museums and Arts service

- **File:Boudiccastatue.jpg** *Source:* https://upload.wikimedia.org/wikipedia/commons/f/fc/Boudiccastatue.jpg *License:* CC-BY-SA-3.0 *Contributors:* Picture taken by A. Brady *Original artist:* A. Brady

- **File:Bramhayani_(Bhairab_Naach_mask).jpg** *Source:* https://upload.wikimedia.org/wikipedia/commons/2/21/Bramhayani_%28Bhairab_Naach_mask%29.jpg *License:* Public domain *Contributors:* Own work *Original artist:* Shakeelstha (talk) (Uploads)

- **File:BrigitteCelt.jpg** *Source:* https://upload.wikimedia.org/wikipedia/commons/1/1c/BrigitteCelt.jpg *License:* Public domain *Contributors:* Own work (Original text: *self-made*) *Original artist:* Paul B (talk)

- **File:British_Museum_Egypt_101-black.jpg** *Source:* https://upload.wikimedia.org/wikipedia/commons/f/fc/British_Museum_Egypt_101-black.jpg *License:* CC BY-SA 3.0 *Contributors:* Own work *Original artist:* Einsamer Schütze

- **File:British_Museum_Ganesha_Matrikas_Kubera.jpg** *Source:* https://upload.wikimedia.org/wikipedia/commons/6/6c/British_Museum_Ganesha_Matrikas_Kubera.jpg *License:* CC-BY-SA-3.0 *Contributors:* Transferred from en.wikipedia to Commons. Transfer was stated to be made by User:Giggy.
Original artist: The original uploader was Redtigerxyz at English Wikipedia

- **File:British_Museum_Huaxtec_1-2.jpg** *Source:* https://upload.wikimedia.org/wikipedia/commons/4/49/British_Museum_Huaxtec_1-2.jpg *License:* CC BY-SA 3.0 *Contributors:*

- British_Museum_Huaxtec_1.jpg *Original artist:* British_Museum_Huaxtec_1.jpg: Gryffindor

- **File:British_Museum_Queen_of_the_Night.jpg** *Source:* https://upload.wikimedia.org/wikipedia/commons/2/22/British_Museum_Queen_of_the_Night.jpg *License:* CC0 *Contributors:* BabelStone (Own work) *Original artist:* ?

- **File:Bronze_siva.png** *Source:* https://upload.wikimedia.org/wikipedia/commons/9/94/Bronze_siva.png *License:* Public domain *Contributors:* ? *Original artist:* ?

- **File:Bust_Athena_Velletri_Glyptothek_Munich_213.jpg** *Source:* https://upload.wikimedia.org/wikipedia/commons/e/ea/Bust_Athena_Velletri_Glyptothek_Munich_213.jpg *License:* Public domain *Contributors:* User:Bibi Saint-Pol, own work, 2007-02-08 *Original artist:* Unknown (Greek original by Kresilas)

- **File:CSA-T5-\protect\char"0024\relax100-1861.jpg** *Source:* https://upload.wikimedia.org/wikipedia/commons/7/77/CSA-T5-%24100-1861.jpg *License:* Public domain *Contributors:* Image by Godot13 *Original artist:* National Museum of American History

- **File:Camunda5.JPG** *Source:* https://upload.wikimedia.org/wikipedia/commons/f/f9/Camunda5.JPG *License:* Public domain *Contributors:* Transferred from en.wikipedia to Commons by Redtigerxyz using CommonsHelper. *Original artist:* Mohonu at English Wikipedia

- **File:Candi_Sambisari,_Hindu_Temple_of_Java_Indonesia_2013_e.jpg** *Source:* https://upload.wikimedia.org/wikipedia/commons/d/d9/Candi_Sambisari%2C_Hindu_Temple_of_Java_Indonesia_2013_e.jpg *License:* CC BY-SA 3.0 *Contributors:* Own work *Original artist:* TeshTesh

- **File:CarthageBillion.jpg** *Source:* https://upload.wikimedia.org/wikipedia/commons/9/97/CarthageBillion.jpg *License:* CC BY-SA 3.0 *Contributors:* Own work *Original artist:* Chuy1530

- **File:GD-EG-KomOmbo016.JPG** *Source:* https://upload.wikimedia.org/wikipedia/commons/9/92/GD-EG-KomOmbo016.JPG *License:* CC BY-SA 2.5 *Contributors:* ? *Original artist:* ?

- **File:Gauri'{}s_procession_commencing_from_the_Zanani-Deodhi_of_the_City_Palace.jpg** *Source:* https://upload.wikimedia.org/wikipedia/commons/5/50/Gauri%27s_procession_commencing_from_the_Zanani-Deodhi_of_the_City_Palace.jpg *License:* CC BY 3.0 *Contributors:* Own work *Original artist:* Avinashmaurya

- **File:Gnome-mime-sound-openclipart.svg** *Source:* https://upload.wikimedia.org/wikipedia/commons/8/87/Gnome-mime-sound-openclipart.svg *License:* Public domain *Contributors:* Own work. Based on File:Gnome-mime-audio-openclipart.svg, which is public domain. *Original artist:* User:Eubulides

- **File:God_marriage_AS.jpg** *Source:* https://upload.wikimedia.org/wikipedia/commons/4/42/God_marriage_AS.jpg *License:* CC BY-SA 2.5 *Contributors:* ? *Original artist:* ?

- **File:Goddess_Kali_By_Piyal_Kundu1.jpg** *Source:* https://upload.wikimedia.org/wikipedia/commons/f/f1/Goddess_Kali_By_Piyal_Kundu1.jpg *License:* CC BY-SA 3.0 *Contributors:* Own work *Original artist:* Piyal Kundu

- **File:Goddess_Nike.jpg** *Source:* https://upload.wikimedia.org/wikipedia/commons/a/a6/Goddess_Nike.jpg *License:* CC BY-SA 3.0 *Contributors:* Own work *Original artist:* Marek.<a href='//commons.wikimedia.org/wiki/Special:Contributions/Marek69' title='Special:Contributions/Marek69'>69</a> <a href='//commons.wikimedia.org/wiki/User_talk:Marek69' title='User talk:Marek69'>^{talk}</a>

- **File:Goddess_Nike_at_Ephesus,_Turkey.JPG** *Source:* https://upload.wikimedia.org/wikipedia/commons/7/7e/Goddess_Nike_at_Ephesus%2C_Turkey.JPG *License:* Public domain *Contributors:* Own work *Original artist:* Maxfield

- **File:Golden_Apple_of_Discord_by_Jacob_Jordaens.jpg** *Source:* https://upload.wikimedia.org/wikipedia/commons/2/20/Golden_Apple_of_Discord_by_Jacob_Jordaens.jpg *License:* Public domain *Contributors:*

  [1]

  Original artist: Jacob Jordaens

- **File:Greek_Roman_Laurel_wreath_vector.svg** *Source:* https://upload.wikimedia.org/wikipedia/commons/e/e9/Greek_Roman_Laurel_wreath_vector.svg *License:* CC0 *Contributors:* Laurel_wreath_fa13.gif By Фёдор Таран (http://fa13.com) [Copyrighted free use], via Wikimedia Commons *Original artist:* dalovar

- **File:Hangaku_Gozen_by_Yoshitoshi.jpg** *Source:* https://upload.wikimedia.org/wikipedia/commons/7/71/Hangaku_Gozen_by_Yoshitoshi.jpg *License:* Public domain *Contributors:* This image is available from the United States Library of Congress's Prints and Photographs division under the digital ID jpd.01786.

  This tag does not indicate the copyright status of the attached work. A normal copyright tag is still required. See Commons:Licensing for more information. *Original artist:* Tsukioka Yoshitoshi

- **File:Haryali_Teej.jpg** *Source:* https://upload.wikimedia.org/wikipedia/commons/3/3f/Haryali_Teej.jpg *License:* CC BY-SA 3.0 *Contributors:* clicked by me in guru brahmanand Ashram Kurukshetra **Previously published:** na *Original artist:* Mavensgroup

- **File:Head_and_upper_body_of_the_goddess_Sekhmet,_Kelvingrove_Art_Gallery_and_Museum,_Glasgow..JPG** *Source:* https://upload.wikimedia.org/wikipedia/commons/9/96/Head_and_upper_body_of_the_goddess_Sekhmet%2C_Kelvingrove_Art_Gallery_and_Museum%2C_Glasgow..JPG *License:* CC BY-SA 4.0 *Contributors:* Own work *Original artist:* Osama Shukir Muhammed Amin FRCP(Glasg)

- **File:HinduismSymbol.PNG** *Source:* https://upload.wikimedia.org/wikipedia/commons/1/1f/HinduismSymbol.PNG *License:* CC-BY-SA-3.0 *Contributors:* Created by Tinette user of Italian Wikipedia. *Original artist:* Tinette (talk · contribs)

- **File:Hyndla_og_Freia_by_Frølich.jpg** *Source:* https://upload.wikimedia.org/wikipedia/commons/9/99/Hyndla_og_Freia_by_Fr%C3%B8lich.jpg *License:* Public domain *Contributors:* Published in Gjellerup, Karl (1895). *Den ældre Eddas Gudesange*. Photographed from a 2001 reprint by bloodofox (talk · contribs). *Original artist:* Lorenz Frølich

- **File:Iansã.jpg** *Source:* https://upload.wikimedia.org/wikipedia/commons/8/87/Ians%C3%A3.jpg *License:* CC BY-SA 2.5 *Contributors:* Sculpture by Tatti Moreno, in public place *Original artist:* Picture taken by Eurico Zimbres

- **File:IdolofDurgaPooja.jpg** *Source:* https://upload.wikimedia.org/wikipedia/commons/2/22/IdolofDurgaPooja.jpg *License:* CC BY-SA 4.0 *Contributors:* Own work *Original artist:* Rakeshmallick27

- **File:India_statue_of_nataraja.jpg** *Source:* https://upload.wikimedia.org/wikipedia/commons/2/21/India_statue_of_nataraja.jpg *License:* CC BY 2.0 *Contributors:* http://www.flickr.com/photos/rosemania/86746598/in/set-72057594048518296/ *Original artist:* Rosemania

- **File:Ishtar_Eshnunna_Louvre_AO12456.jpg** *Source:* https://upload.wikimedia.org/wikipedia/commons/c/ca/Ishtar_Eshnunna_Louvre_AO12456.jpg *License:* CC BY 2.5 *Contributors:* Marie-Lan Nguyen (User:Jastrow), 2009-01-14 *Original artist:* ?

- **File:Ishtar_vase_Louvre_AO17000-detail.jpg** *Source:* https://upload.wikimedia.org/wikipedia/commons/6/6a/Ishtar_vase_Louvre_AO17000-detail.jpg *License:* Public domain *Contributors:* Own work *Original artist:* Marie-Lan Nguyen

- **File:Itzpapalotl_1.jpg** *Source:* https://upload.wikimedia.org/wikipedia/commons/e/e8/Itzpapalotl_1.jpg *License:* Public domain *Contributors:* This raster graphics image was created with Adobe Photoshop CS *Original artist:* Unknown

- **File:Jeanne_Hachette_Dubray_2007_06_17.jpg** *Source:* https://upload.wikimedia.org/wikipedia/commons/7/7c/Jeanne_Hachette_Dubray_2007_06_17.jpg *License:* Public domain *Contributors:* Own work *Original artist:* Jastrow

- **File:Joan_of_arc_miniature_graded.jpg** *Source:* https://upload.wikimedia.org/wikipedia/commons/3/39/Joan_of_arc_miniature_graded.jpg *License:* Public domain *Contributors:*

- Colour-graded to reveal more detail using GIMP software "curves" tool *Original artist:* ?

3.3 Content license